Every Step She Takes

ALSO BY ALISON COCHRUN

Here We Go Again
Kiss Her Once for Me
The Charm Offensive

Every Step She Takes

ALISON COCHRUN

ATRIA PAPERBACK

New York • Amsterdam/Antwerp • London •
Toronto • Sydney/Melbourne • New Delhi

ATRIA
PAPERBACK

An Imprint of Simon & Schuster, LLC
1230 Avenue of the Americas
New York, NY 10020

First Atria Paperback edition September 2025

Interior design by Kris Tobiassen

Manufactured in the United States of America

1 3 5 7 9 10 8 6 4 2

Library of Congress Cataloging-in-Publication Data is available.

ISBN 978-1-6680-2125-5
ISBN 978-1-6680-2126-2 (ebook)

This one is entirely for Jordan, my love.

It was worth taking the scenic route to find you.

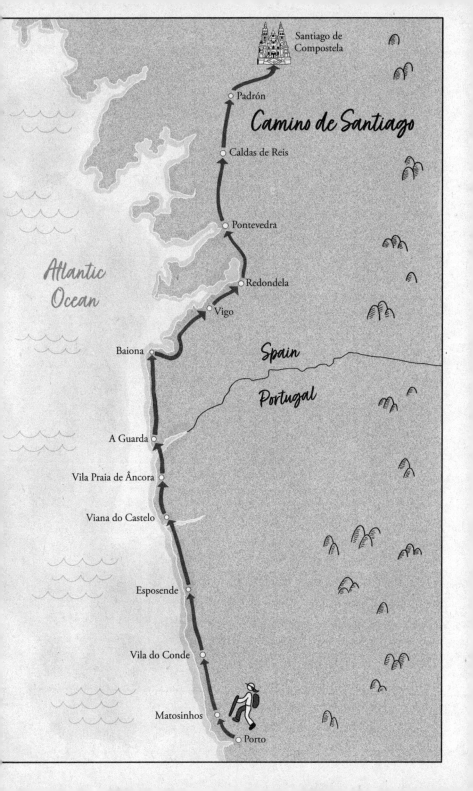

Santiago de
Compostela

Padrón

Camino de Santiago

Caldas de Reis

Pontevedra

Atlantic
Ocean

Redondela

Vigo

Baiona

Spain

Portugal

A Guarda

Vila Praia de Âncora

Viana do Castelo

Esposende

Vila do Conde

Matosinhos

Porto

Every Step
She Takes

ONE

Sadie

Nothing good happens when I drink red wine, and I'm already on my second glass of Chateau Ste. Michelle when the man sitting across from me starts talking about cryptocurrency.

This is why I told my sister no more tech bros.

I'm not sure if he is *for* cryptocurrency or against it or simply trying to educate the ignorant masses, but I nod along to his lengthy diatribe while discreetly checking my phone under the table. Only thirty-eight more minutes.

In thirty-eight minutes, I will fake a dental emergency or a dead cat or an early-morning meeting. In thirty-eight minutes, I will use one of my innumerable standby excuses for bailing on a first date, and before too long, I'll be in bed with a lavender face mask, watching HGTV and doomscrolling before falling asleep by nine o'clock.

In thirty-eight minutes, I'm allowed to call it. That's the misguided agreement I made with my sister.

"And, of course, you know what an NTF is," my date continues after a sip of his Imperial IPA. I just keep nodding and drinking my wine. So very, *very* misguided.

It was red wine that got me into this mess in the first place.

My sister, Vi, is a travel influencer who treats my house like a way station, but she kindly graced Mom and me with her presence over the holidays, in between her eastern Europe tour of Christmas markets and her spelunking trip to New Zealand. After sharing an entire crockpot of her homemade glühwein, Vi and Mom started grilling me about my love life, like they always do. My happiness— or, more accurately, my lack of abject misery—is guided by one simple rule: never discuss my love life with my family.

This used to be easily accomplished, because I had no love life to speak of. While my middle school friends were getting their first crushes, I was still playing Barbies with Vi; while my high school friends were getting their first boyfriends, I was maintaining a 4.0 and working six days a week at my Nan's antique store. In college, there were casual flirtations that never went anywhere, and a few drunk kisses that I usually regretted even more than the hangover.

Then my Nan died, and my whole life changed, and there wasn't any *time* to think about romance or relationships or what I even wanted. But that never stopped my mother from trying to set me up with every man under fifty who crossed her path. It never stopped my little sister from coercing me onto the dating apps.

Discussing my love life with them only reinforces their delusion that I want their help.

But thanks to fucking *glühwein*, I did discuss it. I drunkenly told them that I am giving up on romance once and for all, that I don't want to date anymore, and that I am perfectly content by myself.

Not surprisingly, this drunken declaration did not go over well. My mother cried about never having grandchildren and my sister confidently vowed to find me the perfect man.

I burped brandy and cardamon as I told her the perfect man does not exist.

"That's because you're too picky," Vi said. That's what she *always* says. As if I should just settle for the first man who's nice to his mom and doesn't send unsolicited dick pics. As if I haven't *tried* to develop feelings for all the men I've dated. Most of my friends from college have husbands now; several have kids; they all file joint taxes and have a built-in plus-one to weddings and an emergency contact who doesn't frequently travel to remote locations with no cell service. Developing feelings for one of these men would be the path of least resistance.

"Maybe I don't need a man to be fulfilled," I told them. My certainty was, unfortunately, undermined by a drunk hiccup.

"Maybe you need to give your dates a fair *try*," my mom insisted.

"Maybe you need to let *me* find you a man," Vi said, rubbing her hands together in an ominous fashion.

Maybe you both need to let me live my life without your constant meddling. Is what I *would* have said, if I was ever honest with my family.

Thus, a glühwein-motivated arrangement began to take shape because Vi has the confidence of someone who has never been told *no*. A benefit of being a younger sibling, I think. She always had a safety net to catch her. When our parents fought, I was there to distract her with an art project and a Broadway musical soundtrack played at full volume. When my dad took off and my mom couldn't get out of bed for nearly two years, I was the one who French braided Vi's hair before soccer games and packed her school lunches. She always had me.

That's how she turned her love of travel into a full-time job as a successful influencer under the handle cestlavi. It's how she became a freelance writer at some of the biggest travel publications in the country. It's how she bullied me into this agreement.

I would let my sister set me up on as many dates as she wanted before my thirty-fifth birthday. But if she couldn't find the perfect man *for me* by then, both her and my mom had to accept that I'm happy on my own.

There were rules: I had to promise to keep an open mind about each man; I had to give each date at least an hour before dismissing him; and I had to kiss every man who initiated it, so I could find out if we had chemistry.

Vi called this the *butterfly factor*. As in, "What if you think he's a dud, but then you kiss him and feel *butterflies*?" Because my sister is ridiculous.

While I was reluctant to sign up for five months of horrible, hops-flavored first kisses, I was even more reluctant to argue with my sister. So, thanks to familial pressure and the lubricating wonders of mulled wine, I agreed.

I went from going on one or two dates per year to going on *four* dates in the month of January alone, slotting in an hour wherever I could: after a twelve-hour workday; on a Saturday morning after spin class; between tearing out the old carpet in my bedroom and retiling the kitchen backsplash.

First, there was the marathon runner who insisted we hike Tiger Mountain so he could not-so-subtly assess my overall health, turning a first date into the Presidential Fitness Test of my middle school nightmares.

Then there was the guy who took me to a film festival in West Seattle to watch *Full Metal Jacket* and stuck his hand down my shirt during the scene where Vincent D'Onofrio dies, effectively ruining all nipple-play for the rest of my life.

And there was the Zillow executive who insisted we sit on the same side of the booth, like a serial killer. At minute fifty-two, he started stroking my love handles while telling me that he loved women "with a little something to hold on to."

But for every walking red flag, there was a decent-enough man too. I've been on sixteen dates since Christmas, endured nine butterfly-less first kisses, and when the timer ran out on my obligated hour for each date, I found a polite, if abominably dishonest, reason to leave. Like I always do.

And at a certain point, when you can't make it longer than an hour with sixteen different men, you start to wonder if maybe the problem isn't with them at all . . .

But now my thirty-fifth birthday is in four days, so my sister pulled out the stops with the seventeenth man, who is currently taking another sip of beer.

Grant Foster owns a successful tech start-up, volunteers at an after-school program that teaches kids how to code, and eats dinner with his grandparents once a week. He has a border collie and an electric car; he's financially stable; he goes to therapy and *talks* openly about going to therapy; and he's conventionally handsome, with Chris Hemsworth's physique, Chris Pine's eyes, and Chris Evans's smile. He's the best parts of all the Chrises, and he's the kind of man I *should* be attracted to, minus the current tangent into tech-mansplaining hell.

I don't know even what my boxes are, but I know the man sitting across from me checks all of them, and I'm *still* counting down the minutes until this date is over. (*Thirty-two.* I check again while he's explaining the difference between blockchains and Bitcoin mining.)

Part of me wants this date to fail. I want the clock to run out on my sister's scheme, for another birthday to come and go without my life changing in any significant way, for my family to never again ask about why I haven't met *the one* and finally abandon me to my self-chosen spinsterhood.

But there's also a part of me that wants Grant to be that *one.* I want this to work, because that would be so much easier than the alternative: questioning the reason why it *doesn't* work, why it never works.

"I'm boring you," Grant says suddenly. I didn't think he was paying any attention to me, so his abrupt recognition of my existence causes me to spill some of my wine. He must've caught me checking the time again. (*Twenty-nine minutes.*)

"I'm sorry. I tend to get tunnel vision when I'm talking about my passions." He bashfully glances down at the scuffed table, and I feel a surge of compassion for the guy.

"It's okay," I reassure him. "Just wait until I get going on the intricacies of reupholstering a chair. Besides, I totally wanted to know more about non-fungus tickets."

"Non-fungible tokens," he corrects.

"Tokens, yes, right. I wanted to learn about those."

He flashes me the Chris Evans smile. "No you didn't."

"No, I really didn't," I admit, and he laughs at himself. Most men *never* laugh at themselves. Grant rolls his broad, muscular, Chris Hemsworth shoulders, and they strain against the fabric of his Henley, and *maybe* this can work.

"I want to know more about you," he says, leaning forward so he can hear me over the noise of the bar. "Tell me: Who is Sadie Wells?"

And shit. I want to go back to the lecture on fungus tokens, because I don't have the faintest fucking idea how to answer that question.

I swallow hard and try to hide the stress hives breaking out along the backs of my hands. He's not *trying* to trigger an existential identity crisis, but I'm nothing if not an over-achiever.

"Who is Sadie Wells . . . ?" I repeat as if I'm ruminating on my answer, not inwardly wishing I had a self-destruct button. Because somewhere around date nine back in March, when a marine biologist who looked like Jonathan Bailey didn't stir anything in me, I started to realize I don't really know myself at all.

"Who am I?" I take a long drink of red wine to stall. It's a Thursday night, and the bar on Queen Anne Hill is crowded with thirtysomething, working professionals. Confident, successful people who probably know how to answer basic questions about themselves without breaking out in stress hives.

"Yeah," Grant continues to prod. "I want to know the *real* you."

It's a noble goal, to be sure, but sixteen dates in four months have taught me that even *I* don't know who Sadie Wells is. I check the time again. *Twenty-seven minutes.*

"Your sister mentioned you're a small-business owner," he says after another stretch of awkward silence.

"Yes!" I blurt, desperate for this conversational lifeline. "I run an antiques store."

He eyes me over his pint glass. "Aren't you a little young to work with antiques? Isn't that sort of . . ."

"For old people? Uh, yeah. Mostly."

"So how did you end up running it?"

At least this is a question I can answer, no identity crisis required. "My great-grandparents bought a Victorian house in Queen Anne when they came here from Ireland in the twenties, and my Nan inherited it. She was obsessed with preserving the original detailing of the house and hunting down antique furniture to match its history. When my grandad died when I was six, my Nan used his life insurance payout to convert the downstairs into an antique and recycled furniture store. And then when she died, she left both the house and the store to me."

"Fascinating," he says, and the handsome bastard seems to genuinely mean it. "Tell me more about the store."

I'd rather not. "Uh, it's not . . . very interesting."

"I think everything about you is interesting," he insists with a flirtatious grin. At least, I think his grin is of the flirtatious variety.

The problem is, I don't know how to tell him more about the store without ripping my heart open for this stranger. I can't tell him that when I was a kid, back when Nan and Grandad were alive, that old house felt warm and welcoming, their laughter always loud enough to drown out my parents' screaming matches. But now that they're both gone, it feels like living alongside ghosts, and no matter how many home renovation projects I do to my creaky house, nothing changes that.

But I can't talk about this with an amalgamation of Chrises. Hell, I can't even talk about it with my mom and sister.

"Tell me about your start-up?" I non sequitur, and Grant gets swept up in another passionate monologue about his work. I study his rugged stubble, his kind eyes, and I try, try, *try* to feel some level of attraction.

When that doesn't work, I reach for my wineglass again.

"But I never want my job to be the only thing that defines me," Grant is saying. "What are some of your hobbies?"

"Uh . . ." It's another stumper. "I-I don't really have time for hobbies."

I used to have time for hobbies. I used to have interests and *passions*. Well, one passion.

I grew up breathing new life into old, well-loved items under Nan's tutelage. At seven, she had me polishing brass lamps she found at flea markets for resale, and by nine, I could reupholster a chair. By eleven, I was converting old dressers into bathroom vanities and using a table saw unsupervised. I loved every minute of it.

It seemed like an act of magic, to take a discarded piece of furniture that no one wanted anymore and turn it into something beautiful. It was all I ever wanted to do with my life: give second chances to broken dressers or water-stained tables or ripped couches.

But when I was twelve, my dad took off, and my mom fell into a long, dark, depressive episode, so I had to take over her duties at the store too. I scoured the *Seattle Times* obituaries to get leads on upcoming estate sales, haggling with next of kin. I learned to use QuickBooks when other kids were using their

Nintendo Game Boys, and when I got accepted to the University of Washington, there was no question about what I was going to study. I would major in business. To help Nan.

Only, before I even finished my undergrad degree, I lost my Nan too.

One day she was single-handedly hauling armoires up the stairs, and the next day she'd fainted behind the register after skipping breakfast. It turned out to be aggressive, stage-four breast cancer. She was gone within a month. And the house, the store, her entire legacy . . . She left it all to me.

I was only twenty-one when I inherited a business that was failing and a house that was falling apart.

There was a lot less time for furniture restoration projects after that. Less time for friends and dating and self-reflection. Less time for having any kind of life outside that dusty store.

Until this bet with Vi gave me sixteen hours of self-reflection while sitting across from men I didn't want to kiss, and I started questioning absolutely everything.

"What about travel?" Grant prods. "I usually try to take two or three big trips every year. I think it's important to travel abroad and to experience different viewpoints," he pontificates. "I can't believe how many Americans have never even left the country."

Unfortunately, *I* am one of those Americans. "I would like to be able to travel," I mumble. "Um, I've never really had time for that either. I've always been too busy running the store."

I honestly can't remember the last time I had a day off, let alone multiple days off in a row to take a vacation. I've had to settle for living vicariously through my sister's adventures.

"Well, maybe I could convince you to take a trip someday," Grant says. *Forty minutes into our first date.* A knot of anxiety forms in my stomach, and it gets worse when he reaches over to put his hand on top of mine. I flinch, and he *definitely* notices the hives.

"Uh, sorry, it's a . . . a stress response," I tell him before promptly reclaiming my hand and hiding it under the table.

Grant misconstrues this detail. "Are you nervous about this date? That's so *cute*."

He says it sweetly, but I feel infantilized all the same, and I want to correct him. I'm not nervous about this date; I'm petrified at the thought of going home and telling my mom and sister that yet another setup didn't work out, when I don't have the right words to explain *why*.

I still have nineteen minutes to go, but the words come out before I can stop them. "Actually, I'm so sorry, but I have an early-morning meeting and—"

"At your antiques store?" Grant frowns.

"Yes. It's with my assistant manager, Jane. She's a real person." I probably shouldn't have added that last part, but I plow on as I start gathering my purse and my coat. "I'm so sorry."

"No, it's okay," he says. He pulls a few twenties out of his wallet and leaves them on the table, signaling to our waiter that we're leaving.

"You can stay," I tell him.

"No, I can walk you to your car."

"I-I didn't drive here."

"Then I'll walk you outside," he says with measured politeness, and that's how I end up standing awkwardly outside the bar with him forty-six minutes into our date, on an evening that has no business being this cold this far into spring. I shiver.

"So," he says, sliding his hands into the pockets of his peacoat. "I really like you, Sadie. But I get the impression you're maybe not into it."

And damn this man with his emotional maturity and direct communication style. There's a reason why I prefer to lie and ghost; because otherwise I'll lie and people-please. "No!" I squeak. "I'm not *not* into it. It's just . . . this meeting! I'm stressed about this meeting! Really!"

He locks his Chris Pine eyes onto mine. "Then, do you think . . . may I kiss you goodnight?"

And despite everything, I want to kiss Grant and feel the butterflies Vi's always talking about. I want to kiss him and feel all the things they sing about in love songs. I want this kiss to save me from ever having to find the right words for my mom and sister.

I want this kiss to save me from having to find the right words *for myself.*

So, I nod.

Grant leans in. He smells like eucalyptus and emotional intelligence, and when his mouth presses against mine, I will myself to feel something, feel *anything.*

Instead, I feel as empty as my house of ghosts.

"What could you *possibly* have found wrong with this guy?" my sister demands when she finds me sneaking another glass of pinot from the fridge exactly fifty-nine minutes after my date started.

"There was nothing wrong with him," I start.

"Then what happened?" My mom is hot on Vi's trail, and she flies into the kitchen wearing her bathrobe and nothing else. I get an unseemly flash of her crotch before she plants herself on a barstool beside the island. And this is why most grown adults don't live with their families.

Or allow their families to live with them, as the case may be.

"He looked so handsome in those Instagram photos," my mom says dreamily.

"He was," I grumble into my wine.

"He was the perfect fucking man," Vi snaps.

"But he wasn't the perfect man for me." And after seventeen dates, I'm starting to think there really is *no* perfect man for me. Because I'm maybe not attracted to men at all.

But if that were the case, wouldn't I already know this about myself? Why didn't I figure this shit out in college like every other self-respecting millennial?

Vi slams her chopsticks down onto the quartz countertop, because she's decided to eat some suspicious leftover grocery store sushi. "Give it to us straight," she demands, and it's an interesting choice of words, given the circumstances. "Why didn't it work with that sexy man? Did you talk about upholstery too much?"

"I talked about upholstery the right amount. It's just—"

I wasn't attracted to him.

I don't think I've ever been attracted to a man.

I'm . . .

I'm *what*? I don't have the slightest idea how to finish that thought. How do you figure out your sexuality in your thirties? There's no GSA for grown-ass adults.

In four days, I will be thirty-five, and more than anything, my birthday feels like a horrible reminder of how little I've changed since I was twenty-one.

"Grant and I want different things in life," I lie. *And lie and lie and lie.*

"What *do* you want, sweetheart?" my mom coaxes.

And shit. I walked right into that one. "Oh, you know . . ."

They don't know, and I don't know, and I feel like the walls are closing in. I'm stuck between a Grant and a hard place, with no hope for escape.

"This isn't over." My sister hobbles on her crutches to the fridge and pulls out an energy drink. At 8 p.m. "I still have a few more days to find you the perfect man. I'll just double down on my efforts and—"

"No!" The word escapes from the deepest part of my gut, the part that goes hollow at the thought of going on any more dates with any more men *ever again*. I just don't know how to explain this to my sister or my mom.

I feel like I need to have the right answer, the specific label . . . that I need to be *certain*. I feel like if I don't have the perfect words to explain whatever this is to my family, they won't listen.

And I need *time* to find those words.

So, I pivot. Hard. "No, don't do that, Vi. I-I wouldn't want you to overexert yourself. With your toe, I mean." *Totally saved it.* "What did the doctor say about the X-ray results?"

My little sister unleashes a dramatic sigh and welcomes the attention. "Eight weeks! He said I'm going to be in this boot for eight weeks!" She gestures to the foot she has propped up on one of my stools. They're midcentury modern barstools that I tracked down at an estate sale in Ravenna, and I just finished sanding and restaining them, but none of that matters to Vi. "Can you believe that? *Eight weeks* over a *toe*? Who even breaks their big toe while parasailing?"

"I would guess a lot of people."

My mom twists a cloth napkin in her hands. "I wish you wouldn't do such dangerous things, especially in foreign countries," she laments, because Molly Wells is a collection of anxiety disorders in the shape of a woman held together by Wellbutrin and romance novel audiobooks.

Vi brushes off her concern. "The extreme adventures company seemed legit."

"The one that was operated out of a rusted bus in Venezuela?"

"Yes." Vi is oblivious to my sarcasm. "The doctor said I shouldn't travel for *two months*. What am I supposed to do with myself for two whole months? Work in the store with you?"

"Your disgust is noted."

Vi has always jumped on any excuse to be away from the store and the family responsibilities that come with it. As a kid, that meant karate and Girl Scouts and an elite soccer team. In high school, she went on summer volunteer trips to the Dominican Republic and did a semester in Tokyo her junior year. The day she graduated, she got on a plane to backpack Europe for ten weeks and didn't call home once. It's been that way ever since. She boomerangs home sometimes to catch up on sleep and laundry and her regularly scheduled judgments of my life choices.

Victoria Wells never overthinks. She just *acts*. Which is probably why she was able to casually come out as bisexual at nineteen between bites of my homemade cottage pie. Without angst. Without questioning. Without having a fucking existential crisis about it.

And that's the other thing. Vi is bi. If I were queer, wouldn't she sense it somehow? Wouldn't she have tried to set me up with a woman at some point?

Vi exhales in horror. "I can't be stuck here like you. I was supposed to leave for Portugal and Spain in four days! I worked so hard to make this trek happen and I've been looking forward to it for *months*, and now *this!*"

"You're going to Portugal?" my mom asks nervously, as if Vi has announced a planned trip to an active war zone. "Why?"

"It's the guided tour of the Camino de Santiago," Vi snaps. "It's been in the works for over a year now, and the tour company is paying me *generously* to do the trip and post about it. I pitched the story on the Camino to the *Seattle Times*, and they're considering running it next month. *In print*. Plus, I had a whole daily blog planned, with affiliate links and sponsors." She melodramatically presses the back of her hand to her forehead in anguish. "So much planned social media content. *Wasted*."

Vi often cries over sponsored content, but it's clear this opportunity is important to her. Her Instagram might be 80 percent bikini shots in front of various waterfalls, but that's because she knows how to game the algorithm. She's always wanted to be a travel writer, and she's smart enough to know that bikini selfies are how to get there.

Besides, she looks fantastic in a bikini—like Nicola Coughlan in *Bridgerton* meets every *Sports Illustrated* cover model ever—and she never misses an opportunity to remind the world of this fact. It's all part of being a travel influencer and midsize fashion icon.

"I can't just *bail*. Writing for the *Times* would be a huge deal, and I don't want to disappoint the tour company." Vi wails like an injured otter before reaching for her can of legalized methamphetamine. Her long acrylic nails fumble with the tab for less than a second before she gives up and hands the can to me. I open it for her, and I'm immediately assaulted by the smell of blueberries and lighter fluid. The logo on the can says *Bitch Fuel*, with a slogan that unironically tells me to "fuel my inner boss bitch."

But I don't have an inner boss bitch. At best, I have an inner canary in a coal mine that I've been ignoring for far too long.

"I can't believe I'm going to miss this trip!" Vi cries as I pass her the opened energy drink. "Can you imagine? All that sunshine and fresh air? Walking all day and drinking Portuguese wine every evening? Escaping it all for a while?"

And I can imagine it, actually.

"What if I do it for you?" I hear myself say.

Vi slurps her Bitch Fuel and belches subpar sushi. "Do what for me?"

"The trip. The Camino or whatever." An idea is starting to take shape in my red-wine brain. "I could go and document everything for your Instagram and blog, and I'll take notes so you can still write the article for the *Seattle Times*."

My sister's green eyes go wide. "You . . . you would do that for me?"

"I would do anything for you."

My mom shakes her head. "No, no, you can't do that, Sadie. You've never left the country before. You don't even have a passport."

"I do, actually." Unused and buried at the bottom of my sock drawer.

"But you haven't trained for this Camino-thingy," my mom counters.

"It's just walking," Vi interjects.

"Sadie hates walking."

"No I don't!" Sure, most of my walking happens on the tread-mill while watching old episodes of *Love It or List It*, but still. I do yoga twice a week with my mom, and my job is basically strength-training in the form of moving solid-wood furniture. How hard could it be to just *walk*?

"But . . . but what about the store?" my mom cries in a final, anxious attempt to keep me here. "Who will take care of the store?"

Something stubborn takes shape in my chest, maybe because I'm tired of being the safety net. "You and Vi," I answer plainly. "You can both handle it while I'm gone. It's only for . . ."

I don't even know how long this trip is, and that's probably a sign I should abandon this impulsiveness.

"Two weeks," Vi fills in.

"Two weeks," I repeat. "Don't you think you can handle everything for two weeks, Mom?"

I can see a thousand anxious thoughts blooming behind my mother's eyes, but she doesn't voice any of them.

"Are you serious about this?" Vi asks with so much hope in her voice.

"Dead serious," I say with growing conviction. Because maybe this is what I need. Maybe I'll be like Cheryl Strayed, and this will be my *Wild*. I'll have two weeks away from the store, and my family, and the pressure to date men so I can finally figure myself out.

Or I'll be like Diane Lane in *Under the Tuscan Sun*, and I'll buy a crumbling villa and never return to the real world.

"I'm doing it," I say one more time, to convince myself.

Even with the broken big toe, Vi manages to catapult herself off the stool and smother me in a hug. "Thank you, thank you, *thank you*!"

"Who knows?" my mom adds, because she can't fucking help herself. "Maybe you'll meet a hunky Spanish man and finally fall in love!"

I down the rest of my pinot. "Yeah. Maybe."

C'est La Vi with Me

| HOME | ABOUT ME | DESTINATIONS | BLOG POSTS |

Find Yourself on the Camino de Santiago

Vi Wells
April 16, 2025 116 comments

As always, Nomads, this post contains affiliate links, and I receive a small commission if you purchase anything from these links. I only promote products that have helped me embrace my life of adventure!

If you haven't already heard of the Camino de Santiago, then listen up, Nomads, and prepare to dust off your Keens. You're about to become as obsessed as I am with this travel trend!

Historically, the Camino de Santiago (also known as The Way of St. James, or just "The Way") was a series of routes throughout Europe all ending at the glorious Cathedral of Santiago de Compostela in northwest Spain, the location of St. James's final resting place. Once traveled by medieval Catholic pilgrims, the Camino is now a popular long-distance trek for travel lovers of all ages, cultures, abilities, and backgrounds. Last year, nearly 500,000 pilgrims arrived in Santiago from all over the world, and this year, I can't wait to grab my Osprey backpack and join those ranks.

While the Camino was originally viewed as an act of sacrificial piety, the modern Camino is the perfect place to escape the demands of everyday life. Pilgrims attest there's something meditative about walking for weeks through beautiful countryside, quaint villages, and the staggering coastlines of Portugal and Spain. Evenings are reserved for resting your feet over tapas and cerveza while making friends with fellow trekkers who might just become your "Camino Family." Unlike other long-distance hikes, such as the Pacific Coast Trail, you won't have to rough it on the Camino. The routes travel through towns where espresso and wine are always available, and pilgrims rest their heads on pillows each night at various hotels, hostels, and albergues (hostels specifically for pilgrims). Even if you don't complete the trek for religious purposes, there is something undeniably spiritual about The Way.

At least, that's what draws Brazilian-born Inez Oliveira to the Camino year after year. Oliveira completed her first Camino—the most popular route, the Camino Frances—at age twenty-two, and fell in love with the transformative nature of the trail. Almost a decade ago, her experience inspired her to launch Beatrix Tours, a company that's grown to include organized trekking tours in over 15 countries. But CEO Oliveira still serves as a guide for small groups of pilgrims along six different Camino paths. She's found the Camino often attracts travelers who are spiritually lost in some way, and her tours are unique in that she provides guided prompts for self-reflection along the way, making the Camino both a literal journey and an emotional one.

"Many come to the Camino at a crossroads in their lives and they do this walk to find answers, and often a way back to themselves," Oliveira explained to me in a phone interview. "I am blessed to be their guide on the path of self-understanding."

I will be joining her two-week trek on the coastal route of the Portuguese Camino from Porto to Santiago in May, and I can't wait to get away from it all and find myself on the Camino. I was lucky enough to interview Oliveira about her approach. For our full Q&A, click on the link.

TWO

Sadie

I am not Diane Lane.

This becomes apparent in the seventy-two hours I have to prepare for this red-wine-fueled life choice. Diane Lane didn't have to drop two grand at REI for a new Osprey 40L backpack, new hiking boots, and moisture-wicking everything because she had a sister who didn't trust her with her top-of-the-line trekking supplies. Diane Lane didn't have to endure a crash course in Instagram influencing from said hypercritical Gen Z sister. She didn't have to worry about regulating her mother's emotions while dealing with her own mounting panic, and she didn't have to pull an all-nighter to ensure her assistant manager wouldn't burn down her Nan's life's work in her absence. Diane Lane didn't have to ask her psychiatrist for emergency Xanax for the flight. Probably.

And Diane didn't spend her thirty-fifth birthday wandering around a Hudson News because her anxiety forced her to get to the airport four hours early.

No, in *Under the Tuscan Sun*, Diane Lane made her mental breakdown look tragically beautiful. I make my mental breakdown look, well . . . tragic.

I arrive at my gate an hour before boarding just as the woman at the front counter picks up the phone to make an announcement.

"Welcome to British Airways flight 520 to London," she trills in a lovely accent. "We will begin boarding momentarily, but we want to remind you that this is a full flight. Overhead storage space will be limited, so we're looking for fifteen passengers who'd be willing to check their bags free of charge."

My bag weighs at least thirty pounds and is already crushing my shoulders, so I briefly consider ditching it when my phone buzzes in the pocket of my yoga pants. It's a mildly threatening text from Vi reminding me to post before boarding. I snap a maybe-artistic, maybe-just-crooked photo of the gate sign before slapping a filter on it and uploading it to the cestlavi account, along with fifteen of Vi's pre-approved hashtags.

Two seconds after I press post, I get another text demanding the next one is a selfie. THE ALGORITHM WANTS PHOTOS WITH PEOPLE, she text-shouts at me. My phone buzzes again as another bubble appears on the screen. AND YOU HAVE TO INTRODUCE YOURSELF TO MY FOLLOWERS.

A beat, and then a third text. I DON'T WANT ANYONE THINKING I TOOK THAT JANKY-ASS PHOTO.

The spiraling thoughts start as my steps echo through the jetway before boarding the plane.

What if I can't find any overhead space for my backpack?

What if I can't navigate my way through Heathrow and I miss my connecting flight to Porto?

What if the plane crashes and I end up in some kind of cannibalistic *Yellowjackets* situation? Or worse, a *Lost* situation, where I won't know what's going on for six years, only to discover I was maybe dead the whole time anyway. At least, I think that's what happened in the *Lost* finale.

What if I'm the only person who is still confused by the *Lost* finale?

What if my seatmate packed a tuna sandwich and wants to *talk to me*?

My anxiety brain thoroughly and efficiently runs through every worst-case scenario, trying to protect me from upcoming disappointment by anticipating it. Because I am Molly Wells's daughter through and through.

When I arrive in front of seat 18B, I discover there's easy access to bin space (though my heavy bag requires the help of three strangers). There is only one seat next to mine by the window, and the older woman on the other side of the aisle has already removed her shoes and started in on a knitting project. She doesn't seem like a talker.

The flight was the one thing Vi couldn't easily transfer into my name when I decided to take her place on this trip four days ago. She planned to buy me a ticket using her airline miles, but the owner of the tour company stepped in and kindly offered to arrange my flight, including an upgrade to premium economy. I guess it pays to be an influencer.

I would never splurge on such an indulgence, but I can't complain about the extra room. Apparently, only straight-size people under five-feet tall are allowed to be comfortable on airplanes, and I am neither of those things.

I take off my coat and shove it under the seat in front of me before cuing my downloaded "sad girl indie" playlist on Spotify and spritzing a small amount of lavender onto my left wrist to calm me. Then I set up my things in the seat pouch in front of me: two Lärabars; my Owala water bottle; Dramamine; a phone charger; a *Lonely Planet* guidebook about Portugal. I glance down at my phone and the screen is an endless stream of notifications from Vi's Instagram, comments and mentions and tags. There are texts from my sister about content, and texts from the assistant manager of the store about inventory, and texts from my mom about whether I packed enough doses of my Lexapro.

I ignore everything, put my phone in airplane mode, and slide it into the pouch too.

The flow of people entering the plane soon thins to a slow trickle, then stops completely, and the window seat next to me remains empty. The flight attendants start closing the overhead bins, and I begin to relax a little as Gracie Abrams croons in my AirPods. I let my elbows spread wide and my long legs stretch out a little farther, enjoying the freedom.

Until out of nowhere, a blue-haired figure materializes in the aisle, swinging a backpack that dangles off one shoulder and accidentally smacking people with a Hydro Flask covered in stickers: several different pride flags, a SHE/HER decal, and a "Protect Trans Kids" glittery rainbow all catch my eye. Giant headphones jostle around her neck, and she *absolutely* looks like a talker.

Anxiety gathers deep in my lower gut. *Please.* Please don't let her be my seat companion.

She slings off her backpack and starts opening and closing overhead bins in search of a spot to stash it. The bag looks like it was once maroon, maybe orange, but has long since faded to a fecal-brown color. It's covered in patches from places around the world, like Van Life's answer to a Girl Scout vest. She makes a triumphant sound when she finds a small spot for the backpack and stands on her tiptoes to cram it in. As she starts punching the bag into its tight space, her shirt and fleece ride up, and her jeans slide down her hip bones to reveal the waistband of her briefs and a tattoo of some kind of vined plant that snakes down her left hip and disappears into her underwear. I force myself to look away as a flight attendant brusquely marches down the aisle to help.

"Thanks, friend," she says to the attendant in a vaguely European accent. She shrugs off her mustard-colored Cotopaxi fleece to reveal a threadbare gray T-shirt and a distinct lack of bra. Her eyes scan the seat numbers until they land on 18A, and her gaze drops down to me. As her mouth widens into a friendly smile, something weird happens in my stomach.

It's not my usual anxiety knot; it almost feels like my stomach lifts into my rib cage the way it always does during takeoff, and I have an inexplicable sense of déjà vu as I look up at her face, like seeing someone from childhood you forgot existed. But I know I've never met this woman. It's an unexplainable familiarity, like an itch in the back of my head that I can't scratch.

"That's me," she says, pointing to the window seat.

Because of course it is. I tug out one AirPod. "Sorry," I say as I unfasten my seat belt and quickly move out of her way.

"Nothing to be sorry about, friend." She smiles breezily.

I settle back into my seat, elbows tucked, legs crossed, AirPods in, eyes fixed forward. It's the body language of the unsociable and emotionally closed off. I can feel her shifting beside me, scrunching up her coat and tucking it into the small of her back. She attempts to squeeze her Hydro Flask into the seat front pocket, but her legs are even longer than mine, so she spreads them wide to accommodate the oversized water bottle, and her knee bumps mine.

With every movement, she jostles our joined seats, making me feel like a small boat on the open ocean.

And that's when I pop a Xanax and wait for it to carry me off into a blissful, anxiety-free sleep.

But then Window Seat leans over me to accept a moist towelette from the flight attendant, and I suddenly feel more awake than ever. Her Seattle grunge aesthetic suggests she should smell like a compost bin, but as she dangles her body in front of mine, I get a whiff of . . . sandalwood? Clean laundry? Sunshine after an afternoon rain?

She smells like opening a window on the first warm day of spring.

It's as I'm sniffing this stranger and thinking about Magnolia Park in early June that I realize she's talking to me. I pull out a single AirPod again, and the music cuts off in my ear. "I'm sorry, what?"

She's still smiling, and she gestures to her long legs. "They really don't make these seats big enough for normal-size humans anymore, do they?"

I'm not sure what to do with this comment, so I sort of laugh, sort of cough in response.

"Where are you headed?" she asks in that same indistinct accent that's either European or merely the effects of chain-smoking during her formative years. "What's your final destination? London?"

"Oh. Uh . . ." This is not a hard question, but my brain has never performed well on-demand. "Porto," I finally tell her, politeness winning out over introversion.

My seatmate presses a hand to her chest. "Me too." Then she rattles off a few foreign words. And *ah*. That must be the accent.

"Oh, sorry, but I don't speak Portuguese."

"Desculpe," she says, still smiling.

"Sorry?"

"Exactly. *Desculpe* is 'sorry' in Portuguese. Seems like something you might want to know." She keeps smiling at me until the pilot comes over the intercom for the welcome speech. "There's only one reason Americans fly straight to Porto," Window Seat continues over the announcement. "Are you doing the Camino?"

I nod.

"Cool. Are you doing the interior route out of Porto or the coastal route?"

I have no idea what that even means. "I-I don't know."

"Just winging it, then?" she asks. "Nice. I did that on the Camino del Notre a few years ago. If you have any questions or want any advice, let me know. This will be my fourth Camino, and a friend of mine actually—"

"Free headphones?" a flight attendant asks, shoving a basket in our direction. I'm grateful for the interruption as we both take a pair. When Window Seat opens her mouth again, introversion triumphs, and I jab the AirPod back in place. I point to my ear and mouth *sorry*.

Then I close my eyes and wait for the Xanax to save me.

The wine is free on international flights.

I learn this when the attendant pushing the drink cart takes one look at my face and asks if I'd like a mini bottle of the generic red in an overtly pitying tone. He passes me two with a wink before getting Window Seat her ginger ale, probably because he's caught me crying during an episode of *Property Brothers: Forever Home* on my seat-back screen.

The Xanax has failed me. We're only two hours into a ten-hour flight, and I'm such a mess of anxiety that another flight attendant comes by to give me a third bottle of red after I polish off the first two. And it's as I'm crying into my wine that it happens. The airplane seems to hiccup in the stratosphere. For a second, I think I'm more drunk than I realize.

The plane trembles a second time. My right hand reaches for the armrest at the same time Window Seat does. Our fingers brush as a shot of Drew's face freezes on my personal TV with the words PA ANNOUNCEMENT bannered across the screen.

"Uh, hello there, folks," says the American pilot. "Looks like we're experiencing some unexpected turbulence, so I'm gonna go ahead and turn on the fasten seat belt sign and ask—"

The rest of the announcement is drowned out by the intense jolt that rattles the overhead bins.

And holy shit. This *is* going to end in a *Yellowjackets* situation. I squeeze the armrest tighter and realize I'm actually squeezing

Window Seat's calloused hand. I'm too panicked to care, and I cling to her as the plane rattles.

This is just anxiety-brain running away with reality, I tell myself. *We're not going to crash.*

The plane rollicks, and the red wine in my stomach rollicks along with it, and for a fleeting moment, my stomach exists in zero-G, floating up toward my rib cage like it did when I first saw Window Seat's face, before my whole body seems to slam back into my seat, with more force driving me downward.

Babies are crying. The captain makes another announcement, and the flight crew hurries to strap themselves into the jump seats. Everyone around me looks worried, even Window Seat, whose dark eyebrows have jumped into her hairline. The old lady across the aisle has put away her knitting and now clutches purple rosary beads, mouthing a prayer.

The TV screens go black, and I finally yank off my free headphones. The full sound of panic hits me. An alarm is going off. The captain's voice crackles in and out as we convulse again.

Doesn't it always seem to go that as soon as you try to figure out your life, your plane plummets into the Arctic Circle? And on my fucking birthday.

I'm going to die before I have the chance to find the right words.

I'm going to die without knowing who I really am.

I'm going to die without anyone else knowing me, either.

"I think I might be a lesbian!" I shout into the chaos. The confession isn't meant for anyone but me, my last chance to test the words on my tongue, to see how they feel before I die.

If anyone does hear me over the din of our imminent deaths, they don't react.

Except Window Seat.

Her rough fingers clutch tighter to mine, and my eyes shift from the blank screen to her worried face. I forgot we're holding hands.

They say your entire life flashes before your eyes in the moments preceding your death, but I don't have much of a life, so instead of a Greatest Hits slideshow featuring every Saturday night I spent working in the store, my pre-death ticker-tape parade is of this stranger's face.

It's a long, narrow face, offset by a Cupid's bow mouth. A dastardly widow's peak. Blue hair, fading to brown and bleach-white around the temples, that's cut into some kind of stylish mullet. A nose ring. A constellation of tattooed stars beneath her left ear, tracing down her long neck. There are probably more tattoos lurking just below the fabric of her gray shirt.

She doesn't pluck her eyebrows, she's not wearing any makeup, and she desperately needs some ChapStick, but she's still beautiful. Or handsome, maybe? A strong jaw and a chin dimple, and that ineffable feeling that she's someone important to me, somehow.

Time unfreezes. Window Seat is still staring at me as the plane shakes like a pinball in the arcade of the gods. "I think I might be a lesbian," I say again, meaning for Window Seat to hear it this time. Because apparently I don't give a shit about having the perfect words when I'm about to die.

Window Seat gives my hand a squeeze. "Cool," she says.

Cool?

Some combination of the wine and the dying makes me keep talking. "I-I don't know for sure if I'm really a lesbian. I went on seventeen first dates with men, and I didn't feel a damn thing for any of them, and for the first time it seemed so obvious that the problem isn't with the men at all."

"Are you sure?" she asks as the plane heaves. "Men are usually the problem."

"The problem is *me*. I-I'm not attracted to them."

"That doesn't sound like a problem."

I shake my head and keep trying to make this stranger understand. "I've been forcing myself to date men my entire life, and

I've always hated it, but I never slowed down long enough to wonder *why*. I . . . I never let myself wonder if . . ." My voice trembles. "I didn't want to question it."

. Window Seat doesn't have a snarky response for that one.

"But if I'm gay, shouldn't I already know that about myself? I mean, I'm thirty-five-years-old today!"

"Oh. Happy birthday!" She grins at me like we're not on the 787 equivalent of the *Hindenburg*.

"Wouldn't I know by now?"

"The messages we receive from society and our families can be very powerful, and the current political climate makes coming out more fraught for a lot of people," she says, perfectly reasonable. At the next patch of turbulence, an overhead storage bin flies open and a woman behind us screams.

I scream louder. "But my family wouldn't give a shit! I grew up in Seattle, and my sister is bisexual, and I have gay aunts!"

But as soon as the words are out of my mouth, I'm thinking about our senior trip to California, when my friend Rachel wasn't allowed to go to San Francisco because that's where the gay people lived. I'm thinking about my friends who were afraid they'd have to share a dorm room with a lesbian and vowed to change in the bathroom stalls every day if it came to that. And the tears come even harder. I turn back to this stranger. "I would know if I were gay. Right?"

Window Seat stares at me with soft brown eyes. They remind me of polished dark walnut. "Would you?"

"It doesn't even matter now! It's too late!"

"Too late for what?"

"For everything! I'm too old, too inexperienced! I'm going to die a *virgin*!"

Window Seat's eyebrows spike all the way up to her widow's peak. "Well, you know, virginity is just a construct of the patriarchy and—"

I blow a raspberry, and she laughs. *Laughs!* On this, the eve of our demise.

"It's not funny! I've never had sex!" I blurt and quickly cover my face with my free hand.

Window Seat somehow remains eerily calm. "It's super common for queer people to miss out on certain adolescent experiences, or to experience them later in life. Our timelines are different than our hetero peers, and many queer people experience a second adolescence when—"

I shake my head again. "I'm too late. It's too late."

"It's never too late to start living as your authentic self," says this beautifully handsome stranger.

"It is if we're all dead!"

Something brushes my shoulder. I wonder if it's falling luggage—preferably something heavy to knock me unconscious for this last part—but when I turn around, I see the flight attendant who snuck me the extra wine staring down at me with the distinct mark of secondhand embarrassment etched into his features. "Miss, I need you to lower your voice," he whispers. "You're upsetting the other passengers."

And that's when I notice the plane is no longer shaking. That it maybe hasn't been shaking for a while now.

A different flight attendant is carefully readjusting the luggage from the open bin, and on the screen in front of me, Drew and Jonathan are fake-bickering again as they install a support beam.

Several things become clear all at once:

The plane isn't going to crash.

No one is going to die.

Except maybe me. From mortification.

Because I just came out to the Beautiful/Handsome stranger who is still holding my hand.

THREE

SOMEWHERE OVER CANADA

Mal

"Fuck . . ."

The woman with the freckles slowly exhales the curse as the disgruntled flight attendant slinks away.

I expected her to apologize for the tenth time, so the shocking profanity makes me laugh. It's probably inappropriate, given the near-death experience everyone thought we were having.

The turbulence was admittedly awful. I'd rank it right up there with landing at the Taipei airport during a typhoon, and that puddle jumper I misguidedly took in the Seychelles because the pilot let me pay him in Jif peanut butter.

But we were never going to *die*.

Freckles, though. She had the fear of death in those saucer-size blue-green eyes. Now, realizing death isn't going to put her out of her misery, her pink skin turns even pinker beneath the constellations of freckles sprinkled across her face.

"I'm so sorry," she gasps in horror.

Ah. *There's the apology.*

"Sorry for frightening small children with your shouts of imminent death?" I ask with a slight cock of my head. "Or sorry for coming out to me?"

Freckles rips her hand away from mine like it burned her, but she was squeezing so tight a minute ago that there's still a faint pressure on my palm after she lets go, like the ghost of a hand still resting in mine.

I try to recall the last time Ruth held my hand like that, but my brain quickly informs me the footage cannot be found. I spent a year with a woman who *never once* held my hand. A year of pretending that I didn't care, that I didn't need that kind of innocent intimacy.

And then Freckles grabbed my hand, and I remembered how nice it feels to be anchored to another person.

Freckles is ignoring me again as she fumbles for the free headphones, her eyes firmly focused on her episode of *Property Brothers*. "Are you really just going to go back to watching HGTV after all that?"

Splotches of red spread down her pale neck. "Yes. Yes, I am," she mutters.

I lean closer and whisper, "You have nothing to be embarrassed about."

This isn't *strictly* true. She did shout about dying a virgin on an airplane. But I feel compelled to make sure this woman knows her lack of experience isn't the embarrassing part. Not figuring out you're gay until thirty-five isn't embarrassing, either.

"Please don't talk to me," Freckles mumbles. "I am busy trying to repress the last thirty minutes."

"Hey," I say gently. I take a risk and tug the cord of her headphones out of the screen to cut off the sound. She doesn't yell at me for doing it, which I take as a sign to keep bugging her. "I hate to break it to you, but there is no repressing something like that. You can't scream *I think I might be a lesbian*, unload all your queer trauma on me like I'm your fairy god-dyke, and then shove it back down again."

"Oh *God*." She covers her blushing face with both hands. "I can't believe I did that."

"Yeah. It's too bad we didn't die."

She drops her hands and turns to face me fully. "That—that wasn't me," she insists. "I'm not that person. That was the wine!"

"And the Xanax, probably." I saw her pop it before takeoff, but it didn't stop her from anxiously tapping her foot for the first two hours. "Bold move, chugging cheap red on top of that."

Her head whips forward again as her polka-dot blush intensifies. "I'm *an idiot.*"

"Nah. I once took Dulcolax instead of Imodium on a sixteen-hour flight to Sydney. You got off easy by comparison."

She doesn't even react to my worst diarrhea-while-traveling story because she's too busy hyperventilating in her seat. At this point, I should probably let this poor woman go back to her *Property Brothers* episode. Let her stew in embarrassment for the rest of the flight.

And I would, if it wasn't for the silence. The first two hours of the flight were unbearably quiet, even with my music at full volume in my headphones. There's an emptiness that creeps in whenever I'm alone these days, making room for my too-loud thoughts.

I can't handle hearing my own thoughts right now, and Freckles is the perfect distraction.

I nudge her with my elbow. "Hey. What's your name?"

She huffs a defeated sigh. "Why? Do you want the details for when you write about this whole humiliating saga in your memoir someday?"

"Oh, sweetheart," I tease her, "you're not making my memoir. I've lived a very interesting life."

Freckles purses her lips, and it takes me a second to realize she's suppressing a laugh. So she *is* capable of laughing at herself.

"I'm Mal," I try, extending a hand toward her.

She stares at it for a moment, as if she doesn't remember the way she clung to me during the turbulence. "Mal? As in *bad*?" she asks, like I'm the human embodiment of a bad omen. There's something about her genuinely frightened tone that makes the words wedge themselves between my ribs like knives.

Mal as in bad.

The thoughts grow too loud to drown out.

I hear my father's rumbling voice, yelling in Portuguese. *What did I do to deserve such a bad daughter?* I see the disappointment etched into his face every time I failed to live up to his expectations. The way he'd tighten his fists at his side, the way he wouldn't talk to me for days at a time if I screwed up. He always wanted me to know that he could take it all away if he wanted to, until the day he finally did.

The memories feel like a tightened fist around my throat, like a boulder sitting on my chest.

"I'm Sadie." Warm fingers suddenly slip between mine, and Freckles's sweaty hand tethers me back to this airplane. I focus on the woman shaking my hand, because that makes it easier to stay in the present instead of lost in a past I can't change.

Her auburn hair is pulled into a loose ponytail with a clip, a few wisps falling around her temples from the almost-crash. Her shoulders are tensed halfway up to her ears, and she's still blushing. Freckles has one of those young, angelic faces that makes her look perpetually sixteen. And those fucking freckles. She's wearing makeup, but they're still visible beneath her thick foundation. She must have a million little reddish-brown freckles covering every inch of her exposed skin. You could play connect-the-dots with those freckles and create an unsolvable maze. You could paint by numbers all over her peaches-and-cream skin.

If we *were* going to die, hers would've been a wonderful face to be my last. I'm trying *not* to stare at what's below that face, but I am fairly certain her body is equally divine. Soft and curvy, the plump, pale skin of her stomach visible between her high-waisted yoga pants and crop top.

Okay, fine, maybe I am staring.

"Sadie," I repeat. Her name tastes like sweet tea. "So maybe a lesbian, huh?"

She groans again. "No. I don't know. Maybe? Or maybe just queer? Or . . . I googled something called asexuality, and that could be it. But I just don't . . . how are you supposed to figure it out?"

It takes all my willpower not to smile as she works herself into another bluster.

"You could try talking about it with your fairy god-dyke."

That gets her to snort a laugh. "Seventeen dates," she says. "I let my sister set me up on *seventeen* dates, and I couldn't make myself feel *anything*, and at some point, I felt like I was looking at my whole life through this different lens. I've never been attracted to men, but I've never considered that there might be another option."

This particular bluster involves frantic hand flailing, and I'm not sure why I find it so utterly charming.

"But I couldn't figure out how to tell my sister any of this, so I kept going on those stupid dates until I couldn't stand it another minute. And now I'm *here*."

I think Sadie is crying again, the way she did when the Property Brothers built that piano alcove before the turbulence. "Why did I spend so many years repressing all of this?" She takes a sharp breath. "I shoved it down to a place so dark and deep, it could never reach me. And now I can't even think the word *lesbian* without crying."

"Because you don't want to be a lesbian?" I hedge.

"Because if I'm a lesbian, then I tortured myself dating men *for nothing*." She fumbles to hide the evidence of her tears, as if she didn't draw my attention to them two seconds ago. As if she hasn't been breaking off bits of her heart and sharing them with me like the other half of a Bueno bar. "I've punished myself for not making it work with men. But now . . . I mean, I've never even kissed a woman."

For one deranged second, I wonder what she would do if I kissed her right now on this airplane.

It's probably not the right time, on account of the tears and extreme emotional distress. And all the wine.

She sighs. "I guess there's no point in imagining an alternate-universe Sadie who isn't starting from zero at thirty-five." It feels like the rest of the plane has faded away into the white noise of the engine and it's only the two of us in this intimate little bubble where this total stranger keeps trusting me with her vulnerabilities.

I fumble for something useful to say and land on, "Maybe you can try to forgive yourself for not being ready instead."

Sadie blinks and blushes and tries so hard to hold back her tears. "Ready?"

"Yeah. Maybe you weren't ready to know you're gay." I shrug. "Maybe it's not too late. Maybe you're right where you're supposed to be."

Sadie shakes her head in disbelief.

"I'm telling you this as a concerned queer elder: you are not too old," I say slowly, clearly, hoping she will finally hear me. "Growing up, our heterosexual peers got to experiment and explore and figure themselves out, but thanks to the twin horrors of homophobia and heteronormativity, many of us missed out on that whole developmental phase."

Sadie twirls her hair thoughtfully, and I watch the red strands wind around her pale finger like ribbons on a present.

"You weren't able to have a queer adolescence, and that's not your fault."

"I don't really know if . . . I mean, maybe . . ." She twirls and twirls. "Maybe I'm not even a . . . *lesbian.*" She whispers the last part like it's a dirty word, and like she didn't shout it many times when she thought we were all about to die.

"Maybe you're not." I shrug again. "But in my experience, not many straight people feel the need to come out in the midst of a near-death experience," I say, and I watch as she folds in on herself, scrunching up her shoulders again, tucking in her elbows, trying to make herself small in her seat.

"I-I . . . I'm sorry," she stutters, "but I'm . . . tired. Do you mind if I just . . . ?" She points to the paused seat-back screen.

"You can do whatever you want, Sadie."

She slots one headphone into place, her eyes glued forward. The silence fills my head like old television static, a haunting emptiness my darkest thoughts are all too eager to fill.

"Can I watch with you?" I ask, pointing to her screen.

She hesitates, fiddling with the second headphone a moment before she offers it to me like some kind of olive branch. Sadie with the freckles allows me to share her headphones and her armrest as I lean in closer to watch Drew and Jonathan lament the Soto family's cramped kitchen, grateful for all the noise that fills my head.

"Do you think they'll take out that wall and put in an unnecessarily large kitchen island?" I ask her.

Sadie's jaw is clenched, and after a long stretch of silence, I'm convinced she's going to ignore me again, even though we're attached by cheap airline headphones. But then she smiles, just a little bit. Just in the corner of her mouth. "Drew and Jonathan? Never."

C'est La Vi with Me

HOME	ABOUT ME	DESTINATIONS	BLOG POSTS

The Ultimate Camino Packing List

Vi Wells
April 29, 2025 68 comments

As always, Nomads, this post contains affiliate links, and I receive a small commission if you purchase anything from these links. I only promote products that have helped me embrace my life of adventure!

If you've been around this blog for a while, you know there's nothing I love more than a travel hack! And if that hack helps me save space in my carry-on? I'm a goner!

How you pack for the Camino de Santiago can depend on many different factors, such as the Camino path you're trekking, the duration of the trek, and the time of year you plan to go. For example, if you plan to spend 40 days doing the Camino Frances in October, your packing list is going to look very different from a packing list for doing the Portuguese Coastal Camino for 14 days in May (like I'm doing).

It's also important to consider where you plan to stay each night before drafting your packing list. Some pilgrims choose to stay in municipal albergues, where you pay as little as 10 euros for a bunk bed in a room with anywhere from 6 to 30 pilgrims. If that's your plan, you'll likely want to include a sleeping bag, pillow, and maybe even a sleeping pad on your packing list, along with a quick-dry towel and shower shoes. However, I'm traveling with Beatrix Tours, and all of our accommodations include private, double, or triple rooms (depending on your price point) with en suites, so all of my bedding will be provided for me.

There are a million Camino packing lists out there written by pilgrims who have done this trek dozens of times, and you can find some of my favorite ones here. I also wanted to share some of my must-have travel items that will certainly be making the trek with me!

- This 40L Osprey pack.

- My Keen hiking boots—both stylish and practical for long days on the trail.

- My favorite yoga pants by FitCheck. They come in a dozen beautiful colors, and their sizes go up to 4XL, because they know that us thick girls want to look hot while exercising too.

- This dress from Columbia. It rolls up super small in your bag, doesn't wrinkle easily, and will look great for nights out after a long day of walking.

- My <u>portable sound machine</u> by Hatch. It's meant for babies, but I think it's perfect for drowning out noise at a loud hotel (and it comes in this adorable mint green).

- My favorite <u>moisture-wicking undies</u> from Duluth Trading Company. Not only do they keep me dry in my downstairs, but they're cute enough for any surprise rendezvous you might have with fellow travelers. 😉

- This <u>incredible travel makeup bag</u>. What can I say? Even when I'm roughin' it, I like to look good. How else do you think I find myself in surprise rendezvous?

FOUR

LONDON, ENGLAND
Tuesday, May 13, 2025

Mal

Freckles snores. *Loudly*.

She passes out around the third kitchen transformation involving two-toned cabinets, and she doesn't wake up again until they shove her breakfast between her forehead and the seat-back tray. And even then, she simply relocates her head and keeps snoring until we begin our final descent. As she fumbles for her things, she doesn't acknowledge me or the discarded headphones tangled around the armrest between us. By the time we land in London, it's almost as if that brief bubble of vulnerability never existed, like this woman never opened up to me at a cruising altitude of thirty-four thousand feet.

"I hope you find what you're looking for on the Camino, Sadie," I tell her before we part ways.

Her eyes flicker over my face like she can't quite recall where she knows me from. "Thank you," she finally says in a clipped tone. It's our aisle's turn to deplane, and she stands to pull a pristine Osprey backpack down from the bins. It must weigh a ton, because she almost falls over when it comes down on her head. I leap up to help, and our hands brush one last time as she manages to wrangle her arms through the straps.

"Bom caminho," I say in Portuguese. *Good journey*.

She frowns at me in confusion and turns around to march down the aisle. By the time I grab my bag from a few rows ahead, she's gone.

Jet-lagged and stale, I step into the terminal to find Heathrow *Heathrow-ing*. The airport is its typical self: overcrowded, over-perfumed, and overstimulating, all flashing florescent lights and overlapping noises spilling out of different stores.

I love it. Absolutely everything is a distraction from my noisy thoughts.

A few feet from the gate, the terminal transforms into a ridiculous luxury shopping mall, with life-size posters of famous actors selling Prada and Versace and Coach. Handbags and watches, fragrances and coats, and, of course, VAT-free cigarettes sold by the caseload.

There's nothing quite like the rhythm of an international airport. The harmony of a dozen different languages, the frantic tempo of shoes and luggage wheels against the lacquered floors as people hurry to catch their flights; the melody of suits shouting at invisible people in their ears as college students have hushed conversations over their travel guides. I've always loved the possibility of it all, the potential. The hustle and the energy. Airports are like purgatory. You're nowhere and everywhere, suspended in a temporal no-man's-land until you step onto your next flight.

Each gate is like a magical portal to a different world. This door will take you to Vienna, that one leads to Johannesburg. Every door will take you away from whatever past you need to escape.

Airports have been one of the only constants in my life.

Some people chop off their hair after a bad breakup. I book international flights.

When my first love broke my heart at eighteen, I got on the next train that would take me to the Edinburgh Airport and booked a flight to France. When my undergrad girlfriend and I realized we were better off as friends, I went on a solo road trip around Iceland. When I got dumped by my grad school professor, I trekked the Annapurna Circuit in Nepal. I got cheated on, so I went to Patagonia.

Heartbreak doesn't hit the same when you're on your way to experience something brand-new. Most problems seem small when you're standing at the foot of the Pyramids or the Colosseum or Chichen Itza. Nothing helps me forget an ending better than the new beginning promised by a boarding pass. Keep moving, keep exploring, keep focused on what's next, never what's passed.

So when Ruth dumped me a week ago, I knew what I had to do. Even if the breakup wasn't actually the bad part.

I let myself get swept up in the current of Heathrow until my phone vibrates in my fleece pocket, and I look down to see Michelle's face floating above the red and green phone icons.

"Mal, where the fuck did you put the colander?" Michelle screeches over the distant sound of pots and pans clanging. Closer to the phone, a baby starts crying. "Oh, no. Oh, shush shush, baby boy," she coos softly. "I know, I know. Mommy shouldn't have raised her voice. And she shouldn't have used an adult word. But sometimes, Auntie Mal drives her to it."

"Hello, Cedar." I make kissy noises into the phone, hoping the baby can hear me. "Did Mommy look for the colander in the cupboard next to the oven?"

"Of course she did. *I* did." Michelle sputters in frustration. "And I'm not talking about the shitty—I mean, *poopy*—plastic one we bought in undergrad. I need the nice metal one. What kind of forest ecologist would I be if I used *plastic* kitchen utensils?"

"A tired one who is doing her best?" I try. "And aren't Kwame's parents coming over for dinner *tomorrow* night?"

"It's called meal prep, Mal!" Michelle hisses.

"At"—I glance down at my phone again to confirm that it's not even nine in the morning here in London, which means it's—"two in the morning? Michelle, why are you meal prepping at this ungodly hour?"

Cedar cries out again, and Michelle makes a few more shushing sounds before she continues. "Cedar woke up and he won't go back to sleep, and I have the submission deadline on that climate paper coming up, but I can't work on my data sets with a baby strapped to my chest, so instead I'm getting ready for Kwame's parents, because for some inexplicable reason, I told them I would make the yams!"

Her voice has become increasingly frantic over the course of this rant, and I can picture her so perfectly: she's probably standing in the kitchen of her mom's old house in Ballard, her three-month-old strapped to her chest in his Ergobaby carrier. I'm sure she's bouncing up and down to soothe him while she throws open the ancient cupboards we painted white four years ago, when her mom bought a condo in Palm Springs, and Michelle took over the mortgage on her childhood home. I flew into Seattle from Guatemala City for the housewarming and ended up staying over a month to help her fix up the place. She was in the second year of her PhD, and she didn't have the time or the money to fix the rotting front porch or replace the galvanized steel pipes.

Time and money are the two things I always have in spades.

That was before Kwame moved in with her, before I met Ruth and ended up staying in Seattle for over a year. Before a week ago, when Ruth kicked me out of the condo I bought her—the one I'd put in her name, like a lovesick fool—and I had to start crashing on Michelle's couch.

Before I booked a plane ticket and fucked off, like I always do.

I'm sure the newborn exhaustion is evident in Michelle's brown eyes, but her unwashed wisps of blond hair always look intentionally tousled, never greasy, like her years of camping for forestry field research were the perfect gauntlet to prepare her for motherhood. She's probably standing in front of the giant window behind the sink, where the sill is lined with dozens of plants. Some of them are connected to Michelle and Kwame's research, some are herbs for cooking, and some are simply beautiful.

In a few hours, the sun will hit those yellow walls and turn the whole house honeysuckle, and the kitchen will smell like fresh mint, rosemary, and thyme.

A strange homesickness slices through me. Strange, because I've never lived in one place long enough to consider it *home*, and I've never let anyone get close enough to be missed. Except Michelle.

And, by extension, Kwame and Cedar. Though to a lesser degree.

I take an audible deep breath and hope Michelle does the same five thousand miles away.

"Kwame's parents aren't going to know which colander you used at two a.m.," I try to reassure her.

She sighs. "True."

"And do you *really* want to be the kind of wife who bends over backward to please your in-laws?"

"Frack no."

I smile into the phone at her censored curse. Overheard, a chime sounds and a pleasant feminine voice announces a gate change for a Lufthansa flight.

"I take it you made it to Heathrow, then," Michelle notes in a quiet voice. Perhaps Cedar is falling back to sleep.

"Yes," I say, equally quiet as I dodge a rogue wheeling suitcase.

"Have you eaten anything yet?"

"I'm on my way to find food, *Mom*chelle." The terminal opens into a hexagonal food court, and I beeline my way toward a cafeteria-style place I remember serving black coffee.

"*Food,* not just black coffee," she scolds in demonstration of her terrifying psychic friendship powers. When I arrive at the eatery, I grab the largest cup for coffee, but I also grab a banana. For Michelle.

"I don't need you to micromanage my eating habits from five thousand miles away," I snap, even though I sort of do. Grief does weird things to your appetite, and sometimes I forget about food all day until it's midnight and I can't sleep because my stomach is an angry pit of despair.

Not that I'm grieving. Not exactly.

I position my cup beneath the coffee carafe, but then I force myself to put a sausage roll on my tray.

"Yes, you do," Michelle snaps back, because she knows me far too well. "I'm worried about you. This whole trip feels a lot like fleeing again."

"I'm not *fleeing*. I was going to fly out for the funeral in three weeks anyway, and now I'm arriving early to do a quick Camino."

"It's the funeral part of that sentence that concerns me."

My hands tighten around my tray, and I find myself frozen in the middle of this airport cafeteria. The fucking funeral.

In three weeks I'll have to publicly mourn the man who gave me life and then ruined it. I'll have to sit in a church, under the watchful eyes of someone else's god, and say my final goodbyes. People will come up to me, want to shake my hand, want to tell me they're sorry for my loss, even though I didn't lose anything when he died; I'd already lost it all twenty years ago.

The other end of the phone is silent, and the thoughts swarm like bees. My ribs squeeze against my lungs, and I temporarily forget how to breathe until, blissfully, a man with a cockney accent screams at me. "You gonna pay for that, love?"

My body and brain come back online like a rebooted computer, and I walk my tray over to the register. I pay with my phone, and when I finally respond to Michelle, my voice is even. "Oh, by the way, I drank the last of your oat milk and left you some money to replace it."

"I don't give a darn about the oat milk." She pauses, then clicks her tongue. "Are you referring to the hundred-dollar bill under my Yellowstone magnet?"

"Of course."

"That isn't remotely how much oat milk costs," Michelle says in the disgusted tone she usually reserves for commenting on the contents of her son's diapers. "You're doing it again, you know."

"Doing what?"

"Running away from your feelings. Falling in love with the first pretty girl you see and chasing her halfway across the world because that's easier than sitting with your thoughts and feelings."

I gasp indignantly into my giant coffee. "There's no girl. No one said anything about a girl."

"There will be a girl soon enough. There always is."

"I don't know what you're talking about." I'm temporarily distracted by a head of red curls that flashes in the corner of my eye. I turn, but it isn't her.

"There was probably a girl on the plane." Michelle's voice is deep and dry, like a perfect white wine.

"How *dare* you? I'll have you know there was horrible turbulence the whole flight! We almost crashed! We almost *died*."

"No, you did not."

"No, we did not," I concede. "But if we had died, wouldn't you feel guilty about these false accusations?"

"I've known you for almost nineteen years," Michelle says pointedly. "Don't act like this isn't a thing you do."

It is a thing I do. If anyone knows my dysfunctional romantic habits, it's Michelle. She was the undergrad girlfriend who necessitated the three-week Icelandic road trip. She was once a girl who lived halfway across the world, and I fell in love with her instantly.

It was Berlin, spring semester, during a study-abroad program. Michelle was a college junior studying environmental science at Western Washington University. I was a twenty-year-old haphazardly accumulating credits in everything from psychology to agriculture to linguistics at an American school in Madrid.

She was a lesbian who loved astrology, reality television, and dancing until four in the morning in faux-leather pants and feather boas.

I wasn't interested in labels, and I loved loud parties, new beginnings, and her.

I loved her so much, in fact, that when the study-abroad program ended, I followed her back to the tiny Pacific Northwest town of Bellingham, Washington, just to be close to her.

In true sapphic style, we immediately got an apartment together. And our romance lasted a whopping six weeks into our lease before we broke up.

But unlike every other person I've impulsively fallen in love with since, I never fell *out* of love with Michelle. Our love simply shifted. We became best friends who stayed close, even as I flitted around the country, around the world. Michelle got into the University of Washington's Forest Ecology program and settled in Seattle where she grew up. I took dozens of jobs at dozens of nonprofit organizations around the world and settled nowhere.

Eventually, I decided I liked the label *lesbian* after all; Michelle met Kwame and realized she's bisexual. And a year and a half ago, I came to Seattle for Michelle's wedding, met Kwame's cousin Ruth, and did the insta-love thing all over again.

Michelle has seen me at my absolute worst. She knows all my annoying habits, all my secret neuroses, all my childhood trauma, and no matter how many times I've tried to push her away, she never budges. She's the only person I can be my true

self with, the only person who never leaves. Michelle is my pla-
tonic soulmate.

"You make me sound like some kind of slutty womanizer," I
complain now through bites of sausage roll.

"You're not a womanizer," she quickly corrects. "You're a
serial monogamist, and I think you should try being single for
more than a day this time."

I swallow. "For the sake of full transparency, I should probably tell you that there was, in fact, a woman on the airplane . . ."

"I fucking knew it."

"It wasn't my fault! She had *freckles*."

Michelle sighs again, and this one carries a potent mixture
of exhaustion, exasperation, and a hint of maternal disappointment.

"Don't get your panties in a twist. I'm never going to see her
again."

"Worry about your own damn panties," she snaps.

"I don't want you to worry about me, M," I tell her seriously.
"Ruth dumped me, and I'm taking a trip to heal my broken
heart. It's not that complicated."

"Ruth didn't have the ability to break your heart," she says,
effortlessly cutting through my emotional smokescreen. "But
your *dad* . . ."

"I don't give a shit about my dad," I insist, "dead or not."

Michelle's tone abruptly shifts to cartoonish placating. "That
was a nice, big fart, baby boy! Yes! Yes, it was! Get that gas out of
your cute little belly!"

The tension of our conversation dissipates into wild laughter
as Michelle continues to celebrate her baby's flatulence.

Sometimes, I think Michelle puts me on the same level as
her colicky, constipated newborn. And maybe that's fair. She
has a PhD and a postdoc position at UW. She's doing critical
research on forest resiliency and global climate change. She's a

world-changing Aquarius, and I'm just an aimless Gemini who doesn't know the cost of oat milk.

"I'm not Cedar," I tell her when the laughter stops. "You don't have to take care of me."

"Of course I'm going to take care of you. That's what friends do." Michelle's voice goes soft, but no part of her is babying me. "Just like how you've always taken care of me when I've needed it. Whether you want to deal with it or not, your girlfriend dumped you the same day your dad died and left you this massive, unexpected inheritance, and if you don't deal with that grief, you're going to—"

"How can I grieve someone who never accepted me?" The words stop Michelle's tirade in its tracks. I wish my tone was flippant, but I've never been good at staying flippant with Michelle.

The memory roars in my ears, in my heart.

The first time I fell in love with a girl, I held nothing back. I was seventeen, and I believed Prithi was *the one*. We were roommates at our boarding school in Scotland and started dating in our final year before university. We even made plans to attend Oxford together. I was positively bursting with love, and I desperately wanted my father to know about it. I wanted to shout about my love for the whole damn world to hear.

So, the summer before Oxford, I decided to come out to my father.

I should have known better than to trust Valentim Costa with my real feelings.

"Grief isn't logical," Michelle finally says.

"Look, I'm going to miss my flight if I don't—"

She sees through this lie and barrels on. "I know it's tempting to distract yourself with something—or *someone*—new, but maybe you can spend some time alone with yourself on this trip . . ." Michelle tries in the soft voice she uses for Cedar. "Spend some time *reflecting*. You're the most generous, most loving person I know, but you tend to lose yourself in relationships."

"No I don't," I argue. "When have I ever done that?"

"Well, when we were dating, you pretended to like *Battlestar Galactica* . . ."

She's got me there.

"And I love that about you! You're selfless to a fault. But maybe on this trip, you could be a little selfish. Focus on yourself."

I know she's right about everything. She always is. On the plane, I used Sadie as a distraction, and if she'd given any indication that she wanted me to, I would've easily abandoned my planned trip to follow her on the Camino. I would've spent two weeks falling in love with her.

And then I would've fallen out of love, because that's what I always do, and I'd be right back where I started: with a dead dad who didn't want me, and an inheritance I don't want, either.

In three weeks, I'll have to go to my dad's funeral and finally decide what to do with the legacy he left me. I don't need distractions. I need some fucking clarity.

But I'm not going to admit this to Michelle with any sincerity. "I get it," I say dismissively. "I will have adult feelings and make adult choices. No Romeo antics. No love at first sight, no following strangers to second locations, no getting carried away by fleeting delusions of true love. This will be a romance-free trip."

"Mal!" she shrieks, and Cedar echoes with a bleating cry.

"What? Do you want me to find true love or not? You're sending me mixed messages here, M."

"No, Mal!" Michelle's voice almost trembles with rage into the phone. "Why are there sandy seashells in my metal colander?"

Oh, *right*. That's where I put it.

LIKED BY MOLLYMACDOUGALWELLS AND 13,419 OTHERS
cestlavi

Guest Blogger Introduction Post!

Hey Nomads! As you can see, I'm not Vi. I'm the other, more boring Wells sister, Sadie, and I'll be taking over this spot for the next two weeks as I complete the Portuguese Camino with @Beatrixtours. I'm sorry you're stuck with me while my sister heals from her injury. This is my first time traveling abroad or doing anything even remotely adventurous. I'm nervous and excited, and I hope you will stick around to see how it goes. Thanks for reading, and sorry again.

#cestlaviwithme #travelblog #broadsabroad #travel #portugal #spain #caminodesantiago #solowomentravelers

IMAGE DESCRIPTION: a white woman with long red hair wearing a black zip up and white crop top posing in front of a window at Heathrow Airport

Comments

beatrixtours
We can't wait to meet you and have you as part of our Camino family!

mollymacdougalwells
I am so incredibly proud of you, my girl. Get out there and see the world. Your mama loves you!

zaraisavegan
Whoa you look exactly like your sister just much older

jonassalt
r u even queer tho?

thegregorygraham69
my thick goddess! You do not need to be single any longer. I will love you forever. Check your DMs!

FIVE

LONDON, ENGLAND

Sadie

I need food. Emotionally. Cognitively. Gastronomically.

I need it to soak up the red wine still lingering in my gut. I need it to put an end to the headache that developed as soon as I smelled the eighty different perfumes sold in Heathrow's C Terminal.

If I'm ever going to locate my connecting flight to Porto, I need brain fuel, especially since I slept through the breakfast they served on the plane.

I wander through the overstimulating airport, trying to find something edible that doesn't cost twenty pounds, because my wine-soaked brain can't handle exchange rates. I eventually stumble upon a cafeteria that looks promising, but as soon as I grab a tray, I spot Window Seat at a nearby table.

Mal. My bad-luck charm.

She's wearing her giant headphones, and she's talking animatedly between gulps of coffee. She doesn't see me, but my stomach drops anyway at the sight of those expressive eyebrows, that bowed mouth, those star tattoos behind her ear.

And it hits me like a solid oak armoire falling down a flight of stairs: I *came out* to this woman. That wasn't a Xanax-induced hallucination. After years of dismissing every suspicion, ignoring every impulse, and repressing every damn feeling, I told the first ostensibly queer woman I saw that I'm a lesbian because three glasses of wine and a Xanax convinced me I was dying.

Probably. I'm *probably* a lesbian.

Or . . . *maybe* a lesbian?

Maybe I'm queer, or maybe I'm just having a nervous break-down.

Except what did Mal say? *In my experience, not many straight people feel the need to come out in the midst of a near-death experience.*

Another flush of embarrassment sweeps over me.

I told a beautifully handsome, effortlessly confident stranger that I've never had sex. She must've thought I was ridiculous.

The funny thing is, Mal didn't make me feel ridiculous at all. She treated every misguided word that came flying out of my mouth, no matter how absurd, like it was important.

Across the cafeteria, Mal glances up from her coffee, and I instinctively duck behind the partition to avoid being seen. Like a child.

When I stand up again, I catch a glimpse of her hazel eyes. The V of her lips is curled into an easy, amused smile as she talks to the person on her phone. Mal isn't merely Beautiful/Hand-some; she has the air of someone who is completely at home in her own body. She moves her lean frame and her slender limbs with purpose, with intention. I bet she's never apologized for taking up space in the world.

I can't believe I told her I'm a lesbian.

And based on my picture-perfect memory of her mouth, I can't believe *I* didn't suspect I might be a lesbian a long-ass time ago.

As soon as I take my phone out of airplane mode, I'm flooded with messages from Vi. I find a bathroom with weirdly podlike stalls and rummage through my pack for my toiletries. In front of the mirror, I assess the severe damage.

I look as disoriented as I feel. Heathrow is a timeless vortex, and I don't know if it's morning or evening, if I'm hungry or just hungover. If I even exist at all. I do know that my skin looks both dry and greasy somehow, that my eyes are puffy and red, and that I'm sticky everywhere.

I've never been this brand of tired before, not even after a twelve-hour day on my feet at the store. I force myself to brush my teeth, freshen my makeup, and redo my hair. Then I find the one place in the terminal that has natural light and take a selfie.

HAPPY NOW? I text Vi once the introductory post is uploaded.

ARE YOU HAPPY? She texts back. YOU LOOK LIKE SOMEONE JUST PUT A GLASS ON YOUR GEORGIAN COFFEE TABLE WITHOUT A COASTER.

IT'S CALLED A BUTLER'S TABLE AND IT'S MAHOGANY, YOU PLEBE.

It's a three-hour flight from London to Porto, and by the time we land, I've been reduced to a hungover, jet-lagged, food-deprived zombie who can barely function. The utter hell of the customs line doesn't even register until I'm at the counter and a buff Portuguese man looks up from my passport and asks, "Business or pleasure?"

He's speaking English, but I blink at him uncomprehendingly. "Are you here for work or leisure travel?" he rephrases.

"Pleasure. Uh, I mean, leisure," I manage, and he firmly stamps my passport.

I'm back on autopilot, sleepwalking to baggage claim, getting swept up in the crowds of people moving toward the exit. I somehow put one foot in front of the other until I can see windows, sunshine, and the outside world. The Porto Airport is nothing like Heathrow. There's not a Coach store next to a Burberry, there's no overwhelming perfume smell, and no one runs into me without apologizing. The central atrium is compact and relatively empty when I come through the final security doors.

"Ms. Wells!"

My brain doesn't register my own name until it's said three times at increasing volumes. "Ms. Sadie Wells!" A hand on my shoulder. "Hello, Ms. Wells!"

Some foggy instinct tells me that I'm supposed to turn toward the voice, and I spot a woman wearing a tie-dyed Beatrix Tours T-shirt and high-waisted linen pants. "Wow! You look exactly like your sister! I recognized you immediately!" She throws her arms into the air like she's either praising Jesus or celebrating a tequila shot. "Welcome to Portugal!"

"Hi," I say, half-dazed, stretching a hand toward this woman. "I'm Sadie."

"Inez Oliveira!" She brushes aside my hand and opts to take me by both shoulders, planting a kiss on each of my cheeks. She smells floral and sweet, and her skin is soft, and her lips are on my face, and I'm definitely blushing as she kisses my cheeks. "I'm your guide to the Camino and your own spiritual awakening for the next two weeks!"

My brain scrambles through the two frantic Duolingo lessons I attempted on the way to the airport. "Bom dia!"

Inez keeps smiling at me. "Bom *d*ia," she corrects, emphasizing the hard *d* sound. I pronounced it *bom gia*, the way the green bird taught me. "Bom *g*ia is the Brazilian pronunciation," she explains. "I'm from Brazil originally, but here, people say *bom dia*. And technically, it's almost three in the afternoon, so we say boa tar*de*."

I learned the wrong version of Portuguese. Damn green bird. "Desculpe," I apologize. At least I know that one.

"It's nothing!" she says, reaching out for my shoulders again to give them a friendly squeeze. Inez has the energy of an eighties Jazzercise instructor, the voice of a televangelist, and the face of a Brazilian supermodel. She wears her hair in a long Afro that frames her face like a halo, her dark-brown skin shimmers with some kind of glittery makeup, and her wrists jangle with chakra beads and crystal bracelets.

"We are waiting for one other pilgrim—" She cuts off mid-sentence, and her already glowing face somehow lights up even more. "Maëlys!" she shouts at someone behind me. It sounds like she's saying *Mileys*, like there are two Miley Cyruses coming toward us.

But no. There are no Miley Cyruses.

I hear a raspy voice say, "Inez! Did I keep you waiting?"

And I recognize that voice.

She comes fully into view. Blue mullet and tattoos, her pack slung over one shoulder and her giant water bottle swinging like a bell. We must have been on the same connecting flight.

"Sadie!" Inez trills. "This is Maëlys Gonçalves Costa. She'll be walking the Camino with us!"

Maëlys. Mal. As in a maelstrom. My face is positively on fire.

I didn't just come out to a random stranger on a plane; I came out to someone on my Camino tour.

Someone I will be stuck with for the next two weeks.

Mal

"Freckles!"

The word flies out of my mouth before I can stop it. Out of the corner of my eye, I see Inez's confusion, but my gaze is focused on the deep red blush spreading down Sadie's neck.

The coincidence of it is almost too much. She's standing there with her stiff trekking pack, looking at Inez for an explanation, because *she's on the tour*.

Michelle is truly *always* right.

Even jet-lagged, hungover, and exhausted, in the unflattering lighting of the Porto Airport, with a look of utter panic on her face at the sight of me, Sadie is the dangerous kind of pretty. The kind of pretty that makes me want to fly her to Greece so I can watch her watch the sunset on Santorini. The kind of pretty that makes me want to get a dog or a Costco membership or a RAV4. The kind of pretty I fall for every damn time.

If I'm going to focus on myself this trip, I need to be far away from Sadie and her freckles.

"Hello again," I finally say. Very neutral, very detached, very not-Romeo-like.

Inez bobs her head between us. "Oh. Do you already know each other?" she asks in that thick Brazilian accent that reminds me of summer, good espresso, and the first time we met.

I was eighteen, heartbroken and angry as hell at the whole damn world. I had a pair of Vans and my old JanSport backpack, and I set out alone on the Camino Frances from St. Jean Pied de Port. Inez was twenty-two and trekking solo after finishing university in Barcelona.

At first, we just walked together casually, finding each other on the trail each day, sticking together when it was convenient and parting ways when it wasn't. Then, one night, we ended up at the same albergue that turned out to have a horrific case of bedbugs that scarred us both emotionally. So the next night, we splurged and split the cost of a real hotel room, with no bugs and a bathtub where we could soak our aching bodies. We were inseparable after that, walking the rest of the way to Santiago side by side, staying in the same albergue or shared private room each night.

There was nothing romantic about our partnership; I was too young for her and still madly in love with Prithi, even if she had ripped my heart in half with her bare hands. Inez hadn't transitioned yet, and she wasn't in a good place mentally. Romance wasn't even on her radar. But we became a Camino family, and there was something about that bond that felt *better* than romance.

We've mostly stayed in contact through WhatsApp messages, and we've only seen each other in person a handful of times since that first trip, but when I felt the itch to escape Seattle, she was the first person I called. That's how I ended up on her Portuguese Camino tour at the last minute.

"We don't know each other," I finally tell Inez as Sadie stews awkwardly beside us. "Not really. We were just on the same flight."

"Oh yes, of course! I booked your tickets together!" Inez beams at us like our fateful meeting in this moment is the greatest joy of her life. "And now you are about to become partners on the road to self-discovery! Pluto has moved into Aquarius, which means it's the perfect time for transformation, rebirth, and inner contemplation!"

God, how I've missed her mystic bullshit.

"Sadie was also a last-minute addition to our tour," Inez explains. "Her sister is a travel influencer who was going to cover the tour for her blog, but then she broke her foot abseiling, so Sadie is taking her place and doing the blog for her!"

"It was parasailing and her big toe, but um, yeah." Sadie stares down at her feet.

"Mal and I met on my first-ever Camino," she says, continuing her introductions. "She's originally from Portugal, and she spent summers here with her father, so she's a good resource to have on our trip!"

I try to mirror Inez's smile, but I've been on Portuguese soil for all of thirty minutes, and already people are reminding me of my shit father and those shit summers.

"Isn't this so exciting!" Inez claps her hands together and bounces on her toes. "In just a few hours, we'll embark on a journey toward Santiago and toward living as our most authentic selves!" Then Inez goes so far as to poke Sadie in the ribs. "I hope you're ready to shed all preconceptions about yourself and dig deep into the core of who Sadie Wells really is."

Sadie's heartbeat is nearly audible in the Francisco Sá Carneiro Airport, and I find myself wishing I could reassure her again. I wish I could reach out and hold her hand, because dealing with Sadie's emotional turmoil is so much easier than dealing with my own.

But I don't.

"Come!" Inez excitedly throws her arms into the air. "To the road of self-actualization."

A taxi takes the three of us into the heart of Porto, where we're meeting up with the rest of the tour group at the Sé Cathedral: the same cathedral where my father's funeral will be held in three weeks.

As we drive along the Douro River sparkling in the midday sun, I try not to think about the last time I came to this city, this country. It was over five years ago now, for my father's seventieth birthday. I was living in Amsterdam at the time, volunteering at an LGBTQ+ call center for teens in crises. When the invitation arrived, I had no intention of flying to Porto for one of my father's self-indulgent celebrations. But working with queer kids who were trying to resolve their family trauma tricked me into thinking it might be time to resolve my own.

My dad called, begging me to come to his party. So, against my better judgment, I did.

But he only wanted me there as a prop, as physical proof that he was a good father. I was something to parade around to his friends when I was in a charming mood, something to hide away whenever I wasn't. That's all I ever was to him: an accessory, like his Gucci sunglasses and Jaeger-LeCoultre wristwatch. If I didn't reflect what he wanted people to see, well . . . then it was better if no one remembered that Valentim Costa had a daughter at all.

The taxi drives past the Dom Luís I Bridge, and the medieval city center comes into view, with its terra-cotta roofs and narrow white, red, and yellow buildings checkered along crooked streets. On the hill overlooking Ribeira, the towers of the Sé Cathedral loom large.

"It looks like King's Landing," Sadie murmurs with her face plastered to her window.

"That's Croatia, actually."

Sadie squeezes the backpack on her lap and flushes red. "I-I've never been to Europe before."

My head turns back to my window and I see this spectacular city through her awestruck eyes. The dazzling river, the turquoise sky, and the city spread out on those hills, seemingly held together by magic and history.

Portugal is quite beautiful, if you don't have ugly memories here.

The taxi deposits us in a narrow alley near the church, and Sadie can barely get out of the car with her oversized pack. Then she waddles up the steps toward the cathedral under its massive weight, which is even more comical.

"Do you need help?" I offer, as Inez skips ahead to find the other members of our group. Because surely I can offer to help this woman without wanting to pick out Ikea furniture together.

"I've got it," she grunts.

Her confidence is undermined by the way she pitches and sways with every step. I follow close behind, ready to catch her if necessary. It takes a while, but we eventually make it to the cobbled courtyard and find Inez standing by a Camino marker. The concrete pillar is only about a meter tall, with an image of a yellow scallop shell engraved against a square blue background, the symbol of the Camino de Santiago. Below that is a yellow arrow pointing to the direction of the path.

Inez is talking to a man who must be her administrative assistant, based on his impractical jeans and espadrilles. He has a clipboard and Inez's pack at his feet—the same 30L Deuter pack she wore a few years ago when we met in Sweden to walk the Way of St. Olaf. I check in with Mr. Espadrilles, and he confirms my traveler's health insurance before he asks me to sign one last waiver saying Beatrix isn't responsible for any injuries I may sustain on the journey.

The courtyard is crowded with tourists and pilgrims, most of them clearly at the start of their treks. A few people hover close to Inez—a masc-looking person in tiny bike shorts doing jumping jacks; a pretty femme with a curly bob, huge tortoise-shell glasses kept in place by a beaded string, and a giant camera dangling around her neck like it's 1992; a stout, older butch with trekking poles who looks like she just stepped out of a Columbia Sportswear catalogue—but it's unclear if they're all on Inez's tour or if they're waiting for their chance to take their picture at the first trail marker of their Camino.

"Beatrix travelers!" Inez calls out, and the eclectic assortment of people moves closer as she secures her Afro out of her face with one of her adjustable hair ties. "If you haven't already picked up your pilgrim credentials, please head inside the cathedral to get them."

I turn toward the cathedral, and Sadie trails after me like a lost puppy. "Why does the Camino start in a church?" she asks as we step inside the cool, dark vestibule.

And surely answering her question is innocent enough. "Because it's a religious pilgrimage," I tell her. "Did you research *anything* about the Camino before taking your sister's place?"

Even in the dim light, I can see her blush deepen. "At this point, I think you know I did not."

"And technically, the Camino doesn't start here," I explain as we queue behind a gaggle of Germans with their yellow guidebooks. "The Portuguese Camino starts in Lisbon, but most pilgrims begin here in Porto because Lisbon adds an extra four hundred kilometers, and there isn't as much pilgrim infrastructure on that part of the route."

She nods like she's trying to memorize every word I say. "And what, exactly, is a pilgrim credential?"

"It's a booklet where you collect stamps along the Camino." We step forward in line, and even though the nun at the front desk greets us in English, I respond in Portuguese out of some weird instinct before I turn back to Sadie. "You must get two stamps each day of your Camino, and you get them from restaurants, shops, and albergues. Those are hostels specifically for pilgrims."

"I know what they are," says the woman who didn't know why the Camino started at a church. The nun hands her the blue-and-white accordion booklet.

"As long as you complete at least the last one hundred kilometers of the Camino, you use the credentials to get a certificate when you reach Santiago saying you completed the Camino."

"Why?"

"Why what?"

"Why do you get a certificate? Like, what's the point of it? Does it get you free stuff or special discounts?"

"No. It's just, like, a souvenir."

Sadie flips through the mostly blank pages of the booklet suspiciously. "I don't get it. Why would I need a certificate saying I finished the Camino? I'll know I completed it."

I don't have an answer for that. I grab my booklet and turn away from her.

By the time we make it back outside, the man in espadrilles is gone, and a small circle has formed around Inez, including Bike Shorts, Giant Camera, and Old Butch. "Six, seven," Inez counts, pointing to me and Sadie as we join the group. "Perfeito! That's everyone! Welcome, pilgrims! Bom caminho!"

Bike Shorts hoots in response, and Inez adorably pumps her fist in the air. "Yes! That's the kind of energy I want to see! I am so happy you have all decided to join me in this transformative experience. I cannot wait to get to know each of you better," Inez singsongs like a Disney Princess addressing her flock of woodland creatures. "Tonight, we will have dinner as a group and do proper introductions, but for now, we have a journey to begin!"

This time, Giant Camera and another femme with peekaboo platinum streaks in her black hair hoot along with Bike Shorts. Inez radiates pure joy.

"Today we have a short, twelve-kilometer walk to Matosinhos, on the coast just outside Porto, to ease us into the Camino. We'll take things slow and give ourselves plenty of time to stop for photos and water. Public restrooms are also marked along the route in the app. Did we all download the Camino app? And if we get separated for some reason, please reach out in the WhatsApp group chat."

There's some confusion as Inez passes around a QR code for the app, and a woman with perfectly coiffed, bottle-blond hair and a full face of makeup loudly struggles with what an app *is*, but Giant Camera steps in and helps. Technology finally sorted, Inez clarifies, "I know some of you literally just stepped off the plane, but you will have the chance to get supplies in Matosinhos this afternoon. Sound good? Any questions?"

There are, in fact, *many* questions for such a small group, and after another thirty minutes of tedious details about the trek, we take a group photo of the eight of us crowded around the trail marker. I end up next to Sadie again, and her long ponytail brushes my bare arm.

"How many Caminos did you say you've done?" she asks me as we begin our descent from the cathedral down toward the river. Her cheeks are pink, and her eyes look the exact color of the sky in this lighting, and she has her zip-up tied around the narrow of her waist, emphasizing her staggering curves. And I definitely need to avoid her.

I grab my headphones and sling them around my neck. "You know, I'm pretty tired from traveling, so I think I'm going to put a podcast on and zone out," I say. Very casual, very indifferent, very much not staring at her freckles.

"Oh," Sadie says as I cover my ears and lose myself in the white noise and the steady steps of our walk away from Porto.

From: Wells, Sadie <sadie.wells@livewellsantiques.com>
Sent: Tuesday, May 13, 2025 9:13 p.m.
To: Wells, Victoria <cestlavi@gmail.com>
Subject: Draft of first blog post?

Hey Vi,

Here's what I have so far for my first blog post. Am I on the right track at all???

Day One: Porto → Matosinhos (7 miles)

About two miles into our journey today, I discovered there were several things I did not know about the Camino when I agreed to do this trip for my sister.

1. I didn't know the walking would start as soon as we got off the plane, and I wish I'd had the chance to shower the jet lag off first.
2. I didn't know that we would be walking an average of 12 miles per day, starting with a 13-mile (!) walk tomorrow.
3. I didn't realize the Camino is a religious pilgrimage, or that it would start in the Sé do Porto Cathedral.
4. I knew, in theory, that I would have to carry my possessions on my back, which is why I bought a $500 pack from REI. But I didn't know

what carrying my possessions would *feel* like. It fucking hurts. My neck is strained from the weight, and my lower back is pinched and aching.

5. I also didn't realize that *walking* hurts. The arches of my feet burned, and my ankles were actively strangled by my hiking boots.

6. I didn't know how hot it would be. It's only May. Chill out, Portugal. (I was also alarmed to discover that unlike everything else I packed, my sports bra is *not* moisture-wicking, and my boob sweat got out of hand very quickly.)

7. I didn't realize how much I hate my long hair until it got damp from all my neck sweat. It felt so thick and heavy, I had to put it into a bun. Which means the back of my neck is now sunburned.

8. I didn't realize how much time I would have to spend with other people . . .

——

Sadie Wells—Owner and Manager of *Live Wells Antiques*
www.livewellsantiques.com
Tuesday–Friday 9 a.m.–7 p.m.
Saturday–Sunday 10 a.m.–5 p.m.

From: Wells, Victoria <cestlavi@gmail.com>
Sent: Monday, May 12, 12:24 a.m.
To: Wells, Sadie <sadie.wells@livewellsantiques.com>
Subject: Re: Draft of first blog post?

What the fuck, Sadie?!

You literally could not be further from the right track! This just makes it sound like I didn't prepare you for the trip!!! And you realize the whole point is to make Beatrix Tours sound good, right?! Stop talking about your boob sweat and describe the fucking scenery or something.

And don't forget to work in the affiliate links I sent you!

Please don't mess this up for me.

Vi

———

Victoria Wells
Travel Writer
~Not all who wander are lost~

SIX

Sadie

I've made a huge mistake.

That's the prevailing takeaway as we trek from Porto to Matosinhos. That, and my growing suspicion that my sister may have glossed over some of the specifics of this trek when I agreed to it.

Namely, she withheld her knowledge of how much I would hate it.

The group trudges along a paved path following the river out of the city. Or, more accurately, *I* trudge, while Inez and the others happily strut. The man in the rather indecent spandex shorts whistles while he dramatically lifts his knees up to his chin with each step. The older blond woman who didn't know how to use her phone loudly monologues at another woman, whose trekking poles clang against the ground as we walk. Then there's the woman who stops directly in front of me every ten steps to take a photo on her archaic camera.

Mal is at least a football field ahead of me, chatting with the gorgeous thirtysomething who has a platinum underdye, an edgy septum piercing, and the most perfect smoky eye I've ever seen. Something other than the sun makes my skin hot when I think about Mal putting on her headphones to avoid me.

Mal has tied a bandanna around her neck for sun protection and has a trucker hat shoved over her blue mullet. Her brown eyes are hidden behind a pair of sunglasses, and her coat and gray T-shirt have both disappeared to reveal a men's tank top that shows off her tanned, muscular arms and a sprawling tattoo across her sternum. She looks like she belongs on the Camino. Even her hiking pants are the zip-off kind that turn into shorts, and although I find this fashion choice offensive on many levels, I can't argue with the practicality. According to my phone, it's only eighty degrees, but in black yoga pants, with this backpack causing a waterfall of sweat to flow down my spine, it feels like the surface of the sun.

At this point, there's nowhere I'm not sweating, but Mal's toned calves appear to be *glistening*. I watch her take long, easy strides like this is a leisurely stroll through the park.

My heart bangs wildly inside my chest. Because I'm over-exerting myself, obviously.

I tear my gaze away from Mal and the others, and let my eyes wander to the river on my left. The small cloud puffs patterned across the sky seem to glow in the afternoon sun, and they're perfectly mirrored across the smooth surface of the water. It's one of the most beautiful places I've ever seen, like a postcard my sister would send me.

When the woman in front of me stops to take another picture, I pull out my phone and do the same. On the other side of the river, there are green hills dotted with a strange harmony of baroque, Romanesque, and neoclassical buildings that make me think of Nan. If she were here, she'd be pointing out the architectural features of every church, every house, and she'd be able to tell me what the inside would've looked like in centuries past. She'd know where the marble was imported from and how the rugs were made and what wallpaper designs were in style back then. Unexpected grief reverberates through me.

I wish Nan was here. I wish we'd visited places like this when she was alive, experienced *real* history instead of simply collecting relics from the past in a dark store.

Eventually the river widens and the rocky terrain along the path shifts to sand. We reach the beach, and the ancient buildings of Porto give way to the more modern architecture of suburban Matosinhos. Even through the agonizing sensations in my neck and shoulders, I feel a small sense of pride at surviving our first day.

Up ahead, the group comes to a stop alongside Inez, who has paused in front of a statue. Or, more accurately, five statues: stone carvings of women facing toward the sea with their arms outstretched, their expressions twisted in anguish. There's something exquisitely sad about the artwork, about those five figures, one collapsed directly onto the sand.

"Monumento Tragédia no Mar," Inez says as we all stand there in silence, staring at this personification of devastation. "There was a shipwreck here in Matosinhos in 1947 that killed over 150 fishermen at sea. This commemorates that loss."

I study this master class in grief, the physicality of it. When Nan died, there wasn't any time to scream at the heavens like these statues. I had midterms. I had a mom who was imploding under the weight of her own loss, and a fourteen-year-old sister who needed someone to show her that everything was going to be okay. I'd just inherited a business and a house and the dreams of the person I loved most in the world. There wasn't time for anything.

But right now, I feel like I could stand in front of these statues forever, basking in the bravery of their open grief.

Mal turns her back on the statues first, and one by one, the rest of us follow, leaving behind the display of mourning.

Before we check into our hostel for the night, Inez leads the group to a restaurant with a giant sign advertising its "pilgrim menu" and boasting the fact that they're open for an early dinner. A host guides the group to a patio with long banquet tables, and everyone else comments on the charming pergola and the outdoor fireplace, but I only have eyes for the carafes of ice water waiting for us.

I pour myself a glass and gulp it down before everyone else even sits, since it takes a while to finagle eight hiking packs around the table. The woman with the camera chooses the spot on the bench next to me, and I can't even hyperfixate on how pungent I must smell because I'm busy refilling my glass, allowing the water to slowly bring me back to life.

When I finally look up and see all the unfamiliar faces lined up and down the wooden table, I'm overwhelmed by the sudden, mounting social pressure and the growing anxiety that I always feel in situations like this, when I don't know what to say or what to do. So, I find the one familiar face: Mal's, with its staggering widow's peak and its Cupid's-bow mouth. She ended up directly across from me in the musical chairs of choosing dinner seats.

"Welcome to Matosinhos!" Inez announces from the head of the table. "This will be dinner for tonight. I'm sorry it's so early."

It's six o'clock, but okay.

"We have an early morning tomorrow, and a long day of walking to Vila do Conde, so make sure you fill up tonight."

A menu appears in front of me on a shabby piece of paper, the offerings broken into three categories: first plate, second plate, and dessert. Even though it's in English, I'm still confused. I would ask Mal how it works, but she seems to be avoiding my gaze, so when the server arrives beside me, I wait for camera woman to order first, then say, "I'll have the same," without the slightest clue what I'll be eating.

Minutes later, the server returns with several bottles of wine for the table, along with giant baskets of bread. The last thing I need after being awake for thirty-six hours is more wine, but the bread is another story. I grab a plain white dinner roll and marvel at how it could possibly be the best thing I've ever consumed.

"Let's start with a toast!" Inez holds up a glass of red wine, and the rest of the table does the same, except Mr. Indecent Shorts, who is busy doing quad stretches next to the table.

"To the journey!" Inez declares. "Saúde!"

"Saúde!" everyone echoes, and I fumble for my water glass to join in on the cheers.

"When I talk about the Camino with people who are unfamiliar with it," Inez monologues, "most people assume it's one path that leads you to Santiago. But the Camino is a dozen different paths all heading in the same direction. You can start in France or Spain or Portugal. You can walk one hundred kilometers or five hundred or a thousand, if you want, and there are different variations along the way. Religious pilgrims would start the journey from their own front door, and whatever path they took—that was their Camino."

She pauses for a moment to take another sip of her wine, and all seven pairs of eyes stay glued to her, waiting for her to finish. There's something lovely about the cadence of her voice, something mystical and effortlessly captivating about her. "I love that about the Camino." She sighs. "Everyone is walking to the same place but getting there in their own way, at their own pace."

Several murmurs of agreement ripple around the table. Mr. Indecent Shorts even stops stretching for a moment to nod enthusiastically. Inez takes another sip of wine and smiles. "I am blessed to be your guide for this individual journey that we will take together. Now."

She claps her hands together. "I like to begin each tour with introductions. I am Inez Oliveira, and my pronouns are she/her. I'm a Cancer, originally from São Paulo, but I moved to Europe for university and never left! I'm a trans lesbian, and I live with my wife in Lisboa when I'm not trekking. I'm the founder of

Beatrix Tours, and I've done eight different Camino routes a total of sixty-three times. This will be trek sixty-four."

"Saúde to that!" shouts the older white lady with the blond coif.

"Obrigada." Inez does a small curtsy. "I would love for each of you to tell us your name, where you're from, and any other details you want to share. You do not have to disclose anything about your gender or sexuality, if you don't want to," she adds. This caveat confuses me even more than the menu, but no one else seems bothered by it. Mal bites off a hunk of bread across from me, looking nonplussed.

I am very plussed. "I do want you to tell us what brought you to the Camino, though," Inez adds. "In my experience, no one comes to the Camino only to walk. We are all called to the Camino for one reason or another. I was twenty-two when I did my first Camino, and I was not in a good place. I was horribly depressed because I was stuck living as a man. I was called to the Camino so I could escape the societal pressures that were trapping me in a false life."

More people "Saúde," and she disarms them with another radiant grin. "So, what called each of you to the Camino?"

There's an awkward beat of silence before the blond woman raises her hand. "I can go first. Hello, everyone, I'm Rebecca Hartley! I'm originally from Dallas, Texas, but I've lived in Marietta, Georgia, for the past thirty years with my husband, raising our four kids."

Rebecca Hartley looks exactly like someone with four kids who lives in Georgia. She's probably in her late sixties, but with a skin-care regimen that has magically preserved her regal face. Her hair is big, her accent is thick, and her tracksuit is Barbie pink and designer. She takes a deep breath and finishes her introduction. "And I was called to the Camino because I recently came out to my family as a lesbian."

I choke on a hunk of bread. It's the last thing I expected this woman to say.

Rebecca's blue eyes fill with tears, and she reaches for her napkin to staunch them. "Y'all, it feels so amazing to say that out loud." She blots the makeup beneath her eyes. "I've been living a lie for so long, and I was fixin' to live that lie forever. But my youngest is graduating from medical school and finally moving out of her old bedroom, and I can't use my kids as a reason to suffer through my marriage anymore. So, I finally asked for a divorce."

The table erupts in applause for Rebecca, but I can't seem to make my arms move to join in. I'm numb from hearing this woman's coming-out story, and when my eyes fall on Mal again, I find her looking directly at me.

"Thank you. Thanks, y'all." Rebecca waves her napkin like a Southern debutante. "It's been hard since I came out. My youngest has been great about it, but my other three kids are struggling to accept it, and my ex-husband, well . . . his opinion don't matter no more." More applause. "I think I was called to the Camino because I wanted to go somewhere I can be myself without worrying about how it makes others feel."

"You can always be yourself with us!" Inez is sobbing now, and she gets up from the table to go give teary Rebecca a hug. Then half the table is hugging Rebecca, and *what's even happening*? It's like I'm in a very progressive after-school special, but for geriatrics.

"Who the hell is going to follow that?" Cool Septum Piercing jokes.

Another woman who looks like she's in her late sixties clears her throat. "Hello. I'm Ro Hashmi, they/them. Non-binary. Bisexual." They start in a gruff monotone, and I feel like shit for misgendering them, even if it was only in my head. "Born in Pakistan. Currently in Trenton, New Jersey. Was a computer programmer. Retired now. Also have four children. My corgis."

Each sentence comes out of their mouth like a terse jab. "I was called to the Camino because I like to walk."

"Is that . . . all?" Inez asks slowly, clearly promoting them to share the way Rebecca did.

"Yes," Ro answers curtly.

Inez shrugs. "Okay, then!"

"I'm Vera Lopez," says the woman sitting next to me with the camera. She also has a European accent, but like Inez, her English is flawless. "I live in Madrid, but I grew up in Burgos, Spain. The Camino Frances went through my street. As a kid, I used to watch all the pilgrims pass by the front of our house, and I would make up stories about all their grand adventures. I decided it was finally time to write my own story. Oh, and, uh, and I'm aroace. I hope it's okay that I'm here."

I don't know what *aroace* means or why it would disqualify her from being here, but once again, no one else seems confused.

"It's more than okay!" Inez erupts cheerfully. "We're so happy you're here, Vera."

Introductions are interrupted when the first round of food arrives. From what I can tell, the plate in front of me is a salad that consists of sliced tomatoes under a bed of iceberg lettuce. I pick at my food as the cool septum-piercing woman introduces herself as Ari from Portland, Oregon: a Filipino, trans, polyamorous pansexual. She says she's a beekeeper-slash-barista who is studying palmistry and is happy to do free palm readings for anyone who's interested. It's maybe the most Portland thing I've ever heard.

I glance around the table. Everyone has introduced themselves except for me, Mal, and Mr. Indecent Shorts. And so far, everyone is queer. Which seems statistically unlikely, unless . . .

I lean closer to Vera. "Um, sorry, but do you know . . . ? Is this a queer tour . . . ?"

Vera swivels in her seat and stares at me with the first perplexed look of the night. Before she can answer, Inez pounces on my sudden engagement. "Yes, Sadie? Are you ready to introduce yourself?"

"Um, no, I was just . . ." I fumble with an excuse, but in my jet-lagged state, I can't think of any way to escape the inevitable. "Sure. I-I can introduce myself. I'm Sadie from Seattle. I own an antique furniture store, and I enjoy restoring and repurposing old pieces with, um, reupholstery and stuff." I awkwardly wave to the table. Red, angry hives have already popped up along the backs of my fingers. "I, well, uh, I'd never heard of the Camino until five days ago. My sister is a travel influencer, and she was supposed to do this tour, but she broke her toe, and I volunteered to take her place."

A huge, potentially life-ruining mistake.

"Oh, so both you and your sister are queer?" Ari asks. "Very cool."

"Um, well . . ."

"Sadie is straight!" Inez interrupts with her usual exuberance. And she sounds so sure of this fact, I almost believe her. "She's an ally, of course, and she's excited to help her queer sister write about this tour!"

Everyone stares at me like I've sprouted three heads, which is physically possible at this point. Something is happening to my body—something horrible and unfamiliar—and it could be an *Animorphs*-style Cerberus transmogrification.

I sit on my hands to hide my stress hives. "I'm sorry," I croak, "but is this a gay tour?"

"Of course!" Inez smiles. "Beatrix is a tour company exclusively for lesbians, sapphics, and other LGBTQ+ women and gender-queer folks."

I have three stomachs as well as three heads, and each of them are filled with acid and anxiety. Because I don't belong here.

I have no business being on a *queer tour* with people who are confident in their identities.

Inez eyes me from the head of the table. "Did you not know . . . ? Did your sister not tell you this is a queer tour?"

I bite down on my lip and try not to cry. I'm so tired, so hungover, so overwhelmed, and I just learned that in my attempt to run away from my gay panic, I ended up *on a gay tour*.

Ro loudly grunts. "Isn't the whole point that this is supposed to be a safe space for us? How can we have a straight person on the tour?"

"Are you, like, *Straight* with a capital *S*?" Ari asks. "Or, like 'straight.'" She uses air quotes on the second *straight*, as if I'm supposed to know the difference.

"There is something very gay about reupholstery," Vera notes.

"Like, you don't really only date cishet men, do you?" Ari sounds horrified at the thought.

I don't know how to answer her. I don't know who I date, or what I want, or how to talk about any of this without choking on my tears.

The anxiety is everywhere, spreading from my brain to my stomach to the tips of my fingers and toes. Everyone is looking at me, debating my sexuality, and *this* is the real plane crash. This is the near-death experience.

Even if I could survive the Camino, I could never survive *this*.

A clanging sound echoes up and down the table, silencing everyone and everything, including the anxious thoughts drilling down inside me. I glance up to see Mal holding her pint glass and a butter knife. "Excuse me," she says, clanging the glass one more time. "But I haven't introduced myself yet."

With that, all the attention shifts away from the three-headed, heterosexual freak to Mal. She briefly meets my eyes and gives me a discreet wink. This redirection isn't accidental. She's coming to my rescue.

And that's when I do start crying. Small, quiet tears I'm able to hide because no one is looking at me except her.

SEVEN

MATOSINHOS, PORTUGAL

Mal

This obviously doesn't count.

I said I'm going to avoid Sadie Wells on this trip, and I will. But I couldn't just sit here while she collapsed in on herself like a dying star.

She didn't know this is a queer tour. The universe has a fucked-up sense of humor, and it's clearly decided to make poor Sadie the butt of its jokes.

So, yeah, I impulsively slammed my knife handle against my glass to save her from scrutiny. But this doesn't count as flirting or anything.

"Excuse me. But I haven't introduced myself yet," I announce louder than necessary, ensuring that the entire table is looking at me, even the Italian in the tiny shorts who is doing wall sits against the stone façade of the outdoor fireplace like that's a perfectly normal thing to do in a public establishment.

"Hey, everyone!" I turn on the charm, making eye contact with everybody in turn. As a kid, I would sit in the back of the room at board meetings, memorizing the way Valentim could make each member feel special and uniquely seen. "My name is Mal Gonçalves, she/her, lesbian-ish. And I came to the Camino because I got dumped."

"Aww, biscuit," Rebecca coos in condolence.

"Thanks, friend, but it's okay. My ex and I weren't right for each other for a lot of reasons."

So many reasons. What was it Ruth said in that final fight?

You're directionless.

You're floating.

I need to be with a real adult.

Ruth loved my spontaneity and my restlessness when it meant trips to Thailand and Marrakesh and Paris; when it meant surprise gifts and tango lessons and extravagant nights out. But when it meant introducing me to her friends and colleagues as her unambitious girlfriend who lived off a trust fund and aimlessly drifted between nonprofit jobs, she liked it a lot less.

I loved Ruth in the beginning, when everything was new and exciting, but those feelings never last.

"Fleeing the country after a breakup is sort of my MO," I tell Rebecca with perfect indifference.

"Are you Portuguese?" Vera clocks instantly.

"On my dad's side." I take a sip of my beer. "My mom is British and Spanish, but she's lived in New York since I was six. I lived with her until I went to boarding school in Scotland, and now I live in Seattle."

Or I *did* live in Seattle. Now I don't really live anywhere.

Vera studies me with a crinkled brow. "You look *really* familiar," she says slowly.

"I lived in Madrid for a few years when I attended an American university there. Maybe we crossed paths then," I quickly explain, and I hope it will be enough to stop her from considering it further.

The server returns to the table with our main dishes and deposits a plate of buttered clams in front of me. I haven't missed much about this country, but it does have some of the best damn seafood in the world, and I tuck in without another word of introduction.

"I have something to confess!" Tiny Shorts shouts from where he's doing Tree pose. "I also did not know this tour was for the lesbians. I thought it was for all the gays."

"And who are you?" Ro asks in their intimidating monotone.

"Oh. Yes," he says in a thick Italian accent. "Ciao! I am Stefano Demurtas. My pronouns are he/him. I am from a town called Alghero on the beautiful island of Sardinia, but I now live in Napoli. I am international triathlete and do Ironmans all over the world, but last December in Taupo, I got injured. I had knee surgery and now cannot do anything strenuous for six months. So, I am here!"

Ari raises an eyebrow. "Walking two hundred miles . . . ?"

"Yes!" Stefano lunges forward on one leg, an act that is made obscene by his very tight bike shorts. "I do not like to be still. I like always to be moving."

"We can see that."

"Stefano . . ." Inez drags his name out hesitantly. "And you are . . . ?"

"An Aries," he answers with another lunge.

"Um, great, but I meant . . ." Inez comfortably shifts in her chair and defaults to professionalism. "Beatrix Tours has a firm policy about not requiring travelers to disclose their gender or sexuality, and I strive to create an inclusive environment, but . . . I assumed you . . . are you not a trans man?"

"Ah, no. I am cis gay man."

"Oh." Inez's permanent smile falters. "Well, this has never happened before . . ."

"But per favore! Please!" Stefano begs with his hands in Prayer pose beneath his chin. "Do not kick me off the tour! I want to do Camino with all you beautiful people."

"It's not against our policy, exactly, but the website very clearly states that Beatrix caters to lesbians and LGBTQ+ women . . ."

Stefano waves his hand. "I did not read website."

"Clearly." Ari snorts into her wine.

Inez attempts a more diplomatic response. "Perhaps you'd be happier doing the Camino on your own . . . ?"

"Alone is no good," Stefano wails. "I do not like alone or still. I do not like silence."

This sounds like something I would say, and I'm slightly concerned that the person I relate to most at this table is the one who added protein powder to his wine, but I'm even more concerned about Inez. She's never been one for confrontation, and if everyone protests having a cis man on the tour . . .

"Gender is a construct," I blurt, drawing the attention back to me again. "If Stefano wants to hang out with a bunch of cool sapphics, I say let him!"

He blows me a series of grateful kisses.

"I agree," Vera adds with a shrug. "Everyone should feel welcome."

Ari adds, "Yeah, if it's not against the policy, who cares?"

Stefano responds with more dramatic air-kisses. "Bella! Veronica and Arielle! Grazie!" He doesn't know their names, but he falls to his knees and professes his undying love for them anyway. "You are most beautiful flowers, le mie bellissime amiche."

"Don't push it, buddy," Ari snaps at him. Stefano rises and pantomimes zipping his mouth closed.

Inez nervously fiddles with her yellow chakra beads, and I lean around the back of Ari's chair. "It's your company," I tell her. "You get to decide what to do here, and you don't have to explain yourself to anyone."

Her hands settle. "Of course Stefano can stay. Everyone is welcome on the road to self-understanding."

Everyone cheers, and Stefano waves to our server. "More wines! Grazie!"

Several more bottles are uncorked, and when Sadie passes me a bottle of cabernet from across the table, I don't notice her freckles or the Quinta Costa label on the wine. The noise of the group saves me from noticing anything at all.

Our lodging for the night is a hostel directly across the street from the restaurant, and when the wine is finally emptied, the half-drunk group swans over with our giant packs. The entryway and communal area of the hostel are Scandinavian minimalism by way of a one-star accommodation, and even though it's not an actual albergue, everyone milling around seems to be pilgrims like us. The beautiful, twentysomething staff of expats all wear black, while the walls are white, and the furnishings are a pale wood. The only color comes from the flyers advertising pub crawls and hostel-inspired nights on the town. There's a sleek, modern bar along the far wall, and a slew of tables where guests drink their evening cerveza.

It's exactly what I expected from the accommodation on our Camino tour: bare-bones and no-frills.

Inez checks us all in, then begins passing out room keys as she gives us the rundown of tomorrow's plan. "In the morning, we will meet here in the lobby at eight o'clock sharp for breakfast. You will need to have all your things packed and be ready to start our trek at that time. We depart promptly at eight thirty." She fiddles with the keys in one hand and her phone in the other. "Now, Stefano, Ari, and Vera signed up for a triple room."

"Migliori amiche!" Stefano shouts, throwing one arm over each of their shoulders. Vera accepts the key, and she, Stefano, and Ari do an inebriated swagger down a hallway on the ground floor. Another key goes to Ro, who seems less than thrilled when Rebecca follows them up the stairs.

When it's just me and Sadie left in the lobby, Inez dangles a silver key in my direction. "Your room is on the fourth floor."

Sadie tries to stand upright, but some combination of her pack and the extreme case of jet lag makes that difficult. "Where's my room?" she slurs sleepily.

"Fourth floor," Inez repeats. "You're rooming together."

Sadie is suddenly very awake. "Excuse me? *Together?*"

"Yes. Your sister signed up for a double room. Didn't she tell you?" Inez asks, but it's clear at this point that Sadie's sister didn't tell her fuck all about this trip.

"No. No, she didn't." Sadie shakes her head and refuses to look at me. "I'm sorry, but I can't . . . I can't room with her. Or anyone."

"I'm not thrilled about it either." The words come out harsher than I intend, but Sadie isn't the only one who's disappointed with our room assignment. How am I supposed to avoid this woman if she's sleeping in the twin bed next to mine for the next fourteen nights? I'll have to listen to her snoring and smell her shampoo after she showers and see her freckles every damn morning.

"Sorry," Sadie sniffles. "It's not personal."

"It sounded a little personal," I grumble.

"I'm sorry, Mal." Sadie stares at me with a sadness that rivals the statues that welcomed us into Matosinhos, those women who were so unafraid of their own grief. She turns back toward Inez. "It's . . . it's fine. I can share a room."

Inez flicks her gaze over to me. "Is this arrangement going to be okay for both of you?"

Absolutely not.

"Absolutely!" I reassure Inez. Sadie nods too, and Inez slumps in visible relief. "Thank goddess. I can't handle any more unexpected surprises today."

"I'm sorry I caused you so much additional stress," Sadie quickly apologizes, working herself into another spectacular bluster. "I promise I will handle this all better once I've had a good night of sleep." She adjusts her heavy pack and almost falls over again. "Do you mind just pointing us in the direction of the elevator?"

I turn to Inez. I'm not going to be the one to tell her.

"How is there no elevator?" Sadie cries as we face the steep, narrow staircase up to our room.

"A lot of budget hotels in Europe don't have elevators."

"That's fucking ableist."

"Do you want me to carry your bag for you?"

"I don't." She grabs onto the straps and tries to stand up tall. And then she starts falling backward as soon as she takes a step. After a few false starts, she finally gets enough momentum to make it up the first flight of stairs. I should leave her there on the landing up to the second floor, but I don't.

We arrive at the rickety wooden door with the crooked number 42 nailed to the front ten minutes later. I slide the key into the lock and push open the door to reveal a standard one-star European hotel room. It's a clean but cramped space with two twin beds, a tiny bathroom visible through a pocket door, and not much else.

Sadie freezes in the doorway and stares at the semi-depressing, one-hundred square feet. And she finally, fully, breaks down.

Heavy, full-body sobs tremor through her as she remains immobilized in the doorway. I set my backpack down on one of the beds and hover beside it, unsure what to do. There is a part of me that wants to go to her, to hold her hand the way I did on the plane. I want to sit with her, listen to her.

But I also know myself. I know that comforting is my romantic gateway drug, and if I hold Sadie now while she cries, it will only be a matter of time before I want to hold her in other ways too.

I can't let myself go down that road with her, and not just because I'm swearing off Romeo-antics. Sadie is a fragile baby gay, a gosling who's only now learning how to walk, and I don't want to be the asshole hawk that swoops in and traumatizes her.

I'm great at falling in love and horrible at staying in it, and in the end, someone always ends up hurt. I wouldn't want that person to be Sadie.

So, I don't comfort her. Instead, I say, "I'm going to give you some space," as I'm already halfway out the door.

"What are you doing here?" Inez asks me, switching seamlessly into Portuguese an hour later.

I gesture at her across the table with my Super Bock beer. "Enjoying a beer with an old friend," I answer back, though my Portuguese is hardly seamless these days.

Inez casts a glance around the mostly empty lobby of the hostel. "I don't mean *here*. Why are you on this tour?"

"I told you. I got dumped."

Inez narrows her eyes, like she's trying to read my aura to uncover the truth behind my usual bullshit. "I was sorry to hear about your dad," she finally says.

"I wasn't." There's a bottle of Vinho Verde in front of Inez, the label printed with my last name and the logo of Portugal's coastline. That logo, the wine within that bottle, and the company it represents . . . those were the only things Valentim Costa cared about.

When I came out to him, he told me, in no uncertain terms, that I couldn't be both gay and his daughter, and I took him at his word. I've spent the twenty years since that rejection embracing my queerness and disavowing the part of me that was him. I rejected all the Costas—my paternal grandparents, my aunts, my cousins. I rejected any ambition, any sense of familial duty, any love I might have had for Portugal or wine or him. I used my trust fund to travel the world and fall in love with as many women as possible, because I knew that would really piss him off.

And I always fall out of love with those women before there is any possibility of being rejected again.

"Yet you came home after all these years," Inez says now.

"This isn't home. And I came to do the Camino," I correct her. I snatch up the wine bottle and begin to pick at the label. "The Camino helped me once. I'm hoping it can help me again."

"Did it help? It seems like it only taught you how to run."

"You *walk* the Camino," I joke.

Inez watches me peel off the wine label in tiny, sticky pieces that litter our table, and I wait for her to call out my bullshit, to push me to be honest with her, the way Michelle would.

But she never does. Inez is not Michelle, and I've trained her to never expect genuine vulnerability from me. Like most people in my life, Inez accepts what I'm willing to show her. That's how I want my friendships. Usually.

Tonight, though, I'm thinking about the woman on the plane who confessed all her most precious secrets to a stranger. I'm thinking about the statues of grieving women. I'm thinking about all the things I haven't let myself feel.

"He left it to me," I hear myself say.

"Who left what to you?"

"My father. Valentim." Bits of the label stick to the pads of my fingers, and I try to wipe them on my clothes under the table. "He left me Quinta Costa. The entire business, his entire fortune. A dozen vineyards, the majority shares, just . . . all of it."

Inez stares at me blankly at first, as if we're not speaking English or Portuguese, but some third Martian language that resembles neither. "You said he disowned you. Why . . . why would he do that?"

"That's the question that's been haunting me since I got the news."

It's not like my dad completely cut me out of his life after I came out to him. He sent birthday cards with extravagant gifts each year; he called me to complain about the family of finches living in his fireplace at the vineyard in Vigo; he emailed me random articles about things I'd loved when I was ten years old. For all intents and purposes, he acted like the fight never happened, even if the unspoken chasm between us was evidence that it had. We never talked about anything real, we rarely saw each other, and we never mentioned the fact that I'd spent the first eighteen years of my life preparing to take over the family business, then spent the next eighteen years drifting aimlessly from job to job, from country to country, from woman to woman.

I hated him for it—for rejecting me and acting like he hadn't—but I kept picking up the phone when he called, unable to fully sever that fragile connection.

He never told me he was sick. Up until the bitter end, he was leaving me voicemails about a Cabrera vole that kept sneaking into his vegetable garden. And then he was gone, and I was getting a phone call from a stepmom I'd never met, telling me what happened, telling me about his trust. None of it was going to her. All of it was coming to me.

Even in death, Valentim Costa saddled me with his emotional baggage.

"Does this mean you're now CEO of Quinta Costa?" Inez asks. "Should I start addressing you as 'sir'? Or 'Your Majesty'? What is the appropriate form of address for a capitalistic overlord?"

"The board named Valentim's fifth wife as interim CEO while I figure out what I want to do with the company."

"What are you going to do with it?"

I shrug and aim for flippancy. "Sell it? Run it into the ground? Burn each vineyard that he loved more than me, one by one?" I suggest, not flippant at all.

"Sounds like you're in a healthy place with all of it." Inez nods her head up and down like an infinitely wise bobblehead. "Now the spontaneous Camino is starting to make sense. You're searching for someone to take your mind off"—she waves her hand in circles in front of my face—"all of *that*."

"Not someone. The Camino."

"Uh-huh." She clucks in disbelief. "You forget that I've met you before."

"I'm changing my ways."

She clucks again. "Just promise me that when you do your typical Mal thing, you'll choose someone other than Sadie to fall in love with. I don't need that kind of mess on my tour."

"I have no idea what you're talking about."

"Don't think I didn't notice the looks the two of you were exchanging at dinner."

"There were no looks. Like you said, Sadie is straight."

"She's definitely gay for you." Inez rolls her eyes. "And who isn't? You're sapphic catnip. You have Kristen Stewart's face, first-season Shane's hair, and Tig Notaro's body."

"Tig Notaro's personality too," I add.

She scoffs. "Don't flatter yourself."

"I'm sorry, but did you not just imply that I can turn straight girls with my mullet and dad bod?"

"Your outsides are inarguably fabulous, but the insides could use some work."

I throw the wadded-up label scraps at her and pretend those words don't hurt.

Ruth loved to teasingly call me her *himbo*, a hot body and an empty head. She was joking—she always *said* she was joking— but after a while, it became clear that she was only interested in my body and my bank account, that in her eyes, I had nothing else to offer her. I was *both* the sugar daddy *and* the arm candy, and neither felt great.

"Promise, Mal. Fall in love with someone else. Her sister's blog has a huge following, and the publicity could really change things for me and Beatrix. I need Sadie to have a good time and write nice things about this tour. As the company's sole investor, you should care about this going well."

"I'm not an investor."

Inez empties the label-less bottle into her wineglass. "What do you call it when you write a check to cover all the start-up costs for a new company?"

"Spending Daddy's money," I answer, and *ha*. There it is. Perfect flippancy. "I wasn't really the only investor, was I?"

"You think banks were lining up to give a small-business loan to a dirt-poor, Afro-Brazilian trans woman looking to open a tour company for queer women?"

"You should know that I only wrote that check for the tax break."

"There's no tax break for loaning money to a friend."

"There's always a tax break if you're rich enough." I reach for my pint glass only to discover it's empty. "And I told you ten years ago, it's not a loan. You never have to pay it back. You don't owe me anything, Inez. Not even a spot on your tours."

"I owe you *everything*." She tugs at her shirt with the Beatrix Tours logo. "None of this would exist without you."

"Don't mention it."

"Mal, you—"

"No, seriously," I cut her off. "Please don't mention it ever again. It makes me weirdly uncomfortable."

Inez lifts her glass toward me. "You want people to think you have a heart of stone, but you have a heart of pure gold, my friend."

"I recently inherited a lot of gold," I say, and Inez snorts a laugh. This is where I want to stay: in the shallows where I make jokes and Inez laughs.

"Not Sadie, okay?" she repeats, her tone sober.

I wish I had another beer, another label to rip up, another distraction to keep the thoughts from slipping in through the cracks.

"Not Sadie," I agree. "I was thinking about Rebecca, actually . . ."

"Don't."

"What? She keeps it *tight*. That's a GILF if I've ever seen one."

"Please stop."

"Or maybe Ro. We could make love while their corgis watch, then snuggle up for a Ken Burns documentary after."

"Why are you like this?" Inez covers her face to hide her laughter.

I laugh too, and then I order another beer.

At the end of the night we hug, and Inez slips a healing crystal into the pocket of my fleece.

"What is this? Were you carrying this around all day?"

She ignores my teasing. "It's amethyst. For willpower."

THE CAMINO CREW

Inez Oliveira

Boa noite, beautiful pilgrims!

I hope you get the rest you need to face our first full day tomorrow!

9:54 p.m.

Inez Oliveira

Tomorrow we will also have our first sharing circle! Part of this tour is guided self-reflection as we make our journey. Each day, I will ask the group a question to prompt self-reflection, and I will invite you to share. 9:57 p.m.

Ro Hashmi

DO WE HAVE TO SHARE? 9:58 p.m.

Inez Oliveira

I know it can be scary to be vulnerable, but connection is one of the greatest gifts the Camino offers us. 10:03 p.m.

Ro Hashmi

BUT DO WE HAVE TO SHARE???
10:05 p.m.

Rebecca Hartley

Dear Camino Friends,

It was lovely to chat with y'all at dinner. Thank you for being so accepting. I can't wait to share with you more tomorrow.

Love,

Rebecca 10:12 p.m.

Ro Hashmi

BECAUSE I DID NOT SIGN UP FOR GROUP THERAPY 10:13 p.m.

Ari Ocampo

ro you dont have to write in all caps . . . it makes it look like youre screaming at us 10:15 p.m.

Rebecca Hartley

Dear Ari,

They are screaming, dear. They are screaming at their phone as they send their messages. It's quite alarming.

Love,

Rebecca 10:21 p.m.

Ari Ocampo

and rebecca youre not writing a letter to a lost love away at war . . . we know who you are 10:22 p.m.

Vera Lopez

I have extra Compeed if anyone needs it for their blisters 😅 10:27 p.m.

Stefano Demurtas

 12:08

10:29 p.m.

Ari Ocampo

stefano why the hell did you just send a 12 minute voice memo?? 10:31 p.m.

Stefano Demurtas

Going for a little run 10:32 p.m.

Stefano Demurtas

Can't text 10:32 p.m.

Ari Ocampo

i cannot with all of you 10:33 p.m.

Stefano Demurtas

Hkrncofgarlg 10:33 p.m.

Ro Hashmi

BUT DO WE HAVE TO SHARE??????

10:41 p.m.

Mal Gonçalves

I'm sorry, but your nonsense has driven Inez to take solace in a bottle of disgusting wine. She will address all further inquiries in the morning. Get some sleep, weirdos. 10:57 p.m.

EIGHT

Sadie

The facts are these: I'm starfished atop a scratchy blanket, wearing one of my ratty UW T-shirts and no pants, hair half-wet, with absolutely no idea where I am.

My brain searches for something familiar. The blue glow of my alarm clock or the yellow tinge of Queen Anne streetlamps coming through the blinds, the soft feeling of my plush duvet and five-hundred-thread-count sheets, the hum of my air purifier. But there's nothing.

The world outside is mostly dark.

I fling out an arm for my phone. My elbow knocks it onto the floor, and then I knock myself onto the floor when I lean over to reach it.

It's as my face hits the cold laminate flooring that I remember I'm in a sparsely furnished, depressingly monochromatic hostel in Matosinhos, Portugal.

I slowly recall the events that led to my current half-naked, half-wet state of semiconsciousness. An excruciating eighteen hours of travel; another three hours of walking with a thirty-pound pack; arriving at this hostel and feeling so exhausted, I could barely keep my eyes open. I remember cramming my body into the smallest shower I've ever seen. The warm water felt divine at first as I hunched under the short shower head, but then my neck started to hurt, and I had to skip my conditioner treatment when the hot water ran out.

After the shower, I laid on top of my scratchy duvet and zero-thread-count sheets in only my underwear and forced myself to write a draft post for Vi's blog as my heavy eyes kept sliding shut. I remember telling myself to blow dry my hair before falling asleep, but based on the current state of said hair, that did not happen.

I pick up my phone and clamber back onto the bed. It's not even 5 a.m. yet, but I feel wide awake. I open Google and try to find the closest place to get coffee and breakfast, but nothing seems to open before 7 a.m.

On cue, my stomach rumbles deeply. Across the room, there's a gurgle, followed by a cough. And fucking hell. *That* is when I remember I'm not alone.

I fall onto the floor again in a misguided attempt to conceal my half-nakedness from Mal before I realize that the room is completely dark, and Mal is still very asleep.

Everything else from yesterday comes rushing back in, and the shame isn't too far behind it.

In the dark, I reach for my backpack and drag my belongings into the world's tiniest bathroom. I click on the light and after blinking a few times, I catch sight of the woman in the mirror. Her hair looks like an abandoned bird's nest, and her face is washed out by the sallow light of the bathroom. Her eyes are some combination of wild and exhausted, and she looks frightened, nervous, and entirely unsure of herself. I splash cold water on my face and then whip out my phone.

"How could you not tell me?" I hiss as soon as my sister answers my call.

"Huh?" Vi sounds groggy even though it's only 9 p.m. back in Seattle, and Vi has never gone to bed before midnight.

"How could you neglect to mention this is a gay tour?" I whisper-scream as loudly as I can without waking Mal on the other side of the thin pocket door.

Vi yawns. "I dunno. I didn't think it mattered."

Of course she didn't.

"Well, it . . . it does matter, Victoria."

"I told Inez you're straight, and she said it was fine for the promotional trip."

I wish I had the right words to explain to my sister why it *does* matter. I wish I could tell her that I'm *not* straight without feeling like a massive fraud. How can I have such intense imposture syndrome over the feelings in my own heart?

"If anyone should be mad, it's me." Vi sounds fully awake now and extremely indignant. "How could *you* not tell me how hard it is to work in the store?"

"I think it might be something I've mentioned once or twice . . . a day. For the last twenty years."

Vi makes a languishing noise, and I can imagine her dramatically throwing herself onto the pile of decorative pillows I bought for her bed. "Jane had me working the register for twelve hours straight, and it was nonstop mean old people and mean rich people!"

"That sounds like our clientele."

"It's only been two days, and I'm so tired. And Jane yelled at me every time I was on my phone."

Good for Jane. If my assistant manager can handle Vi, she can definitely handle running the store until I get back.

"You're tired?" I practically yell. "You didn't remotely prepare me for this trek! I'm already sore, and we're supposed to walk thirteen miles today!"

Vi sighs wistfully. "I would give anything to switch places with you."

I almost agree with her on instinct, but I catch myself. I'm currently sitting on a closed toilet seat at five in the morning so I don't wake my roommate. My lower back, neck, and shoulders hurt the way they do after a long day of rearranging the sales floor. I'm starving, and I have no idea how to procure food in a foreign country, and I'm already out of Lärabars.

But do I really wish I was back in Seattle, equally exhausted after a day of work? Alone in my room rewatching *House Hunters* because I'm so burnt-out, I can't do anything but dissociate?

Part of me does. Part of me wants to tell Vi I can't do this, part of me wants to book the next flight home, burn my pack and hiking boots in effigy.

But there's another part of me—quiet but getting louder by the minute—that sort of wants to see where this road might take me.

"I think I made a huge mistake in coming here," I whisper into the phone.

"Good," Vi says. "It's time for you to start making some mistakes."

There's more free bread at breakfast.

I distracted myself from my empty stomach all morning by revising my first blog for Vi and posting to her Instagram. I wrangled my tangled hair into a single French braid, did my makeup, and tried slapping Band-Aids over the blisters forming on my feet.

By the time Mal woke up, I was already heading out the door with all my stuff in search of food.

At the hostel's continental breakfast, I load my plate with bread, weird cheese slices, and ham that seems to be of the lunch meat instead of breakfast variety. I'm not sure if I'm supposed to make a sandwich with it at eight in the morning, but I watch the woman with the camera—Vera, I think her name is—eat them separately at her table with Ari, so I intend to do the same.

I find some fresh fruit, grab a pack of Muesli to shove in my pocket for the next time I'm stuck without food, and find the coffee carafe off to the side of the banquet table. Then I awkwardly hover with my heap of food as I try to navigate the social situation of choosing where to sit. The lobby is full of people wearing hiking clothes and eating together in small groups. Ari and Vera are at one table. Inez is at another with Ro and Rebecca, listening politely as Ro complains about the difference between American and Portuguese continental breakfast. Stefano is wearing another pair of shorts that are basically a Speedo and doing squats next to the table while he eats yogurt. And then there's an empty table tucked into the corner . . .

As soon as I make moves toward my own slice of quiet paradise, Septum-Piercing Ari calls out my name. "Hey, Sadie!" she waves. "Come sit with us!" I begrudgingly oblige.

"How did you sleep?" Vera asks just as I take a giant bite of my bread.

I chew quickly and when that fails, I cover my mouth with my hand. "Hard," I answer.

"*Same.*"

"More importantly," Ari interrupts, using a rolled-up piece of ham to point at me. "How could you sleep at all with your fine-ass roommate five feet away?"

"Oh, uh . . . Jet lag?"

Vera tsks. "You do realize that not everyone experiences sexual attraction, right? And Sadie said she's straight."

I didn't, actually. Everyone else has said it for me.

"Mal's hotness transcends sexuality," Ari declares, brandishing her ham slice scepter. She swivels back to me. "Don't you agree, Straight Sadie?"

"Is Mal hot?" I ask, as if the thought hasn't occurred to me.

"She is."

"She *really* is," Vera agrees. "Even I can appreciate her aesthetic beauty."

"Sì, sì," Stefano adds, appearing at our table like a jack-in-the-box with zero-percent body fat.

Ari shakes out her hair in a distinctly sultry fashion. The platinum streaks in her black hair conjure hipster Cruella de Vil vibes, but her overall aesthetic is cooky high school art teacher from the nineties. But the art teacher you secretly had a massive crush on. "Sadie, as the token straight of this tour," Ari says, "figure out what Mal's deal is for me."

"Her . . . deal?"

"Yeah. Like, is she seeing someone? Are they monogamous? Would she be down for something casual? How does she feel about butt stuff?"

Vera smacks Ari's arm. "Don't make her ask that!"

"I will ask her about butt stuff for you," Stefano volunteers as he sinks into another squat.

My face is hot, and I'm sure the hives are springing up on my cheeks in red splotches. It's how I react every time people talk about sex around me.

I've always had a small group of female friends, but sometime in my mid-twenties, it became anxiety-inducing to meet up with the girls from business school for happy hour, because all they talked about was sex. They'd exchange horror stories about awkward one-night stands and ask for advice about boyfriends that never went down on them, and I would sit in petrified silence the whole time, praying no one would ask me any direct questions about my sex life.

The more time I spent with them, the more alienated I felt. The more *behind* I felt. So, eventually, I stopped hanging out with them at all. I stopped hanging out with anyone outside my immediate family, really.

"I swear I recognize her from somewhere," Vera says to her banana.

"Who?"

"Mal. Like, maybe she's European famous or something . . ."

"I've never seen her before, but with that hot-ass face and that hot-ass ass, I wouldn't be surprised if she was."

Vera scrunches her face in concentration. "She's definitely rich."

"How can you tell?" I ask.

"She paid for everyone's dinner last night," Vera says. "Didn't you notice?"

I was so jet-lagged, I wouldn't have noticed if Mal did a naked limbo on top of the table.

"And she paid with an AmEx Black card."

"You're like a little detective, aren't you, V?" Ari rubs her hands together mischievously. "Perhaps you shall be my Mal spy."

"I will not."

I keep my attention focused on my breakfast, once again praying no one will ask me any more direct questions. Maybe Mal is famous. Maybe that's why I had that weird sensation of *knowing her* when I first saw her on the plane. Maybe that's why *every time* I look at her, my stomach pole-vaults into my rib cage.

Inez stands on her chair and claps her hands together to get our attention. "Good morning, my beautiful pilgrims!" she sings. She glances around the room. "Everyone here is beautiful, but this announcement is specifically for the beautiful pilgrims on the Beatrix Tour. This is the last call for toilets and coffee. We're meeting out front in five minutes!"

As she finishes her announcement, Mal comes running down the stairs with her bag slung over one shoulder. Her hair is wet and slicked back, showing off her widow's peak. She's wearing her Hokas, brown hiking pants, and a white T-shirt beneath her open fleece. She's distinctly *not* wearing a bra again.

And she is, regrettably, very hot indeed.

* * *

Matosinhos is beautiful in the morning. As we set out for the day, the sun filters between white-washed buildings that reflect the golden light and make the cobblestones sparkle. There's a floral smell to the air, perhaps from the purple flowers in the trees, and it mixes with the salty crispness of the sea.

Even though it's already eight thirty, the city is only starting to wake up. Old men in aprons sweep the sidewalks outside their storefronts, small delivery trucks unload the day's fresh meat and produce, and school children in uniforms parade down the street in small clusters, their parents trailing after. Inez leads us in the direction of the yellow arrows, through sleepy streets and sunshine, as people call "Bom caminho!" to us pilgrims.

Our group adds to the music of the morning too. The clang of Mal's water bottle; the anachronistic click of Vera's camera; Inez's commentary and Rebecca's humming and the clang of Ro's trekking poles; the sound of eight pairs of asynchronistic feet clomping along the Camino. There is something comforting about being part of this morning routine.

The comfort ends, though, when our pathway along the beach turns from sidewalk to boardwalk. Each time my hiking boots hit the wooden slats, pain shoots from my ankles to my calves. I try to cling to the pleasure of the blue sky and the roaring sea, but after an hour on the boardwalk, I've lost all optimism.

The group stretches out along the boardwalk as everyone walks at their own pace, and I am the caboose, trudging along miserably. At one point, Stefano jogs back to me and offers to carry my pack the rest of the way.

"But you have your own pack to carry," I point out.

"I will run ahead and drop my pack off at the hostel, and then run back for your pack," he says. And the idea of him *running* with his pack makes me so angry, I almost do let him carry both bags.

Inez has everyone take a photo of our feet fanned around a bronze engraving in the middle of the boardwalk that has the phrase *bom caminho* in several languages. *Buen camino. Good journey.*

There is nothing good about this journey.

We don't take a proper break until we reach a town called Boa Nova a little after ten. There's a café tucked under a checkered awning, and Inez wrangles two sidewalk tables together so we can rest. Everyone drops their packs in a heap and trickles inside in search of coffee and a bathroom.

I line up behind Rebecca and search for a menu where there seems to be none. This place is nothing like my local Seattle coffee shop. The café has the low lighting of a bar, which it might be, given the beer tap in the corner. A few locals stand at the counter sipping from tiny white espresso cups, and everyone is speaking Portuguese except us.

"Do you want help ordering?" a voice asks close to my ear, and I nearly jump out of my skin at Mal's sudden closeness.

"Uh, no . . ." I stammer. "I'll be okay."

When I reach the counter, a stern woman rattles off a monologue in Portuguese while I blink dumbly at her. Duolingo didn't cover this in the first two lessons.

"Hi, um, coffee?" I try. And I throw in a "desculpe" for good measure.

"Café?" she repeats back to me, and I'm not sure if she's talking about a drink or a building.

"Yes? Please."

"Café," she says again, this time performing charades with an imaginary cup of coffee.

"Sí. Or, uh, sim. Por favor."

"Faz favor," Mal whispers behind me.

I fumble for a few bills I withdrew at the airport. I have no idea how much a cup of coffee costs, so I hand her a ten euro.

The woman stares at the outstretched money and proceeds to laugh at me. "Não. Não."

We're playing charades again, and this time, she keeps pressing two pinched fingers into the palm of her hand. "Um," she says. "Um."

"Um, *what*?"

Mal clears her throat and steps forward, placing a single euro coin on the counter.

"Obrigada!" the woman shouts, sweeping the coin into her apron. She says something else to Mal, but the only word I catch is "Americana."

"Americana," Mal echoes, and they both laugh. I feel infinitesimal. Like a silly, stupid American in the presence of Mal's cool worldliness.

The only thing worse than the laughter is the world's tiniest cup of espresso that the woman hands me. It tastes like licking freshly ground coffee beans, and I discreetly dump it out before I return to the outside table.

"Café means espresso," Mal says as she follows me outside.

"Pilgrims!" Inez beams at us as we sit down. We're the last two people to rejoin the group, and Inez eagerly launches into one of her spiritual speeches. "Welcome to our first sharing circle! As we established last night in the WhatsApp chat"—she shoots a pointed look at Ro—"you do not *have* to share, but I hope you will." Her gaze shifts to Mal. "The friends you meet here can become your forever family."

A gremlin voice in the back of my head wonders if Mal and Inez have a romantic history from back when they met on the Camino all those years ago. I stare at Inez, searching for clues in her cheerful expression.

"Now," Inez continues. "Today's trek to Vila do Conde is twenty-one kilometers, or thirteen miles, and it is the first of many long days ahead of us. For our first sharing circle, I want you to consider what scares you most about the Camino."

"Scares us?" Ro repeats with a tight frown. "Is the Camino scary? I thought it was supposed to be safe."

Inez offers them a reassuring smile. "It is very safe. I'm talking more about *emotional* fears."

Rebecca raises her hand. Today's tracksuit is an impeccable powder blue. "You don't have to raise your hand," Inez says encouragingly.

Rebecca lowers it. "I am scared I won't be able to do it," she says with a little tremor in her voice. "I've never attempted anything like this before, and I'm worried I won't be able to walk two hundred miles."

Rebecca looks like she does Pilates five times a week. She'll be fine.

"I'm scared that after all these years, the reality of the Camino won't live up to my expectations," Vera shares next, and we hopscotch around the loose semicircle.

Ari: "I'm afraid of not being fully present in the moment while I'm here."

Stefano: "I'm scared of being bored."

Ro: "I'm scared of these sharing circles."

Mal: "Blisters."

"And how about you, Sadie?" Inez asks, swiveling to face me. I thought I'd successfully concealed myself behind Mal, but no such luck, apparently.

"I, uh, um . . ." I start, very articulately. "I-I thought you said we didn't have to share."

C'est La Vi with Me

Are You Afraid of the Light?

Sadie Wells
May 14, 2025 6 comments

Day two of the Camino had us walking 13 miles from Matosinhos to Vila do Conde, mostly on the boardwalk following the Atlantic coast north of Porto. The shore permanently at our left was both rocky and green as we started, but it eventually became soft sand. The ocean absorbed the color of the sky, shifting throughout the day from pale blue to dark gray to blinding azure. As we trekked along the boardwalk past small towns, always following the yellow scallop shell and arrow, our tour guide asked us to reflect on what scares us the most about the Camino. Little does she know, all I ever think about are my fears.

A Non-Exhaustive List of Things that Scared Me on the Camino Today:

1. Walking.
2. More specifically, having to walk 13 miles while knowing I'll have to walk 14 miles tomorrow.
3. The possibility of passing out in the middle of the path from all this walking when it literally would've taken twenty minutes to get to Vila do Conde by car.
4. I was scared of how strong the sun felt by only ten in the morning.
5. I was scared I was going to visibly sweat through my underwear and yoga pants (Good news! They both moisture-wicked like their lives depended on it.).
6. I was scared someone was going to try to talk to me while I was that sweaty.

7. I'm scared of the fact that I will have to carry my belongings for the next thirteen days like some kind of pack mule.

8. I'm scared that I might not be strong enough to carry all my belongings.

9. I'm scared of our tour guide's prying personal questions.

10. I'm scared that every hotel we stay in will be a bleak, colorless void of sad.

11. I was scared that something truly horrible was happening inside my hiking boots.

From: Wells, Victoria cestlavi@gmail.com
Sent: Wednesday, May 14, 2025 12:24 a.m.
To: Wells, Sadie sadie.wells@livewellsantiques.com
Subject: Re: Second Blog Post Draft

This is a step in the right direction, but it still doesn't make Beatrix sound great . . . remember, you're supposed to inspire people to want to take this trip. Can you at least pretend like you're enjoying yourself?

Victoria Wells
Travel Writer
~Not all who wander are lost~

NINE

Sadie

I'm terrified to look. Right now, my feet are like the proverbial cat in the box, and as soon as I peel back my wool socks, I will know if once and for all they are dead. I will have to face the reality of what I've done to my poor appendages.

My feet are stretched out in front of me on the cool laminate floor of our private albergue, the shower humming behind me as Mal rinses off. For the moment, I can pretend that nothing is bleeding.

Thirteen miles is *brutal* when carrying the world's heaviest pack. I thought the boardwalk was the worst thing I could imagine, but then I had the pleasure of walking on cobblestones for the last stretch into Vila do Conde, and they were an absolute bitch. For a while, my feet went blissfully numb and felt like they were no longer attached to my body physically or spiritually, but then the cobblestones brought fresh hell. I truly thought I might collapse and never be able to stand up again.

There are probably a thousand blisters lurking beneath my socks, and I am quite certain the pinky toe on my right foot has detached itself and has been rolling around in my shoe since lunch.

And if I am missing a toe, I should probably do something about it.

Deep breath. I pull one foot closer to me and start to unfurl the sock from my mangled foot. The sock resists, as if the wool fibers have fused to my sweaty skin. With a sharp tug, it comes free.

The first thing I notice is that my baby toe is still blissfully attached to the rest of me, though the toenail wasn't quite so lucky. The puckered skin beneath looks angry but isn't bleeding. The second thing I notice is the smell.

Gagging, the rest of my foot comes into focus. It looks like raw ground beef. The skin is red and wrinkled. There's a giant blister on my big toe, another one on the side of my foot. There is a third blister on my heel that looks like a malignant tumor. Across the top of my foot and around my ankle bone, huge bruises are forming where my hiking boots have crushed my will to live.

I let out a strangled cry as I reveal the left foot, which is just as bruised and busted. Somehow, *seeing* the physical evidence of my injuries makes them hurt more, and I bite down on my lip. Nothing is bleeding. At least *nothing is bleeding.*

I chant this in my head over and over again, trying to reassure my anxious brain that it's all going to be okay, but the pain is too much, and I let the miserable tears fall.

I am not Diane Lane or Cheryl Strayed. This isn't my *Wild*, and I'm not sure why I thought it could be. I sit on the hard floor and weep for my deceased feet. And then I weep because I somehow tricked myself into believing this trip was my perfect escape. I wanted to believe I could somehow outrun *myself.*

I weep for the girl who never let herself question or wonder or explore; the girl who kept busy, kept repressing, kept forcing herself to date men because that's what she thought she had to do.

I weep for the woman who is thirty-five and too far behind to ever catch up. I weep for all that lost time.

The bathroom door opens with a creak. Mal emerges in her loose tank top and sleep shorts. With all my sobbing, I didn't hear the shower stop.

Rubbing my hands under my puffy eyes, I try to hide the evidence of my tears. Unfortunately, it's impossible, on account of the snot oozing down my face. I'm so tired of crying in front of this woman.

Mal pauses just outside the bathroom, studying me with her sepia-tone eyes.

"Don't look at me!" I yell, though the words get distorted, again because of snot.

Mal crouches in front of me so we're at eye level, and she releases a heavy sigh. "Will you please let me help you, friend?" Her raspy voice is surprisingly gentle.

I don't want her help. I don't want to give her more reasons to see me as ridiculous and useless.

"Sadie," Mal says, tone firmer. "Let me help you."

I'm not sure if it's the stern way she says my name, or if it's because I am in no position to refuse assistance, but I slowly allow my legs to extend in her direction. "Okay," I whisper.

Mal shifts so she's sitting crisscross in front of me, and then she reaches for my right foot. "Good lord, don't touch my feet!" I recoil. "They're repugnant!"

"I've seen worse," Mal says, and she touches my foot anyway, both of her hands carefully caressing my right foot, and I didn't expect the contact to feel so intimate. It's only the two of us, sitting close together on the floor of our shared hotel room, and she's massaging my foot, and her hands are smooth, and her grip is firm. When her hands touch me, there's the same tingling recognition I felt before, but there's also something else. Something new. A sensation in my lower stomach that feels like hunger and satiation at the same time.

She's delicate with my blisters as she begins rubbing my arches with her thumb. Then she flexes my foot against her palm, slowly at first, working out some of the stiffness.

It's not only the massage that feels intimate, I decide after a minute of these soothing movements. It's her eyes. The way she stares at my foot with such intense focus, like she's trying to learn the language of my skin and sinew. She finally drops my foot, and I can finally breathe again.

"Well, the first thing we've got to do is get you better shoes." She seems wholly unaware of how sexy that foot massage was.

"My boots are from REI. And they were really expensive."

"Incidentally, that is not the sole marker of a good shoe." Mal picks up my left foot and begins absently going through the same movements. "You bought hiking boots, which are great for, you know, *hiking*. But we're *walking*, and it will be mostly on boardwalks, sidewalks, roads, and other hard surfaces. You don't need all the ankle support. In fact, I think the ankle support is restricting your movement. You need something that will cushion your feet from the repetitive pressure of your body slamming against the ground. And it doesn't help that these seem to be brand-new?"

Embarrassed, I nod.

"A Pacific Northwest girlie should know better than to ever exercise in shoes that haven't been broken in. Your poor, poor toes. And these arches!"

Demonstratively, she strokes my left arch. Involuntarily, I shiver.

"What size shoe do you wear?"

I cannot believe I'm expected to carry on an intelligent conversation amid these weirdly sensual touches, but I clear my throat and try. "Size nine, usually."

"Perfect." Mal stops touching my feet once and for all and quickly gets up to fetch her dirty Hokas from over by the door. "These should fit you. I want you to try wearing these tomorrow."

I sputter at this generous offer. "B-but then . . . then what will you wear?"

"I can wear my hiking sandals." Mal shrugs. "It's only a fourteen-mile day."

Only.

"At least we'll give your feet a reprieve from these torture devices." She picks up one of my hiking boots and then tosses it over her shoulder with a flourish.

"I-I can't let you do that for me."

She breezes right past my protest. "And your wool socks are quality, but the most important thing is to keep your feet *dry* while trekking. Here." She tosses me something. "Try these under your socks. Don't worry. I haven't worn that pair yet."

I hold up the thin socks she's handed me. "Toe socks?"

"Trust me. They'll feel weird at first, but they'll stop your toes from rubbing together while sweaty. It makes a huge difference."

Suddenly, the pair of toe socks in my hands feel like the nicest gift anyone has ever given me.

"Oh, and did you pack any Vaseline? Never mind, actually. Mine is right here."

"Why are you doing this for me?"

She stops riffling through the pouches of her bag and turns toward me. "What do you mean?"

"Um, well, it's just . . ." I twist the toe socks in my hands. "Well, you've seemed annoyed with me ever since you discovered we're on the same trek."

Mal purses her lips in a very annoyed fashion. "Why would I be annoyed with you?"

"Because I'm the drunk woman who weirdly came out to you when I thought I was dying, and now you're stuck with me." I cringe at myself. "Because I'm a ridiculous fool who knows nothing about the Camino or Portugal or what shoes to wear."

"You confuse the shit out of me, Freckles," Mal explodes, and the tub of Vaseline in her hands goes flying.

It takes me a second to realize that *Freckles* is a proper noun in this context. That *I'm* Freckles. By the time I put it together, Mal is ranting again. "How can someone who owns and runs her own small business have zero self-confidence?"

"I'm sorry," I mutter. Mal huffs and then plops herself down on the floor beside me.

"I'm not annoyed with you, Sadie," she says softly, "and I'm sorry if I made you feel like I was."

"Oh." I don't know what else to say.

"And I'm doing all of this for you, my sweet baby gay, because that's what we do for each other. As your queer elder, I have to look out for you."

"Queer elder? What are you, like two years older than me?"

"Queer elder is more a state of mind than an age," she says. "It's like I've been trying to tell you. As queer people, we operate on different timelines. *You* are on a different timeline, and that's okay."

I rotate the pair of socks in my hand. "Thanks," I grumble. "For, um . . . for acting like I'm queer."

Mal snorts. "What are you talking about? You *are* queer."

"Not on this tour."

"*Ah*. Right. Because everyone keeps calling you straight."

"I *hate* it," I admit. "And I don't know why, because I don't want them to know I'm gay. I don't even really know if I am gay or bi or pan or whatever! And it's not like I've ever dated a woman or anything."

"You don't have to date a woman to be queer," she says, pulling her knees up to her chest on the floor beside me. Her elbow brushes mine, and why does even the smallest, accidental touch make me feel like a stranger in my own body? "Attraction and action are different things."

"But how can I even be sure if I'm gay if I've never kissed a woman?"

"Straight people are allowed to know they're straight without kissing anyone," she points out. "And I didn't kiss a girl until I was seventeen, but I knew I was queer the first time I laid eyes on Julia Styles in *10 Things I Hate About You.*"

I pull my legs up to my chest, too, and hug them tight. "My Nan opened the store when I was six," I hear myself say, "and I spent my whole childhood helping her run it. And then my mom, well . . . she sort of got . . . sick. After my dad left."

"Sick?" Mal prompts without demanding I share.

I share anyway. "Depressed. My mom has always struggled with depression and anxiety, but that . . . that was a really hard time. I had to take care of the store and my sister *and* my mom, and I was only twelve. And at twenty-one, I inherited all of it."

"Inherited?" Apparently, Mal's strategy is just to repeat key words back to me until I elaborate on them. I'm not sure why it's working.

"My Nan left everything to me. Before I even finished under-grad, I had a store to run and a house to maintain. I-I never had time to question anything. And at a certain point, I didn't *want* to question anything, because I had this sneaking suspicion that if I did, my entire idea of myself would crumble all around me."

"I see." Mal nods slowly. "So you didn't just miss out on a queer adolescence. You missed out on *any* adolescence."

"I guess . . ."

Mal clears her throat. "I can relate to that a bit, actually," she says. I turn my head to study her face in profile, waiting for her to share more, but her gaze remains fixed forward, and she doesn't offer any other personal details. She hasn't shared *anything* personal about herself, now that I think about it. Mal projects this outgoing, carefree demeanor, but there's something in the set of her jaw right now that suggests there's more going on just beneath the surface. Almost as if the right sandpaper could scrape away her varnish and reveal the true grain pattern underneath.

I want to peel back the varnish, but not everyone wants to share their most intimate secrets within forty-eight hours of meeting someone, so I drop it. "What do you do when you missed your chance to be a messy teenager?" I ask rhetorically.

Mal releases her knees, and her long, bare legs spill out in front of us. "You give yourself permission to be a messy thirty-five-year-old." She's her happy-go-lucky self again. "You have your second adolescence *right now*!"

I gawk at her. "Um . . . *how*?"

She jumps up excitedly. "You said you came on this trip to escape real life. So, for the next two weeks, what if you relive all those experiences you were denied as an adolescent?" She begins pacing our cramped room. "Like sneaking out and going to a party, and having a crush, and holding hands with a girl."

"What girl?"

"We'll find one," she says dismissively as she continues her enthusiastic laps across the floor. "You can get bangs and pierce something you shouldn't and kiss a stranger, if you want. You can do whatever you want. Mess up and make mistakes and just *be*."

I snort. "That sounds nice, but I'm not really . . ."

Not really *what*? Why does what she's describing feel as impossible as finishing this two-hundred-mile journey?

Mal stops excitedly twirling around the room and looks down at me. Whatever she sees on my face shatters her brief glee. "But first, we've got to take care of these feet," she says soberly. "Did your sister tell you to pack Compeed?"

"Yes!" I try to get up to grab the bandages from atop my bed, but my calf muscles seize, and I end up right back on my ass.

"Where?" Mal asks. She doesn't even laugh at the fact that I can no longer stand on my own accord. I point to the blue cosmetics bag on my twin bed. She grabs it. "After your shower, we'll get your feet as dry as we can, slather them in Vaseline, and cover them with socks. Then in the morning, we'll cover your blisters with Compeed. It should work like a second skin and will last for a few days. Come on." She sticks out her hand. "I'll help you get into the shower."

"I can get in the shower by myself," I mumble.

"Oh yeah?" Mal grins. "Show me how you can stand up on your own again?"

In the face of her mockery and my debilitating exhaustion, I stick out my tongue at her.

She laughs. "Let me help you up," she insists, and I do.

"First, shower," she says. "And then we can get to work fixing your pack."

"What's wrong with my pack?"

Everything, it turns out, is wrong with my pack.

After a long shower, Mal makes me spend an hour cutting my belongings in half. She holds up each item like the Marie Kondo of long-distance trekking, asking me if I *really* need it. But I need everything I packed.

"You absolutely do not need *two pairs of jeans.*" Mal takes them out and throws them onto the floor. "They're heavy, they take up too much room, and everyone will laugh at you if you trek wearing jeans. We're leaving these behind."

This goes on. She chucks one of my cardigans, two of my crop tops, my blow-dryer, and all my skin-care products except my sunscreen.

"That moisturizer is ninety-five dollars!"

Mal puts it directly into the trash. "I'll Venmo you."

Vera's comment about Mal having money flashes in my mind, but then I'm diving to save my electric toothbrush from the junk pile.

"That thing is way too bulky! You can get a small, cheap one from the farmácia for a euro."

"I can't get rid of anything else!"

"You can and you *will*." She gets rid of my *Lonely Planet* guidebook, my crossbody purse, my white sneakers ("Could you have packed anything more *impractical*?"), and my makeup bag.

"Wait! I can't part with my makeup!"

"We are *trekking*. There's no better time to divest from the beauty industry."

"But I *like* being invested in the beauty industry." I hug the cosmetics bag to my chest.

"Just make sure you're wearing makeup for the right reason," she says with some of Inez's spiritualism in her voice.

"What's the *right* reason?"

Mal doesn't answer because she's suddenly distracted by my three coats.

She accepts that I need the iPad and notebook to work on my sister's blog, but she throws out the dress Vi made me pack ("You can get drunk in yoga pants."), the sound machine ("Is this for a baby?"), and half of my underwear ("You're supposed to stink on the Camino. That's half the fun!").

The next morning, there is a stack of my so-called shit on my remade twin bed. She writes *donation* on the back of a receipt and sets it on top of the stack. Apparently, pilgrims leave things behind at albergues all the time, and items are passed along to people who need them.

When we set out for the day at eight in the morning with the rest of the group, my pack is at least ten pounds lighter. Mal has redistributed everything, putting the heaviest items on the bottom, and adjusted the straps to the right height for my body. She secures the small strap across my chest, even though it smooshes my boobs, and the pack feels almost weightless on my shoulders, my hips holding most of the burden. *I* feel almost weightless.

The toe socks are conspicuous at first, as are Mal's shoes, but after the mile, my feet settle into this new rhythm. My calves still ache, my forehead is sunburned, and I'm the most physically exhausted I've ever been, but there's something almost hypnotic about the walk. I *almost* enjoy it.

The walk from Vila do Conde to Esposende starts with a stretch of wooden boardwalk along the beach, but the blue skies and sparkling ocean help ease the annoyance of it today. May in Seattle is unpredictable, but here, May is glorious. Warm, with a light breeze coming off the water, everything green and saturated and remarkably *alive*.

On the outskirts of town, we stumble upon a market with wares clearly targeting pilgrims that packed horribly. Shorts and raincoats, sunscreen and hats. Mal grabs one of the hats—a cheap baseball cap with an anthropomorphic oyster shell embroidered on the front—and shoves it onto my head.

"You can't do the Camino without a hat."

It's the single ugliest accessory I've ever seen. I love it.

Ari studies us as Mal pulls my ponytail through the back of the cap, and I attempt to hide my blush beneath the stiff bill. Ari cocks her head to the side, then snorts. "That oyster shell looks like vulva."

"Will you please help me order real coffee?" I beg Mal at our midmorning stop.

"You don't want to water anymore plants with your espresso?" She smirks at me. "You can order a cappuccino most places," she explains as she leads me inside the café, where patrons are drinking espresso and beer in equal measure, even though it's before noon. "Or you can ask for café com leite, coffee with milk."

"Yes, that," I say. She approaches the counter and begins speaking Portuguese with the middle-aged man behind the counter. I have no idea what they're saying, but I find myself watching the way her bowed mouth moves around the unfamiliar sounds.

"Are you hungry?" Mal switches back to English and turns to me.

I have never been this hungry in my whole life. Apparently walking all day works up an appetite. "I could eat," I tell her. She orders something, and a minute later, a white plate with six round pastries appear in front of us. "What are those?"

"Are you fucking kidding me?" Mal shouts, and the drunk and/or over-caffeinated customers stare at us. "You've been in Portugal for forty-eight hours, and you haven't tried pasteis de nata yet?"

"What's a pasteis de nata?" I ask at a reasonable indoor volume.

"The only thing I like about this country," Mal answers. She picks up one of the pastries and shoves it toward me aggressively. "Try it. Right now. I want to watch."

"That's . . . weird . . ." I take the small treat from her and study the flaky crust and the custard-like middle.

"It's not weird. You'll get it when you taste it."

I gingerly take a bite, and *oh my fucking Christ.*

The flavor explodes across my tongue. The buttery crust, the lusciously decadent custard, the hint of spice. Cinnamon, maybe, or nutmeg. I temporarily leave my body as the sweetness flows through me, and when I return to earth, I am moaning obscenely into my last bite of pasteis de nata. I've somehow blacked out and eaten three of them standing here at the bar, and now Mal is staring at me with an unreadable expression.

But the custard is so delicious, I'm not even embarrassed by my reaction. "Okay," I tell her, licking my fingers for any lingering taste. "I get it."

Mal clears her throat. "Nothing like it, right?"

I want more, but we have to rejoin the group for sharing circle.

"Today, I want us to create our intentions for this trek," Inez says in her sage voice once we're all gathered together. "The third day is one of the hardest. Your body is sore and tired, and you're not yet used to the daily distances. When it gets challenging today, I want you to return to your intention. I want your intention to be your true guide on the Camino."

Ro snorts derisively into their croissant, and Mal angrily throws a pasteis de nata at them.

While Inez's constant prompting for self-reflection can feel heavy-handed at times, this morning her words niggle at something in the back of my mind.

I agreed to this trip because I wanted to escape, and if she'd asked me my intention yesterday, I would've said it was simply to survive the Camino.

But now I'm here, on a sidewalk café in Europe, with the taste of custard lingering on my lips. There are cobbled streets and sunlight and trees. There's a long path in front of me, and a Portuguese lesbian beside me who just wants to help, and I feel like I can aim for something better than *surviving*. I've been in survival mode since I was twelve years old.

I think I can do better than *escape*.

Maybe Mal was right, and for the first time in my life, I can simply *be*.

Maybe it's time to make some mistakes.

LIKED BY MOLLYMACDOUGALWELLS AND 13,419 OTHERS
cestlavi

Hey Nomads! Please allow me to introduce you to the love of my life: the pasteis de nata. She's small, but she is mighty.

And make sure you feast your eyes on my latest blog post about eating my way to Esposende, where I rank everything I've eaten on the Camino so far. (It turns out walking almost 14 miles in a single day makes you surprisingly hungry . . .)

#beatrixtours #cestlaviwithme #travelblog #broadsabroad #travel #portugal #spain #caminodesantiago #solowomentravelers #pasteldenata #foodporn

IMAGE DESCRIPTION: a white plate with two custards, sitting on a yellow tablecloth

TEN

Mal

"I'll do it!"

Sadie bounces up next to me in a flurry of sunburned limbs. She must've jogged to catch up, because her face is beet-red, she's sweating even more than usual, which is saying something. Her chest heaves up and down as she gulps in desperate breaths, and *holy hells*. That's all it takes for my brain to replay the pornographic way she ate nata at morning tea. The way her eyes blew wide with wonder and pleasure, the way she savored each bite on her tongue, the way she gasped and moaned, completely unselfconscious and unapologetic, maybe for the first time all trip. Maybe for the first time in her whole life.

I should've known she'd react that way to the world's greatest pastry. When Sadie thinks no one is watching, she stares at the scenery with unbridled joy. She smiles at the blue sky every morning, and she's taken at least two hundred pictures of the beach that's always to our left. Seeing the coastline through her eyes makes it feel new to me too. It makes me feel like I did as a kid, growing up near these shores, in awe of everything.

I squeeze my eyes shut for the length of one deep breath, then look back at Sadie without picturing her mouth dotted with custard. "You'll do what?"

"The queer—" She cuts off as she pinches her side and pants. "The queer adolescence thing. I'll do it. I-I want you to help me make up for lost time."

"It's not about making up for lost time." I hand her my water bottle, and she stops walking to take a long drink. Water sloshes out the side of the bottle's wide mouth and drips down her chin. "It's about reliving the coming-of-age experiences our heteronormative society denied you."

"Sure. That." She wipes the water off her chin with the back of her hand, and I don't let myself stare at her wet mouth. It's been a long, quiet morning walking on boardwalks and sand, sidewalk and dirt paths, and now the Camino has taken us through a bamboo forest, the midday sun filtering through the trees in golden slats. It's been a day of creeping silence: the silence of dead dads and homelands and roots that have been cut and lost. The silence of spinning thoughts about intentions and inheritances; of memories I wish I could forget.

In all that silence, I forgot about the particulars of my conversation with Sadie last night. I forgot about coming out of the bathroom to find her crying on the floor of our hotel room, and I forgot how desperate I felt to make her feel better.

Twenty-four hours. I couldn't even make it *twenty-four hours* without comforting Sadie.

"I want those queer experiences," Sadie says to me. It's not a whisper, not an apology. There's no hesitation in her voice. Even though Vera is only a few meters behind us, pausing to take photos of the way the light bends around the trees, Sadie speaks at her normal volume.

Which, granted, is still fairly quiet.

"Okay . . ." I stretch out the word so it's three syllables, and I'm not sure if I'm acknowledging her statement or agreeing to be her fairy god-dyke for real.

"Great!" Sadie claps her hands together the way Inez always does, as if her excitement is too big for her body to contain. And I guess I've agreed to do it, then. "Where do we start? Should I kiss a stranger at a bar tonight? Or maybe you should teach me how to flirt with a woman first?"

Sadie's face is all freckles and sweat and youthful exuberance. To Sadie, the prospect of flirting with a woman is as exhilarating and new to her as pasteis de nata.

Everything is new to her, and I've always chased newness.

"We start," I tell her, "with your hair."

"What's wrong with my hair?"

Sadie stares at me from across the lunch table, twirling a strand of her thick auburn hair.

"There's nothing *wrong* with your hair. You have great hair. That's the problem."

"It's a problem that I have great hair . . . ?"

"Yes. We need to fuck up your hair." I lower my voice and lean closer, even though the rest of the group is loudly counting in unison as Stefano does push-ups on the floor of the restaurant. Ari bet he couldn't do one hundred push-ups before our food arrived. He's currently on 342, and no one is paying any attention to Sadie and me. "Fucking up your hair is a queer rite of passage."

"Three hundred forty-five!" everyone shouts.

Sadie is double-fisting her curls. "You're saying that in order to be queer, I need to have bad hair . . . ?"

"No, no." I take a gulp of my ice water and search for a better way to describe this. *349.* "Growing up, I always had long, naturally brown hair, because my father never let me cut or color it. I wasn't allowed to choose what I looked like, because my father saw me as an extension of his own image." I reach for my water again. That's a little more than I meant to share, and I take a drink to gather myself. "So, after I kissed my boarding school roommate for the first time, I shaved my head without telling him."

Sadie's eyes are the size of the sexually suggestive oyster on her hat.

I hold up both hands. "I'm not saying you have to shave your head! I'm saying that for a lot of people, coming out is about seizing autonomy over your own body."

"Three hundred sixty!" The chorus rings out.

"Especially for those of us who were socialized as women." I dodge an excited air punch from Ro of all people. "Our lives revolve around other people telling us what to do with our bodies from a young age. To me, queerness is about existing outside those gender norms. It's saying *fuck you* to the rules that dictate how we look and how we act. It's true freedom."

365.

I watch the mental gears turn inside Sadie's head. She has a tell when she's grappling with something that challenges her view of herself: she bites her upper lip with her bottom teeth, like a nervous, inverted beaver.

"Three hundred sixty-nine!" The group chants just as the server comes through the back curtain carrying a heavy tray on each forearm. Stefano springs up, fresh-faced and not remotely perspiring, and effortlessly relieves the server of one tray with a flirtatious wink. Ari curses and slams a twenty onto the table.

Our lunch spot for the day is a family-owned diner that closed for a few hours so we could take over the cramped space. Linoleum flooring and Formica tabletops and red plastic chairs—it reminds me of the kind of place I would sneak away to as a teenager so I could eat a plate of french fries and pretend to be a normal kid for a while.

Today I ordered a Francesinha, for nostalgic reasons. Sadie ordered the same, for anxiety reasons, and I let her, because no one has ever looked sexy while eating a Francesinha.

"I'm not sure what alarms me more," she says when Stefano places the sandwich in front of her. "The fact that it's so wet, or the tiny green olive sticking out of the swamp like an eyeball."

"Don't insult the olive. It brings the whole dish together."

Sadie pokes at her very wet sandwich with her fork before finally loading up a bite that's mostly cheese, soggy bread, and tomato sauce. "It's not . . . totally revolting," she says after she forces herself to swallow.

"Rave review."

To me, the sandwich tastes like summer afternoons reading the latest Meg Cabot in a corner booth. It tastes like a sidewalk café in Porto, like nights when my father was out of town on business and his house manager, Luzia, would feed me a home-cooked meal. It tastes like comfort and five different meats.

"This whole fucking up your hair thing . . ." Sadie points at me with her fork. "Is that why you have a mullet?"

"Are you implying that my mullet is fucked-up?"

"It's blue."

"My mullet is *cool*. Like Joan Jett. Or Kristen Stewart playing Joan Jett."

"Or like my high school geometry teacher," Sadie adds.

"Oh, was your geometry teacher a smoking-hot dyke?"

She snorts. "Definitely not." But then she starts chewing on her top lip again as she reconsiders the sexuality of her former teacher, her whole face tightening like a fist.

"Sadie."

She's so lost in thought, it takes her a minute before her eyes come back into focus on my face. "Hmm?"

"I need you to admit that my mullet is sexy."

Her pinched eyebrows smooth out, then crumble. She lets out a small laugh. "I'm afraid I can't do that."

"Yeah, we'll see."

Sadie's face flushes the color of her Francesinha, and a heat spreads across the back of my neck, too.

"Ari, I need you to settle something for me." I turn toward the pretty Portland barista and find she's already looking at me with her smoky eyes. "I'm explaining to Sadie that fucking up your hair is a queer rite of passage."

"Oh, totally." Ari nods solemnly. "I got frosted tips in eighth grade."

"*Merde*," Stefano curses. He has conjured hand weights from somewhere and is doing bicep curls between bites of his halibut. "When I first thought I might be gay, I styled my hair like David Cassidy. I thought it was manly."

Everyone at the table turns to stare at Stefano. "David Cassidy?" Rebecca repeats. "From *The Partridge Family*?"

"Wait. How old *are you*?" Ari asks.

Stefano clutches an imaginary string of pearls. "A lady never owns her age."

"What are we talking about?" Ro asks as they come lumbering back from the bathroom.

"Fucking up our hair in our queer youth," Ari answers.

"I had the Weird Al," Ro grunts. When Rebecca gasps, they shrug. "What? It was the eighties."

"When I finally accepted that I'm aroace, I threw away my hair straightener, curling iron, and all my hair products," Vera adds, gesturing to the natural wave of her curly bob. "I used to spend *an hour* on my hair every morning, because my mamá told me it was the only way I'd ever find a husband."

Sadie's fingers tangle themselves into her ponytail again as everyone shares hair stories, until Rebecca sets down her glass of Vinho Verde with a pointed thunk. "I'm as gay as Dolly in 'Jolene,' but I'll be damned if I ever fuck up my hair on purpose." She pets her blond halo like a starlet in an old movie.

Everyone laughs, and Sadie finally releases her hair shackles.

"See?" I tell her gently. "A rite of passage."

"Why would Sadie care about queer rites of passage?" Ro asks. "She's straight."

Ro has all the subtlety of an acme anvil falling on the road-runner, and when I glance up at Sadie again, I expect to find her hair strangling her wrists. But she's holding her fork instead as she saws off a piece of sandwich and dangles the bite in front of her mouth. I wait for the panic to return to her expression, wait for her to blush or fluster or slink away to the bathroom to hide.

But Sadie doesn't do any of those things. She looks at Ro and conjures their casual shrug from before. "I'm thinking about fucking up my hair."

"I can't do this."

Sadie clutches the starched towel draped across her shoulders like a smock and looks up at me with the full weight of her terrified eyes.

"You can totally do this." I slice the scissors open and closed a few times, trying to pump her up, but the gesture looks more menacing than intended, especially because they're a cheap pair of kitchen scissors we found at the Foinz.

She winces at the two shiny blades. "But what if I don't *want* to do this?"

I pocket the scissors like a cowboy holstering his gun. "You absolutely do not have to do anything you don't want to do," I tell her, emphasizing each word so she knows I mean it.

"Yes, you fucking do!" Ari shouts from the other room. She's sitting on my bed with a bottle of Quinta Costa she's sharing with Vera. The hostel bathroom isn't big enough for anyone but me and Sadie, but a small crew insisted on joining us.

"You don't," I say again. Sadie looks up at me from her make-shift salon chair, also known as the toilet. "If you don't want to cut off your hair, you don't have to."

"But it's a queer rite of passage," she mumbles.

"There isn't one single right way to be queer."

Sadie arches her head so she can glimpse her silky hair in the mirror above the sink. One hand releases the towel so she can stroke her fingers from crown to tip, admiring the strands that luxuriate all around her. "It's pretty, isn't it?" she asks, tilting her chin at her reflection.

It's so fucking pretty. "Uh-huh."

She shakes out her hair, and it swishes around her in mesmerizing waves. "Everyone loves my hair," she says, more to her reflection than to me. "It's always the first thing people notice about me."

"But do *you* love your hair?"

"Yes," she says to the woman in the mirror. "But also, it's so *hot* when we're walking, and it's so thick and heavy, it's giving me a headache to wear it up."

"Do you want to know what I think?"

She finally pulls her gaze away from her reflection and stares up at me with those terrified eyes.

"If your favorite thing about your hair is that other people think it's pretty, I say . . . let's fuck it up." I snip the scissors in her face once more, and her trance breaks.

She steals one last glance at her reflection, then faces me, resolute. "Okay, yes. Let's fuck it up."

"Hell yes!" Ari shouts from the other room.

"Finally," Stefano grunts. He's in the middle of a Vinyasa flow on the weathered hardwood floors of our Esposende hostel, and for an age-ambiguous man somewhere between forty and sixty, he's shockingly limber as he moves from plank to cobra.

Sadie repositions the towel around her shoulders, and I carefully take a strand of her silky hair between my fingers.

"Are you sure *you* can do this?" Sadie squeaks at me.

"I've been cutting my own hair for twenty years."

"That is not reassuring."

She tenses as I flip her hair at the ends and ready the scissors. From this close, it's easy to see the twitch of her jaw muscles and the small lines around her pursed mouth. I'm so close, in fact, that I can count her individual freckles; I can feel her nervous, shallow breaths; I smell her lingering shampoo after her post-Camino shower. It smells like wildflowers.

I'm so close to her, I can see her blush spreading down the column of her throat, and I feel a little dizzy, knowing that blush is because of me.

I clear my throat. Without further ado, I lob off a long chunk of her hair. We both watch in a mixture of horror and fascination as the red strands fall to the linoleum.

"Do we like it?" Sadie asks for the dozenth time.

She keeps reaching up to her shoulders to grab the invisible strands of her memory. The gorgeous, thick hair that ran down her back is gone, replaced by a choppy bob that sits about two inches above her pale shoulders. I also gave her feathery bangs that sweep across her blue-green eyes and then frame her face on the sides. It somehow makes her look both younger and older, with her cute, rounded cheeks and her staggering curves no longer hidden behind a curtain of her hair.

"We *love* it," Ari croons.

Vera also nods emphatically. "We really *really* love it."

Stefano rattles off a few words of rapid-fire Italian. I only understand about half of it, but from his tone, it sounds complimentary.

Sadie can't stop reaching for what isn't there. "It's not too short?"

"If you keep searching for approval, you're going to give me a complex," I tell her as she ruffles her new bangs. "I think I did a damn good job."

"You did. Of course you did," Sadie rushes, "but I've just never . . . it's so *short*."

It's not *that* short, but it was easily eighteen inches of Sadie that we left on the bathroom floor, so it makes sense that she's going to need time to adjust. I know she doesn't regret it, because when Inez knocks on the door and everyone is distracted by letting her in, I catch Sadie stroking her new hair and smiling to herself. It's not her awkward smile, or her apologetic smile. It's the smile she gives the blue sky and the sunshine when no one else is watching.

"Who ordered the ham and Swiss?" Inez asks from the doorway, and Vera's hand shoots up. After our heavy lunch and a long day in the sun, no one felt like going out to dinner, so Ro helped Inez collect sandwich orders, and now they're helping her pass them out to their correct owners.

"Sardine sandwich, right here!" I hold up my hand, and Ro holds my sandwich like a football and launches it across the hotel room with a perfect spiral.

"*Meu Deus!*" Inez shouts once all the sandwiches are divvied up. She claps her hand to her mouth as she stares at Sadie. "Your hair! It looks amazing!"

Sadie's cheeks explode in fiery splotches. I guess I'm not the only one who can make her blush like that.

She reaches up for nothing, and then lets her limp arm fall. "Uh, thank you, Inez. Mal did it."

Inez's eyes shift over to me on the floor, and I can already hear the lecture that will be coming my way tomorrow. "Enjoy your dinner," Inez says, turning toward the door.

"Stay!" Vera calls out. "Stay! Stay! Ro, you too! Eat floor sandwiches with us!"

And that's how we all end up sitting on the floor of the hostel room eating subpar sandwiches. Rebecca joins after her shower, hobbling into the room with a towel wrapped around her hair. "My blisters have blisters," she cries out, and Sadie passes her a pillow to sit on.

Everyone is either punch-drunk from the exhaustion of the last three days, or *drunk*-drunk from the extra bottles of wine that somehow materialize. Stefano tells a story about getting travelers' diarrhea on the twenty-fifth mile of an Ironman race in Ecuador, including a very vivid and hilarious reenactment of what took place behind an unsuspecting tienda.

Inez tells stories about the best and the absolute worst tour groups she's taken on the Camino. Then Rebecca has everyone howling as she describes the social politics of her HOA, and Ari tells stories about working as a barista in Portland, which are honestly more horrifying than Stefano's desecration of that Ecuadorian tienda.

And it's a nice night. Inez goes to bed first, and then Ro offers Rebecca an arm to help her up off the floor. It's a surprisingly sweet gesture from such an unrelenting curmudgeon. They say goodnight, and one by one, the group winnows. When Ari saunters out after kissing me on the cheeks eight times as a goodbye, it's just Sadie and me.

She's quiet and withdrawn, the way she always seems to be after the whole group has been together. I putter around for a minute, cleaning up food wrappers and rogue bits of hair from the floor. When she's still quiet after all that, I gently nudge her. "What are you thinking about, Freckles? Profoundly regretting the haircut?"

Her hand reaches for invisible hair, but she shakes her head. "No, no. I was . . . I was thinking about my geometry teacher, actually."

I snap my fingers. "She *was* a smoking-hot dyke! I *knew it!*"

Her lips crack into a smile, but then she's chomping on her upper lip again. "I honestly don't know . . ."

I sit down on the edge of my bed across from her and wait for her to say more. "Her name was Mrs. Daniels," she continues after a long, heavy silence. "She had this black-and-gray, helmet-shaped mullet, and all the boys in our class used to make fun of her. It took me a while to understand *why* they made fun of her, because she was such a good teacher, perfectly nice, sometimes even funny."

Sadie draws her legs up beneath her, staring at some fixed point on the wall. "Back in ninth grade, I didn't know the stereotype. I-I didn't know that having a mullet made you a lesbian, but I quickly learned that being a lesbian made you a joke."

Her words land on my chest like a punch. I can see it so clearly: a fourteen-year-old Sadie, with that same innocent face and those same freckles, simply trying to find the area of a triangle. Maybe she wasn't even questioning herself then. Maybe she didn't look at Mrs. Daniels and see some part of herself mirrored back at her. But she was surrounded by ignorant teenagers who made it clear that being a lesbian was something to mock and ridicule, and there's no way she didn't internalize that.

Did Sadie always make herself small, or is it something she learned to do out of fear that if she took up space, people might truly notice her? And if they noticed her, maybe they'd realize she was a joke too.

"I'm not even sure if Mrs. Daniels was actually gay," Sadie muses. "Everyone just assumed she was. We called her *Mrs.* Did she have a wife?"

"Was gay marriage even legal in Washington state then?"

"Oh." Sadie blinks at me. "No. I guess not."

She pauses again, gnawing on her lip. "Do you think she knew she was the punch line of freshman boys' jokes?" Sadie asks. "Do you think she cared?"

Sadie sucks in a sharp breath and she looks at me expectantly, as if my answer will somehow rewrite the lesson she learned in that classroom all those years ago. "I think we all care a little bit," I tell her. "Some of us are better at hiding it."

Sadie bobs her head up and down as she considers this. I get the feeling she isn't done, so I hold myself as still as I can until she finds her voice again.

"A few years ago I had this dream that I was engaged to Jack Antonoff."

It's not what I expected her to say next, and I nearly fall off my bed as I try to make sense of her non sequitur. "Jack Antonoff? The Bleachers guy?"

"And the guy who produces most of Taylor Swift's music, yes."

"Weird choice for a dream fiancé, but okay."

"That was the thing," she tries to explain in a classic Sadie-bluster, all flushed cheeks and frantic hand movements. Her blue-green eyes are glossy and terrified. "I didn't want to marry Jack Antonoff. In the dream, I was on the New York subway for some reason, and I kept telling everyone that I didn't want to marry him, but no one would listen, and I couldn't escape the engagement. Or the subway. I was just . . . stuck."

She takes another sharp breath and releases it instantly, a hissing noise escaping her lips. "The next day, I told my sister and my mom about the dream, like it was this funny anecdote. Like, isn't it so random? I had a dream about Jack Antonoff! And we all just laughed about it." She pauses for a second, her eyes locked on her own blistered bare feet against the floorboards. "But the dream wasn't funny. I don't remember all the details now, but I do remember feeling absolutely terrified that I was going to have to marry Jack Antonoff. I said it *wasn't* funny, Mal!"

I'm trying to stifle my laugh, but I'm finding it very difficult. No one has ever sounded quite so devastated at the thought of marrying Jack Antonoff. "Except it kind of *is* funny."

"It was a *nightmare!*"

"Okay. Okay."

"It is funny, actually," she admits, but there's no humor in her voice. Her tone is hollow, far away, even though she's right here, just five feet away on the other twin bed. "It's funny that I'm only just now realizing that dream wasn't about Jack Antonoff at all."

I stop laughing. "No," I say, my tone matching hers. "It doesn't seem like it was."

Sadie gathers up her now-short hair and tries to pull it into a ponytail, but bits keep sliding out. Eventually, she gives up, and lets it fall around her face again. "I felt like I was stuck on this path I didn't want to be on, and I thought I could never get off it."

"But now you are off it," I remind her.

"Yeah, and I have no clue where I'm going."

"You're going to Santiago de Compostela." That gets her to crack a smile, and she's so heartbreakingly beautiful in this moment, I don't know what to do with myself. She's scrubbed clean from her shower, not a stitch of makeup on her face, with a million freckles and her hair adorably short. She's almost unrecognizable from the woman I met on the plane a few days ago.

But she is the same woman. Still scared and unsure and so hard on herself for not having figured it all out sooner.

There's another tug in my chest, like a cord yanking me toward Sadie. I follow the pull as I climb off my own bed. "Can I sit here?"

She nods, and I lower myself onto her bed. I press my shoulder against hers, and I hope the contact says everything I'm struggling to put into words.

"Why did I force myself to date men for so long?" she wonders aloud. The question seems rhetorical, so I spare her another lecture on compulsory heterosexuality. "I *always* hated it. I went out with this one guy a few times in my early twenties, and he would send me these thoughtful, romantic texts. Things like, 'the moon is beautiful tonight, and it makes me think of you.' And I felt sick every time I read those texts. The thought of a man thinking about me made me *sick*."

"In your defense, that text is gross."

She does some combination of a laugh and a sniffle, and without warning, drops her head to my shoulder. It's such an innocent gesture, but it's also an achingly intimate one. Something that only happens between close friends or lovers. Sadie and I aren't either of those things, and I'm overwhelmed by the way she keeps trusting me with parts of herself.

I'm also overwhelmed by her wildflower smell, and her smooth hair against my cheek, and her soft body pressed against mine. I put an arm around her shoulders, and this gesture is also innocent, also intimate.

"Thank you," Sadie whispers again as I squeeze her in a tight sideways hug. Then I put a hand on her leg, and she puts her hand over mine, and we're sort of . . . holding hands. On her bed. In our pajamas.

I try to ignore the way her hard nipple keeps brushing my arm through her cotton T-shirt every time she takes a deep breath. I force myself not to enjoy the feeling of her smooth, plump thigh beneath our hands.

But then she takes another deep breath, every part of her pressing against every part of me, and all my noble intentions go straight to hell. Some kind of half-strangled noise inadvertently escapes my lips, and Sadie lifts her head to look up at me.

"Are you okay?" she whispers. She's *so close*, I can taste her breath.

It tastes like the tuna sandwich she had for dinner, actually, and the fact that I'm still turned on really says something.

"I'm fine," I finally tell her through a clenched jaw. I'm holding my body as still as possible. I'm in a prison of barely maintained self-restraint, a prison of my own making. Her blue-green eyes flutter down to my mouth, and the anticipation makes every part of me tingle.

"Mal?" she whispers back at me.

"Hmm?"

"Thanks for fucking up my hair." She ruffles her bangs again, and an image flashes through my mind. Sadie on a twin bed like this. Me fucking up her hair in a very different way. I feel for the amethyst crystal Inez gave me, always in my pocket. *Willpower.*

"You're welcome," I croak. Very innocent. Very restrained. Very *not* intimate. Then I climb off the bed before I can do anything regrettable. No part of her is pressing against any part of me, and I should be relieved.

I am actually quite devastated.

Sadie studies me like she can't figure out why I keep taking steps away from her. Then she smiles again. "Any chance you want to watch some *Property Brothers* with me before bed?"

She unplugs her phone from the bedside table and holds it up to me. And I *am* relieved. Nothing effectively kills the mood like inviting Drew and Jonathan into the space between us.

M&M CHAT

Today

Mal

I almost kissed her 11:19 p.m.

Michelle

Who? 11:24 p.m.

Mal

The woman from the plane 11:25 p.m.

Michelle

I thought you were never going to see
her again 11:37 p.m.

> **Mal**
>
> Come on
>
> Neither of us believed that
>
> It turns out she's on my fucking tour
> 11:38 p.m.

Michelle

Of course she is 11:44 p.m.

> **Mal**
>
> YOU'VE GOT TO HELP ME
>
> I was THIS CLOSE to kissing her
>
> What do I do????? 11:45 p.m.

Michelle

Don't panic. I have a perfect strategy
for this.

The next time you find yourself in
a situation where you want to kiss
her . . .

Don't. 11:53 p.m.

> **Mal**
>
> I do not comprehend
>
> 11:54 p.m.

Michelle

I know it's a foreign concept for you

But sometimes, people experience
attraction and they don't act on it 11:59 p.m.

Mal

That doesn't sound right 12:00 a.m.

Michelle

And if that doesn't work, then every time you look at this woman's mouth, think about your dead dad and the multimillion-dollar company you just inherited 12:11 a.m.

Mal

But I don't want to think about that . . . 12:12 a.m.

Michelle

Yeah. That's kind of the point. 12:18 a.m.

ELEVEN

Sadie

It's only a haircut.

There's nothing profound about it, nothing revolutionary. Yet I keep reaching up to confirm those eighteen inches are really gone. I keep catching sight of myself in passing windows and remembering that I left all that hair on the bathroom floor in Esposende. When I see my reflection, I both don't recognize myself and feel like I'm seeing myself for the first time, somehow.

I don't look better, exactly. Mal used kitchen scissors, after all, and the ends are choppy and uneven in places, the slightly crooked bangs loudly announcing that I'm *going through something*. But I love the haircut all the same. It makes me feel rebellious.

It makes me feel the way it did when Mal forced me to leave behind all the items in my pack that weren't serving me. I'm lighter, my steps easier, my head clearer.

I don't look better, but I *like* how I look better, and I didn't realize that was possible.

The walk from Esposende to Viana do Castelo is the most beautiful part of the journey so far. We walk through quiet, cobbled streets on our way out of town in the morning, past lines of children making their way to school, past white churches with terra-cotta roofs and blue tile accents, past lovely town squares that sparkle in the early morning sun.

We all pose for a group picture in front of a blue-and-yellow sign with a dozen different directional arrows (Santiago: 208 kilometers), and then the group falls into its usual walking pattern, with Stefano jogging ahead and then looping back to walk with Inez and Mal at the head of the group, like he's an overly eager dog that doesn't want to wander too far from his owners. Ari bounces between Mal at the front and Vera at the rear, where she always is because she stops every few yards to take pictures of crumbling churches or bird of paradise flowers or random old men sitting on benches. Ro and Rebecca hover in the middle, keeping pace with each other step for step.

I float between walking with everyone and with no one. Sometimes I push myself so I can walk with Mal, and we talk about her past Caminos and my home renovations projects. About how she knew she was gay and about all the times I should've suspected I might be something other than straight. But when my legs get tired, I fall back and chat with the retirees about antiques and upcycling, laughing along as Rebecca's cheeriness clashes with Ro's crankiness.

Even with my lighter pack, lighter hair, and Mal's shoes, my calves and feet still ache by the third mile, and eventually, I can't keep pace with the retirees, either. I fall back as we trek along the staggering coastline, trying to soak in the deep blue sky and the hills of bright green and a paddock of fluffy white sheep right beside the turquoise ocean. Vera stops to take two dozen photos of the sheep, her camera making its signature *click, click, click.*

"I bet that's a beautiful one." I pause beside her to take a drink of water. Vera reviews the photos in her viewfinder and is clearly discontented with what she sees, because she raises the camera again. Except instead of taking more pictures of the sheep, she turns the camera to me.

"Do you mind?" she asks, her index finger hovering over the button.

"Oh, um, no. Go ahead."

Click, click, click. Vera glances down at the viewfinder again, then looks back up at me. "The hair really suits you," she says plainly. "You look like yourself."

Then she tilts the camera so I can see one of the pictures. It's both me and not me, with a half smile and a patchy sunburn and a dorky hat shoved over my short hair. I don't look like I'm posing. I'm just . . . *being*.

It's like I'm looking at myself through Vera's eyes, and she somehow sees me more accurately than I do.

"You're an amazing photographer," I tell her. I take in the whole image of Vera: her big glasses with their beaded chain; her Velma haircut; her moisture-wicking hiking turtleneck. She looks like a slutty librarian Halloween costume. Or like Rachael Leigh Cook in *She's All That*. Like she's waiting for someone to rip off her glasses and prove she was hot all along. Except Vera seems perfectly happy without Freddie Prinze Jr. and the popular girl makeover. How does anyone feel that comfortable being totally and completely themselves?

"Thank you." She repositions her Canon and takes a few more photos of the sheep.

"Can I ask you something kind of embarrassing . . . ?" I start as Vera angles her body back toward the path. "What does aroace mean?"

She swivels toward me with a look of alarm on her face. "Oh."

"Sorry. Is that a stupid question?"

"No! Not at all. I just didn't expect it." We fall into step with each other as Vera considers her answer. "Aroace stands for aromantic and asexual, which means I don't experience romantic or sexual attraction."

"So, you don't date or . . . have sex?" I hear how the question sounds as soon as it's out of my mouth. "Wait. Sorry. That was really invasive. Don't answer that."

"That *was* an invasive"—she laughs at me—"but I actually don't mind answering it." She pauses again, this time to take a photo of a hawk drifting across the placid blue sky. "There are aromantic people who date, and there are asexual people who have sex, but no, I don't do either of those things. I don't feel any need to do those things."

Her words feel like a splash of cold water trickling down from the crown of my head. I've always hated dating, always run away from the possibility of sexual intimacy, never even felt the desire to have sex with anyone.

There was this time, senior year of college, when I decided I wanted to have sex, just to get it over with already. His name was Josh C., only ever Josh C., because we already had a Josh in our marketing seminar study group. One day, I misguidedly feigned interest in his lengthy tirade about Zack Snyder's *Watchmen* adaptation, and he invited me over to watch the director's cut with him.

Just the two of us. He made that part very clear.

Everyone else in the study group agreed. This was obviously code for sex.

I absolutely did not care about *Watchmen*, but I figured Josh C. was my chance to lose my virginity. So, I waxed everything, bought a new bra, wore a low-cut shirt and did some light googling. I went to Josh C.'s dingy apartment off the Ave and braced myself to have sex.

And . . . he genuinely just wanted to watch the director's cut of *Watchmen*.

The closest we got to anything physical was when I said I was cold, and Josh C. put a blanket over both our legs.

Afterward, when I debriefed the night with the girls in my study group, I couldn't make sense of what I'd done wrong. Why didn't that horny twenty-two-year-old want to touch me? I blamed myself, assumed there was something wrong with me.

Only now am I starting to wonder if Josh C. didn't touch me that night because he could tell I didn't want him to.

Men have kissed me goodnight, and I've had my fair share of unwanted, drunk tongue on a bad first date. The occasional boob-honk or ass grab. But no one has ever kissed me like they want *me*, no one has ever touched me with passion or longing or a burning need. But I've never had a burning need to touch someone else, either.

"Can I ask you another question?" I turn back to Vera. "How did you figure out you're aromantic and not just someone who hates dating?"

"Well, I've never dated at all, so I don't actually know if I hate it or not." She shrugs as we stop again. I'm not even sure what she's taking a photo of this time. "But I don't need to date to know I'm not romantically attracted to people. It's never appealed to me. I could never understand why my friends wanted to hold hands with boys or why our friendship wasn't enough for them. I can't imagine needing any of that."

I think about all the times I've told Vi and my mom that I don't mind being single, that I'm okay focusing on work, that I don't want a relationship. I've said it so many times, I've convinced myself it's true. But is it?

"And, um . . . the asexuality thing?" I mumble. "How did you, uh . . . how did you know that?"

"It can be tricky, because people often confuse asexuality with a lack of libido or sex drive, but I have a sex drive. It's just not directed at anyone." Vera stares at me through her camera. "Are you questioning if you might be asexual?" She asks it so plainly, so devoid of judgment. Maybe it's because I feel like I'm talking to a black lens, but I find it easy to speak plainly too.

"Sort of, yeah, actually."

Vera takes another photo of me, but she doesn't speak. Her silence is like a door that's been left ajar. I step through it.

"I feel like I'm too old to be questioning, like I should have the answers already."

"Why?" she asks, still behind her camera. "Are you going to be tested on it later?"

I sigh. "No, it's just . . . I've only ever dated men, and I've never been attracted to any of them," I confess to her camera lens. It click, click, clicks. "So I could be asexual, but I could also be . . ."

Vera lowers her camera and asks the next logical question. "Have you ever been sexually attracted to a woman before?"

"No," I answer quickly. Because I haven't. Not really.

Sure, I've had celebrity crushes, and I've had unusually intense friendships with other girls that in retrospect *may* have been crushes. But I've never looked at a woman and imagined touching her.

I've never *let* myself look. I never let myself imagine.

Last night comes into focus: sitting on a toilet seat as Mal leaned over me with a pair of kitchen scissors. Mal standing between my open legs to get the right angle, Mal tilting forward to reveal her prominent collarbone, the tops of her small breasts, the compass tattoo across her sternum. Mal smelling like sandalwood and spring in Seattle, fingertips on the back of my neck, fingernails across my scalp, all while I sat perfectly still, terrified to move, terrified to breathe. Terrified of everything.

And later: Mal on the bed, her body heat and her sardine breath. Her hand on my thigh, my head on her shoulder, a simple intimacy that felt anything but simple in that moment. It felt enormous, and terrifying, and—

And *oh*. Oh shit.

"Asexuality exists on a spectrum. You might experience limited sexual attraction, or only experience it rarely," she says. "It's not black and white, but in my experience, nothing is."

We start tracing the coastline again. Rebecca and Ro are out of earshot, and Inez and Mal aren't even visible. They haven't been for the last ten minutes. What does it mean that I'm always aware of where Mal is in space?

"I was initially afraid to sign up for this trip," Vera says quietly. "I know there are people in the community who don't think asexual people are queer. But to me, queerness is about existing outside of the heteronorm when it comes to sex and love, and no one is more out of the norm than aroace people. The entire world revolves around sex and romance, and not participating in those things can be so incredibly isolating."

Feeling alienated at every girls' night out, keeping everyone at arm's length, training the people in my life to never ask too many questions. "Yeah," I agree. "It really can be."

"You have a crush."

The accusation is whispered in my ear an hour later as I walk up an impossibly steep hill, and I trip over my own feet. I nearly go down, but a hand latches on to my elbow and keeps me from eating asphalt.

When I'm stable again, I turn to see Mal smirking at me. "I-I don't . . . I don't know what you're talking about."

"Oh, really?" The smirk intensifies. It's unfair that she has a face so suited to playfully mocking expressions. Her eyebrows are spring-loaded for surprise and her bowed mouth easily twists into a sideways smile.

The only thing my face is suited for is blushing and telegraphing my every thought. I assume I'm doing both now, which is why Mal says, "Don't be embarrassed! I also have a habit of developing crushes on every pretty girl who's nice to me."

Her hand is still on my elbow, and I gently tug it away as we continue up the vertical hill, my thighs and glutes burning as ferociously as my blush.

"And if she's completely off-limits. Oof." Mal presses a hand to her chest, drawing attention to that cavernous clavicle and her usual bralessness under her gray tank. "Be still my beating heart."

I wish my beating heart would be still, but it's hammering wildly inside my chest as several things become abundantly clear.

One: I do have a crush.

Two: And it's on Mal.

And three: Mal humiliatingly knew about it before I did. She knows I have a fucking crush on her.

"Off-limits?" I echo.

"Yeah, that's what makes it perfect! It's a totally safe crush for your second adolescence!"

"Perfect?" I can barely breathe, and I'm not sure if it's from the hill or my increasing mortification.

"You have your first lesbian crush!" She punches me in the arm in a celebratory fashion, and this is becoming the weirdest interaction I've ever had with another person. "At least, I'm assuming it's your first lesbian crush."

We finally reach the top of the hill and turn left toward what appears to be a neighborhood or the outskirts of a small village. Below, we have a remarkable view of the coast. I use the view as an excuse to pause and take a drink of water.

If I've ever had a lesbian crush before, it's been a secret to everyone, including me.

And if I've had a crush before, it didn't feel like *this*.

"Letting yourself develop a crush is a big step in your queer adolescent journey." She throws an arm around my shoulders in an entirely too-platonic fashion. "This is awesome."

It's not the hill or my humiliation that steals the air from my lungs this time. It's the look on Mal's face. She isn't smirking or playfully mocking me. She's truly, sincerely, *happy* for me, and happiness is painfully beautiful on her.

I turn away from all that beauty and continue following the coastline north. Mal quickly falls into step beside me, the clang of her Hydro Flask keeping time like a metronome. "What's wrong?" she asks after a stretch of silence.

My eyes are anywhere but her face. "Nothing. It's just . . . it's awkward . . . that you know how I feel."

"It shouldn't be!" Mal jumps in front of me so I'm forced to look up at her. "Please don't feel awkward! I'm your fairy god-dyke. It's okay for me to know this stuff. We have princess–fairy god-dyke confidentiality."

She walks backward for a few yards so we're face-to-face, her eyes level with mine. It almost feels like we're tied together with an invisible string, like she's leading me somewhere I'm not ready to go.

"If I'm being completely honest," she starts, looking me in the eye with zero regard for where she's going, "Sometimes I feel the same way."

Something strange happens in that instant. I take another step forward, but my foot never makes contact with the ground. I'm floating, suspended in air, suspended in time. "You . . . you *do?*" I hear myself say. God, I *sound* like an adolescent.

"Totally. It's hard not to have a crush on Inez. She's sunshine personified."

My feet are firmly back on solid ground. "Inez?"

"You have good taste, is all I'm saying. Inez is the fucking best."

She still isn't watching where she's going, and she backs herself into a Camino trail marker, stumbling sideways.

Inez. Mal thinks I have a crush on *Inez*.

Inez, who is off-limits because she's our tour guide. Inez, a pretty girl who's been nothing but nice to me.

Inez. I *wish* I had a crush on Inez.

Mal continues to stumble, and I almost reach out to steady her like she did for me, but she catches herself before she falls and effortlessly slides back into step beside me. "Whatever you're feeling right now," she says, as if she didn't nearly land on her ass. "Let yourself feel it."

I keep putting one foot in front of the other. I don't look at her. I *won't* look at her right now, because I don't want her to see the devastation that's surely dashed across my face.

"I know we've only known each other for, what? Four days? But I get the impression that you've spent the last thirty-five years ignoring your body. Ignoring your gut, not listening to what it's been trying to tell you."

We take another step and I still don't look at her.

"Sometimes, as scared queer kids, we cut ourselves off from our bodies entirely to survive," Mal says. "So, whatever you're feeling right now, whatever you feel when you look at Inez—if you blush or get sweaty palms or butterflies or whatever—let yourself feel it. Learn how to listen to what your body is telling you."

I'm blushing and my palms are sweaty, but I don't have butterflies. I have a stomach full of rocks.

I take another step, and another, and another, and Mal's water bottle bangs out a death march. "Hey. Sadie." Mal's hand is on my elbow again, pulling me up short. "I'm sorry. That . . . that was presumptuous of me. You're upset."

"I'm not upset."

"Then why won't you look at me?"

I look at her. And fuck it. *There* are the butterflies. A thousand tiny wings are flapping inside me as they lift my stomach into my chest. "I'm not upset," I say again, forcing myself to keep looking at her stupidly earnest, Beautiful/Handsome face.

"It's only that I'm not used to talking about these sorts of things," I tell her, and it's the truth.

It's *part* of the truth.

"You can always practice talking about these sorts of things with me." Her thumb gently swipes my arm in a gesture I think is meant to comfort me, but it sets my teeth on edge. "That's what I'm here for."

That is what she's here for.

"Thank you," I finally say. "I promise to talk to you about my crush . . . on Inez . . . when I'm ready."

Mal's hand falls away from my arm and she flashes me a strained smile. "I'll be here," she says, "whenever you're ready."

We catch up with the rest of the group in the postcard-perfect village of Carreço when we stop at a bright and airy bakery for morning tea. I order a cappuccino and two pasteis de nata, and then I manipulate things so I end up sitting next to Vera, as far away from Mal as possible.

"For today's reflection," Inez starts, "I want us to talk about listening to our bodies."

I snort into my mug, and foam splashes onto my nose. Across the table, Mal lets out a sharp laugh, and Inez glares at her.

"Our bodies are the most important guide we have on the Camino," Inez continues, "and they contain more wisdom than we realize. We need to connect to the sensations of our bodies so we can be attuned to the messages they are sending us. Close your eyes with me. Turn inward. What is your body saying?"

Too much. I feel sweaty and shaky and anxious. My stomach is full of rocks and butterflies, floating and sinking, and the last thing I want to do is listen to it.

Quite frankly, I need my body to shut the fuck up.

M&M CHAT

Today

Mal

False alarm, everybody!

No need to panic! It was a false alarm!
10:13 p.m.

Michelle

I'm about to train 15 technicians how
to use the remote sensing equipment
before field work starts next week, and
I do not have time for vague lead-ins
10:19 p.m.

Mal

Sadie has a fatty crush on Inez, so I'm in
the clear 10:20 p.m.

Michelle

And Sadie is . . . ? 10:24 p.m.

Mal

The woman

With the freckles

That I almost kissed 10:24 p.m.

Michelle

You did not mention she had freckles.
You don't stand a chance, my friend.
10:25 p.m.

Mal

But I do! Because she's into Inez!

I'm no longer at risk of kissing her
10:25 p.m.

Michelle

Is she still on your tour . . . ? 10:27 p.m.

> **Mal**
>
> Yes 10:27 p.m.

Michelle

And is she still your roommate . . . ?
10:28 p.m.

> **Mal**
>
> Well yes but I can't control that
>
> I'm not going to bug Inez to switch my
> room after everything she's done for me
> 10:28 p.m.

Michelle

And is this woman with freckles
currently sleeping ten feet away?
10:29 p.m.

> **Mal**
>
> What's your point here? 10:29 p.m.

Michelle

Your complete lack of self-awareness
is impressive 10:29 p.m.

TWELVE

VIANA DO CASTELO
Saturday, May 17, 2025

Mal

"Sadie. Sadie! Wake up!"

There's a sharp snort followed by an unattractive throat clearing as Sadie jerks up in bed, blinking into the low light of our room. It's dark beyond our Viana do Castelo albergue, but I clicked on the bedside lamp when I decided to chase this impulsive urge.

"What? What is it?" she grumbles, wiping her head around the room in search of a cause for this 4 a.m. wake up. "Is everything okay? Is there a fire?"

"Why would there be a fire?"

"I don't know!" She rubs the sleep out of her eyes. "Why would you be waking me up for anything less?"

"Come on."

She closes one eye and squints at me with the other. "What?"

"Come on," I say again. "We're going for a little walk."

"This whole trip is a walk."

I shove my feet inside my hiking sandals and toss my Hokas on the floor beside her bed. "This is an extra walk."

"*Why* are we doing extra walking in the middle of the night?"

"As part of your queer adolescence, obviously. We're going to hike up to Santa Luzia hill and watch the sunrise."

Sadie doesn't move from her nest of sheets and blankets. "No," she says, and then she flops onto her back.

I'm confused.

This seemed like such a marvelous idea as I tossed and turned until three in the morning, listening to the soundtrack of Sadie's snores. The views from Santa Luzia hill are incredible, with a sweeping panoramic of the city and the sea and the River Lima that connects the two. It seems wrong to be here, in this town, and miss the chance to see it. I don't want to miss the chance to share it with her. Even if we were up until midnight talking about everything and nothing and watching *Property Brothers*.

And damn. She appears to be back to sleep already.

"Come on," I try again, moving close to nudge her shoulder with more enthusiasm. "Sneaking out in the middle of the night is a quintessential teen experience!"

Sadie pulls the duvet up over her head. "It's not even sneaking out," she grumbles. "We're allowed to leave our rooms whenever we want. Because we're *not* teens."

"Yes, well, it's the essence of the thing. Besides, we have curfew. We're all supposed to be in our rooms from midnight to six a.m. for safety."

"Well, if it's for safety, we should probably abide by the rules."

"Said like a rule-follower who's never defied her parents."

My taunting still isn't enough to rouse her, so I switch to physical coercion. I latch on to the duvet still covering her face and attempt to yank it off. The problem is, awake Sadie might be as stubborn as a bull, but *sleepy* Sadie is as stubborn as every fucking bull in all of Pamplona combined. I pull on the duvet, and she pulls right back twice as hard.

"I thought you wanted quintessential adolescent experiences!" I screech as I struggle to outmuscle her.

"Adolescents need sleep!" she screeches back with one more vicious yank of the duvet. I lose my footing, and she ends up pulling me along with the blanket. Our little game of tug-of-war ends suddenly when I fall on top of the duvet and her.

Sadie yelps. "What are you doing? Get off me!"

My brain scrambles for a way to play this off as intentional, but it's four in the morning, and my elbow just collided with what I hope was her stomach.

She quickly disabuses me of my hope. "Ouch! That was my boob, you boob!"

"This is the natural consequence of your actions," I tell her with all the casualness I can muster while my face is buried in blanket.

She flails beneath me, and I flail on top of her, and somehow that's the moment I register our bodies are only separated by the thin fabric of this duvet.

I wonder if she realizes it too, because she goes still beneath me. I roll off her and wedge myself between her body and the wall on this tiny twin bed. Neither of us moves for the length of three labored breaths, and then I pull the blanket down from over her face.

She looks pissed. Her hair is mussed, with her bangs sticking straight out like an awning over the rest of her face, and her eyes are furious but awake. She looks—

Off-limits.

"Was this strictly necessary?" she whispers. Our faces aren't even a foot apart on her pillow.

"Depends," I whisper back. "Did I change your mind?"

"Let me make sure I understand. You want me to get up at . . ." She checks the time on her phone. ". . . four in the morning, so I can walk *more*?"

"Yes."

"And sleep less?"

"That would be correct."

She unleashes a string of ingenious curses, and I sit up beside her, folding my hands beneath my chin. "Please?"

"I'm already getting up," she harrumphs, throwing the blanket off herself and onto me. As she rises from the bed, her sleep shorts bunch together, giving me a view of the dimpled flesh of her upper thighs.

Sadie adjusts her shorts, then turns to glare at me. I do a thoroughly good job pretending I wasn't staring at her arse. "Let's go," I say very calmly, very indifferently, very not aroused. "I'll race you to the stairs."

"Stairs? You didn't say anything about stairs."

I insist that we tiptoe past the door to Inez's room like the rebellious teens we're pretending to be, and Sadie reluctantly humors me. The lobby of our private albergue is dark except for the faint glow of the front desk and the blue computer light reflecting off the glasses of the clerk. We creep past them too, and stealthily slip into the predawn.

Viana do Castelo is eerily vacant at this hour. It's not a big enough city to have a nightlife, and no one in Portugal wakes up before six. As we wander toward Santa Luzia hill, it's as if we're the only two people in the world. I usually hate this kind of silence, this quietly meditative time of day, but with Sadie clinging to my side, it's slightly more tolerable.

Of course, she's only clinging to me because the headlamp I'm wearing is our primary source of light.

"About these stairs . . . ?" she starts.

"How did you think we were going to get up the hill?"

"Not via fucking stairs," she grumbles, tripping over cobblestones in the dark and swearing again.

"During the day, you can take a funicular to the top," I tell her, pointing ahead to the tracks that run up the side of the hill rising above Viana do Castelo.

"Great. Let's do that."

"It doesn't open until ten a.m."

"Sounds like we should turn around, then."

I tighten my grip on her arm, which she has threaded through mine. "After hours, you have to climb these stairs they've built into the hill. There's only, like, seven hundred or something."

"Seven hundred stairs?"

"You've already walked forty miles. What's seven hundred steps?"

She harrumphs again. Sleepy Sadie is irritable in a surprisingly refreshing way. She's usually so concerned with pleasing others, but she seems to have no interest in pleasing me this morning. Maybe the queer adolescence is working; selfishness *is* the most critical cornerstone of youth.

"Tell me more about reupholstery," I say, trying to distract her from the physical strain that awaits us.

"Uh-uh." She huffs. "It's your turn to share things."

"What do you mean?"

"I've already told you a thousand embarrassing things about myself," she says as she reluctantly trudges up the first few steps. "I got drunk on red wine and told you I'm a clueless virgin who didn't realize she's queer even though she used to masturbate to Eliza Dushku in *Bring It On*."

"Um, you did not tell me that last part, actually."

"I didn't? Well, the point stands. I want to hear some of your humiliating secrets."

"Okay . . ." The stone stairs narrow after the first switchback, and our arms detach so we can walk single file up the steps. It's cold without her pressed against my side, and I zip my fleece. "I've also masturbated while thinking about Eliza Dushku."

"I'm serious, Mal!" she squawks from behind me.

"So am I! Those leather pants she wore in *Buffy*? That's formative queer awakening stuff right there."

"Come *on*," she whines into the dark. "Tell me something *true* about yourself."

Something true. There are a million true things I could share with Sadie as we climb these stairs. I could tell her about my own inheritance; I could tell her about my own shit-head dad; I could tell her about Ruth, or about all the other women I used as distractions; I could tell her that I want her to be my favorite distraction of all but that I'm trying to change.

Her footsteps stop, and I turn to see her resting a few steps below. She throws up her hand to shield herself from my head-lamp, and I swivel it to the side. "This is me," I say with a half-hearted flourish, unable to give her anything else. "I don't have secrets. You get what you get."

She huffs again and forces herself to keep climbing. "I don't believe you."

"Why not?"

"Because sometimes you look at the ocean like you're angry at it."

I trip over a step and stop again. "What?"

She collides with my back, and we pause only one step apart. "Sometimes, it seems like you love this place, and other times, you get this look on your face like you want to fight every damn tree. Your jaw tightens right here." Her index finger brushes the hinge of my jaw where I didn't even realize I was clenching my teeth. Her skin is cool, and when she touches me in the dark, I become aware of every treasonous atom in my body.

"And sometimes," Sadie whispers, "you look so profoundly sad."

I angle my face so her hand falls away. "I'm not." Then I angle my whole body away from her and continue up the stairs.

"Hmmm . . ." she says to my back.

"What's that noise? What does *hmmm* mean?"

"It means that everyone has a little bit of sad in them all the time, and it's interesting that you're denying yours."

I swallow around a golf ball that seems lodged in my throat. "I'm not that complex, Freckles."

"I think you are," she says, before she starts coughing from trying to talk and climb these hell stairs simultaneously. I pass her my Hydro Flask. "But you seem hell-bent on making me think you're just a pretty face."

I swivel fully around. "You think my face is pretty?"

Even in the dark I can see the shadowed hint of her blush. Sadie takes a long drink of water, and several deep breaths before regaining control of her respiratory system. "Tell me *one* true thing about yourself."

"Fine. I think your face is pretty too."

She shoves my water bottle aggressively back into my hands. The stainless-steel rim tastes like her spearmint ChapStick. "You know, these stairs are the fucking worst," she barks.

"Don't hate me, but I don't even think we're halfway there."

"I might hate you," she says, and we drag ourselves up another two dozen steps in silence. "How about this?" She punctuates each word with a gasp for air. "I get to ask you one personal question."

A spike of fear shoots through me, but I try to sound flippant when I say, "Deal."

Sadie considers her one question as we climb. I expect her to ask why I'm angry at the ocean or why this place makes me so fucking sad, and I don't know how I'll answer her with the honesty she deserves.

"What do you do for a living?" she finally asks, and the banality of the question catches me entirely off guard.

"What do I do for a living?" It's such a commonplace question, and it should be easy to answer. But for me, it never is. "Uh, well . . . I don't actually do . . . *anything*. At least at the moment."

She quiets for a few more steps before she asks. "You mean, you're unemployed?"

A logical assumption and far preferable to the truth. "Not unemployed so much as . . . not employed."

Between puffs of breath, I can practically hear Sadie thinking about this. "You don't work? Like, at all?"

"I've had a lot of jobs," I rush to tell her, thinking about what Ruth said. That I'm a directionless, purposeless lump.

"I worked for Smith College in the housing department while I got my master's there. I worked at a queer youth center in Amsterdam, and for Planned Parenthood in Dallas, and for an NGO in Bangladesh, and for a DV shelter in Wyoming, and—" I cut off, because I realize my résumé doesn't make me sound any less directionless or purposeless. "In Seattle, I volunteered for a few different organizations, but I couldn't seem to settle into any of them. I've done a lot of different things in different places, but nothing that could be considered a career, I guess."

Sadie's judgmental thoughts feel so loud on this hill. "What do you do for money, then?"

I focus on the dark in front of me so I don't have to think about the expression on Sadie's face as I say. "My grandfather started a business, like your Nan. Only, it ended up being quite successful."

Quite. What an absurd understatement.

"It was very successful," I amend. "And he left me a small fortune when he died. At twenty-five, I came into my trust, and I've been living off that for the past thirteen years."

Another excruciating pause. "Wait, so you actually are wealthy?"

"Uh, considerably."

"I guess Vera was right."

I wheel around and blind her with the headlamp again. "What did Vera say about me?"

Sadie throws a hand up over her eyes. "Nothing. Just that you clearly come from money, even though you dress like someone who finds their clothes in a dumpster."

She's insulting me, quite cruelly, but I don't think I've ever liked Sadie more than I do in this moment. Because every time someone learns I have money—learns I'm Maëlys Costa, of the Quinta Costa fortune—there's a shift in how they treat me. I can feel it in my bones like a change in barometric pressure.

But Sadie, bless her, after being awoken at an ungodly hour and forced to climb Satan's staircase, is still cranky as hell with me, millionaire or not. The horizon is turning pale purple behind the hills to our east, and I can make out those eponymous freckles in the predawn light. "Come on. I want to make it to the top before sunrise."

"I will go at whatever speed I want, thank you very much."

I adopt an exaggerated Italian accent. "Climb on my back. I will carry you up the hill. I carry sandbags up Mont Blanc for fun."

"Shove it, Stefano." She pushes past me so she can lead for a while, setting her own slow, steady pace. "Do you enjoy not working?" she eventually asks.

"No," I answer. It's the most honest thing I've said to her all morning. Hell, it's the most honest I've been with myself since my dad died.

"Why not?"

"I just . . ." *Hate feeling unsettled. I hate feeling untethered. I hate that I'm floating and that I don't know how to stop.* I try to breathe around the swollen lump in my throat. "It's just not how I thought my life would be."

For the first eighteen years of my life, I was told I only had one possible future, one path: to inherit the family business, to take over the wineries, to be a Costa. Then, when I came out to my dad, that future—the one I'd always quietly resented—was ripped away from me. And even though I never wanted it, I didn't know what to do without it.

But I don't tell her any of this, and Sadie doesn't push it. She doesn't demand more information than what I'm willing to give. I almost wish she would.

I don't want to talk about my dad, *and* I need to talk about my dad, and I have this strange feeling that Sadie, of all people, might understand.

Except I don't know how to give away pieces of myself without prompting, the way she does. I don't know how to relinquish anything real about myself without the other person forcing it out of me.

I've fallen in love dozens of times, on a half dozen continents, but I've never learned how to be honest in the way that matters, not without fear that people will reject me, the way my dad did.

But Sadie, who's never been in love as far as I know, can be vulnerable in a way I've never experienced. Maybe because of what happened on the plane. Or maybe because she's more honest about herself than she realizes.

Clearly, I'm the one who is truly in a state of arrested development.

"I guess I don't really know what I'm doing with my life," I finally tell the lavender sky, and it's as vague as everything else I've offered her about myself. "And I'm almost forty. You think you're behind . . ." I chuckle at myself, because it's better than crying on this dumb hill.

"Don't be ridiculous," she grunts miserably. "You're not behind, Mal. You're—*oh*."

We've reached the top of the steps, and the view spills out in front of us like a treasure map being unfurled across a table. The pastel light makes the endless green look hazy, turns the sea a mysterious gray-green, and highlights the sky in pale oranges and pinks, like the colors of the lesbian flag. "Oh God, it's *beautiful*,"

Sadie exhales, dropping herself onto a bench so she can stare out at the world.

And this right here. *This* is my favorite part of traveling. I love getting to experience something new with another person, to witness the amazement on their face as the world becomes a little bit larger for them.

Maybe that's why I'm so good at falling in love and so terrible at staying in it; why I've worked two dozen jobs but never stuck with anything. I live for the awe, but the awe never lasts. Eventually, the newness stops feeling quite so exquisite, and I have to move on to the next new thing.

But Sadie—seeing the world through Sadie's eyes—almost feels like it could be exquisite forever.

I sit down on the bench beside her, passing her the water bottle. We both drink and stare into the distance as the sun comes up on this impossibly pretty day.

"I don't think you're behind," Sadie says with her gaze still fixed toward the horizon. "I think you're exactly where you're meant to be."

With that, she turns to face me, and her eyes are lit up like the pastel sky. "Because if you weren't, I never would've had the chance to experience this."

We sit shoulder to shoulder in silence for over an hour, breathing and watching, and even the silence is exquisite with her.

"I might have the tiniest bit of a crush."

Inez smacks me in the arm with her water bottle.

"Okay, first of all, that hurt more than I think you realize," I say, massaging the burgeoning bruise. "And second, hitting me was completely unnecessary. I'm already hitting myself. Figuratively speaking."

"Good," Inez hisses.

We're standing outside the albergue, sharing a clandestine 8 a.m. cigarette while everyone else finishes breakfast. Smoking is the one bad habit in my life I've been able to break, but every now and then, usually in times of stress when I'm traveling in Europe, I get tempted to see what I've been missing since I quit.

The answer is: not a lot. In my mind, cigarettes were the magical cure-all of my youth. A stress-reliever, an anxiety-preventer, a distraction from unwanted thoughts, something to do with my unsettled hands. But the truth is, I don't think the cigarettes had anything to do with it. I was just better at repressing things when I was younger.

Still, when I caught Inez sneaking one outside, I joined her anyway.

"Don't you worry," I reassure her now, after I take a long, disgusting drag. "There's plenty of self-flagellation happening in here." I tap a finger to my left temple. "Dormant Catholic guilt has been reactivated."

Inez narrows her eyes at me. "I don't feel sorry for you."

"You shouldn't. But . . ." I tap out the ash from the end of my cigarette against the railing of the stoop, and then sort of hold it aloft, not smoking it but giving off the impression that I could simply be between puffs. "Is it really such a bad thing? That I have an innocent crush?"

"Sim," she says, switching our conversation into Portuguese. "Because with you, there is no such thing as an innocent crush."

THIRTEEN

VILA PRAIA DE ÂNCORA

Mal

The silence without Sadie is a different story.

She spends the trek from Viana do Castelo to Vila Praia de Âncora dawdling behind the rest of the group with Vera, taking pictures and stopping to chat with every old man who wishes them a *bom caminho*.

Vila Praia de Âncora is one of my favorite towns on the northern coast. It's a quaint beach community with incredible surfing that's still relatively unknown by non-Portuguese tourists. On the white sand beaches, you're only likely to meet locals, pilgrims, and the occasional Portuguese traveler on holiday. We would vacation here sometimes, my dad and me.

When I was eleven, he purchased a vineyard north of here on the other side of the Spanish border, and we'd spend at least a few weeks at that vineyard outside Vigo each summer, training staff and testing grapes to see how they were progressing for the upcoming *vindima,* when people from all over would come to stay at my father's vineyards and help with the harvest. He made the season into a spectacle, of course.

If the flavor of the grapes in Vigo pleased my father, sometimes we'd add a few extra days to our trip and come down to Âncora. And if the grapes were sweet and not bitter, my father sometimes even let us take his sailboat to make the journey. Just the two of us, my father barefoot as he taught me how to adjust the sails out on the ocean. He'd let me take over when we reached the Minho River between Portugal and Spain, and if the grapes had been *really* good, he'd compliment me on my skills, call me a natural. Then we'd spend a long weekend swimming in the Atlantic, reading books on the sand, and eating oysters and ice cream until my stomach hurt.

So, I love Vila Praia de Âncora, but I also hate it, like I hate all the places that hold my happiest memories with my father.

I spend most of the eighteen-kilometer walk trying not to think about those memories. I share AirPods with Ari and listen to a podcast about the history of ketchup. I reminisce with Inez about our previous Caminos together, and I go for a jog with Stefano during morning tea, and I let Ro tell me more about their corgis than I ever wanted to know.

But no matter what I do, the silence of the walk is anything but exquisite.

It's a comparatively short day, so we arrive in town a little before two and get lunch in the central square across from the city's main church. Flowers of deep magenta are in bloom and ornament every available surface in the square. I eat pizza, and I don't think about the way my father would sneak a single flower from these displays to tuck into my hair.

But I do think about it, and the golf ball in my throat swells to tennis ball–size.

And that's when I decide I can't handle any more silence. I need loud. I need busy and crowded. I need distractions.

I need a Sadie-size distraction.

"I think you're ready," I tell her after we've checked into our hostel on a narrow street that connects the central square to the beach. As soon as we arrived, Sadie fell into her post-Camino routine, checking for new blisters and tending to old ones before getting in the shower for twenty minutes to scrub the Camino off her smooth skin.

Now she's cross-legged on the floor, going through her yoga stretches, but I can't force myself to sit down. Stillness is just as bad as silence.

"Ready for what?" she asks, doing a sideways stretch for her lower back.

"Ready for flirting."

Sadie snaps back into her forward-facing cross-legged seat and stares up at me. "I don't think I am, actually."

"Is that what you're wearing to dinner?"

Sadie glances down at her outfit: a pair of yoga pants that stick to her curves like glue, a white crop top, and her black zip-up. "What's wrong with my outfit?"

"It doesn't exactly scream *flirting with a random hottie at a bar*."

"Why would I want my outfit to say that, exactly?"

"Because that's what we're doing tonight. After dinner. I already got Ari and Stefano on board."

She stretches her legs out in front of her and stares at her knees. "Tonight?"

I nod. "I know you're harboring a crush on Inez, but since she's off-limits, I think our best bet is to go to a bar and have you get your flirt on." I do a shoulder shimmy to emphasize this point.

"Flirt . . . ?" she repeats. "With a woman?"

"No, Sadie, with a man. Preferably one with a full beard and lots of muscles. A real Jason Momoa type."

Her gaze snaps back up to my face, and she looks truly petrified. I would feel guilty for teasing her if I slowed down enough to feel anything at all.

"Yes, Freckles, with a woman. Isn't that what you want?"

Her splotchy blush begins to bloom across her throat, her cheeks, the whites of her arms, like a hundred flowers opening in the sun. Almost like the sunrise this morning, painting everything in pink.

"Yes," Sadie croaks. "Yes, that's what I want."

* * *

Dinner is at a sidewalk restaurant with a view of the water, and I guide Sadie to the far end of our communal table so we can have a little privacy. "When you were dating men," I start while she surveys the menu, "did you ever make the first move?"

Sadie shoots an anxious glance down to the table, and I follow her eyes to where Inez is ordering a few pitchers of sangria for the table. When her gaze returns to me, she keeps her voice low. "Do I look like I've ever made a single move in my life?"

Sadie looks like she doesn't even know what a move *is*.

"Men always made the first move, then?" I ask, matching her almost-whisper. It's unnecessary: Ari is telling a loud story about the time she met K.D. Lang and Stefano is doing burpees, much to the ire of the restaurant waitstaff, and much to the delight of a table of fit young men across the patio.

"On dates, you mean? I guess, yes. I've always waited for men to initiate the kiss. Mostly because I never wanted to kiss them," she grumbles. "But beyond that, moves have never really happened . . . like, a man has never tried to initiate *sex* with me."

She only mouths the word *sex*, and I wish I didn't find it so damn charming. "I find it very hard to believe that a man has never tried to have sex with you."

"Why?"

"Because you're very beautiful, Sadie."

She winces at the compliment. I brace both hands on the table. "Do you believe you're beautiful?"

"I know I'm beautiful." She shakes out her shortened hair, and I'm so utterly and hopelessly *charmed*. "I just . . . I have a complicated relationship with that word . . ."

"With the word *beautiful*?"

She winces again as the server puts a giant pitcher of sangria between us. Apparently, Inez ordered a liter for every two people.

Sadie fumbles with the heavy pitcher and sloshes sangria into her glass.

"The thing is, whenever someone tells me I'm beautiful," she says as she gives herself a generous pour, "there's always this hint of surprise in their voice. Like they can't believe I'm beautiful. Like I'm beautiful *in spite of.*"

"I truly have no idea what you're talking about."

Sadie is unequivocally, inarguably pretty, like the requisite freckled redhead in a J.Crew ad. She's even prettier right now than she was the first time I studied her face on the plane, with her spunky short hair and her sunburned face and her freckles sneaking through her makeup. "In spite of *what?*"

She takes a gulp of sangria and almost chokes on a chunk of peach. She makes a little sweeping gesture over her torso. "In spite of how fat I am."

"You're not fat!" I say, perhaps a little too loudly. Ari's story cuts off midsentence, and everyone turns to stare at our end of the table.

Sadie groans. "Damnit, Mal. That's literally the *worst* possible response." She becomes a human face-palm emoji. "I thought you were better than that."

"How . . . how was that the wrong response?"

She slams back another drink of sangria like it's a tequila shot. "Fat is not a bad word," she says firmly. "It's not an insult. It's not positive or negative. It's just a fact about my body."

"But you're not even *that*—" I try, but she cuts me off with a fiery glare.

"I'm midsize, if that's what you mean."

"I'm really sorry," I say, and Sadie picks up a dinner roll from the basket in front of her and chucks it at my head. Everyone at the table laughs.

"You're still not getting it!" Sadie snarls post–bread projectile. "Don't be *sorry*! There's nothing wrong with being fat. There's only something wrong with how other people view my fatness—what they assume it means about me." She picks up another hunk of bread from her basket and takes an unapologetic bite.

Someone at the table grunts, "You tell 'em, kiddo." I think it's Ro.

Sadie sits up straight in her chair, looking poised and regal. "When people tell me I'm beautiful, it's always in this infantilizing way. Like, *no, Sadie, you're so beautiful.* Like they deserve a fucking medal for seeing my beauty through the ugliness of my body."

"Your body isn't ugly." It's probably the wrong thing to say again, but I can't help it. Sadie's body is as beautiful as the scenery on the Camino, like the rolling hills and staggering rocks, like the undulating waves and the softness of the earth. Her body is glorious, and it didn't occur to me that anyone might not see it that way.

But I'm also genetically predisposed to be thin with minimal effort. I have the metabolism of a teenage boy, and I get muscle definition from a single day of manual labor. So, I guess I don't have the faintest idea what it's like to live in Sadie's body.

I pick up the bread she threw at my face and take a bite. "Thank you," I say instead. "For taking the time to correct me."

She glowers at me, like she's suspicious of whatever is going to come out of my mouth next. And maybe she should be, because I just can't fucking help myself sometimes. "But Sadie." I lower my voice and hope the rest of the group can't overhear. "Is that how *I* said it? Was I being infantilizing?"

Her glass is poised below her bottom lip as she pauses. Her eyes look almost turquoise tonight, like the ocean a few meters away. She presses the glass to her lip, then pulls it away again, leaving behind a half-moon imprint of her ChapStick. Her teeth catch her upper lip.

"No," she finally says. Her voice is quiet too. "No, that's not how you said it."

She sets down her sangria and reaches for the menu in front of her with her usual fluster. I reach for my menu too, and notice the entire thing is in Portuguese. "What are you hungry for?" I ask.

She turns the menu over to the backside, which is blank, then sighs. "I have no idea."

"This place has great seafood," I suggest, even if those five words are enough to conjure memories of my dad buying oysters, prawns, crab, and clams by the crate-load and bringing them back to Porto to boil in a giant pot on a night his chef was off—one of those rare nights he wasn't hosting or working or showing some new woman around the vineyard. It would be just the two of us, with napkins tucked into our shirts like bibs, cracking open the shells on the kitchen counter and eating lobster over the sink.

I clear my throat. "I've heard the octopus is especially good."

Sadie grimaces with impressive cultural sensitivity. "Octopus?"

"It's a famous dish in Portugal. You should try it before we cross the border into Spain tomorrow."

She chews on her bottom lip and stares at the menu like a better option will materialize. When the server eventually reaches our end of the table, though, Sadie squares her shoulders, sits up straight, and looks them dead in the eye. "Polvo à lagareiro, por favor."

She looks exceptionally proud of herself as she hands the menu back to the server. "You can't order coffee with milk, but you know which item on the menu is octopus?"

She points to a chalkboard menu behind me with the specials listed in both Portuguese and English. "Ah."

I weigh the ratio of deliciousness to childhood trauma as I debate my order, then get the bacalhau à Brás anyway. And since I'm indulging in my father's favorite dish, I decide I might as well pour myself some sangria too. The red wine, fruit, and brandy swirl on my palate. It tastes like endless summer afternoons.

"So, before I so rudely got us off track with my internalized fatphobia," I say now that the rest of the group has moved on from our drama, "we were talking about making moves. You said that dudes never made the first move with you, and you never made the first move with them? So, how did you ever date?"

"Poorly and infrequently," she answers. "And mostly using the apps."

"You've never met someone in a bar and struck up a conversation with them?"

She chokes on her wine. "Has *anyone* ever done that?"

"I have," I say with a shrug. "I *do*. I've never used a dating app before."

She spills some sangria onto the white linen tablecloth. "Wow. I didn't even know that was possible."

"I'm great at starting new relationships, but I'm terrible at sustaining them."

Sadie watches me take another slow, thoughtful sip of the sangria, holding the flavor on my tongue. "What do you mean?"

"I'm excellent at the falling-in-love bit. The part where everything is new and exciting. Where you can just stare into the other person's eyes for hours and stay up all night talking about everything and nothing."

That's always been my favorite part. I like Mondays. I like New Year's and the first day of spring and the beginning of the school year. I like the first few chapters of every book I've never finished reading and the pilots of TV shows I will never actually watch. I hate endings and goodbyes, but not as much as I hate the dreadful middle part where everything slows down. I hate February and Thursdays and doing the same thing day after day, because that's where the silence lives.

"First kisses are easy," I explain to Sadie. "It's the one hundredth kiss, or the one thousandth kiss that's hard for me."

"First kisses are *not* easy," she mutters.

"But they are! Firsts are always the best part. The first glance, the first touch, the first time . . ." Sadie glances down at the sangria stain on the tablecloth to hide her blush. "I love the beginning, when you're drunk on the mere existence of this new person you get to discover. It's like traveling to a new country. There's infinite possibility in front of you."

She considers this as she pours herself more sangria. "I bet your thousandth kiss is fantastic," she says, and it's my turn to spill some of my sangria, to watch the red wine bloom on the white linen.

"I only meant . . ." Sadie blushes and blusters, but I don't get to know what she meant by that because Stefano starts shouting my name from the other side of the table.

Well, he's shouting "Mel," but still.

"These kind gentlemen have told me about a gay-friendly bar down the road," he says, leaning back in his chair to talk around Ro and Rebecca. He sweeps his hand over to the table of hot men who are still hanging on his every move. "We should check it out, yes?"

"Hell yes we should," Ari says, staring right back at the boys.

It's then that I start to suspect that this sangria might be unusually strong. Because I realize Stefano is *sitting*. In a *chair*. Everyone at the table seems a little loose, a little giddy.

I turn to Sadie. "Maybe take it easy on the—" I start, before realizing our shared pitcher is already down to the dregs of ice and fruit. The server returns to the table and deposits my salted cod in front of me before handing Sadie her octopus. And *shit*.

"This is a whole-ass octopus!" Sadie shouts before the server is even out of ear shot.

"It does indeed seem to be."

She pokes at the small creature on her plate with her fork, and all eight tentacles jiggle. "You didn't tell me it was going to still be in the shape of an octopus!"

"I didn't know! Usually, they serve you a few tentacles at most."

"It has a face! At least, I think that's the face." She pokes it again. "What does an octopus face even look like?"

"It looks like that."

She wipes literal sweat off her brow with her napkin. "I can't eat this!"

"Maybe just close your eyes?"

"There are suckers!" She presses the tines of her fork to the row of suckers along one large tentacle. "Am I supposed to chew on these things?"

Inez pipes in. "This is why you should consider going vegan."

"I'm going vegan after seeing that thing," Ro adds darkly.

The server returns with more sangria, and I dump half the contents into my own glass before Sadie can pour herself anymore.

"I was trying to be brave, and this is what happens? A whole damn octopus." She stares deeply into the creature's dead eyes.

At least, I think those are the eyes. It really is hard to tell.

"Why do I get the feeling this octopus is going to be a metaphor for the entire night?"

FOURTEEN

VILA PRAIA DE ÂNCORA

Sadie

The octopus is definitely a metaphor.

I'm not exactly sure what the metaphor is, exactly, but I know that what seemed like a good idea now feels like chewing on tentacle suckers. I can't *flirt* with a *stranger* at a bar. I can't flirt with a *woman*. I can't flirt with *another woman* in front of the woman I actually want to be flirting with.

My crush on Mal is becoming a sentient being with its own free will, and it's no longer obeying my attempts to silence it.

When she fell on top of me in bed this morning, my butterflies came rushing back in. And when she sat next to me on a bench watching me watch the sunrise for an hour, my body almost reached for her body. And it can't do that. *I* can't do that.

I might have a vaguely bisexual haircut, but that doesn't mean I'm ready for any of this.

"I can't do this," I blurt out while Mal is in the middle of exchanging oyster recipes with Vera. Mal sets down her sangria glass and turns to me like a parent addressing a child that's interrupted them in the middle of an adult conversation.

"You don't have to eat the octopus, Freckles," she says.

I shake my head. "No, no, it's not that. I-I can't learn to flirt!"

Apparently, I've said this loud enough that Ari a few seats down responds. "You don't know how to flirt?"

My cheeks feel hot from sangria and shame, and I press

my cool hands to them as everyone looks at me again. At least the group has thinned a bit. After finishing two pitchers of sangria, Ro offered to walk Rebecca back to their room, though they were both so drunk, it was unclear who was helping whom. And Stefano has been flittering between our table and a group of twentysomething British dudes who are biking the Camino, so it's only Inez, Ari, and Vera who are staring at me now.

And Mal. Always Mal. They all seem to expect me to say something, but I can't remember what the question was. "Mal is going to teach me how to flirt," I say, hoping that about covers it.

"Oh, is she now?" Inez asks. There are several empty seats between Inez and Mal, but the way she glares at her cuts through the dead space.

"Are you looking to flirt with handsome man?" Stefano asks as he bounces back to our table. "I am most excellent wingman. Arjun!" he calls over his shoulder, and a boyishly attractive man appears beside him. Stefano slings an arm around him. "Susie, this is Arjun. Arjun is a heterosexual. Arjun, this is Susie. She is also a heterosexual."

"Her name is Sadie," Vera slurs.

"Not Susie," Stefano says to Arjun, "but still heterosexual."

"Hey," Arjun says with a grin that reminds me of the dead octopus still sitting on my plate.

And it must be 90-proof brandy in that sangria, because I start shouting at Stefano. "Not heterosexual! Not Susie, and *not heterosexual*!"

Ari gasps. "Plot twist!"

"I am completely blindsided by this news," Mal says, loudly and unconvincingly.

"No she isn't," I say, because I've clearly forgotten how to filter myself. "Mal knows, and she's going to teach me how to flirt with women tonight."

"Come, Arjun. I have miscalculated." Stefano leads the confused man away from our table and leaves me with the wreckage of my drunken outburst.

Ari stares at me with her cool septum piercing and her cool hair and her cool smoky eye. "So are you bi, then?"

"I-I don't really . . . know."

Ari shrugs. "Oh, cool." And then she takes another drink of sangria, as if it really is cool that I am clueless about this entire part of myself.

"I-I feel like I've lost so much time," I hear myself drunkenly confess.

Stefano pops back over to us. "Lost it? Where did you put it?"

It's unclear if Stefano is being profound or if there's a language barrier at work.

"You cannot lose time, Shari, because none of us possess it."

Profound, then. Sort of.

"We just fucking told you her name is Sadie, dude!" Ari screams.

"Scusi! Scusi! I have name blindness!"

"You seemed to remember Arjun's name just fine."

There's more yelling, more arguing, as Mal discreetly hands over a credit card, and the British boys grow impatient, urging us away from our table and toward the bar. Arjun has seamlessly shifted his attention to Ari, and she basks in it like the goddess she is.

That's when I finally realize how nice everyone looks tonight. Ari is wearing her usual hiking outfit, but she's painted her lips deep red. Inez always looks fantastic, but her high-waisted linen pants and barely-even-a-shirt crop top flatter her lean, muscular body. Vera looks stunning in a tennis skirt and moisture-wicking polo, but Vera would look stunning in a burlap sack.

Stefano is wearing his usual too-tiny shorts, but based on the reactions he's getting from Arjun's friends, the shorts are working for him.

And then there's Mal. She didn't do anything different for going out tonight. She's not wearing any makeup, and her mullet is its usual level of unstylishly tousled. Her clothes are neither nice nor clean, but for some reason, she's still the most beautiful person I've ever seen.

"You're all so beautiful," I unintentionally say aloud, my eyes still turned to Mal. Stupid sangria.

"Thank you, Sadie," Vera says earnestly.

Stefano nods in agreement. "This is what I am always saying. Not now, Oliver," he says to the British boy clamoring for his attention. "I am with my beautiful girls."

"Some of us are very, very beautiful," Ari purrs. Her eyes are fixed on Mal too.

Oliver is on his knees next to Stefano's chair. "You are the most beautiful," he gushes, and Stefano bops him on the nose.

"Wait, I'm confused," Mal says, studying the interaction between Stefano and Oliver. "Y'all, is Stefano . . . *hot*?"

"Objectively, yes," Vera immediately answers.

Ari nods. "A total daddy."

"I cannot comment on that," Inez says professionally, as she throws back half a glass of sangria in a single gulp, then hiccups again. "But also, yes. Yes, he is."

"I am very hot, indeed," Stefano clarifies for the group, and to demonstrate, he stands up and lifts his shirt to show off a comically defined set of washboard abs on his ageless body. He's like a gay, Italian Rob Lowe.

This is apparently the final straw for our server, who comes over scolding us in Portuguese, and we finally clamor out of our seats, talking over each other. No one seems to care that I don't know if I'm bisexual or asexual or gay. They're too busy arguing over their favorite Chappell Roan songs.

I feel both dizzy and firmly planted, both nervous and hopeful, both drunk and completely sober.

Maybe this night won't be an octopus, after all.

Mal grabs my hand to guide me through the labyrinth of patio tables and out to the sidewalk, and my drunk brain savors the feeling of her palm in mine. Mal doesn't have the hands of a trust-fund kid. She has the hands of someone who knows how to use a garden hoe. They're callused and strong. Capable. I imagine they'd feel good all over me.

Which isn't something I've ever imagined before.

"You don't have to do that, you know," I say.

"I don't have to hold your hand? I'm not sure that's true, Freckles. You almost took out that server. This way." She tugs me along as we follow the British boys to the bar.

"Pay," I say, thinking this makes perfect sense, syntactically.

"What?"

"You don't have to pay for everyone, just because you can."

Her hand twitches in mine, and I crane my head to see her jaw clench for a few seconds before she relaxes into an easy smile. "I know I don't have to. I like to do it. I don't have expensive taste, really. I travel, I support causes that are important to me, and I take care of my friends when I can. Besides," she says breezily, "it's fun to blow my dad's money on a bunch of bad-ass queers and think about how pissed that would make him."

I squint at her in the setting sun. That last part, I suspect, is the closest I've gotten to the real Mal, to the person behind the easygoing nomad façade. The words are casual and teasing, but when she mentions her dad, there's something beneath her flippant tone—bitterness and resentment, I think. But she makes me dig for the real feelings, scanning for clues in the subtle shifts in her eyebrows, her jaw, her stupidly pretty mouth.

I want to tell her that she doesn't have to fight so hard to keep these uglier feelings hidden away, because she'll be beautiful no matter what. But my sangria-soaked brain can't focus on saying actual words. It can't do anything but stare at her mouth.

Ahead of us, Ari has consented to a piggyback ride from Stefano, and he weaves around sidewalk signs and people, who glare at them both. Behind us, Vera and Inez are laughing wildly. But right here, it's just me and Mal, and her hand is still in mine. Another thought pierces through the alcohol: I'm holding hands with a woman.

A tingle shoots up my arm from the place our skin touches. I'm walking down a public street, holding hands with a woman I *want* to hold hands with. And shit, it feels *good.* I feel giddy and nervous; I feel the way I suspect my middle school friends did the first time they held hands with a boy.

The first time I held hands with a boy in seventh grade, I felt sick with anxiety the entire time, and I practically ran to my bus, dragging him along as fast as I could, because all I wanted was for the moment to end.

I feel a little sick holding Mal's hand right now, but it's sick in a *good way.* It's the nausea of reaching the top of a roller coaster before the drop, the thrill of standing on the edge of a rock on Lake Washington before plunging into the water below.

Mal leans over to whisper. "You don't have to flirt with anyone at the bar, okay?"

I tilt into her and our shoulders collide. She feels like a sturdy wall keeping me upright.

"I don't want to pressure you to do anything you're not ready for. Let's just have a fun night with friends," she continues. "That's an equally important part of adolescence."

I don't say anything in response, and it takes me a while to realize that maybe I should have.

"You okay, Freckles?" Mal asks even closer, the words tickling the shell of my ear.

"I think I might be really drunk, actually."

Mal laughs. "You're not the only one."

To prove her point, Stefano does some kind of jog-samba combination with Ari still on his back as he asks, "Are we dancing tonight, bellissimi amici?"

"You can dance if you want to, my friend," Ari answers. "But I certainly won't be."

"If I dance, you dance!" Stefano declares, and then he runs to catch up with Arjun as Ari screeches the whole way.

The twentysomething British pilgrims lead us to a bar on the water with an open patio shaded by an undulating white canopy. A live band plays Fado music, and the black tables on the patio are crammed with people of all ages, locals and pilgrims alike. There's a large, wood-paneled bar on the far side, and we all make a beeline toward it.

"Let's get you some water and carbs to start," Mal whispers against my ear again.

"And wine," I add.

Mal orders a plate of fries, a beer, and, somewhat reluctantly, a glass of wine for me. Vera and Inez grab their drinks and shout something about finding tables, but we stay at the bar even after the fries and mayo dipping sauce are put in front of us. I don't know I'm ravenous until I take my first bite of fried potato.

"So good," I grumble through a mouthful.

Mal smiles, and then her hand comes up to my face, her thumb brushing the corner of my mouth. "You had a bit of mayo," she says.

She's propped against the bar with her body angled toward mine, and I can't explain it, but the way she's leaning right now is the sexiest thing I've ever seen.

"Do you think you have a type?"

"A type of what?"

Her smile widens. "A type of woman that you're attracted to."

The type of woman who knows how to sexily lean against surfaces, apparently. I swallow a hunk of potato. "I-I don't think so."

"Okay, well, what do you like about Inez?"

"I don't like Inez," I say without thinking. Even after the words come out of my mouth, the mixture of sangria and loud music makes it difficult for me to figure out why they're the wrong words. "Oh! You mean my crush on Inez! Yes. Right."

"Right. What is it about Inez that makes her special?"

My brain is a useless maelstrom of alcohol and anxiety, and I can't think of a single damn thing about Inez at all. "I, um, I like her . . . hands." It's the first thing that comes to my mind, because I like Mal's hands. I especially like the way one of her hands grabs me by the waist to pull me away from a drunk Australian who almost knocks me over on his way to the bathroom.

"Her *hands*?" Mal laughs. "Okay, Freckles. What else?"

I close my eyes and try to picture Inez's face over the din of the bar and the din inside my head, but I can only see one face. "I like her mouth. It doesn't fit the rest of her face, but I like that. It's like a surprise in the middle of her face."

"Her mouth is a surprise . . . ?" I can hear the smile in Mal's voice, but I keep my eyes squeezed shut.

"I like her accent, and the purposeful way she moves her body. She's terse, like a poem. Everything she does is so deliberate, no movement ever wasted."

"Her body is like a poem?"

I nod. "She's selfless and kind, and I like how she makes me feel . . . *seen*." The honesty of this statement catches me off guard. "I've spent my whole life trying to be invisible and small," I say with my eyes closed as tight as possible, "but when she looks at me, I feel like I *exist*."

Mal doesn't repeat my words this time, and when she speaks, there isn't a smile in her voice. "Sadie, open your eyes."

I obey, my gaze trained on the glass of wine in my hand.

"Look up at me," Mal orders firmly, and it takes me a second to work up the courage, but I obey this command too. Now that the sun has gone down, her eyes are almost onyx, and her gaze is locked on my face. I squirm under the sudden seriousness.

"What?" I blurt. Mal doesn't say anything, but she's still staring at me, and I want to look away. I'm *desperate* to look anywhere but her face.

But I don't. I can't.

There's a sudden flurry of limbs as someone wedges themselves between us. It's Ari's limbs, Ari who is unintentionally pushing me away from Mal. "What are you two doing over here?" The question seems directed to both of us, but Ari is only talking to Mal. She presses herself fully against Mal's body as she cajoles, "Come join us!"

Ari starts to yank Mal away from me, but Mal reaches for my hand. Ari pulls Mal, and Mal pulls me, and we make it across the patio in a chain of joined hands. There are two tables pushed together and covered with more glasses than there are people. Arjun is there, and so is Oliver, sitting on Stefano's lap. Inez and Vera appear to be playing quarters, but when they see us, they both throw their arms into the air to welcome us.

Ari pulls Mal down into the chair next to hers, and I awkwardly hover next to the table until Inez snags an extra chair from the table behind her and swivels it around for me. "Here, Sadie. Sit. Sit."

The chair is as far from Mal as possible, which is for the best. But it feels like the worst.

"Where were the two of you?" Inez asks me, gesturing to Mal with the black straw from her cocktail.

"Uh, just . . . fries," I say.

Three seats away, Ari drapes herself over Mal, and the fries turn to acid in my stomach. I have to remind myself that I like Ari. I like her a lot. And I know she likes Mal. She made that clear in Matosinhos. She's probably Mal's type too. She's funny and free-spirited, somehow both direct and elusive in turns. She's funky and hip. She's confident and experienced and so damn sure of herself.

I like Ari, but that doesn't mean I want to watch her fall face-first into Mal's lap.

I jump out of my chair. "Stefano! Come dance with me!"

He jumps out of his chair too, even with Oliver in his lap. "I thought you'd never ask!" He squeals as he takes one of my hands in his, clutching my waist with the other. We spin in a wide circle and somehow end up on the small dance floor, right in front of the stage where the live band is playing a cover I vaguely recognize.

Despite the carbs and water, I'm still wildly drunk as Stefano happily twirls me around, and the people and tables and twinkle lights all twirl along with us. I'm about to be sick just when Stefano brings the world to a standstill again. He holds me tight against his muscular chest and moves us slowly through some kind of tango, and my stomach steadies itself.

"Don't worry, my beautiful friend," Stefano coos in my ear. "She doesn't like her."

I arch back so I can see his face, hoping his expression will clarify this nonsensical statement. "Who does like *who*?" I slur in confusion.

"Your Mal. She doesn't like Ari. Not the way she likes you."

My sangria-soaked brain gloms onto only part of what he's said: *your Mal.*

I drop Stefano's arms and take a step backward at the same time Oliver appears, ready to whisk Stefano away. Inez and Vera are in front of me, doing silly dance moves, but I'm frozen in place.

Ari joins us, dragging Mal behind her, with Arjun trailing behind. She dances provocatively against Mal's body, and I shouldn't care.

I don't *want* to care about any of this.

I'm thirty-five, not fifteen, and this night is starting to resemble the drama of a middle school dance. I'm too old for crushes and jealousy and crying on the dance floor.

Of course, I never did any of that at a middle school dance. I never had a *real* crush—just the ones I pretended to have to fit in with my friends. I never liked a boy enough to be jealous, and I never cried over one, because I never actually cared.

Standing in the middle of this cramped dance floor, watching Mal's hands touch Ari the way I imagined them touching me, I find myself almost missing that. I miss the indifference of dating men. It was so much easier than whatever this is.

Mal looks up, her hands still on Ari's hips, her eyes suddenly on me. My eyes were already on her. I'm too drunk to look away in time, so she catches me staring. I force myself to pivot toward Vera, force myself to shimmy alongside her, to laugh when she laughs, until a hand is on my waist again, a raspy voice in my ear. "Hey," Mal says, her lips on the shell of my ear. Because it's loud. Because she has to be this close for me to hear. "We got interrupted earlier."

Her hand slides to my lower back, and I feel like a puppet as she turns me around to face her. I am suddenly reminded by my anxious brain that thirty minutes ago, I described her body as a fucking poem.

God, I miss men.

"Ari is very beautiful," Mal says as we sway to another cover song, and I am two seconds from lying down in the middle of this dance floor and letting everyone trample me. The Fado band starts playing a cover I do recognize. It's "Like a Prayer" by Madonna. A strange, hauntingly sad version of it.

"Is she your type?" Mal asks with her hand still on the small of my back. I don't know what to say. Mal is trying to pick up our conversation from the bar when we left it, but I can't seem to get back there. The words feel too clumsy to hold.

"Do you think Ari is beautiful?" Mal presses.

I put a hand on Mal's arm to steady myself. "Yes," I say, because Ari is *objectively* beautiful. She has a heart-shaped face, large chocolate eyes, and brown skin that shimmers thanks to impeccable makeup. I find her a few feet away, dancing with Arjun, but even as she gyrates her body seductively, I can't seem to move past *objective*.

Ari feels like a celebrity in a magazine: I can recognize her as attractive, but I can't seem to conjure the feeling of attraction. My appreciation for her is purely intellectual. It doesn't stir anything in me. It's not physical, not visceral, not . . . sexual. I've never felt that way about anyone. Not even Eliza Dushku, really, even when I touched myself to the thought of her in a cheerleading uniform. I still felt this . . . *distance*.

Maybe that's why it's taken me thirty-five years to question if I'm queer.

Maybe I am asexual, after all.

Except there is one glaring fault in that logic, and she's got her hand on my lower back. Whatever misguided feelings I have for Mal, they live inside my body in a way no feelings ever have with anyone else. She's in the flush of my cheeks, the twist of my stomach, the throbbing *ache* that makes my legs restless.

"If you *were* to go flirt with Ari right now," Mal is saying, and I try to quiet my riotous body. "What would you say?"

I bite my lip. "I-I don't know."

"I'm not going to make you do it," she reassures me as we gently move back and forth to the song. "I'm purely curious."

"I wouldn't know what to say."

"Hmmm," Mal murmurs, moving even closer to me. "Okay.

What if you were flirting with *me* right now? What would you say to me?"

I haven't the faintest fucking idea. I stare down at my feet like they might hold all the answers. "Nothing. I-I really don't have any clue how to flirt."

"I know we're up against a steep learning curve here, but you've got to start somewhere."

I lick my lips. Everything feels dry. "I-I can't."

"Sadie, look up at me."

I slowly, reluctantly, do.

"Eye contact is the first step in flirting," Mal says, and I feel like her stare is turning me inside out. We're too close together for this kind of eye contact. "If I meet a woman at a bar, and I'm into her, I make sure to look her in the eye while we're talking. And if she holds my eye contact, I figure there's a chance she might be into me too."

I look away. "But . . . but how do you know for sure if someone is into you?" I ask, because I need to immediately do the opposite, so Mal doesn't figure out about my misguided, juvenile crush.

"The mature thing to do is ask her directly if she's feeling it," Mal says with her usual casualness. "But it can be scary to put all your cards on the table like that, and I usually want to have a good idea of what she's going to say before I go for it. So, I test the hypothesis further, by flirting with her."

I start biting my lip again.

"For example," Mal continues. "I might stand close to her, to see how she reacts."

She's so unbelievably close right now, as close as she can be without our bodies actually touching anywhere but the place her hand is anchored on my back, the place my hand is tethered to her arm.

"And if she doesn't move away," Mal says in a quiet voice, "I might find an innocent excuse to touch her. Maybe I'll act like I need to hold her hand."

I think about Mal holding my hand as we walked down the street.

"Or maybe I'll say she has food on her face, so I can touch her cheek."

Mal's thumb in the corner of my mouth.

"I might find an excuse to whisper in her ear," Mal whispers now, her lips brushing my earlobe. "And depending on how she responds to those touches, I might put a hand on her waist, or the small of her back."

Her hand singes my skin through the fabric of my yoga pants.

"And if she likes my hand on her back," Mal says, so quietly I can barely hear her over the music and the blood rushing in my ears. "If she leans into me, or even better, if she touches me back"—My hand falls away from her arm—"then I might try to kiss her. I might stare at her mouth . . ."

Mal's eyes drop to my mouth.

"And I might lean in even closer . . ."

She's already so close, and my entire body is a jumbled mess. I miss the safety of men, because this feels dangerous. I'm petrified that she's about to kiss me.

I'm even more petrified that she won't.

I've only kissed men I didn't want to be kissing, and I'm desperate to know what it's like to kiss a woman. To kiss someone I actually *want* to kiss. To kiss Mal.

I think kissing Mal might answer questions I didn't even know I had, so I lean closer too.

And Mal steps away. Her hand isn't on my back. Her eyes aren't on my mouth. She's a solid two feet away from me. "And that's flirting. That's all there is to it," Mal says plainly, lifting her hands in with a casual shrug to indicate that this—the last ten minutes, this entire night—were nothing more than a demonstration, a lesson on how to flirt.

Every touch, every lingering glance, every second of her

closeness was all for the sake of my queer adolescence. Mal was never actually going to kiss me.

I feel so silly for thinking she might, for briefly wondering if my crush wasn't so absurd after all.

I feel fifteen and humiliated. I feel like crying on the dance floor.

I feel . . . surprisingly grateful, I realize. Because for the first time in my entire life, I *wanted* someone to kiss me. And it felt so fucking good to *want*.

I grab Mal's hand and, without explanation, I pull her away from the dance floor, past the black tables and the wood-paneled bar, dragging her down the boardwalk until our feet land in the sand. I keep going until the music becomes a faint sound over the waves, until the lights from the boardwalk bars fade, and it's just the two of us on the twilight beach.

"Sadie, what's going on?" Mal asks when I drop her hand and wheel around to face her. She's standing there with her mouth half-open, her eyebrows crinkled, and I'm so damn furious that she has the audacity to be so beautifully handsome.

"I have a hypothesis to test," I tell her.

This is a mistake. Something I will regret in the morning.

But I've never made a mistake like this before, and like Vi said, I'm long overdue.

I look up at her confused face in the moonlight. "I need you to kiss me."

FIFTEEN

VILA PRAIA DE ÂNCORA

Mal

"You need me to *what*?"

Sadie on sangria is something else. She's looking me directly in the eye, bold and unflinching. "I need you to kiss me," she says again. "For science."

An unhinged laugh escapes my mouth, but Sadie doesn't flinch.

"Please," she adds. "Please kiss me, so I can test my hypothesis."

"Wow. That might be the sexiest thing anyone has ever said to me."

She folds her arms across her chest. "I'm not trying to be sexy. I'm trying to be . . . semantic."

I almost laugh again, but then Sadie takes a step closer to me, and the sound dies in the back of my throat. Her eyes are burning in the dark like twin suns, and in the moonlight, I can still see the millions of stars spread across her cheeks.

"You're the one who wanted to be my fairy god-dyke. Now I need you to Bippity-Boppity-kiss me so I can know, once and for all, if I'm gay."

Those words settle over me like a sobering cloud. "Sadie," I sigh. "You don't have to kiss a woman to know if you're a lesbian."

"I know that," she snaps impatiently. "But I want to. I *need* to know what it feels like."

Her tone slips into the kind of sadness that makes me want to reach for her, but I suspect reaching for her is part of what's led to our current beach standoff, so I hold back. "I-I can't kiss you."

"Why not?" The sadness is gone, and annoyance rises in her tone. "You didn't have any problem flirting with me all night to prove a point."

I scrub my face with my hand. She's right. Sort of.

But I wasn't flirting with her all night to prove a point. I was flirting with her because I couldn't help myself. I held her hand because I wanted to, and I stood close to her all night because she smells like wildflowers and summertime, and I touched her because she feels so damn good. I flirted with her, and then half-heartedly tried to turn it into some sort of deranged flirting lesson when I realized I was about to fuck it all up and kiss her on that dance floor.

The problem with a-pitcher-of-sangria Sadie is that I'm *also* a-pitcher-of-sangria Mal.

I got drunker than I should have. I touched her more than I meant to, and I got caught up in the way she responded to my touch. I got carried away by her freckles and her newness, and I would have kissed her, if not for Michelle's voice in my head, reminding me that this is what I always do.

Sadie is a pretty girl and a perfect distraction.

Which is why I can't kiss her now, even if she's begging me to. I'm worried kissing Sadie Wells will make it that much harder to stop elegizing her freckles.

I take a deep, cleansing breath of salt air. "I'm sorry I flirted with you. I shouldn't have done that."

Sadie shifts her gaze toward the ocean, hiding a look of hurt.

I don't want to hurt her.

I really, *really*, want to kiss her.

"This night didn't quite go how I planned in my head," I confess, shoving my hands into the pockets of my fleece to stop them from reaching for her.

She snorts. "It's been a real fucking octopus of a night."

"We should've read the signs."

"The Octopus Omen," she says, her arms wrapping tighter around her chest. She moves her hands up and down the length of her folded arms, shivering slightly.

"Oh shit, you're cold." She took off her zip-up when we got to the bar, and now she's only wearing her white crop top. I shrug off my fleece and bridge the three steps between us. "Take this."

"I'm fine," she says between teeth chatters. I hold up my fleece, and she steps into it without further protest. I wrap it tightly around her without realizing this means we're standing too close again, as close as we were while dancing. Sadie's hair smells like a garden, her mouth smells like wine, and her skin smells like sunscreen and sweat, like every happy summertime memory.

She smells like all the summers I spent here, in Portugal, with my father. Summers spent running around vineyards in the sweltering afternoon sun. Summers spent holding the first sip of wine on my tongue before my father drilled me with questions about acidity and tannins. Lonely summers spent hiding in the gardens during my father's lavish parties, lying on my stomach in the grass, reading a book by flashlight and wishing that he would notice I was gone, waiting for him to come find me.

He never did, and eventually I learned to stop waiting.

Sadie smells like all of the real feelings I'm trying to ignore. And here I am, practically hugging her as she puts on my fleece.

"The last guy I kissed . . . his name was Grant," Sadie says quietly into the small space between us. "He was one of the guys

Vi set me up with. And he was honestly *perfect*. He was everything I'm supposed to want, and I didn't want him."

The sadness returns to her voice, and I can't fight the urge to hug her on purpose, to wrap my arms around her and hold her close.

"So many men, and I never wanted any of them. And I started to believe that I'd never find love, that I'd never find my person. That I'd never get married or have a family of my own. That I'd never get to have any of the things I wanted because I couldn't make myself be attracted to men. So I started telling myself I didn't want those things at all."

She goes quiet in my arms, her cheek pressed to my shoulder. "I've forgotten what it feels like to want something."

She raises her head. She's so close that she takes up my entire field of vision, blots out everything else. All I can see are those eyes, those freckles, those two front teeth piercing her upper lip.

"Right now," she says in a hushed but firm voice. "I really want to kiss you."

And I can't really argue with that.

Sadie

"Okay," Mal says, exhaling wine and fruit. "Kiss me, then."

And I'm not going to overthink this.

We're on a moonlit beach with the sea and the stars, and I'm wearing Mal's jacket, and it smells like candlewood and sugar and sweat, a mixture of her and this place we're in together. She's right here, with her arms encircling me, and I want to know how it feels to kiss a woman—*this* woman—just this once.

I'm going to kiss her.

I have no idea *how* to kiss her, and now I'm definitely overthinking it.

"Um, I-I don't have much experience in . . . in this," I mutter, and the intimacy of the moment goes out with the tide.

Mal chuckles lightly as her hand finds my waist beneath her coat. "Kissing is like flirting," she tells me quietly, "you've got to start by actually looking at me."

I level my gaze with hers. My stomach leaps into my chest again.

"Then you can touch me . . ." she coaches.

Anxiety surges through the sangria fog. "Touch you *where*?"

Her mouth is back on my ear. "Anywhere you want."

A shiver of anticipation ricochets through me. I lift my right hand and clumsily put it on her bare forearm, where it was when we were dancing. There's absolutely nothing sexy about the way I clutch her tibia, but she doesn't falter. "Then you lean in . . ."

I lean and Mal leans, and . . . I nearly headbutt her, for Christ's sake. I'm in my head instead of my body, fumbling every move.

Her grip tightens on my waist. "And then you just kiss me, Sadie," she says. And I try to. I arch my head to the side and press my mouth to hers. Only, I barely catch her mouth, and my lips end up mostly on her chin. It's as terrible as all those kisses with men over the years.

Humiliated, I try to pull away, but Mal's hand firmly holds me against her. She slowly shifts us both and gently presses her mouth to mine. And . . . and it's not terrible at all.

I'm stiff in her arms, not sure if I should move or how, but she somehow decodes my anxiety, and her other hand comes up to gently cup the place where my neck meets my shoulders, her thumb resting on my cheek. The tension spools out of me.

Her mouth is soft and firm at the same time, like her hands. She parts her lips just enough to coax my bottom lip with hers, and it's *nothing* like all those kisses with men.

Time slows down on this dark beach, like I'm watching game footage of this kiss in slow motion. I can feel Mal trying to teach me with every touch, every subtle shift. I follow her lead and allow my mouth to soften against hers.

I'm kissing Mal. I'm kissing a woman.

What the fuck am I supposed to do with my hands?

They're hanging limply at my sides like a pair of dead fish. Reading my mind somehow, Mal takes one of my hands in hers. If it's supposed to make me relax, it has the opposite effect. Mal's skin is so warm, it ignites my entire body. Something hot and restless glides down my spine, pooling heat in my lower stomach.

Mal guides me like a marionette, taking that hand and putting it on her right hip. My other hand gravitates to her left hip. I'm gripping her in place.

My hands clutch the soft flesh and sharp bone beneath her hiking pants and some heady instinct takes over.

I pull our bodies flush. My mouth opens wider against hers, and I can feel the heat of her breath, taste the sangria we shared, feel the tip of her tongue as it enters my mouth and licks, before retreating in a way that makes me want to chase her.

I do chase her tongue with mine, and I'm rewarded with a hot, hot, burning heat that courses through my body.

It's the opposite of kissing men in every possible way. I want more, not less, and I feel wild with that need. The heat of mouths and tongues and hands and all the places our bodies meet. I moan into her, like she's a pasteis de nata, but sweeter. *So much sweeter.*

She meets my moan with her own breathless growl and arches her body against mine.

I try to remind myself that Mal is kissing me for educational purposes; that she's only kissing me because I literally begged her to. This moment might mean the world to me, but it means nothing to her. I *need* to remind myself of that fact.

Only Mal is kissing me back like it could mean *something*. Time has sped up again, and my brain can't keep up with my body, with all the things it wants to do and is doing. I'm kissing Mal frantically, clutching her hips like I might drown if she doesn't keep me afloat.

When Mal finally breaks away, her breath comes out in sharp exhales. She clears her throat and tries to detangle our bodies. "Did that confirm your hypothesis?" she asks with scientific detachment, as if she hadn't stuck her hand halfway up my shirt.

I shake my head with zero detachment. "I think I need multiple data points." And I pull her back to me, sloppily capturing her mouth with mine. Drunk and dizzy, I kiss her, and she kisses me back, and I maybe grind myself against her hip bone. I'm not overthinking this.

My hands are about ten steps ahead of my heart, which is desperately trying to remind me that this is only an experiment, but it's hard to focus on that when Mal is touching me everywhere I wanted her to.

When she pulls away again, I collapse into her in a boneless heap. I want more—*more and more and more*—but I force myself to let go of her hips. She lets go of my waist.

Mal clears her throat so intensely it sounds like she dislodges her lungs. "That seemed . . . *educational*," she says, dignified, despite her swollen bottom lip. "Do you have the data you need?"

"Absolutely." I manage a curt nod, even though it feels like the sand is shifting beneath my feet. My whole *world* is shifting. "So it turns out, I might really be a lesbian."

Mal laughs into my short hair, my exposed neck. "You don't say, Freckles?"

SIXTEEN

A GUARDA, SPAIN
Sunday, May 18, 2025

Sadie

A horrible banging echoes through my head when I wake up the next morning, and it takes me a minute to realize it's not merely the throbbing effects of my sangria hangover. Someone is banging violently on our hostel door.

"Sadie! Mal! Wake up!" It's Inez's voice shouting at us from out in the hall. "You were supposed to be downstairs ten minutes ago!"

Shit. I fumble for my phone on the bedside table, and the screen plainly tells me it's ten after eight. I slept through my alarm.

Wait, no. I was so drunk, I forgot to *set* my alarm.

I jerk up in bed, and the motion sends the entire room spinning.

Sangria? Never again.

In the opposite twin bed, Mal attempts to get up, but gets caught in a tangle of sheet and duvet and ends up hopping halfway across the room before she falls into a pile of blankets and bare limbs.

"Fuck!" she grumbles.

Fuck indeed. I need to get up, get packing, get downstairs, but I'm afraid if I move, I will have to see that octopus again on the other end. My only comfort is that Mal looks as shitty as I feel as she stumbles into her hiking pants, forgetting to take off her sleep shorts first. Her mullet is plastered to the side of her face, her skin is unnaturally pale, and she keeps hissing words in Portuguese. I don't have to speak the language to know she's cursing.

"Are you up now?" Inez shouts through the door.

"Uh-huh." Mal grunts. "Up! We're up!"

"You have five minutes to get downstairs."

Five minutes. Five minutes to make everything stop spinning. Five minutes to get over the worst hangover of my life and be ready to *walk all day.*

At the very least, I need to start by walking to the bathroom to brush my teeth so I can get the taste of sweaty toe socks out of my mouth. I carefully shift my legs over the side of the bed and ready myself to stand, a process that takes an embarrassingly long time. Then it's an agonizing shuffle to the bathroom, where Mal is standing over the sink, splashing water onto her face. "Can I . . . teeth?" I barely manage to ask.

"Good idea."

Mal slides over so we can both brush our teeth in the tight bathroom. Our tired eyes meet in the mirror above the sink, and I'm pleasantly reminded that not only did I get regrettably plastered in the middle of a two-hundred-mile trek, but I also regrettably kissed the roommate I'm still sharing a small space with for the next nine days.

I kissed Mal. Experienced, confident, beautifully handsome *Mal.* I kissed her like a fumbling teenager with *no* experience and very little understanding of human anatomy. I kissed her like a horny, eight-handed octopus monster.

Shame whirlpools in my stomach at the memory of the eager way I clung to her on the beach, the way she had to guide my hands, my tongue. The way she had to coach me through something as juvenile as a kiss.

I wanted to make a mistake, and I sure as hell didn't half-ass it.

Mal's toothbrush dangles from her mouth as she stares at my reflection. She looks like she might say something, her mouth slightly ajar, her eyes fixed on the reflection of mine.

I feel like *I* should say something, but I have no idea what.

I'm sorry I bullied you into kissing me last night?

I'm sorry I enjoyed it so damn much?

It was a huge mistake, and we never have to talk about it again, and please don't hate me forever?

Bravely, I opt to say nothing at all as we continue brushing our teeth in silence. When she finally spits into the sink, she wipes her mouth on the back of her hand, and states the obvious. "So, this is kind of weird, isn't it?"

I spit out my toothpaste too. "Very weird."

"But it doesn't have to be weird."

"I'm listening . . ."

"We kissed," she says with a shrug. "It's not a big deal."

"Totally not a big deal," I lie.

"It's like you said," Mal continues as she wrangles her greasy hair into a half ponytail. "I'm your fairy god-dyke, and last night was like turning a pumpkin into a carriage, or . . . something."

"Totally." I can be as casual and flippant as her. Watch me nod my head with complete indifference. "Though I don't recall the part of *Cinderella* where she makes out with her fairy godmother."

A grin flickers on her face. There's toothpaste in the corner of her smile. "That's because Disney is always straight washing that shit. In the original Grimm Fairy Tale, they totally had a Holland Taylor–Sarah Paulson thing going on."

"Ah, of course." I nod, and Mal nods, and we're standing two feet apart in a tiny European bathroom, nodding like a couple unhinged bobbleheads, and it's *still* weird. I can't stop staring at her mouth. At the curve of it, at the toothpaste smile, at the perfect *v* of her upper lip. I licked that spot last night. I took the curve of her mouth between my teeth and tried to find the right equation to measure its parabolic arch.

"I'm sorry I forced you to kiss me," I blurt in an attempt to silence my mouth and math-related fantasies.

"No, you didn't." Mal takes a step toward me, then two steps backward and bumps into the shower door. "I-I chose to kiss you. You know, for science."

"Right. For science."

We're both still nodding, and I'm starting to worry we'll never be able to *stop* nodding at each other. We're going to be stuck in an awkward nodding loop until the shame from last night finally fades. *If* it ever fades.

"And the experiment was successful," Mal adds. "It . . . it helped, right?"

I nod and nod and nod. "Totally. Very helpful. I-I think I just needed to . . . you know . . ."

"Kiss a woman," she fills in, and those words are enough to conjure a visceral memory of her hot hands and her wet mouth and the pulsating *ache* in my lower stomach.

"Ehm, yes. That."

She nods, and God, she even makes nodding sexy. I try to look anywhere *but* her mouth, but it's a small bathroom, and she takes up the entire space with her long limbs and her perfect hair, her tattoos and her nipples beneath the thin fabric of her shirt. There's literally nowhere safe to fix my gaze, and when I glance back up at her face, I find she's looking at me too.

There's another violent knock on the door, and we both jump. "I swear to the goddess, I will break down this door!"

"It's only nine miles," Inez says from behind the giant pair of sunglasses she's wearing indoors when we make it downstairs eleven minutes later. "A Guarda is nine miles away. We can make it nine miles."

Ari groan-burps in protest as she pours Liquid I.V. into a water bottle.

"That shit doesn't actually do anything," Ro points out.

"Leave me to my delusions, Hashmi!" Ari screams in a very proportional response.

"No loud noises," Vera mumbles, rubbing her temples in slow circles.

"What did y'all get up to last night?" Rebecca asks innocently, as if she doesn't know *exactly* what the sangria did to all of us. Then she starts passing out hangover kits she put together in paper bags before the rest of us woke up this morning. Inside, I find a water bottle, paracetamol, and several carb-heavy items from the breakfast buffet. Lastly, she hands me a paper cup of black coffee.

And thank goddess for Rebecca.

Inez turns to me, and I can see my wrecked face in the reflection of her glasses. "Would you mind, um, *not* writing about last night? You know, for the blog?"

Writing about last night is the *last* thing I want to do. "I promise," I reassure her, and her hungover grimace softens a bit.

"We can totally do this," Inez says again, and no one believes her. "Wait . . ." She looks around the hostel lobby, scanning the faces of her ill charges. "Where's Stefano?"

There's a chorus of confused grumbles. "Maybe he went home with Oliver?" Ari suggests before the door to the hostel opens. Stefano struts inside wearing his tiny shorts, sipping water from the CamelBak straw attached to his pack. "Buongiorno!" He greets cheerfully. "Sorry I am late. It was a beautiful morning for a sunrise 10k."

Everyone glares at him before Ari says what we're all thinking. "I really fucking hate you."

* * *

I should feel like shit. Between waking up at four yesterday to hike Santa Luzia and staying out all night drinking, walking the Camino should be the hardest thing in the world.

But as we follow the coastline out of town, each step feels invigorating and energizing, like it's slowly bringing me back to life. I love the sun and the sea and the predictable routine of putting one foot in front of the other. The water and coffee clearly help my mood, as does the giant croissant Rebecca put in my breakfast bag, but they can't explain why I feel almost giddy, why I can't stop grinning to myself.

The Camino is not the reason why I keep pressing two fingers to my smile, remembering the heat of Mal's mouth against mine. It's not why Vera takes a photo of my goofy expression and asks me if I'm still drunk.

And I *am* still drunk. Drunk on Mal Gonçalves.

I have a giant, uncontrollable, all-consuming crush on Mal, the kind of crush that makes me so distracted, I trip over my feet three times in a row, and on the fourth time, I skin my knee so badly it bleeds. The kind of crush that makes it hard to focus on anything but her lean legs and long stride. I'm separated from Mal by two retirees and one hundred yards, but it feels like her body is still pressed against mine on that beach.

Is *this* how my middle school friends felt about their crushes? No wonder they never shut up about boys. If I had someone to talk to about this, I don't think I would ever stop.

It's our last day on the Portuguese coast, and I try to concentrate on memorizing the beauty here. In another mile or so, we'll take a boat across the border into Spain and find ourselves one giant step closer to Santiago de Compostela. I'll miss the tiny, old Portuguese men who hobble past us with their "Bom caminhos!" I'll miss the unrelenting kindness of everyone we've met along our journey. I'll miss the sound of Mal effortlessly switching between English and Portuguese at every café and restaurant. But most of all, I'll miss pasteis de nata.

I order an entire plateful when we stop for morning tea, and I make sure to savor every bite before they're gone forever.

The path moves away from the coast and into the woods, taking us along a soft trail of trees for another mile before the path abruptly cuts across a stretch of sand. We end up on the bank of a river. There's an inconspicuous dock with a few small boats bobbing in the current beside it and people waiting in disorderly lines.

"All right, my beautiful and/or hungover pilgrims!" Inez announces. "The boats cost six euro! Get on whichever one has room, and we'll meet up on the other side in Spain!"

I get swept up in the current of people heading toward the boats. Someone takes my cash.

Another man speaking Spanish takes my hand and lifts me into a boat, where I'm surrounded by people I don't recognize, all singing in Portuguese. I quickly learn they're all nurses, and they're doing the Camino as a team-bonding experience.

I look up and see that Mal is next to Inez in a different boat, that the whole group is separated. The motor churns and the noise drowns out all other sounds as we cruise across the river, water spraying up into the boat, making it impossible for me to see. I grab on to my hat and hold it in place amid the wind and the waves.

The trip is wild and wonderful, and when my feet are on solid ground again, I'm in a new country.

The town of A Guarda is on a hill overlooking the Atlantic, and we schlep our bags up to our hotel for the night in a chorus of deeply exhausted groans. It's clear we're all carrying hangovers in addition to our heavy packs, and the 9 miles it took to get us here were challenging.

It's a little after one when we arrive, but Inez has a personal relationship with the owner of our hotel, so we're able to check in early. Perhaps the greatest joy of my life is discovering our hotel has an elevator. Granted, it's only big enough for one person at a time, and you have to open the doors yourself, but everyone except Stefano happily waits their turn to be carted up to the third floor.

"I suspect it's going to be an early night for most of us," Inez says before we all part ways.

"You suspect correctly," Vera tells her as she stifles a sangria-scented burp.

"So, let's meet up for lunch in an hour, and then we'll retire early. We can all do our own thing for dinner, if we're still awake at seven."

"Deal," Ro grunts, "but under one condition: no one orders wine at lunch."

Everyone agrees, and an hour later, we're together again, walking the few blocks to Restaurante La Casa de la Abuela. It's in an unassuming building next to a tattoo parlor, but once inside, we discover a rustically charming place with eclectic furnishings and herbs hanging over the bar. The restaurant is spread out over several rooms and patios, with old family photos decorating the walls. It reminds me of my house of ghosts, but warmer and more inviting.

The owner greets Ari like *she* is family, before guiding us through rooms with stone walls and wood-beam ceilings. Each space is full of upcycled furniture items. There are wine barrels converted into tables, repurposed chandeliers, and living room furniture functioning as banquette seating. Seeing the way the pieces work together to create something surprisingly chic makes me miss Nan's antique store for the first time all trip.

Well, not the store, exactly, but my tiny workshop in the back of the store, the place where I used to reinvent old items the way this restaurant has, honoring the past while also creating something new.

The owner seats us on an expansive patio, and the rest of the group is in the middle of a conversation I missed while daydreaming about furniture restoration. "I have sixteen, I think," Ari is saying as we all settle around an old dining room table that's been dressed up with a pink, woven tablecloth.

"Sixteen what?" I ask.

"Tattoos." Ari chugs some ice water as she considers this. "No, wait. Seventeen."

"I have *tre*." Stefano winks from his chair where he's doing seated calf raises. "But they are places your eyes cannot go."

"How many tattoos do *you* have?" Ari asks Mal, leaning across the table to stroke the bird tattoo on Mal's right wrist. The memories of last night rise in the back of my throat like the red wine and brandy. Memories of Ari touching Mal while they danced together; memories of Mal touching me.

"I've lost count," Mal says, before pulling her arm away to reach for her water.

"I've always wanted to get a tattoo," Vera says wistfully. "But I've never been able to commit to something that I would want on my body forever."

"Not me." I casually reach for a menu, but it's in Spanish, yet another language I don't know. "Growing up, I always swore I'd never get one."

"Well, that sounds like a challenge." Ari lays down her menu, and when a server comes by, she orders in flawless Spanish. Then Inez orders tapas for the whole table to get us started—patatas bravas and croquettes, as well as lots and lots of bread to soak up our lingering hangovers—and I get by with just enough Spanish to order myself a Coke. When it arrives, I take a sip, and *oh my damn*. Even Coca-Cola tastes better here.

"We could get tattoos," Ari casually suggests. "There's a shop next door, and the sign said they accept walk-ins."

I snort into my mind-blowingly delicious soda. "I don't think I'm that brave."

"It's not about bravery for me," Mal says, taking a sip from her own Coke, her bowed mouth puckering into an O around her straw. "I just really hate my father."

"Let's *actually* do it!" Vera perks up now that she ingested half a basket of rolls. "Let's get tattoos together!"

"Darling," Rebecca drawls, popping an antacid before taking a sip of her herbal tea. "After last night, I think we've made enough poor decisions due to peer-pressure and group-think."

"I would also advise against—" Inez starts, but Vera and Ari grab on to each other's hands in excitement.

"I'm serious!" Vera insists. "We could all get matching Camino tattoos!"

"Certo! Sì!" Stefano gleefully agrees. He's already up out of his chair even though the tapas haven't arrived yet.

"I'm in," Ro grunts with a surprisingly relaxed shrug.

"I *love it.*" Ari pumps her fist in the air. Mal reaches over and lowers it back to the table.

"Absolutely not." Mal returns to her casual perusal of the menu. The server arrives to take our final orders, and the only thing I want is more potatoes, so I ask for the only other *patatas* on the menu. "I love getting impulsive tattoos as much as the next queer, but we don't know anything about this tattoo shop and its practices, and A Guarda isn't exactly a sprawling metropolis," Mal continues. "Plus, I don't think our hungover brains are doing their best thinking right now."

"It has a 4.5 rating on Google," Ari notes, staring down at her phone.

"And this is a horrible time of the year to get a tattoo," Mal adds on. "You can't expose it to the sun."

"So we'll get it somewhere the sun don't shine." Ari winks at her.

Mal shakes her head. "And trying to keep the tattoo clean while sweating is going to suck."

"Come *on*," Vera pleads, pouting in Mal's direction as if she is the true arbiter of what we do, not Inez. "Aren't we supposed to challenge ourselves to do things outside our comfort zone? That's our reflection prompt for today."

"Hmmm." Rebecca thoughtfully stirs her tea. "When you put it like that, I suppose I could get a small tattoo, somewhere private, just for me."

"Fuck yes, Rebecca!" Ari shouts, completely sober and still committed to this reckless decision.

"For liability reasons, I want to emphasize that I was not promoting permanent physical changes to your body," Inez chirps. Mal studies the worried expression on Inez's face before she speaks again.

"You all can get tattoos." Mal leans back in her chair, and it should be illegal how good she looks doing this. "But I'm going to sit this one out."

"No, no! We've all got to do it! The entire Camino Crew! Sadie, you're in, right?"

I chew on my upper lip. I'm not the kind of person who has tattoos. I wear cardigans and reading glasses; I study the Arts and Crafts movement in architecture *for fun*; I genuinely enjoy doing my taxes. I'm asleep every night by nine, and I'm simply not cool enough to get a tattoo.

Except. I reach up and touch the ends of my short hair, feel the slice of bare neck above my shoulders.

Except three days ago, I didn't think I was the kind of person who would cut off all her hair with kitchen scissors in a foreign country. And I definitely didn't think I was the kind of person who'd drunkenly kiss a woman on a beach.

What was it Inez said at the sharing circle this morning while I was distracted by the nata? The Camino isn't about finding yourself; it's about creating yourself.

"I know that look." Mal interrupts my thoughts with a low, warning growl. "Don't do it, Freckles. This is a very bad idea."

"It is a bad idea," I agree, "but I think that's why I have to do it."

"*Noooo*," Mal groans at the same time Ari does another fist pump and shouts, "Yes!"

Inez shakes her head repeatedly. "Legally, I can't have any part in this. I am going back to the hotel."

I nudge a reluctant Mal with my shoulder. "Part of adolescence is making mistakes, right?"

She shakes her head at me. "I've created a monster."

I reach over the empty basket of bread between us and put my hand on hers. "And Mal?" I wait until she meets my gaze, until her hazel eyes are completely fixed on mine. "You have to get a Camino tattoo with me."

SEVENTEEN

A GUARDA, SPAIN

Mal

As the tattoo needle scrapes across my skin, I have a few regrets.

I regret letting myself get bullied into this. I'm thirty-eight years old, and I should be immune to peer pressure at this point.

I regret allowing Ari to do the research on this tattoo parlor, where the artist was happy to tattoo seven people without signing a single consent form. There's no way this is vegan ink.

I regret letting Vera design the tattoo. I mistook the camera as a sign of artistic talent, but what she draws up is a rudimentary sketch of the scallop shell and arrow that guides our path. And now that rudimentary sketch is eternally inked into my skin between the matching pinecone tattoo I got with Michelle and the intertwined rose and honeysuckle I got for my eighteenth birthday, right there on my left bicep.

But mostly, I regret Sadie.

I regret the way I caved the second she touched me. I regret the way I held her hand as we watched Ari go first. "Is it going to hurt?" she asked with the smallest, more endearing lip quiver.

"Yeah. It hurts every time."

She looked up at me with an open mouth, and all I could think about was how her eyes are the exact color of the place where the sky meets the sea on the horizon. "*You* think it hurts? Then why do you have so many?"

"I told you. I *really* hate my dad." She squeezed my hand in panic.

"Tattoos hurt like walking the Camino hurts," I told her. "It's a hurt that feels worth it. And like the Camino, if you do it once, you become obsessed with doing it again."

Kind of like falling in love. That's what I regret the most: falling for Sadie, despite my best efforts not to. I know love is bad for me—I know it's a self-destructive pattern, a distraction, a way to avoid being alone with myself and my thoughts—but I'm addicted to the newness, to the magic of a first touch, a first kiss.

And what a fucking first kiss it was. All nervousness and hesitation, sweetness and surrender. It felt like *my* very first kiss; Sadie made me feel like a teenager, discovering it all for the first time alongside her.

I regret kissing Sadie last night, and I regret *not* kissing her again in the bathroom this morning. I shouldn't have given into her drunken request to test a hypothesis *and* I should've tasted the toothpaste on her tongue while I had the chance.

Sadie bit down on her upper lip. "I don't think I can go through with this," she said as she watched Vera's eyes start to water.

"You can," I said. Because it was a bad idea *and* she had to do it. "You can install a kitchen backsplash and walk sixty miles and chop off all your hair. You can definitely get a tattoo. Besides, it's a small tattoo. Less than ten minutes."

Her sky-sea eyes were full of doubt, and I thought she might back out, until I heard myself say, "what if I go first?"

And now I have a cliché tourist tattoo on my biceps.

After the tattoo artist wraps Saniderm around my arm, it's Sadie's turn in the chair. She insists I hold her hand, and she squeezes as tight as she did on the plane when she thought she was going to die. She closes her eyes and refuses to watch as the humming needle punctures the top layer of her skin for the first time.

She squeezes me even tighter. It's obvious that every single prick is agony for her, but she doesn't complain, doesn't even flinch. She just holds on to me until it's over.

As promised, the whole process only takes ten minutes. Bold line work with no shading, the sideways scallop shell and the arrow pointing forward. When the artist is done, Sadie opens her eyes and stares down at the black ink on her red, inflamed skin. There's a look of awe in her sky-sea eyes, a look of wonder. Sadie's first tattoo. All of Sadie's firsts.

In the end, I don't regret a damn thing.

"I've never felt like this before!" Rebecca thrills as we all walk down the hill toward the water, because apparently, the only logical thing to do after getting impulsive tattoos is to eat ice cream. "I got a tattoo! At sixty-nine!"

Ro grumbles a laugh. "Sixty-nine," they chuckle to themselves, and that joke is even more shocking than when Ro rolled their sun-protective, long-sleeve hiking shirt to reveal a dozen tattoos up both arms, including several half-naked women and hyper-realistic portraits of their corgis. I didn't peg Ro for a tattoo gay.

"I feel like anything is possible!" There's a new spring in Rebecca's step, all five feet of her bouncing along cobbled streets. "My whole body is buzzing with potential."

Her sincerity is too much for me to handle. "Well, I hope you know this means you're paying for my tattoo removal in ten years."

Vera throws her arm around me. "Aww, you think we're going to be friends in ten years?"

I roll my eyes as the seven of us push our way into a tiny gelato shop. The usual group chaos ensues: the overlapping too-loud voices, the arguments about ice cream flavors, the excruciating number of samples the Americans insist on trying before they commit to a flavor. Sadie has a full existential crisis about her choice before settling on strawberry in a cup, the same flavor I've watched her eat twice already on this trip. I order a scoop of pistachio in a waffle cone.

There's more chaos as we all struggle to find a place to eat our gelato, and we end up in a single-file line along a retaining wall, our feet dangling above the bay. The water gently laps against the wall. Old Spanish men dot the pier in front of us with their fishing poles, the way they probably do every evening. I stare at the joint between the sky and sea, still blazing blue even though it's almost seven. That was always my favorite part of trips to Spain in the summer. The time change meant impossibly long days, daylight until ten at night, extra hours to be outside.

"Do you want a taste?"

I turn to my right to see Sadie, her sky-sea eyes, and her strawberry gelato, which she holds out to me in offering. Her mouth is extra pink, and I absolutely do want a taste. I take the spoon from her cup. The gelato is sweet and creamy, and I picture Sadie's tongue tasting the same way. I let myself imagine kissing the flavor off her mouth, before I tilt my cone in her direction.

She scowls at the greenish-brown color. "What kind did you get?"

"The only kind there is."

She hesitates, then swipes her tongue along the edge of my cone with one slow, long lick that makes me shiver from the inside out. And damn, I have to find a way to kiss her again.

"*Mmmm.*" She moans the way she did with her first bite of nata, the way she did into my mouth. "That's delicious."

There's a smudge of pistachio ice cream in the corner of her mouth, and she tongues it away, and I'm about two seconds from kissing her right fucking now, on this retaining wall, in front of everyone. She notices the way I'm staring at her mouth, and when our gazes meet from a foot apart, she doesn't look away.

"Wow!" I jump and tear my eyes away from Sadie's as on my other side Ari releases a long, low whistle that rescues me from my foolish lust. "How was I so fucking oblivious?" she shouts at the ocean. I blink in confusion, trying to figure out what I missed while dreaming of Sadie's sweetness.

Rebecca startles, too, nearly dropping her chocolate sugar cone into the water below. "What are you talking about, ladybug?"

Ari throws her head back and laughs manically while everyone eyes her with increasing concern. "Nothing!" She's pinching her side as she struggles to breathe through her deranged, barking laughter. "Just realizing I'm always a Judy Greer, never a Sandra Bullock."

"Um, what?"

"Has Ari lost her pretty mind?" Stefano wonders aloud.

Ari jumps up so she can punch him in the arm. "Hey! You got my name right!"

"Prego," he says smugly.

"You don't get a trophy for basic human decency." She punches him again. "Come on. Let's head back to the hotel for face masks and wallowing."

Ari tugs Vera into standing and throws an arm around her shoulders. "At least I have you, best friend."

"I'm not really your best friend, right? Because I've only known you for a week . . ."

The rest of the group gathers themselves with Ro helping Rebecca slowly rise from the retaining wall. Stefano, meanwhile, springs from his sitting position directly onto two feet like some kind of magical jack rabbit. "This is not gelato." He disgustedly throws his entire dessert into the nearest trash can. "Come to Italy, all of you. I show you real gelato."

"You've got a deal, Dollface," Rebecca sings. I'm still in a dreamy, half-daze, barely listening to the surrounding conversation as I finally push myself up to standing. Sadie does the same, and we linger at the back of the group as everyone zigzags up the crooked streets back toward the hotel. Sadie and I don't speak as we eat our respective gelatos, but it's not an exquisite silence.

It's a silence that feels thick with that interrupted moment when I watched her lick gelato out of the corner of her mouth and I almost lost all control of myself, almost licked her mouth too.

I lift my cone to my mouth again, but before it reaches my lips, Sadie's hand jerks forward, grabs the cone, and pulls it to her own mouth. She licks my remaining gelato, then smiles pistachio green at me.

"Sorry," she says, without sounding sorry at all. "It tastes too good. I couldn't help myself."

The last shred of my self-control melts like the strawberry gelato at the bottom of her cup, and I grab the wrist of the hand still wrapped around my cone—the same wrist where her new tattoo shines under the transparent bandage. Without thinking, I pull her off the main street and into a small alleyway next to the nondescript entrance of a shop. I'm pushing her up against the stone wall beside the entrance, crowding against her.

"Sorry!" Sadie repeats with a squeak, sounding like she absolutely means it. "But it was just gelato!"

"I don't give a damn about the gelato." The words come out in an embarrassing growl. The cone falls to the ground between us as I slide my hand around her waist, and then Sadie's cup falls, too, followed by the clang of her plastic spoon. "I'm going to kiss you," I tell her, but before I even can, Sadie's already kissing me. Her cold, sticky fingers cradle the back of my neck while her mouth crashes against mine.

And *this kiss*—this strawberry- and pistachio-flavored kiss— is somehow even better than last night's. There's no pretense, no preamble, no pretending. We don't have to negotiate the details or cloak drunken desire in scientific curiosity. I'm kissing her because she tastes so fucking good, I just can't help myself.

And Sadie is kissing me back like she wanted this too. Her hands travel from my neck to my shoulders, my shoulders to my collarbone, my collarbone to the sides of my breasts beneath my tank top. Then she grabs a handful of that tank top and pulls me even harder against her. Our first kiss was drunk and sloppy and self-conscious, my whole body focused on easing Sadie's nerves, on helping her relax until she became pliable in my arms, like Play-Doh I could mold. But our *second kiss*.

We're completely sober, and it is broad daylight, and Sadie isn't Play-Doh at all. She's the one sculpting me with her hands, moving me where she wants me, touching me and turning me into goo.

She bites my lip, so I bite her back, pushing her against the wall until she lets out a little yelp of pain, then laughs into my mouth. "Sorry." She says the word against my lips, and I start laughing too. "Sharp stone."

I maneuver her away from the wall, and the sober, broad daylight of it all comes crashing down on me. I clear my throat to ensure my next words don't come out in that same horny growl. "You . . . um, you're getting good at that. Very quick learner."

She starts nodding, and then I'm nodding too. We keep nodding at each other and not touching, and I feel like I might combust. "Yes, well, I have a good teacher," she stammers.

I'm shaking with desperation, with a feral *need*. "You know what they say about scientific experiments . . ."

"Of course. You replicate the experiment to see if you get the same findings."

And shit. We're back to equivocating, back to pretending these are practice kisses, when the last thing Sadie needs is *practice*. She already knows how to kiss me in a way that makes me want all of her, in a way that makes me feel like no amount will ever be enough. And I want to tell her that.

I *need* to tell her that none of it has been practice. But what if they are only practice to Sadie?

"Mallory! Samantha!" a voice shouts, and I take another step away from Sadie before Stefano rounds the corner of our little alleyway. "There you are! They sent me to find you! What are you doing here?"

Stefano smiles at us in a way that makes it painfully obvious that he knows *exactly* what we're doing here. He glances down at our feet. "Oh no! You spilled your disgusting gelato!" Then, he goes so far as to wink at us. "We will tell the others you had a little mess to take care of."

A little mess, indeed.

EIGHTEEN

A GUARDA, SPAIN
Monday, May 19, 2025

Mal

"Practice kisses?"

"I can explain."

"I'd like to hear you try," Michelle says dryly into the phone. I watch my clothes tumble round and round through the transparent dryer door.

"Well, you see, she's insecure about coming out at thirty-five and feels like she's behind because she missed out on—"

"Wait. Stop. I take it back. I don't want to hear you try to explain why you couldn't make it a week without kissing this woman."

"The kisses are for science?" I try. "You love science."

Michelle is not amused. In the background, I hear her fingers clacking against her keyboard with sharp jabs of annoyance. "What happened to focusing on yourself on this trip? Have you decided what to do about Quinta Costa yet? Have you spent any time at all reflecting on your future?"

"Don't be ridiculous. Of course I haven't."

I flop back on one of the laundromat's plastic chairs and sigh. The Lavanderia Momblanco is empty at eight in the morning, and the tumbling of clothes in the dryer isn't enough to keep the silence at bay. Today is our longest day yet—19 miles to Baiona— and I should have slept in. Everyone else is back at the hostel enjoying a leisurely breakfast, but I woke up early feeling restless. I hiked up to the Castelo de Santa Cruz to watch the sunrise, but even the beautiful views of the ocean couldn't get the strawberry-pistachio taste out of my mouth.

When I got back to our hotel room, Sadie was asleep on top of the covers, snoring into her pillow. It felt too dangerous to stay in that room with her. So, I gathered up my dirty clothes and waited outside the Lavanderia until it opened.

Then I called Michelle when I knew she'd be awake feeding Cedar or working on her research. From what I can tell, she's currently doing both.

"I'm worried about you, Maëlys," she says now, pulling out my full name to emphasize her motherly disappointment.

"There's nothing to worry about," I insist for the dozenth time. But I've been up since four thirty and have consumed three espressos already, so I'm not sure this is true. "Sadie doesn't have feelings for me at all. Whatever this is, I'm not at risk of Romeo antics, because it can't go anywhere."

"Uh-huh. So you're telling me you haven't done anything stupid for this woman?"

I can practically feel the tattoo healing through the fabric of my fleece. "Nope. Not a thing."

"You're not pretending to like things she likes, or putting her needs above your own?"

I clear my throat. "As we both know, I have always *loved* watching *Property Brothers*."

"You have said on numerous occasions that the one twin's beard freaks you out."

"Why does it look like those nineties Ken Dolls with facial hair that disappeared with water?"

Michelle chuckles, and for a moment I think I've managed to distract her from my much-deserved lecture. But then she heaves another giant sigh. "You've got to stop running at some point, Mal."

I choke on my next flippant comment. I want to keep evading her questions, dodging her concerns by turning them into jokes. But the truth is, I called Michelle because she is the only person in this world who truly knows me, and I want her to remind me why kissing Sadie again last night was an epic mistake.

I need her to stop me from doing it again.

I've been drifting aimlessly through life, fluttering from one thing to the next, one trip to the next, always searching for a new beginning and running again when I get bored. Or when things get hard. "I don't want to hurt her," I confess.

"I don't want *you* to get hurt," Michelle counters, and then I'm thinking about Ruth again. I fell out of love with her long before she ended things, but that didn't stop her words from fracturing the corners of my self-confidence.

"Mal?" Michelle probes gently in my ear, and I clear my throat. Something wet dislodges there, as if I'm about to start crying in this laundromat.

The timer on the dryer dings as my clothes finally stop tumbling, and I'm grateful to have a sense of purpose for my body again. I snatch one of the hampers, take my clothes out of the dryer, and wheel them over to the folding table.

"I don't want to get hurt again either," I say to Michelle as I hold the hot clothes in my hands.

Michelle is quiet on the other end for a while, and I methodically fold my clothes to the sound of her clacking keys and her thoughtful breaths. In the background, there's a mechanical sound, like something sucking and compressing in a steady pattern.

"Why does it sound like you're in the Tardis right now? Are you pumping?"

"Of course I'm pumping!" Michelle snaps. "All I ever do is pump, so I can build up a freezer supply of milk, so that I'm able to go back into work on a regular basis at some point! I feed

Cedar, then I pump, then I store my breast milk in these flimsy freezer bags, and I'll be doing that every three hours for the rest of my life!"

"Surely you'll be able to wean him at some point before he goes off to college."

"It's not funny, Mal. There's nothing funny about constantly milking yourself like a cow."

I'm on the brink of tears again as she shouts about her boobs. "I miss you, M."

"Then come home," she says. Like it's so damn simple.

Like I have a home to return to.

I'm avoiding Sadie.

That's my new plan.

We leave A Guarda promptly at eight, and after prioritizing laundry, I miss the chance to eat breakfast with everyone else. For the first hour of the Camino, I walk alongside Ari in silence, sharing her AirPods as we listen to a podcast together, even though I want to walk with Sadie and hear about her childhood in her Nan's store, about her meddlesome family, about all the boys she didn't love before.

We stop in a tiny town for midmorning coffee, and even though I want to help Sadie order, I join Stefano in running (literally *running*) down to the beach to briefly soak our feet in salt water instead.

When we rejoin the group at the café, Sadie is sitting next to Inez, her face conquered by a ferocious blush. Because Sadie is kissing me for science, but she has a genuine crush on Inez.

For the next hour, Sadie walks up ahead with her, nodding along to a story Inez is enthusiastically telling with her hands. My gaze is fixed on the staggering coastline. I flutter around the group, landing anywhere except at Sadie's side. I exchange travel stories with Stefano; I listen to suburban stories from Rebecca; I even listen to a lengthy story about one of Ro's corgis who is so old, they have to feed him puree pouches meant for toddlers.

In A Riña, we stop at a small shop for drinks and snacks. I wander aimlessly up the aisles and end up buying nothing. We take our provisions another mile up the Camino, to Jardín Meditativo del Caminante, a park along the path. The group spreads out on a natural bench made of rock for our sharing circle.

As everyone takes out their water bottles and snacks, Ro shoves an orange into my empty hands. "Eat," they demand, and I don't argue. I dig my thumb into the rind and citrus squeezes out all the way down my wrist.

"We are almost halfway into our journey," Inez says, "and I want us to reflect on how far we've come."

Chunks of orange peel fall into my lap as I watch Inez's animated gestures. "What is something you've done in the last six days that has surprised you?"

"Tattoos!" Vera shouts, and everyone laughs. I stare down at the Saniderm wrinkled over that silly tattoo on my biceps.

"Absolutely everything," Rebecca blurts. "I never thought I could do something like this. We've walked eighty miles already, and I'm just surprised I'm still here!"

"I'm surprised by how strong I feel," Ari chimes in. "I haven't always had the best relationship with my body, but on the Camino, my body . . . it's all I have, really. And every day, my body carries me along this path. I'm so grateful for my body, and that's not a feeling I've had before."

Several nods and murmurs of agreement echo around the half circle. "This is so far beyond my comfort zone," Ro says when the chorus dies down. "Not the walking part, but the walking with other people. The . . ." Ro coughs awkwardly into their closed fist. "The sharing. I don't normally do shit like this. No offense, Inez."

She bows graciously from her rock perch. "None taken."

"I just . . . I haven't always been great at, uh . . . expressing my . . . my feelings."

Rebecca reaches over and puts a hand on Ro's shoulder. "You're still awful at it, love."

More laughter. I want to join in with it, but I'm stuck in my head, and the only thing I can do is peel this orange.

"Hell, this is Dr. Phil–level for me," Ro dad-jokes. "I didn't grow up in a family where we talked openly about our feelings. And I think, being Muslim, and queer, and trans . . . well. I learned to ignore a lot of my emotions, because if I acknowledged my emotions, then I might have to face the truth of myself."

My eyes land on Sadie across the half circle, but she's staring down at her shoes. *My* shoes on her feet.

"But I'm trying to be more open," Ro grunts. "Rebecca has this way of getting me to talk every night before bed—" Ro pauses to chuckle as Rebecca fluffs her hair in a self-congratulatory fashion. "And even chatting with Mal about my babies . . ." Ro nudges me with their elbow. "That's hard for me, and I appreciate you listening."

Fuck. I am an asshole. I only listened to Ro talk about their corgis to avoid Sadie. It didn't occur to me that Ro was trying to connect with me in a meaningful way—in the only way they know how.

I stare down at my guilt orange and break off a slice. The juice explodes inside my mouth.

"I'm so proud of you, Ro," Inez says from across the way.

I expect Ro to bristle at being told this by someone twenty years younger, but they simply exhale and say, "Thank you, Inez. For pushing me to be proud of myself."

I'm about to cry again. I try to rub a rogue tear out of my eye, but I've got orange juice on my fingers, and all it does is burn.

"I am proud of myself as well," Stefano interjects. "I am learning to slow down. To stop and smell the roses, as they say."

Stefano is currently standing on the edge of the semicircle, doing push-ups in the dirt while everyone else sits. "I am really learning relaxation."

Everyone laughs again.

"What? *What?*" Stefano asks sincerely as he pulls himself into Mountain pose, searching the faces in the half circle for clarification. "What is funny?"

Inez moves the conversation along. "What about you, Sadie?"

Sadie's gaze finds mine, and after a morning of avoiding her, the sight of her blue-green eyes and her pink blush burns as badly as the orange in my eye.

"Have you surprised yourself on this trip?" Inez prods.

"Yes," Sadie croaks. "Um, yes. Yes, I have." She bites down on her upper lip for a moment, and everyone waits to see if she'll elaborate on her feelings. She usually doesn't.

"I've surprised myself in a lot of ways. My hair, for one." She makes a sweeping gesture to her short hair crammed beneath her cheap baseball hat with the vulva-shaped oyster. "And the tattoo, of course. And, um . . . I've been questioning, I guess. Trying to figure out who I am and what I want."

Sadie smiles shyly, beautifully, as she tries to tuck her hair behind her ear beneath her hat. She's wearing hardly any makeup today. She's all freckles and sunburn and herself. Beside her, Vera wraps an arm around her shoulders and pulls Sadie into a sideways hug, while I'm across the semicircle, grinding an orange into pulp in my hands.

"I'm trying to be kinder to myself," she says, "for not having it all figured out already."

Inez twirls the clear crystal dangling from around her neck. "How boring would life be if we didn't have anything left to discover about ourselves?"

NINETEEN

BAIONA, SPAIN

Sadie

Mal has been avoiding me.

She was already gone this morning when I woke up, and she's made a deliberate effort not to be alone with me all day. And *thank fucking God* for that.

I should probably be offended by her distance after last night's gelato kiss, but I'm too *relieved* to care. I don't want to be alone with her either.

Something strange is happening to my body, something that started taking shape when I first saw this tattoo on my skin. The arrow and scallop shell, representing this new path, the one where I keep moving forward, keep putting one foot in front of the other. The one where I keep taking steps into the unknown.

Right now, the tattoo is distorted beneath the sticky bandage that protects it from my sweat, but even so, it demands my attention. I keep peeling back my sleeve to see if the tattoo is still there. It feels like proof that I can change, proof that no part of me is set in stone. That I can keep discovering myself, keep creating myself, keep *claiming* myself.

The ink on my skin anchors me to my body in a way I've never experienced before.

I am physical. Visceral. Aware of my muscles, my bones, my breath. Aware of the feeling of my feet on the ground as we walk, aware of my blood pumping through my veins and the air in my lungs. And whenever I'm close to Mal, or whenever I look at her, or whenever I do so much as *think* about her, I can feel her presence like my heartbeat against my rib cage. I can feel her hands in all the places they've been and in all the places they haven't.

So, no. I don't want to be alone with Mal any more than she wants to be alone with me, because I don't trust myself not to make another catastrophic mistake.

Fortunately for me, it's our longest day on the Camino so far—19 goddamn miles—and Mal avoids me the entire time.

Unfortunately for both of us, avoiding me has a natural expiration date. Our accommodation for the night is a quaint B&B in the coastal town of Baiona, Spain. It's clear from the sheer number of heart-shaped doilies that the place usually caters to an older, more romantic crowd, but Inez appears to be best friends with the owner, in the same way she does with everyone we meet along the trek.

Mal and I don't look at each other, not even when we make it upstairs to a bedroom with pink wallpaper and a giant soaking tub clearly meant for two. The only saving grace is that there are two beds, though it appears they were previously pushed together into a single king-size bed.

I collapse directly onto one of the beds with no regard for how sweaty I am. "I'm going to soak in this bath," Mal announces as she pulls out her toiletries bag and refuses to look at me.

Without another word, she closes the bathroom door. A few minutes later, the sound of the filling tub echoes through the room. If I keep lying here, I'm going to start picturing Mal in that water, so I force myself to get up.

I half-heartedly perform my post-walking routine, moving through my stretches and blister care. It only takes fifteen minutes, and Mal is still soaking, so I take my iPad out to the narrow balcony attached to our room and start drafting the day's blog post. It's full of adjectives and hyperbole, and it sounds like the melodramatic ramblings of a lovesick tween. I don't post it, but I don't know what else to do with myself.

When Mal still isn't done with her bath, I begin pacing the balcony. I feel antsy, but I'm not sure what I'm antsy *for*.

I don't know how to *be* now that we are alone in this bedroom, even if Mal is hiding behind the bathroom door. I don't know where we stand. I don't know how I'm supposed to resist kissing her again, and I'm not sure I *want* to resist it.

"You've got to have a soak in that tub!" Mal steps onto the balcony in her shorts and a tank top, her hair wet and slicked back, and her ostentatious nipples poking out through her thin fabric. The sight of her makes every inch of my body buzz with nerves and anxiety and desperate *want*.

Her tone is friendly, but she's still not looking directly at me. "There's a Froiz a few blocks from here, and I'm going to do a supply run. Do you need anything?"

I *need* to find an outlet for this restless energy. "Uh, no. I'm all good."

"Cool," she says with a casual shrug. "I'll be back in an hour. Enjoy your hot bath."

Then she's gone, and I wander to the bathroom in a strange daze. I fill the tub with the hottest water possible and ease myself into it. My muscles groan in gratitude as the water envelops my sore body. I try to get comfortable, but as nice as the water feels, I'm still an anxious, tightly wound mess.

The problem isn't my body, not really.

It's my head. My restless, distracted, oxytocin-laden brain. The brain that keeps thinking about Mal's mouth, and her tongue against mine. Her hands on my hips, and her hard nipples brushing against my body. The brain that can't stop replaying the way she pulled me into that alley, the way she shoved me against that wall, the way she *growled* at me.

In the tub, I glide my hands over the places Mal touched: along the column of my neck, up the length of my arms, down my soft stomach, around the curve of my hips. Then, I touch myself everywhere Mal *hasn't*. I cup my breasts, tracing my hardened nipple, and my body tightens, my toes curling under the hot water.

It's far from relaxing, but at least it feels like my body and brain are working together, not against each other.

As I touch my large breasts, I think about Mal's small ones. I imagine her dark areolas, and how it would feel to outline them with my fingertips.

My back arches off the bottom of the tub as the pulse of pleasure moves through me, and I chase the feeling, letting my hand slide between my legs under the water. The merest touch there makes my body clench together, and when I start moving my fingers, my back arches again into the pressure, and I let out the tiniest scream.

This isn't relaxing at all. It's feverish starvation. My fingers move harder and faster, but it's not enough, it will somehow never be enough. I need more, more, more. The ache for release is so strong, my movements almost aggressive. My fingers aren't fast enough. The pressure isn't hard enough. I see Mal's Cupid's-bow mouth, and I imagine all the places she'd put it if I asked her to. I think about the places I want my mouth to be. On the star tattoos behind her ear, in the beautiful pools of her clavicle. My tongue on the lean muscles of her stomach; my tongue anywhere she wants it.

The need in me only grows, and my legs hurt from holding them taut against the sides of the tub. My wrist is miserably tired. "Tip over, dammit!" I grunt, but I can't get there. And that's when the shame creeps in—the shame that tells me I should know my own body well enough to make this work. The shame that tells me I shouldn't be thinking about Mal like this.

The shame that tells me I'm too late, too inexperienced, too far behind in every way.

Except two nights ago, a small voice cuts through the shame spiral. Except two nights ago, I kissed a woman for the first time, and it didn't feel too late. It felt right on time.

My hand stills, then slides out from between my legs. All around me, the bathwater has turned tepid.

I still feel an aching need throughout my body, and I still have *so much* shame to work through, but as I sit in the cooling water, I decide exactly what I have to do about both.

"I think you should teach me how to have sex!"

Mal pauses halfway through the door to our room with a paper grocery bag in her arms. "Um. What?"

"Like practice kissing," I say, "but for sex. I want you to teach me how to have sex."

She steps fully into the room and sets the bag down on her bed. Then she puts both hands on her face, her expression contorted into a perfect impression of Munch's *The Scream*. "That . . . that's a joke, right?"

I'm pacing our hotel room in my pajamas, short hair soaking wet, chest heaving. I probably look half-drowned and fully desperate. So, like, no. It's obviously not a joke at all. "Teach me how to have sex as part of my queer adolescence."

Mal drops her hands from her face and laughs. "There are so many things wrong with that sentence, I don't even know where to start." She shakes her head and sits down on her bed next to the groceries. "Actually, yes I do. I'll start with *hell no*. Sadie, you don't need someone to teach you how to have sex."

"Yes, I do!" I feel manic with the need to convince her, which is, admittedly, a problematic way to feel while propositioning someone for sex. The fact that I have to persuade Mal to have sex with me is a clear sign that I should stop. *Hell no* means *hell no*, and all that.

But in the bathtub, this seemed like the perfect solution to my problems, so I find myself pushing forward. "I'm thirty-five, and I don't have the faintest idea how to have sex with a woman."

"May I recommend watching porn by yourself, then, and leaving me out of it?"

"Porn won't help." I've tried porn before, and there's always so much *squelching*. "I understand the mechanics of it. I need an opportunity to practice the practical application."

She raises her hands into Prayer pose. "And that is one of the many reasons the goddess invented masturbation."

"I masturbated in the bathtub, and it didn't help."

Mal starts to say something but quickly cuts off. "Wait, what?"

I sit down on my bed so we're directly across from each other, opponents in this tense negotiation. "I know it sounds deranged, but the thing is, I've never been sexually attracted to anyone before."

Mal releases a frustrated huff and reaches into the groceries for a bag of chips. "I know you've never been sexually attracted to a man, Sadie. That's part of what we're—"

"No, Mal. I've never been sexually attracted to *anyone*. Including women."

"But you have a crush on Inez. You're attracted to her, right?"

I throw my arms up. "I don't have a crush on Inez, you idiot! I have a crush on *you*! That's what I'm trying to tell you. I've never been sexually attracted to anyone *except you*."

The room goes quiet, save for the sound of the plastic chip bag.

"Do you have to eat those right now?"

"Yes," she grumbles through a full mouth. "These are my emotional support Ruffles."

I take a deep breath and place my hands palms-down on the bed on either side of my legs. "I've never had sex, because I've never met anyone I *wanted* to have sex with. But for some horrible reason, I really want to have sex with you."

Mal chokes and expels a cloud of chip dust, but I press on. There's no point in holding anything back now. I've already made the mistake of kissing her twice. I'm already going to have to switch roommates, because you can't solicit someone for sex, get rejected, and still sleep peacefully five feet away from them. So, I put all my cards on the table. "I feel like you're my chance to finally get it over with."

Mal swallows. "Well, with a sales pitch like that, how could I refuse?"

I grip the duvet in frustration. "I'm saying that I want my first time to be with someone I *trust*. I want to figure it out with someone who makes me feel safe."

She sets aside her half-demolished chips. "Here's the thing. You can't just have sex once and figure it all out. That's not how it works. I still feel like it's my first time whenever I'm with someone new, because sex isn't one-size-fits-all." She says this in the most patient, gentle voice I've ever heard. I roll my eyes.

"I have to learn what each unique person wants, what they like, what gets them off," she explains. "You don't need sex lessons. When the time comes, you just need to listen to your partner, and you need to be honest about what you like."

"But that's just it!" I explode. "I have no idea what I like, because I've never done it before!"

"May I once again encourage masturbation?"

Mal looks bored with this entire conversation, as if I've simply asked her to remove the Compeed from my blisters, and now she'd like to scroll on her phone, *please and thank you.*

I take one more deep breath. "I want to learn how to be sexually intimate with *someone else*. With a woman, after all these years of denying my desires and feeling shame about them." I'm wringing my hands in front of her, and although I'm acutely aware of how embarrassing this is, I say it anyway. "I *need* you to have sex with me."

Mal looks at me with her bowed mouth twisted into some kind of hollow grimace. "I think you have the wrong idea about me," she says quietly. "I'm not Shane from *The L Word*."

I let out a frustrated huff. "I don't even know what that means!"

"It means . . ." Mal's hands grip her knees. "Sex *means* something to me. I'm not into random hookups or meaningless flings. I have sex with people I care deeply about."

"You seem to care about me," I tell her quietly.

"Sadie." She says my name with shocking tenderness and utter exasperation. "I do care about you. But—"

"Then hear me out! The sex won't be meaningless to me. It will mean everything to me, because it will save me from feeling like an inexperienced freak with the next person."

"You're not a freak." Mal pushes herself off the bed with an equally frustrated huff. "The right person will be so fucking honored to be your first time. The right person won't make you feel weird or wrong or inexperienced. The right person is going to lose her mind over the fact that you waited for her."

I cringe. "You mean, like, someone with a virgin fetish?"

"No, Sadie, not . . . *ugh*." Mal tugs at the ends of her mullet, and why do I find her horrible hairstyle *attractive*? She's looking at me with so much compassion in this moment, despite this whole misguided proposition, and maybe that's why. "I mean, like, someone who is a decent human being."

"*You* are a decent human being," I tell her.

"Sadie." She says my name with fondness now. She says it with anguish. "I wish I could make you hear me. Sex does not equal *queerness*. Sex does not equal *normalcy*. Having sex with a woman isn't going to magically make you comfortable in your sexuality."

I get all of that. It's not *about* that. "But you make me comfortable. I don't think you understand how rare that is for me."

Her eyes are full of the same mixture of fondness and anguish. "I think I'm starting to."

"So then, have sex with me, dammit!" I am joking this time. Sort of.

She puffs out a laugh. "Sadie," she starts, and this time, she only sounds tired.

I hold up my hands to stop her. "It's fine. I get it. This— this was a horrible idea. I don't know what possessed me. I'm so sorry."

Mal pushes back her hair like she's intentionally trying to heighten my sexual frustration with her fucking widow's peak. "It's okay."

"I-I'll go talk to Inez." I take a step toward the door and away from that widow's peak. "I-I'll tell her you need a different roommate, and I won't bother you with this ridiculous queer adolescent stuff anymore."

She reaches out for my arm. "Wait. You don't have to do that."

I ignore how this simple touch makes me feel like my entire nervous system is composed of butterflies. "I think it's for the best if we're not roommates anymore."

"But . . . but I don't want a new roommate."

I glance down at the slender fingers encircling my arm. I glance up at her worried expression. "Can I ask you one more question . . . ?"

I chew down on my lip as Mal slowly nods. And I know I shouldn't ask her this, but I do it anyway. "Would you?"

Mal blinks at me. "Would I what?"

"Would you be honored to be my first?"

Silence and stillness and stifling *awkward* creeps in between us. Then Mal exhales a frustrated growl. "Of course I would."

Everything melts inside my body like a pasteis de nata on my tongue. I press my forehead to hers. "Then maybe you're the person I've been waiting for."

TWENTY

BAIONA, SPAIN

Mal

Damn. She's good.

It's a pathetic Hail Mary, a last-ditch effort to convince me to go along with this bonkers scheme by making me feel special, singular, *seen*.

No, the pathetic thing is that it works. The flimsy resolve I've been clinging to since I walked into our room and found her standing there in her sheer pajama shorts finally escapes my grip. I've run out of ways to talk myself out of this mistake.

Honestly, I didn't need to be talked into it in the first place.

Because she doesn't have a crush on Inez. She has a crush on *me*. And I have a ridiculous, misguided, adolescent crush on her too. I feel seventeen and absolutely stupid over a girl.

Sadie *wants* me, and I am so fucking honored.

It doesn't matter that we'll both regret this before we reach Santiago de Compostela. It doesn't matter that one or both of us will end up hurt. All I can think about is kissing her again, touching her, feeling her body against mine, and now she's right here with her plump thighs and this white T-shirt that hugs her every curve, and I'm not going to miss the chance to explore those luscious curves with my fingers, with my tongue.

She's standing here with her flushed cheeks and her heaving breath, and all I can do is imagine making her that way with my mouth. I'm picturing how those freckles would look surrounded by starched hostel sheets as I kiss her in a million new places. God, I want my face between those thighs. I want to find out what combination of hands and tongue, speed and pressure, will make Sadie unravel for me, and then I want to watch as she falls apart from my touch. I want to figure out what *she* wants and then teach her how to touch herself like that.

Sadie is a distraction. She's an unhealthy pattern of behavior. She's a way to forget everything I need to face. But she's also beautiful and kind, and she reminds me that the world is mostly beautiful and kind too. She's maybe the most vulnerable person I've ever met. She's given me more of herself in a week than all the other women I've been with combined, and now she's offering me the chance to show her how she deserves to be loved. I'm not strong enough to resist that.

This is obviously a terrible fucking idea. And I'm obviously going to do it.

I try to clear my throat, but it's thick with lust and longing. "We . . . we would need to be on the same page. About this. About . . . what it is." My voice cracks over the words.

"Of course." Sadie breathes onto my cheek.

I tilt my head back so I can study her flushed face. "This is . . . this is just practice, right?"

"Absolutely. It can be just practice," she says breezily, and I ignore the part of my heart that withers at this.

I push on with professional indifference. "If we're going to do this, we need to be clear. Either of us can say no to sex at any time, no questions asked."

"Yes, obviously. Agreed."

"And a safe word," I choke out. "We should have a safe word."

"How about *octopus*?" Sadie bites down on a smile. She reaches up and touches two fingers to my throat. I don't realize I am clenching my jaw until she glides those fingers down my strained tendon. Everything relaxes under her touch. Sadie doesn't break eye contact, doesn't move her hand away. "Are you done with your rules?" she whispers.

I'm so mesmerized by the smooth column of her exposed throat, her creamy skin, freckles like a trail down to her collarbone, that I can barely speak.

"One more thing," I croak. "You have to promise that we'll stay friends after."

Sadie's fingers twitch on the back of my neck as her eyebrows scrunch together. "You . . . you consider me a friend?"

A chuckle escapes my clogged throat. "Do you think I'd give sex lessons to just anyone?"

She unleashes her full smile, and something inside me shatters, then reassembles itself, a sense of certainty clicking into place. I lean in and kiss that smile. She kisses me back, and it *click*, *click*, *clicks* in my brain.

Sadie grabs my waist and deepens the kiss, and it's tempting to let her be in control, to let her do whatever she wants with me.

I break off the kiss, and Sadie sways into me. "Where do you want to start?" I ask like I'm a tax accountant, not a lovesick fool.

"Um . . ." Sadie's glossy eyes drop down to her feet. "With sex?"

"Yes, but *what*? Sex can mean a lot of different things."

The blush explodes in little blossoms across her chest. It's only been a week, but I'm already fluent in the language of Sadie's blushes. I know these stress splotches mean she has no idea where she wants to start with these lessons. She doesn't even know what's on the table.

"I-I think this is a mistake," she stutters, detaching from me. "This—this is a terrible idea. I don't know why I thought this would work."

"Sadie." I exhale her name. "You just spent thirty minutes convincing me to do this."

"Yes, but I think I underestimated how humiliating it will be."

"There is a steep learning curve, to be sure, but it's not humiliating." When she doesn't laugh at my teasing, I take her chin in my hand and gently tug her gaze up to meet mine. "Will you come lie down with me?"

"Okay," she whimpers.

I lead her back toward the twin beds. I briefly drop her hand so we can push the separate twins together into one king-size bed. I lie down, and Sadie eventually follows, careful to position herself as far away from me as humanly possible. We could fit another person between us. "Saving room for lesbian Jesus?"

"I know that pop culture reference! Hayley Kiyoko." She smiles as she tucks both hands between her head and the pillow. It's damn near the most adorable thing I've ever seen.

I prop an arm under my head to look at her. "Do you like Hayley's music?"

She shifts restlessly on the bed. "Is small talk usually part of foreplay?"

"Anything can be foreplay if it gets you hot," I tell her, trying to find a way to get her to relax. Desperate for a way to get her closer to me. "I once dated a person who always wanted to have sex right after *Jeopardy!* Alex Trebek's mustache really did it for them."

She stifles her laughter into her pillow.

"Actually, it was me," I deadpan. "I was the one who always wanted to have sex after *Jeopardy!* I'm the one who loved the mustache." Then I do the sign of the cross in bed. "Rest in peace, you silver-haired aphrodisiac."

She doesn't hide her laugh, and I risk scooting a little closer. She doesn't scoot away, but her expression sobers. "I've never been in a bed with another woman before," she admits quietly into the three feet between us. "Except my sister, but that obviously doesn't count."

"Didn't you ever share a bed with a friend at a sleepover?"

"I didn't have a lot of friends growing up, and at the few sleepovers I *did* get invited to, I would choose to sleep on the hard floor instead of sharing a bed. It made me too anxious, the thought of sleeping next to another girl."

"*Dude.*" I draw out the vowels like the linguistic equivalent of an eye roll. "You were so gay."

She buries her face in the pillow, but I can hear her laughter spilling out. "I *know*."

I slide a little closer again, and her head snaps up when she realizes what I'm doing. "Is this okay?"

She licks her lips before she nods her consent. She's only one-fourth of a Hayley Kiyoko away now. I wrap my free hand around her waist, and when she doesn't flinch at the contact, I pull her even closer, so we're face-to-face, bodies flush. I leave it at that for a moment, waiting for her to adjust to the touch.

When she relaxes a smidge, I weave my legs between hers. She stiffens again. Holds her breath.

"You feel really good," I say, because she really does.

Some of the tension eases from her body. "Uh, so do you."

We lie like that, with our legs and arms intertwined and our cheeks on the same pillow, waiting for Sadie to relax completely.

Eventually, her breathing elongates and her eyelids grow heavy, and I think we might fall asleep like this. Maybe that's what Sadie needs. Maybe she needs time to work up to sex.

I would be more than content cuddling her all night long.

But then Sadie shifts and my knee accidentally presses between her legs. Her breath hitches, and we're both very awake now.

She rubs herself against my knee again, not accidentally at all. I slide closer until my thigh is entirely between her legs, and she rocks herself until her breath sputters. She stops, starts to pull away, but I hold her in place until she relaxes again, then gently rock my clit against her hip bone, trying to show her that she's okay, that *this* is okay. That she's allowed to feel pleasure in whatever way works for her.

The confusing thing is that it's working for me, too, even through all our clothes.

She feels *so good*. She's so soft, and her skin is like the cool side of the pillow. She smells sweet and summery, and I am seventeen, with a girl for the first time, excited over every little touch.

Sadie rocks against me, pushing her body into mine, grinding harder on my thigh, and it's hotter than ten Trebek mustaches, and I'm spiraling out of control with want.

I want to finally get my hands on the dimpled flesh of those thighs. I want to slide a finger into her shorts and feel her wetness. I want to lick her off my own fingers while she watches. I want her on top of me and underneath me and I want her smell all over me.

I want to taste her, eat her, *devour* her.

But I also never want this exact moment to end. I want to live in this innocent pleasure forever, with Sadie making herself feel good against me. Sadie breathing, Sadie blushing, Sadie making eye contact with me as we tug on each other's bodies. I kiss her, because it seems natural that every part of me should be attached to every part of her. We click together like the gears inside a clock, and something in my brain locks into place.

This is why I never should've agreed to this. I don't know how to have sex without feelings, and I don't know how to have *some* feelings without having *all of them*. Without getting lost completely in the other person.

Sadie goes still, her labored breaths quieting against me. "Is . . . is this okay?" she exhales against my neck.

"Yes," I croak. Very, *very* yes.

She cranes her head back to look at me, and I can see in her sky-sea eyes that I've lost her. That she's in her own head, not here with me on this bed, not against me anymore.

I'm not quite ready to lose her. I'm too scared I'll never get her back.

"Sadie," I say, knowing it comes out in a husky growl, betraying exactly how much I need her. "What do you want?"

Sadie

"What do you want?"

I shrink involuntarily from her at this question. What do I *want*?

If I knew the answer to that question, we wouldn't be on this bed fully clothed. I wouldn't be nervously wringing my hands. Mal wouldn't be completely still, holding me in place, as if she knows the smallest movement could send me running.

"I-I don't know what I want," I mutter into the pillow.

"I don't believe you."

I jerk my head up. "What?"

"I don't believe you," Mal repeats. A tiny smile curves the left side of her bowed mouth. "I think you *do* know what you want. I think you're afraid to ask for it."

"That . . . that's not . . ." I shift on the bed and accidentally rub myself against her leg again. And *that*. That is what I want. To feel like *that*.

"This will be our first lesson, then. I want you to practice talking about your pleasure."

"Can we, maybe, not do that instead?"

Mal shakes her head. "If you can't talk about what you want, how will you ever have good sex?"

"I don't need it to be good," I quickly reassure her. "I just need it to be over with."

"Sadie." She says my name in an annoyed growl. "If we are going to have sex, I'm going to make damn sure it's good for you."

The rough edge of her voice rakes across my skin like finger-nails. And holy hells. It turns out that what I really want is for Mal to scold me again in that deep growl.

"Sex is about good communication. You have to be able to tell your partner what you need, and you have to be able to listen to your partner's needs without letting your ego get in the way."

"Okay, let's practice that." I jump in. "Why don't you tell me what you want?"

Her mouth curls into another smile. "Nice try. This is about your pleasure. What gets you hot?"

That disappointed tone of yours, it would seem. *The way you lean against random shit.*

Mal's glistening calves and her staggering widow's peak. Her tattoos and her mouth. Her spontaneity, her sense of adventure. She's like no one else I've ever known, and I'm someone new when I'm with her.

But I could never *tell* her that.

"I-I can't do this."

Mal is perfectly calm as she asks, "What did you think about when you masturbated in the bathtub earlier?"

"You," I answer without thinking, without filter, without considering the consequences of that confession.

Her flawless calm shatters. "*Me?* Really?"

She's unnerved, and it turns out that gets me hot too. Knowing I have the power to shatter her façade of cool. So, I answer honestly again. "Yes, really. You."

She clears her throat. "Oh, um, I . . ." Now Mal shifts nervously on the bed, and if I'm not mistaken, she's—

"Shit, are you *blushing*?"

"No." She puts a hand to her pinkening cheek. "I just got hot earlier when you were dry humping my leg."

I start blushing too, but I don't feel so embarrassed about it.

"What was I doing in this masturbatory fantasy of yours?" Mal asks with a cocky head tilt against the pillow.

"I-I don't know."

"Yes, you do," Mal growls impatiently. "Tell me."

I'm pretty sure I'd jump off a cliff if she told me to do it in that voice. "You were touching me everywhere," I mumble. "With your hands . . . and . . . and with your mouth."

Her jaw twitches, but she says nothing.

"And I was touching you," I add quietly.

"Where?" she demands to know.

I close my eyes. This is the most embarrassing thing I've ever done, but I can't stop now, not when I need her to keep using that voice. "Your breasts," I admit.

She abruptly glances down at her chest, then back up at me. "My *breasts*?"

"Yes, Ms. Never-Wears-a-Bra."

"I don't wear a bra because I don't need to." She grabs at the absence of boobs in demonstration. "I'm flat-chested."

"Yes, but with the showiest nipples I've ever seen."

"My nipples are showy? What does that even mean?" She rubs her fingers over the ridge of her nipples under her tank top on the bed next to me. Any teasing dies in the back of my throat as I watch her touch herself. She catches me watching, and she must see something in my face that prompts her next command. "Tell me what you want."

I want too much. "I want— I want you to take your shirt off."

Without another word, Mal pushes herself up to her knees and pulls off the tank, ruffling her mullet in the process. On instinct, I turn away, the way I did in every locker room, at that small handful of sleepovers, terrified that someone would catch me staring.

Terrified of what it would mean if I *did* stare.

"Look at me, Sadie," Mal orders in that motherfucking growl.

And I do, taking in the knife's edge of her clavicle, the compass tattoo on her sternum, the snaking vines across her taut stomach, and the hint of hip bones above the waistband of her shorts. I study her ropey muscles and her sun-kissed skin and, finally, her breasts. Like two small teardrops on her chest. Her areolas take up most of the real estate, and they're more of a wine color than the dark brown of my imagination, but her nipples are even darker, even larger, swollen pebbles that make me woozy.

I lose track of time, of all sense of modesty and shame, staring at the realness of her.

"Sadie."

The sound of my name pulls my focus back up to her face, where she's watching me as I watch her, discovering every beautiful mystery she's divulged to me.

"What do you want?" she demands.

"I want . . . I want to touch you."

"Then do it."

When I don't move my tingling limbs, she takes my hand in hers and gently presses it to her chest, right over the compass tattoo. She guides my hand across her rib cage, over her breasts, down her stomach. Then her hand falls away, leaving me to chart my own course.

Time ceases to exist once more as I trace one finger around the knot of her hip bone. She shivers, and I move my hand up the subtle curve of her waist, up toward those lovely nipples.

When my fingertips touch the edge of her left breast, Mal inhales sharply, but she's otherwise motionless, allowing my hand to explore at its own pace. Slowly, I crawl the pads of my fingers across the underside of her breast, then up to those red-wine areolas, ghosting over the goose bumps around her nipple. When I take her skin between two fingers, Mal arches into my touch. The restless buzz is between my legs again, the horrible, wonderful need for relief. I rock my hips against her, desperate for pressure or friction or anything.

"All you have to do is ask," she says, barely above a whisper.

"Kiss me?"

"Where?" she asks, but I'm already reaching for her and pulling her on top of me until her mouth crashes into mine.

Pleasure sears across my lips, sweeps down my whole body in a fiery current. She straddles me, kisses me messily, like she's as overcome by feeling as I am. Her knees are on either side of my hips, and I run my hands up her thighs. I grasp her hips and yank her even closer, trying to rub myself against her like I did before, and I'm rewarded with a wordless growl. Each point of contact between our bodies feels like a shock of electricity.

Mal smothers me with her weight. She's over me, on top of me, her growling voice is in my ear. "Tell me where you want my mouth."

"I want it on my . . . wrist." The word slips out in a frenzy of feeling, and I cringe. *My wrist?* I'm drunk on her red-wine nipples. That's the only possible explanation for why I said *my wrist*.

Mal sits up. The sharp points of her ass dig into my stomach as she reaches for my hand. She lifts it to her mouth and tenderly kisses my wrist bone, just below our matching tattoo.

I laugh underneath her, and our bodies vibrate together from the sound. "Why am I so awful at this?"

"I'm into it, actually." Mal turns my arm so that the delicate skin on the inside of my wrist is facing her mouth. And then she licks slowly, like my skin is pistachio ice cream. "Wrist play is totally hot."

I laugh again. Is there usually this much laughter in sex, or am I doing something horribly wrong?

Another cocky head tilt. "Do you want to see what I can do with my wrist?"

I stop laughing. I very much do.

Her right hand finds the swell of my lower stomach, and we're back to electric touches. "You're so soft and smooth," she murmurs admiringly as her hand inches toward the waistband of my pajama shorts, then lower, fingers stroking the outside of my underwear. I clamp down on my jaw to stop any mortifying sounds from escaping.

She lifts her hips up off me so her two fingers rub against my clit through the fabric. It's pressure and friction and *everything*.

I close my eyes, tilt my head back against the mattress, and try to return to that place where shame and modesty don't exist. I try to let my body experience whatever pleasure it wants as she moves in agonizingly soft, slow circles. And just when I think I might lose my mind, she drives her hips down to increase the pressure against me. I curse. I maybe lose consciousness. It's hard to know for sure.

"How do you want me to touch you?"

"Huh urm lerf." That's as close as I can get to words as Mal draws those maddening circles against my body. She moves her hand beneath the fabric, so there's finally nothing between her skin and my skin, and I feel like I'll die before her hot fingers graze my bare clit.

Then they do, and I wince.

"Oh, shit. Sorry." Mal pulls her hand away for a minute. "I don't have any lube."

"It's fine."

"It's not fine," Mal scolds. She sticks her index and middle finger into her mouth, and sucks, and I definitely lose consciousness this time. When she pulls her fingers out of her mouth, they're slick with saliva. She finds her way back between my legs, and this time, her fingers glide smoothly over my clit.

It's five hundred times better than any time I've touched myself. Mal's fingers are like a confident instrument tuned to my body, responding to my every gasp, my every curse, reading me so perfectly. She's over me, on me, rocking against me as her strokes get harder, then softer, then faster.

I'm dizzy. I'm delighted. I think I'm laughing again. "God diggity damn," I moan, and Mal shifts her hand lower, and— "Oh, ouch!" I screech.

Mal's hand freezes in place. "What? Are you okay?"

"Sorry!" I blurt, and then I attempt to cover my face with the pillow.

"No sorrys during sex!" Mal pulls her hand away from my body and moves the pillow out of my face. "Did I hurt you?"

"No," I lie.

She climbs off me, and I'm overwhelmed by a growing sense of dread that I've ruined everything. This perfect moment. All those perfect feelings.

"Sadie. Talk to me." Her voice is a gentle plea, not a growl, and shit, I think I'm crying.

"Sadie." She grabs my hand and raises it to her lips again. Her mouth is also a gentle plea against my wrist bone. "Are you okay?"

"I'm so humiliated."

Mal laughs lightly. "Do you know how many times I've accidentally farted while being eaten out? *This*—whatever this is—is not humiliating." Her teeth playfully bite my wrist bone. "Look at me."

When I refuse, she grabs the pillow and yanks it away entirely, so I have no choice but to face her. Face *this*. "What happened, Freckles?"

"It, uh, hurt a little when you, uh . . ."

"When I fingered you?" she asks bluntly.

I fight to get the pillow back, but she's holding my hands captive. "I'm so, so sorry."

"No, *I'm* sorry," she says, giving my hands a gentle squeeze. "I should have asked before moving inside of you."

Her directness makes me want to *die.* "Can I please just cover my face?"

She holds tighter to my hands. "You cannot. Why are you embarrassed right now?"

"Because I ruined the sex lesson!"

"We were practicing how you communicate your needs around sex, and I think you were doing a damn good job at that."

I sit up so I'm facing Mal in all of her half-naked glory. "Yeah, but I couldn't even go through with the actual sex part."

Mal makes a giant fart noise.

"Okay. Rude."

"Do you really think it's only sex if I penetrate you?"

"I don't *love* that word, but, uh, yes?"

"Sadie, Sadie, misguided lady," Mal sings. "We *were* having sex. At least, it was sex to me. Before I went and messed it with the P-word."

I *almost* laugh.

"Nothing is ruined, Freckles."

Mal is still holding me by both wrists. She can clearly see the stress hives on my fingers. She must feel the way my hands shake nervously. And still, she doesn't let go.

"What do you want?" she asks me.

What I want is to go back to five minutes ago, when I was writhing under the delicious pressure of her fingers. I want to return to that unselfconscious state where I was cursing and moaning and letting myself feel. But as much as I want to get back to that guilt-free pleasure, I can't.

Mal must sense the shattered moment, because she lifts my wrist again and presses it to her lips. "I love your little blush splotches," she says, caressing the ugly red marks on the inside of my arm.

"Those are hives."

"Mmm." She kisses a chain of hives one by one, all the way up to my elbow. "I love your hives, then."

"That's quite gross," I say. What I really mean is, *that's quite sweet.*

She kisses my arm, and then my collarbone, and then my throat, and then my cheek, chasing the places my anxiety has conquered. Then she kisses my mouth in this gentle, unhurried way that loosens something inside me.

"You know what I want?" Mal asks my collarbone. "I want to see if Drew and Jonathan put shiplap in the Ramos's living room."

The last of my shame seeps out of me. "Well, it's not 2018, so they won't."

"Let's find out." She reaches for my phone on the nightstand and cues up *Property Brothers*. Then, she gets my snacks from the forgotten grocery bag, and I discover I'm starving as soon as I take a bite of granola bar. Mal doesn't put her shirt back on, and I eat in bed while Jonathan swings his sledgehammer, taking down yet another load-bearing wall.

"Asbestos?" Mal gasps on the bed next to me. "Wow, I did not see that one coming."

TWENTY-ONE

BAIONA, SPAIN
Tuesday, May 20, 2025

Sadie

It's not a banging that wakes me up this time, but a buzzing. I scramble through the sheets, trying to locate my phone, and my hands collide with something solid and not at all phone-like.

It's Mal. We fell asleep in the pushed-together beds, watching episodes of *Forever Home*, and when I peel open my eyes, I see that she's still topless, lying on her back with her legs spread wide like a beautiful corpse. Her jaw looks unhinged, and her pillow is wet from her sleep drool, and I can't believe this imperfectly perfect woman touched every inch of me last night.

I watch her almost imperceptible breaths, and then I remember my buzzing phone.

When I finally find it on the nightstand, it's my sister's face on the screen. I slink out of bed as quietly as I can.

"Hello?" I whisper into the phone once the bathroom door is closed behind me.

"Sadie!" Vi shouts, and I hold the phone a safe distance from my ear. "What the hell?"

That seems like my line. I hunker down on the closed toilet and wait to see why she's calling me at five thirty in the morning.

Vi cries out. "I thought you were dead! You've been dodging my calls for days!"

I have not been dodging her calls. I didn't answer *one* phone call, because I was in the bathtub.

"I'm fine," I grumble, half-asleep.

"If you're fine, then why haven't you posted in two days?"

Ah. That's the real reason for her call. She's not worried about *me*. She's worried about her *brand*.

I haven't posted to Instagram or her blog since Vila Praia de Âncora, since the night I kissed Mal on the beach. Guilt and anxiety braid themselves through my body. "I'm so, so sorry Vi. I got really busy."

"Busy?" My sister screeches. "Doing *what*?"

"Um, well, this is a trek, so I've been walking a dozen miles every day."

"You knew that going into this," she snaps.

I want to argue, but I swallow the words. "You're right, you're right. I'm sorry."

And I hate that I'm apologizing to her, especially over this. I've walked nearly a hundred miles with all my belongings strapped to my back; I've endured shin splints and back pain, and I've still kept going. I've learned how to care for my blisters and how to order coffee and how to live in the goddamn moment, no thanks to her. I'm learning how to be okay with not knowing, okay with discovering, okay with asking for what I want. Kind of. Almost.

And still, in the face of my sister's displeasure, I apologize.

My need to please her, to care for her, eclipses everything else.

"I'll make sure to get caught up on posts today."

Vi huffs petulantly in the way only a younger sister can. "What's going on with you?"

"What do you mean?"

"You've worked twelve-hour days your whole life, and all of a sudden, you can't juggle a few fluffy Instagram posts with a leisurely walk?"

We walked nineteen miles yesterday, and we'll walk sixteen today, but I don't tell her this.

"You're being cagey," Vi presses, and I almost tell her everything else instead: everything about Mal and my sexual identity crisis and the queer adolescence. I almost tell her about the kiss on the beach, and I almost tell her what it felt like to be touched last night.

Vi is bisexual, and I know she'd understand, that she'd be supportive. But for some reason, the idea of saying any of it to her feels as impossible as being honest about the trek. "I-I've just been . . . spending time with people on the tour, and, um, you know . . . socializing and stuff."

"Holy shit!" Vi gasps. "Was Mom right? Did you actually meet a guy?"

And here she is, handing me the perfect opportunity. All I have to do is tell her the truth. "Uh, yes, actually . . . sort of . . ." I sputter. "I . . . I met a . . . a guy."

I drop my head into my free hand as Vi squeals on the other end. "Fuck yes you did! Is he Spanish?"

"Portuguese," I say hollowly. At least *that* is true.

"Hot damn! Tell me *everything*! What's his name? How did you meet him?"

"His name is Mal . . . colm. Malcolm," I lie, and the horrible thing is, I'm *enjoying* this. After years of my sister grilling me about my love life, I finally have something to share. Something that will earn her approval. "And he's on the tour."

"Wait, he's on the *queer* tour?"

"Yep. He's . . . he's bisexual."

"Hot," my sister says, and it sounds like the verbal equivalent of a fist bump. "But isn't the tour only for queer women?"

My mouth keeps moving separately from my brain's will. "There was a mistake with his registration, and Inez let him stay. It was a whole thing. It's not important."

Vi whistles. "You're all flustered!"

"It's . . . it's a casual thing."

"Don't bullshit me," Vi snaps. "I can hear it in your voice. You're, like, in love with him."

"It's been nine days, Vi. I'm not in love. That would be ridiculous."

"The heart wants what it wants," my sister trills, and I feel even worse for lying about what I *really* want. "And you want this guy *bad*. I can just tell."

"It's just sex, okay?" I blurt. "It isn't serious. It has to end when we get to Santiago."

Vi tuts into the phone. "I can't picture you having a casual sex arrangement with someone."

"Yeah, well, you don't know everything about me," I tell her. And then, for the first time in my life, I hang up on my sister.

Around the third mile of our journey to Vigo, I realize how desperately I need a rest day. I haven't had a full night's sleep since Esposende, and that was eighty miles ago. Even though I haven't touched alcohol since our night out in Vila Praia de Âncora, I still feel hungover.

It's a bone-deep exhaustion that makes every step forward a struggle, and I get the impression I'm not alone in feeling this way. Vera falls farther behind than usual, and she's not even taking photos of the Spanish coast. Ari lingers behind with her, sitting down on every bench we pass. Rebecca asks for a bathroom after every mile, and I suspect it's just so she can have a break. By the halfway point, Ro's crankiness reaches new heights as they beg Inez to let them take a taxi to our lodgings in Vigo. Even Mal has lost some of the spring in her step. She stays by my side all morning, content to go slower with me.

We haven't talked about last night, but it doesn't feel weird like it did the morning after our first kiss. Instead, the quiet feels charged with our shared secret. I catch her staring at me, and we both smile. When Inez has her back to us, Mal briefly holds my hand. When no one else is watching we kiss in a bathroom stall, in the line for coffee, in front of a sculpture of a rainbow whale made from recycled plastics.

I don't know what we're practicing with these secret kisses, but with each one, I learn a little bit more about what it feels like when I want someone. The way my heart strains in my chest, the way her scent fills my lungs, the way her touch makes me feel at home in my body in a way I've never experienced before. And those goddamn *butterflies*.

So, I take whatever secret kisses I can get, and the rest of the time, I enjoy her unwavering presence by my side.

Only Stefano seems unaffected by the relentless pace, and by lunchtime, three people have taken him up on his offer to carry their bags. He's got a pack affixed to each side of him, and he looks like a bellhop in backpacker hell.

"Rest is critical," Inez tells us at lunch. "We are pushing ourselves physically, mentally, and spiritually on the Camino, and we all must nourish our bodies with rest."

No one says anything, but at least half the table groans.

"For the next two nights, we'll be completing a homestay experience outside of Vigo, and during that time, I want each of us to reflect on what refills our cups."

"Wine, usually," Ro deadpans, and everyone but Inez laughs.

She purses her lips and shoots Mal a strange sideways glance. "Funny you should say that, given where we will be staying."

We aren't staying in the city limits of Vigo, Spain. Shortly after lunch, we turn off the Camino and walk along a two-lane highway for a few miles. We move away from the coast and head inland toward open fields and countryside.

Eventually, Inez leads us away from the highway and up a winding dirt road.

"Where, exactly, are we staying for the rest days?" Mal asks from beside me as we twist around another bend in the road, and there's a sharp edge to her voice I haven't heard before.

"You'll see shortly," Inez answers.

"No, seriously," Mal bites out. "Where the fuck are we going?"

Ro glares back at Mal. "Whoa. Relax."

The road winds past terraces of grapes, and Mal curses under her breath with every step. I can't figure out how she's miserable over a rest day in this picturesque place.

The dirt road curves one more time, and as the group crests a hill, a black gate comes into view, stamped with the monogrammed initials CQ in gold filigree.

Behind the gate, we glimpse a mansion on a lush green hill overlooking the property.

"You've got to be fucking kidding me!" Mal shouts as Inez presses an intercom button beside the gate.

"Are you okay?" I whisper to Mal, but it's drowned out by Vera asking, "Wait, are we staying at a Quinta Costa vineyard?"

"I'm going to kill her," Mal grumbles, and I'm not even sure which *her* she's referring to. I reach out to put a hand on her elbow to calm her, but she's still poised like a spring about to explode.

The intercom buzzes, and the gate opens in a grandiose arch. "I'm sorry, Mal," Inez says in a low voice. She rattles off a few rapid sentences in Portuguese, but they don't change Mal's dark expression.

Inez shifts her focus back to the group. "Quinta Costa is the largest producer of Portuguese and Spanish wines, with twelve wineries spread out across the Iberian Peninsula."

We follow Inez up the path toward the house as she continues. "Several of the vineyards offer overnight stays where guests can learn more about the wine-making process, especially during the wine harvest in September or October. They're also supportive of local businesses like Beatrix Tours, offering us free overnight stays for our rest days."

"Bullshit," Mal erupts.

"Dude, what's your deal?" Ari glares at Mal. "You're kind of being an ass right now."

"*Oh*," Vera says, snapping her fingers together in triumphant understanding. "Oh, of course! *That* is where I know you from!"

"Do we get to drink free wine?" Rebecca wants to know.

The overlapping conversations come to a halt as an older woman comes down the path toward us. "Buen Camino!" she greets with a warm smile. Her silver hair is styled in an elegant bob, and she's wearing a white linen pantsuit, tempting fate with the dusty fields all around us. "Welcome, pilgrims! Welcome to Quinta Costa! I'm Luzia Ferreira, and I'm the manager of the Vigo vineyard you see before you. I will be taking care of you during your time with us."

Mal pulls down the brim of her trucker hat and positions herself behind me as the woman offers Inez twin air-kisses. A flock of porters appear to take our packs inside, and Stefano comically hands off all four of his before Luzia guides the group through a manicured garden up to the house. It's a Spanish-style villa with a wraparound veranda, wide porticos, an expansive courtyard with a tiled fountain, terra-cotta and adobe everywhere.

We're ushered into an expansive foyer, and I'm overwhelmed by architectural details. The floor is Italian marble, the chandelier looks like Tiffany glass, and each piece of furniture, from the ornate mahogany end tables to the art deco statues, are perfectly curated, working harmoniously in the space. Nan would've absolutely lost her mind to see this place.

"Through this archway here is the dining room where your communal meals will be served during your stay. Come."

Luzia urges us along with a soft wave, and we find a dining room the size of a football field, where trays of tapas are spread out. A server offers us complimentary glasses of white wine from stainless steel chilling buckets, and everyone tucks in enthusiastically.

Except Mal, who is still hiding behind me.

"What are you doing?" I turn around to face her, but she bobs and weaves, trying to stay firmly concealed behind me. But all her darting only results in her backpack—which she stubbornly refused to surrender—bumping into an antique bar cart. A crystal decanter rattles, then firmly falls onto the marble floor, shattering. The antique dealer in me knows the decanter was worth at least two thousand dollars, and now it's destroyed.

I gasp, and Mal curses, and then the room goes painfully silent. Luzia cuts off in the middle of a speech about the grapes used for the Vinho Verde, and her gaze homes in on the two of us, where we miserably hover over the mess we made. Her tone is clipped. "What happ—" She starts, before cutting off abruptly. "Maëlys?"

Mal adjusts her trucker hat over her face. "I will replace that," she says in an American accent. And truly, what the fuck is going on with her?

"Maëlys," Luzia says again, moving closer to us. The group quietly parts to let her through, and then she's standing directly in front of Mal, and she doesn't look furious at all. "Maëlys Calista Gonçalves Costa?"

In a huff, Mal pulls the trucker hat off her head. "Ola, Luzia," she grumbles.

And then prim and elegant Luzia collapses into a puddle of tears in the middle of this dining room. "Maëlys! Menina!" Luzia kisses Mal's cheeks at least a dozen times before pulling her into a full body hug.

Vera hoots. "I knew it!"

"It has been far too long, my sweet girl! Let me look at you." Luzia holds Mal by her shoulders and studies her at an arm's length. "*Gira filha.* You look so much like him. Oh, how I've missed you!"

Luzia pulls Mal into another massive hug while my brain scrambles to understand why this woman referred to Mal as her *sweet girl.*

"I will pay for the decanter," Mal repeats as she pats Luzia on the back.

"I don't care about that hideous decanter." Luzia smiles through her tears. "My girl, I am so very happy to see you."

Ari speaks for everyone, like she always does, when she asks, "What. The. Fuck?"

But the fuck of it all is starting to come together in my mind. Mal said her grandfather started a successful Portuguese company; the father she hates so much took it over; and Mal, who hasn't been to Portugal in years, wanted nothing to do with it. All trip, we've been sharing bottles of Quinta Costa wine, and Mal has ordered cheap beer instead.

All trip, she's been vague and elusive about her past, her family, her reasons for being here, and now this strange woman is greeting her like a long-lost daughter.

Because she is. Mal is a Costa. And these marble floors and expensive chandeliers and the shattered pieces of crystal all belong to her.

Mal

We're staying at one of my father's vineyards.

One of *my* vineyards.

Fucking Inez.

Luzia's arms tighten around me, and even though it's only a hug, I feel like she's squeezing my ribs into my lungs, pushing my lungs into my heart, rearranging all my internal organs. I can hardly breathe.

I don't know where to look.

Not at Luzia, who is holding me like I'm the physical manifestation of all her hopes and dreams for the company. Not at Vera, who recognized me all along and finally put it together when she saw me here; and not at Ari, whose expression reflects everyone else's confusion. I can't look at the jagged pieces of my father's favorite Baccarat whiskey decanter, and I definitely can't look at Sadie.

Sadie, who is staring at me like she doesn't even recognize who I am.

I want to tell her everything and nothing at the same time. I want to go back to last night, when she writhed under my touch in bed, and I didn't have to think about wine or inheritances or dead dads.

"You finally came home," Luzia whispers into my ear, and I close my eyes. I want to blot out her face, and Sadie's face, and every aspect of this house, every memory contained within these walls.

The memories and the walls both feel like they're closing in around me.

Those summer trips with my father, coming to this house, walking those rows of grapes while he tested my knowledge of ripeness, acidity, flavor palates. Ten years old, and my father making me taste-test casks until I could accurately identify the correct floral or berry notes, spitting into the spittoon until it was entirely full with red wine; my father leaving me with his staff, with Luzia, while he disappeared for days at a time with whichever European heiress or minor celebrity had his attention at the moment.

But I have good memories of this place too: raiding the kitchen pantry for Bueno bars with him in our matching monogrammed robes; playing chess on the balcony of his private rooms; my father's laugh, his big arms, and the way he would lift me up to show me the property. "This will all be yours, Maëlys," he would say, and he would sound so damn proud of me.

And now it *is* all mine.

"This . . . this is your vineyard?" Sadie asks, and her voice brings me back, grounds me in the present. I unravel from Luzia's hug and look at Sadie's confused face.

"It's complicated," I manage.

"Valentim Costa was your dad?" Vera asks, but the words are slurred by the panicked buzzing in my ears.

"Uh, yes. Sort of."

"How is someone *sort of* your dad?" Ro demands.

"Valentim Costa?" Stefano echoes. "Wasn't he quite handsome?"

"I don't know," I grumble. "I didn't spend a lot of time considering my father's attractiveness."

"He was very handsome," Vera clarifies.

Ari swivels back to me. "This man, your father . . . he's *famous?*"

My mouth can't wrap itself around an answer. "Oh yeah," Vera says. "The Costas are, like, the wealthiest family in Portugal."

"The Silvas are the wealthiest family in Portugal, actually," Luzia corrects, and I can feel everyone's eyes on me. I can tell they're looking at me differently. I'm no longer Mal to them; I'll never be Mal again. I'm Maëlys Calista Gonçalves Costa.

My shirt is choking me, and it's impossibly hot and stuffy in this formal dining room, and I feel like the decanter, like I'm breaking into a million pieces.

"Perhaps we could get everyone off to their rooms," Inez suggests, and I can breathe a little better as everyone looks away, moves away.

Luzia and Inez pass out brass keys to the rest of the tour group, with directions on how to find their rooms on the third floor. One of the keys goes to Sadie, and then Luzia turns to me. "I'll have Felipe set up your old room," she says. She hugs me one more time. "Welcome home, menina."

Nothing about this place feels like home.

"How could you do this to me?"

My shouts echo off the high ceilings and too-big room, the way my father's shouts always used to. Even that comparison doesn't quell my anger.

"Funnily enough, this isn't actually about you," Inez shouts back. "This was the plan before you signed up to join the tour at the last minute. I just didn't know how to tell you!"

"Why was this part of the tour at all? Why do your tours involve staying here?"

She clasps her hands together beneath her chin. "Luzia reached out to me a few years back, asking about a partnership with Beatrix to bring more American tourists through Quinta Costa. They were in the midst of a distribution deal in North America, and—"

"And you sold out? You agreed to work with the man who rejected me for being gay?"

She shakes her head. "No, I agreed to work with a company that wanted to support a trans-owned business."

"Well, congratulations," I spit. "I'm sure he was only using you as a pawn to make the company appear more progressive. You were just someone he could parade around during Pride month."

All the radiant light in Inez's face dies out, and the guilt feels like a corkscrew to my heart. "That was a shitty thing to say," she tells me in a flat voice.

And I know it was. "Fuck. I'm sorry. I didn't—"

"It's okay. You're grieving. I know you didn't mean that." Inez exhales and carefully lowers herself down onto one of my father's many couches, which are meant for looking, not actual sitting. A couch could never just be a couch; it had to be a statement piece, a conversation starter at dinner parties, a minefield for a perpetually messy little girl.

My lip quivers with impending tears, and I bite down. "I wish you'd told me about this."

"If I had," Inez says quietly, "you wouldn't have come."

"Yes, exactly."

She stares up at me from her awkward perch. "You needed to come here, Mal."

I did. But that wasn't Inez's call to make.

My old room has been preserved like a terrifying monument to my preteen self. In every one of my father's houses, I was given a space that was solely mine, and it was often the only room that didn't look like the display floor at a Sotheby's. Valentim always gave me full creative freedom with the design and décor of my bedroom, so each one was like a time capsule revealing who I was when he bought the house.

He acquired this house and this vineyard in 1999, which means I'm staring at a reminder of my wannabe emo-punk-rocker phase, with dark purple walls and black curtains contrasting the four different caboodles full of Wet N Wild makeup. It's a toss-up between what's worse: the giant poster of Limp Bizkit's album *Significant Other*, or the fact that it hangs over the dresser where I lined up all my Beanie Babies.

It's a stale, airless mausoleum, and I push through the French doors out onto the balcony to catch my breath.

The view highlights the elegant terraces of grapes that stretch for kilometers in every direction, and all it does is remind me that this house and those grapes and the wine they'll one day produce are all mine.

But I don't want it. I hated the summers I spent at my father's different vineyards. I hate the smell of fermentation, the stain of grapes under my fingernails, the taste of the thing my father would always love more than me. I hated it, and he *knew* I hated it, so why did the bastard leave it all to me?

I can hear a knock on the door from out on the balcony, and I turn, expecting to find Felipe or Luzia or even Inez. "Come in," I holler over my shoulder.

"Mal?" a voice hedges, and it's not any of them.

I turn to see Sadie standing on the other side of the French doors. Her short red hair is wet and clinging to the side of her neck, and relief pours through me at the sight of her here. I stumble across the balcony and directly into her soft arms. As she holds me gently, my insides shatter all over again, and I start to properly cry for the first time all trip. Hell, for the first time since I got the news about my father.

I fucking hate crying. My chest gets hot, and my face gets sticky, and every breath feels like fire in my lungs. The headache comes instantly, followed by a wave of nausea, but I can't seem to stop the tears. And there's just so much snot.

"Mal." Sadie coos my name and strokes my hair until I finally pull away, rubbing my hands across my face until I can see again. I'm arrested by the sight of Sadie's face in the afternoon light on the balcony. Even though we've shared a hotel room all week, she rarely lets me see her like this, scrubbed clean and makeup free. And holy shit—those goddamn freckles. There are more of them than I thought, millions of them, perhaps from all our time spent in the sun. Dark freckles and light freckles and freckles the exact color of her hair. Big freckles and tiny freckles and clusters of freckles that all swirl into one thing, like an entire galaxy contained on her cheeks.

"Freckles." I exhale the word, and I'm not sure if I'm calling her Freckles or expressing the sheer enormity of them. "I'm so sorry."

Sadie is still sliding her fingers through my hair. "Sorry for what?"

For so fucking much. "I'm sorry I didn't tell you. About Quinta Costa, or about who I am, or about my dad dying."

Her hand falls away. "Your dad died?"

Oh shit. I still hadn't told her about that. "You . . . you didn't notice all the funeral wreaths downstairs?"

It's obvious she did not. "When did he die?"

"Um, I don't know, like . . ." I do the calculations in my head. "Thirteen days ago?"

"Mal!" Sadie gasps. "What the fuck?"

"I think the correct response is *I'm sorry for your loss.*"

"Why would I say that when you don't seem sorry for your loss?" Her observation feels like an oyster knife, cracking my shell wide open, cutting to the core of me, the part I never want anyone else to see. It feels like there is nothing left to hide behind, and no reason to try to hide at all.

"I'm not sorry for my loss," I tell her honestly. "Because I lost my dad a long time ago."

And then I tell her everything else. It's as if I can't hold it in anymore, as if releasing the tears opened some kind of dam inside my heart. It all comes spilling out. About my complicated relationship with my father as a kid—about the good memories, and the bad ones, and all the ones in between that still hurt after all these years. I tell her about falling in love with my roommate at boarding school, about wanting to share my love with my father. And I tell her about the day he told me I couldn't be both gay and his daughter. The day I left. The day he *let* me leave.

We sit across from each other on my childhood bed with its black sheets and Hello Kitty blanket, and Sadie holds my hands in hers and listens to all of it. She makes the occasional sound of sympathy or outrage, and sometimes, she squeezes my hands tighter, like she's reminding me that she's still here, but she never interrupts. She doesn't ask me to explain anything, and I find myself explaining everything.

It doesn't hurt the way I always thought it would, unburdening all of this to another person. Putting the feelings into words doesn't intensify them; it takes some of their power away. *Sadie* takes some of their power. She takes my complex grief, the years of sadness and shame and loss, and she holds them all like she's holding my hands.

Maybe it's because Sadie has experienced complex grief, or maybe it's because she's good friends with her own sadness and shame, or maybe it's because she knows what it's like to inherit something she never wanted, but Sadie is able to hold all of it, all of me, in a way I thought only Michelle ever could.

"Can I ask . . . ?" Sadie starts when I finally finish. "Whatever happened with Prithi?"

"Prithi." I exhale her name. It still holds some power. "She . . . after I left my dad's that day, I went back to Scotland for her. I told her I wasn't going to Oxford anymore, since I was never taking over the business, and I asked her to come with me. I wanted to take a gap year together to figure it all out. I . . . I wanted her to run away with me, basically. And she . . ." I huff a laugh.

Sadie gives my hands another squeeze. "I'm guessing that didn't happen?"

"Worse. She told me I should go back to my dad and grovel for his forgiveness. She told me to go back into the closet. To go to Oxford and to do whatever else my father wanted. She . . . she made it very clear that she wasn't interested in me if I wasn't the heir to Quinta Costa."

This final confession festers between us for a moment until Sadie makes a grave pronouncement. "You have deplorable taste in women."

I laugh fully, and it loosens something stale and airless inside me. "Hey, I'm currently having sex with you, so . . ."

"That doesn't help your case. I'm a mess. Having sex with me is a horrible mistake."

"Yeah, but I think you might be my favorite mistake so far."

We sit on the bed in the aftermath of that confession. Of all my confessions.

Eventually, Sadie lets go of my hands. "We need to talk about the last remaining elephant in the room." She reaches over to my dresser and picks up my elephant Beanie Baby. "What happened here?"

I snatch him out of her hands. "That's Peanut, and he does not appreciate your mockery."

"You must've missed him terribly these past twenty years."

"He promised to write." I hold up Peanut and force him to wave at her with one hoof. "Oh, the nights I wasted sitting by the window, waiting for his letters."

"This room is . . ." She scans the walls, and I want to gouge her eyes out before she notices all my Red Hot Chili Peppers CDs. The *humiliation*. "It's a little bit creepy," Sadie decides.

"It's a lot creepy."

"Based on everything you said about Valentim, I'm surprised he didn't take all this stuff down. Turn your room into a home gym or something."

I would've assumed the same about my old childhood bedrooms. I never expected to find this one exactly how I left it twenty years ago. "I guess that's what happens when you own multiple mansions. You forget about weird, abandoned rooms like this one."

Sadie climbs off the bed and traces her hand along bottles of black nail polish, my CD player, my collection of cucumber melon body spray. "I love all of it," she declares. My chest swells in an unfamiliar way.

Her eyes are on a jewelry box, her fingers sifting through necklaces I never wore, earrings I tried to lose. "Do you miss any of this stuff? Is there anything you want to take with you?"

Sadie is the only thing in this room I want, but I already know I can't keep her. From the bed, I watch her wander, open drawers without asking, touch things without thinking. I don't stop her. There's nothing left for me to hide.

Except a red, lacy thong I bought when I was thirteen and which I hid from my father in the back of my sock drawer. She pulls the cheap lingerie out and shakes it in my direction. "Ooh la la!" she teases in a horrible French accent. "Did you bring lots of girls to this room?"

"Only one." I intend to sound teasing too, but the words come out in that embarrassing growl from last night. Sadie quiets for a moment, the thong falling to her side.

"Technically," she says, "I brought *myself* here. After forcing Inez to tell me which room is yours under threat of writing a negative review."

"I should've known you had it in you to be devious."

She curtsies.

"You know, there is *one thing* I would like to take from this room." I scoot to the edge of the bed.

"And what's that?" She slinks toward me like she already knows.

"A memory," I say, as she steps between my opened legs. "Of you, in this room." I run a hand from her thigh up along her wide hip, the soft curve of her waist. "A memory of your skin, and your freckles, and those little sounds you make . . ."

Sadie turns to the dresser, picks up Peanut, and then faces his black, beady eyes away from the bed and toward the far wall. I laugh, and she flashes me another devious smile.

"Maybe this time, you could practice taking your shirt off in front of me?" I try. "You know, for sexual confidence reasons."

She squints one eye and taps her chin. "Only if you agree to wear this." She tosses the red thong so it lands on top of my head, and we both laugh.

We laugh as Sadie does a very shy striptease, sliding out of her bra and then using several Beanie Babies to conceal her large, pale breasts.

We continue laughing when we discover that I can no longer fit in my thirteen-year-old underwear, and I loudly curse every unholy thong that walks this earth as I inelegantly kick it off my leg. And then we're both naked in my dimly lit childhood bedroom, and we're not laughing at all when I fill my hands with her flesh, when my lips kiss her firm nipple, and then down, down, over her decadent curves, all the way down to the tangle of red hair between her legs. I crouch before her like a pilgrim before a religious icon, and I fully intend to worship her.

When I lick Sadie for the first time, she gasps and grabs onto my shoulders. Her nails dig into my skin as I tease out all those lovely little sounds. She's extremely sensitive, and I tread carefully with each lick, each suck, each kiss, even though everything about this moment makes it hard for me to hold back. Her earthy smell and the taste of her as she becomes wet; her fingernails and her moans; the way she trembles and heaves and lets me love her body without an ounce of self-consciousness.

I fuck her here, in my childhood bedroom, against a dresser lined with Beanie Babies, but there's nothing funny about it at all. It feels *sacred*.

Sadie comes hard and fast, thrusting herself against my face before she crumples into a boneless pile on the floor beside me. I'm not sure what I'm teaching her as I slide my fingers between her legs and coax out a few more tremors, what we're practicing as she kisses me after each little gasp.

And when I make her come again, tangled up in my black sheets, I don't know how either of us will be able to pretend this is for scientific purposes.

TWENTY-TWO

Sadie

"I get why it's called la petite mort," I tell her as I stare up at her ceiling, spread out like a starfish in her preteen bed, relishing in the body that just allowed me to experience *that*. "You killed me. But, like, in a good way."

Mal sits up in a flurry of black sheets. "I am death, destroyer of worlds and Sadie Wells."

I bark out a laugh.

"La petite mort." Mal turns the words over in her mouth, her tongue visibly curling. The heartbeat between my legs sputters with little aftershocks from nothing more than watching her tongue touch the roof of her mouth. "What's that from?"

"Um . . . the French?"

"I mean, what's its history?"

I try to prop myself up so I can look at her, but my limbs are made of Jell-O, and I sink right back into the pillows. "Are you asking me to recite the Oxford English Dictionary definition for you? Because I learned the term from *Emily in Paris*."

"Little death . . ." There's that tongue again. "I don't think orgasms feel like death. They feel more like . . . a little *life*."

"Ah, well, you know the French."

"*Dramatique*." She finishes in an exaggerated accent.

And Mal's right. It doesn't feel like death. It feels like rebirth. Like *creation*. Naked and completely unashamed while Mal stares at my body, I feel like I'm learning more about myself, becoming more of myself.

I'm learning how to listen to my body, how to trust it. How to be at home in my skin without feeling shame for the things it wants. I'm learning what I want, and what it feels like to get it.

"I need a pickle," I blurt.

Mal looks visibly taken aback. "Excuse me?"

"I'm *starving*." On cue, my stomach gurgles in demonstration. "I want a post-sex pickle."

Mal somehow waggles her black eyebrows independently from her stoic expression. "What would Dr. Freud say about that?" An exaggerated German accent this time.

"He would say not everything is about penises." I sit up in a flourish of mock outrage. "Pickles are crunchy, tangy, juicy . . . the perfect post-sex snack."

"She's an expert now, folks," Mal announces to our audience of Beanie Babies. Then she playfully smacks my thigh. "Come on. Let's go."

She rolls off the bed, and I'm briefly distracted by this new view of her body. The topography of her ass, the place where it meets the curve of her lean thighs as she bends down to grab her discarded underwear. When she covers that ass with her black briefs, I snap back to attention.

"Go where?"

"To find you a sex pickle." She cranes her head to glance at me over her shoulder, and the heartbeat in my chest and the heartbeat between my legs both sputter.

We put on just enough clothing to leave the room, and Mal presses a finger to her mouth to silence me as we creep down the hall. We pass a window, and there's faint sunlight coming through the blinds. I briefly think it's morning, and that we somehow had sex all night long, but my Apple Watch quickly confirms it's 10 p.m.

"Fun fact," Mal says as she tiptoes toward a secret servant's staircase at the back of the house. "The reason it stays light out so late in Spain is because during World War II, Franco wanted to be in the same time zone as his buddy Hitler, even if it meant having wacky daylight hours, and the country has been in the 'wrong' time zone ever since."

"There is nothing fun about that fact."

Once we're downstairs, we can hear the overlapping voices of Ari and Vera, Stefano and Inez, floating from the dining room. The rest of the tour group is still eating dinner, but Mal has no intention of letting them see us. We skirt around back hallways until we arrive at a huge, restaurant-style kitchen with bespoke appliances: four ovens, twelve gas stovetop burners, an entire wall of refrigerators. "That's the biggest fucking kitchen island I've ever seen."

"The Greenland of kitchen islands," Mal says, running a hand along a butcher's block the size of a Buick. "Drew and Jonathan could never."

Mal walks toward a pantry with purpose, and I can almost picture childhood Mal coming here in the summer, sneaking out of her room for a late-night snack. She flings open the cupboard door, and I expect to find a few shelves with dry goods. Instead, the cupboard doors disguise an arched walkway that leads into a separate pantry *room* at least a thousand square feet in size.

"What in the Property Brothers," I grumble as she leads me to a room with shelves up to the ceiling. It's like shopping at a Supermercado Froiz, and Mal grabs two cans of Fanta Limón, a bag of Sabor a Jamón Ruffles, and several Kinder Bueno bars.

"Are we allowed to just take this stuff?" I whisper, even though I'm pretty sure this pantry is soundproof and could easily double as a bomb shelter. Or a murder room.

"Technically, since my dad died, these Bueno bars now belong to me." She tosses me a Fanta, and I fumble to catch it. Even after everything she shared with me—even after letting me hold her while she cried—she still sounds so flippant about her father's death. When we finally arrive at the section of the pantry housing jarred food, the only pickles we find are half the size of my beloved dills and floating in a jar with olives, peppers, and jalapeños.

"Should we try them?" Mal asks, posing like the woman on the front of the Kanna jar. So, we take them back upstairs with the rest of our treasures. The pickles are spicy as hell, but the chips are better than anything "ham" flavored has the right to be. We sit on the rumpled bed sharing the snacks and watching *Forever Home* on the fanciest television 2005 had to offer.

"My dad was usually busy with work or with his latest lady friend," she tells me. "So whenever we were at the vineyard in Porto, I would get up in the morning and walk into town to go to the library. I would return my stack of books and check out new ones, and then I'd buy a bag of Ruffles to eat on the way back. You should try the Ketchup flavor. It sounds like it shouldn't work, but it really does."

"You went to the library *every day*?"

Mal nods as she takes a giant bite of Bueno bar. "Yeah, my summers were usually lonely. I could easily get through two or three books a day. I think that's part of why I love to travel. Books taught me the beauty of escaping to other worlds."

"I'm sorry," I say, because I'm not sure how else to respond to the heartbreaking image Mal has painted for me. But *sorry* obviously isn't right, because Mal's expression switches from open and unguarded back to her cool-girl façade.

"Don't be sorry for the sad little rich girl."

A new silence chomps at the previous easiness between us. It's dark outside now, and for some reason, all my self-consciousness comes flooding in with the night.

An hour ago, in this bed, I felt so comfortable with Mal that I was able to let go, to feel, to scream obscenities with abandon. To orgasm with another person for the first time in my life.

But now that we're dressed again, that vulnerability feels tenuous.

Mal has given me *so much* of herself, and it feels like at any moment she could take it all away again. I can either let her pull away or . . .

"I have something I need to confess," I burst out, and Mal turns back to me with her surprised eyebrows and that staggering widow's peak.

"What is it?"

I bite down on my upper lip. "I actually think your mullet is very sexy."

"I fucking knew it!" She tackles me backward onto the bed, climbs on top of me, drives me down into the mattress, and kisses me hard. She tastes like ham and chocolate, like sunshine and escapism.

I can't let her pull away.

"You made me coffee?"

I sit up in bed to find Mal perched on the edge wearing a ratty Dashboard Confessional T-shirt and a pair of gym shorts from what appears to be an old school uniform. She has two large white mugs in her hands, but her eyes were on me when I woke up. If I didn't know any better, I would think she was watching me sleep.

She thrusts one of the mugs into my hands. "I didn't *make* the coffee so much as I watched Felipe make it and then brought it to you. I'm just the Door Dasher in this scenario."

"Please don't tell me you're secretly one of those rich people who can't even boil their own water?"

"More like one of those rich people who can't operate an expensive Italian espresso machine."

"My preferred kind of rich person, then." I take a sip from the offered mug. The coffee has cooled to the perfect temperature, and it tastes decadent, almost divine. A bold, rich dark roast tempered with steamed milk and something sweet. There's a subtle hint of spice too, and it almost reminds me of— "Is this a pasteis de nata latte?"

"I had Felipe add vanilla and cinnamon for you."

Mal made me a pasteis de nata latte. I'm fairly certain if I opened my mouth right now, thousands of butterflies would soar out and fill this entire room. This room that contains so much Mal.

It's a faint morning light streaming through the French doors, and I finally risk speaking. "What time is it?" My butterflies stay where they belong, in my stomach and chest and throat.

"Too early," Mal answers with her eyes on her own mug. "I-I couldn't sleep."

I climb out of the sheets and scoot closer to her. "How come?"

My question is met with heavy silence. Mal takes a drink of her coffee, and then another, and maybe the raw emotional honesty from yesterday is gone, buried deep inside her again.

Or maybe not. "I have a bit of a vulnerability hangover . . . from yesterday. I-I don't usually talk about that stuff." She's staring at her coffee again when she adds, "I've never talked about most of that stuff with anyone, actually."

And *that* feels absolutely massive inside me, as if my ribs are cracking open to make room for it. I scoot even closer to her and drop my chin onto her shoulder. "For what it's worth," I whisper, "I think you're really hot when you're being vulnerable."

Mal snorts. "You always think I'm hot. *Wait!*" She shifts so we're facing each other, the profound sadness gone from her expression. "Is *my* body like a poem?"

I slap a hand over my face and groan at the memory of that night at the bar, when I listed everything I like about this woman under the guise of having a crush on Inez.

"Is *my* mouth like a surprise in my face?" she needles.

"In my defense: sangria."

"Do you like my hands?"

I uncover my face. "Yes," I answer. "Yes to all of it."

Mal's smirk straightens into a thoughtful line. And then she's touching me with those magnificent hands, kissing me with that surprisingly adorable mouth, holding me against her terse body. It's a lazy, tangled-up-in-bed-sheets kind of kiss. Slow, like the first sip of coffee on a Sunday morning when you have nowhere to be. Her fingers slide up and down my back, then into my hair, twisting around individual strands as she plants kisses on my cheeks, my forehead, my neck.

None of it feels like practice. I can't imagine what she's trying to teach me with these indulgent kisses. Patience, maybe? Or foreplay?

Or how to accept affection without your heart exploding?

But as Mal holds me in her arms and kisses me sweetly, I start to wonder if maybe there isn't a lesson here at all. Maybe Mal is kissing me because she wants to. And maybe I'm kissing her because I want her—not just for her mullet and her widow's peak and her tattoos. I want the Mal who listens and sees people; the Mal who is generous and kind and always looking out for the people she cares about. The Mal who held my hand on the plane and rescued me at our first dinner. The Mal who gave me the shoes off her feet without a second thought.

The Mal who is hopeful and spontaneous, the Mal who gets up at four in the morning and climbs a million stairs just to show me the sunrise. The Mal who is careful with her heart because she has to be, because she's been hurt by people who were careless with her.

She kisses me like we have all the time in the world, and I wonder if maybe it's not just sexual attraction, not just an adolescent crush. If maybe the strain in my chest is something more than I can comprehend.

Three rasps on the bedroom door abruptly end the lazy kisses, and when they're followed by the sound of a firm voice calling out, "Maëlys? It's Luzia," Mal defies gravity and flies to the opposite side of the bed in an instant.

"Hide," she hisses.

I do not hide. "Excuse me?"

"I was hoping we could talk," Luzia says through the door, and Mal tries to shove me under the blankets. As if that would fool anyone.

"I'm not going to hide," I whisper, wrestling myself free of her neurotic grasp. "Mal, we're not teenagers. You don't need to sneak the girl in your bed down your balcony so you don't get caught by your weird nanny."

"The balcony! That's a great idea!" Mal rolls off the bed and starts frantically putting on her pants. "Get dressed! We'll sneak down the balcony."

"Maëlys? I can hear you in there!" Luzia shouts. "Please don't ignore me. We need to talk."

Mal flashes me a desperate look, and as someone who's done some fairly ridiculous things to avoid conversations with her mother, I humor her. I pull on my dirty yoga pants from yesterday and zip her coat over my sports bra.

"Maëlys!" Luzia calls out again, but at that point, Mal is already showing me how to climb down the balcony like she's Romeo fleeing Juliet's bedroom before the nurse can find them. There's a conveniently located trellis that I suspect she used to sneak out numerous times. I'm not as elegant in my movements as she is, and I end up losing my foothold two feet from the ground. I tumble onto the grass, but Mal is already pulling me up.

Holding hands, we run through the gardens away from the house, laughing wildly as Luzia's screams get louder. She's on the balcony behind us, watching us flee toward the vineyard like a pair of rebellious teenagers as she shouts for Mal to come back. Neither of us is wearing shoes, and our destroyed Camino feet only carry us so far before we both fall onto the grass in a heap of limbs and laughter. Mal's head is on my stomach and my legs are wrapped around her waist, and we're both breathing too hard to do anything but gasp.

When we do catch our breath, Mal tilts her head sideways to look up at me. "I can't believe you climbed down my trellis."

"Be honest: how many girls have climbed down your trellis?"

She smiles at me in the grass. "Only one."

THE CAMINO CREW

Today

Inez Oliveira

Tour of the vineyard in one hour! Meet Luzia on the veranda! 11:03 a.m.

Ro Hashmi

IS ATTENDANCE MANDATORY?
11:04 a.m.

Rebecca Hartley

Dear Inez,

Will there be free wine samples?

With love, Rebecca 11:07 a.m.

Inez Oliveira

Not mandatory! We should all spend our rest day doing whatever refills

our cups before the final push of our
journey 11:09 a.m.

Ro Hashmi

THEN I AM GOING BACK TO BED
11:10 a.m.

Rebecca Hartley

We will both be there promptly at noon
—Rebecca 11:17 a.m.

Ari Ocampo

vera and i are going into town to
stock up on supplies if anyone needs
anything 11:20 a.m.

Ro Hashmi

MORE COMPEED 11:22 a.m.

Stefano Demurtas

Finishing up my trail run now! Will join
everyone for the wines! 11:25 a.m.

Inez Oliveira

Has anyone heard from Mal or Sadie
today? 12:02 p.m.

Ari Ocampo

no and I don't think we will . . .
12:04 p.m.

Rebecca Hartley

It's cute that they think we don't know
12:05 p.m.

Mal Gonçalves

We can see this, you know . . . 1:47 p.m.

TWENTY-THREE

Mal

We spend the day together.

We lie in the grass, even though it's damp with morning dew beneath us, hiding from Luzia and the rest of the world. Sadie talks about the popular girls in middle school, the ones she secretly studied, perhaps confusing longing for jealousy. I talk more about Prithi, about falling like I'd never hit the ground, about loving without holding back. I talk about growing up in houses so perfectly staged, it was like living in an Ibsen play. She talks about her love for repurposing old furniture for thirty minutes straight, showing me pictures of the things she's created on her phone, and I fall a little more in love with her with each photo. Not because the furniture is beautiful, but because *she* is when she talks about it.

I tell her more about my mom, who was never cruel like my father was, but was never loving like he could be, either. Her perfect indifference to my existence hurts in its own way; when I came out to my mom, she only asked if I was still going to wear my bridesmaid dress to her second wedding. Sadie tells me more about her mom, who loves her more than anything but can't always show up the way Sadie needs her to.

When our hunger and need for more coffee drive us inside, we sneak fresh croissants from the kitchen and eat them on my father's private patio. I give her a tour of the house. The highlights include the portrait of my great-great-grandfather that gave me nightmares as a child, the broken dumbwaiter where I used to hide contraband (like the lesbian pulp novels I found at a used bookstore in Lisbon), and the sculpture of a tree made out of oyster shells with their pearls glued to the top of each one on display in the atrium.

"I call this one the clit-mas tree," I explain with a flourish. "I believe it is the original inspiration for your vulva hat."

Sadie tilts her head to the side to study the sculpture like an art historian. "It really does look like a thousand clits."

"My father spent a quarter of a million on it."

"Naturally."

I kiss her, then, in front of the clit-mas tree. I kiss her in the library, against a shelf of old *Farmers' Almanacs*. I kiss her in my room, and her room, and in every room. And when I run out of places to kiss Sadie inside the house, I take her out to the grounds, and I kiss her there too. Everywhere I never kissed a girl.

Maybe Sadie's not the only one who needs to rewrite her adolescence, because as I kiss her amid the grapes and the memories, it feels like I'm a time traveler going back to fix my personal timeline. When I walk those dusty fields with her hand in mine, I am eighteen and bringing a girl home for the first time. When we find a pair of old bikes in the barn and ride them down the hill to Manny's for gelato, I'm sixteen and on my first date with a girl.

She gets pistachio and I get strawberry, and when we lie in the grass in my secret hiding spot in the garden, our hands and mouths sticky with gelato as we stare up at the blue sky, I'm fourteen and realizing I have my first crush on a girl.

It's an unexpected kind of homecoming. Being here with Sadie—seeing her in this place of complicated memories—almost feels like photoshopping snapshots of my past, doctoring them to include more happiness. It's a glimpse into a different version of my life: one where I fell in love with a girl without it all falling apart.

And when her leg brushes mine under the dinner table that night and stays there, her calf comfortingly pressed against me between bites of salmon, grief suddenly reverberates through my chest.

I wish my dad was here.

For the first time since his passing, I almost miss him. Or, perhaps, I miss the father I wish he'd been, the kind of father who would've been happy to see me happy. The kind of father who would've welcomed Sadie, and this entire ragtag group of queers, with open arms and open bottles of wine.

Over dinner, I grieve for the parts of my life I can never rewrite.

I excuse myself before the group can see that I'm crying, but Sadie follows me out onto the veranda. A soft hand on my shoulder. "Mal? Are you okay?"

I didn't realize I brought my glass of wine with me. "I wish . . . I wish my dad could've met you."

My tears blur my vision, so I can't see Sadie or the way she reacts to this confession. All I know is that she takes a deep breath and pulls me into a hug.

We stay that way for a long time, and when Sadie holds me on the veranda, I'm thirty-eight and allowing a woman to truly see me for the first time.

Later that night, when it's just the two of us in my emo bedroom, Sadie asks if she can learn how to make me feel good too. With every touch, every kiss, every sweep of her body against mine, Sadie is writing and rewriting, deconstructing and rebuilding, and when I come against her tongue, it's with shivers and tears. And this feels like a first too.

* * *

"You've been avoiding me."

Luzia stands at the bottom of the servants' staircase with her arms elegantly crossed, and I freeze mid-step. "No I haven't. I've—"

She cuts off my impending excuse with a stern glare. "You can't lie to me, Maëlys. I survived your teen years. I know your tells."

I pin my lips together, unable to argue with that. After all, it was Luzia who caught me with my first cigarette, Luzia who showed up when I got caught stealing nail polish from the farmacia. Luzia who always knew about the red, lacy thong and never told my father. For my entire childhood, Luzia Ferreira worked as my father's personal manager, which was a résumé-friendly way of saying that she took care of all the shit he didn't want to. I was often that shit.

While my father was either working or entertaining his revolving door of incrementally younger women, and my mother was busy with her social calendar in New York, Luzia was there, desperately trying to ensure that I didn't turn out as self-absorbed as my parents.

"And I always know when you're sneaking out," Luzia scolds.

I finish my descent and stand before her. She's barely five feet tall, and I tower over her like I have since I was eleven, but that doesn't make her any less intimidating. "I'm not trying to sneak out."

I absolutely am. It's six in the morning, and she caught me slinking down the back staircase with all of my things packed. I'd hoped that if I left early enough, I could escape the inevitable confrontation. If I snuck out and met up with the rest of the group at our planned stop for morning tea two miles from here, then maybe I could avoid saying goodbyes altogether.

"Maëlys, I changed your diapers and bought your first box of tampons. The least you can do is have a cup of tea with me before you vanish for another two decades."

She's very adept at the surrogate-mom guilt, and I nod in acceptance. She turns, expecting me to follow, and I slink after her like a reprimanded child. I know exactly where she's taking me. Through archways, through the dining room where she's already put a new crystal decanter on display, through the kitchen that now reminds me of that perfect night with Sadie.

My father insisted his office always be close to the kitchen, because he said he did his best thinking while staring into a fully stocked refrigerator. This office is down an old servants' hallway, probably originally used for the head housekeeper, like something out of *Downton Abbey*. And much like my old bedroom, his office still looks like it does in my memories.

There's already a cart with fresh tea, and Luzia pours two cups, then sits down on one of the highbacked chairs in the alcove. The bay windows behind her face my favorite part of the garden, full of big-leaf hydrangeas in candy-apple red, cornflower blue, and vibrant amethyst. I choose to stand, waiting for my tea to cool and waiting for Luzia to begin whatever planned speech she has in store for me.

"I'm not going to try to talk to you about business," she says gently.

"Well, good. Because I don't know shit-all about business."

She drops two sugar cubes into her tea and stirs carefully. "And I don't want to harp on about the funeral," she continues. "I've taken care of all the arrangements for next Sunday. All you have to do is show up."

Her gaze leaves her swirling tea to fix on me. "You *will* show up, won't you?"

"Yes, Luzia. I will be there."

She returns to stirring. "The only thing I want to talk about this morning is *you*."

"Ah. Right. There it is." I lean against the floor-to-ceiling built-in bookshelves and try to make my tone as casual as my stance. "You want to talk about what a failure and fuckup I've become? You want to hit me with one of those classic lectures about family responsibility and the Costa legacy—"

"Maëlys," she interrupts sharply, but I'm too old to be scolded.

"—Do you want to tell me how it's time for me to finally do my duty and take over the company?" I barrel on over the sound of her protests. "Do you want to yell at me for being selfish and choosing to live for myself? Or for being a spoiled, privileged brat who needs to grow up already?"

"Maëlys!" Luzia slams her teacup back onto the tray, and I fall silent as a small fissure forms in the porcelain. The tea leaks out in a thin but steady stream, flooding the saucer, then spilling over onto a pile of napkins. But Luzia doesn't seem to care about the broken cup or the spilled tea or any of it. "Maëlys," she says, quieter now, but also firmer. "I would never say any of that to you. I don't think those things about you."

The shelves are digging into my shoulder, but I refuse to move from my indifferent position.

"Do you . . . ?" She stares up at me. "Do you think those things about yourself?"

When I don't answer—when I *can't* answer—Luzia turns to the mess on the tray. "I only wanted to talk about how you're doing, and how you're coping with everything."

The only thing worse than leaving my place against the bookshelf is the idea of letting Luzia see me cry. "Here. Let me clean that up." I hurry to the tray, bending over by her feet to conceal my tearstained face as I use the remaining napkins to dry up the spilled tea.

"Don't worry about it," she insists, but I keep trying to destroy the evidence of the mess.

"But it's all my fault."

Luzia's wrinkled fingers brush the hair off my forehead, like they used to when I was a kid. "None of it is your fault," she whispers.

And I do let Luzia see me cry. But only a little.

"You stopped answering my calls," she says, and she lets me see her cry too. "I only wanted to know what you've been up to, menina."

I couldn't answer those phone calls back then, and I can't explain to Luzia now that all I have to show for the last twenty years is three passports completely filled with stamps; a series of nonprofit jobs I always quit after a year; a series of women I fell in and out of love with; an entire life that can be easily packed into a single suitcase; no home, no roots, no purpose. I can't tell Luzia that despite her best efforts, I did turn out like my parents. Cycling through women like my dad; living life on the surface, like my mom.

I'm still kneeling in front of her as Luzia's fingers move softly through my hair.

"I know we can't go back," she says after another stretch of my heavy silence. "I know we can't pick up where we left off when you were eighteen like nothing has changed. I know you must be angry with me for staying by your father's side after what he did, and I deserve your anger. But I would like to maybe . . . have a relationship again?" She's treading so carefully, her words come out like a question. "If that's something you might want too?"

I don't know what I want. That is, and always has been, my primary problem.

"But what if I . . . what if I sell the company?" I ask her.

"You can do that," she says simply. "But that has nothing to do with *this*." She presses her open palm to her heart, then presses it to mine, like she's connecting a string between us. "If you want to sneak away from this place right now, you can. If you want to sell the company and the vineyards and never talk to me again, you can do that too. But menina, if you'd let me, I'd very much like to earn back your trust. Your friendship."

"Damn, Luzia!" I sniffle as a new wave of tears overwhelms me. "What the hell? I leave for two decades and you go get all emotionally intelligent on me?"

She gives me a soft smile. "Not everything here stayed the same."

I wish I had the right words for Luzia, the right way to tell her thank you, and I'm sorry, and I forgive you. I wish I could be as articulate as she is and tell her what she meant to me back then, and what this conversation means to me right now. But the words fail me, and all I do is sit on the ground in front of her like a small kid.

"I like her, by the way."

"You like who?"

"*Who?* Maëlys," Luzia tsks. "The redhead. The girl whose been sleeping in your bed the past two nights."

"Redhead? I don't know any redheads."

Luzia violently ruffles my hair. "You can't hide anything from me."

"Ouch!" I yank my head away from her grasp, but she keeps a hand on my shoulder and doesn't allow me to pull away too much.

"It makes me so happy, menina," Luzia says with a watery smile, "to see you so happy."

And when Luzia Ferreira bends over and kisses the crown of my head, I am thirty-eight and discovering that maybe there *are* small ways I can still rewrite my history.

The last time I walked away from one of my father's vineyards, I planned to never return.

This time, as the tour group passes through the black gate and walks out onto the dirt road, I know my return is as inevitable as my father's funeral in less than two weeks. I won't be able to run away from it all, or repress it, or distract myself from it for much longer. Today, the Camino will take us inland, and we won't return to the coast at all in the next five days.

In five days, we'll be in Santiago, and I will have to decide what to do with Quinta Costa. With my life.

"Don't be angry," Sadie says as we walk down the road side by side, "but I did take one memento from Emo Mal's bedroom."

She pulls something out of her raincoat. "Peanut!" I involuntarily scream. I grab the elephant from her outstretched hands.

"I know your life is too nomadic for the entire collection," she teases, "but I figured you could make room in your bag for one forlorn Beanie Baby."

I press the soft elephant to my cheek, his trunk near my ear. "What's that, Peanut? You only agreed to come because you want to watch Sadie—*Mr. Peanut*!" I gasp. "You perv!"

Sadie swats my arm. "Don't corrupt the innocent elephant like you corrupted me."

"You've loved being corrupted by me."

She blushes at that. I only have five more days of watching those rosy splotches bloom across her face. "No, seriously. Thank you, Sadie." I hold the elephant to my heart so she knows I'm being sincere.

Sadie smiles in return, and I lean over to kiss that sweet smile, forgetting about Inez and Ari and the entire tour group that's spread out around us. Forgetting that in five days, we'll be in Santiago, and whatever this thing is with Sadie—practice or not—will be over.

TWENTY-FOUR

REDONDELA, SPAIN
Thursday, May 22, 2025

Sadie

I don't miss home.

The thought occurs to me halfway to Redondela when my phone buzzes with a text from Vi.

Mrs. Hernandez is here to pick up that curio cabinet you refinished for her. Where is it?

Then, another text. *Also, Mrs. Hernandez is a bitch.*

An overwhelming sense of resentment rises as I stare down at the texts that pulled me out of my meditative morning.

It's drizzling a little, and the fields around us are shrouded in mist like something out of a Brontë novel. I'm listening to my favorite soundtrack as we walk: Mal's clanging water bottle, Ro's clanking trekking poles, Rebecca's pretty humming, Inez's enthusiastic storytelling, and the consistent *click click click* of Vera's camera. My body feels restored after our day of rest, and it's easy to keep putting one foot in front of the other, to keep following those ever-present yellow arrows toward Santiago.

But the texts, and the reminder of the responsibilities awaiting me back home, shatter the rhythm of the Camino, and I realize all at once that I don't miss any of it at all.

I don't miss the store. I don't miss the grueling hours or the constant demands of customers and clients. I don't miss having no life outside of work, and I don't miss living someone else's dream.

This, though. *This* I will miss.

The heft of my pack and the strain in my legs; feeling strong, feeling connected to my body, to the earth, to myself. I'll miss getting up every morning and knowing that the only thing on my to-do list is to walk. The Camino is life stripped down to our most basic human needs: water, food, and sleep. Companionship, sometimes, but also time with yourself.

I've never had more *time* than I do on the Camino. Time to think, time to reflect, time to connect. Time to turn off my brain and do nothing but breathe and walk. And I'll miss that.

I'll miss the vineyard too, and that sacred glimpse into the real Mal. I'll miss sleeping in a queen bed beside her. I'll miss sharing a room because we wanted to, not because we had to. I'll miss lazy morning kisses and late-night conversations. I'll miss Mal. Even if we're just practice.

Maybe it's just vacation brain. Maybe this is how everyone feels when they travel abroad. Maybe this is why Diane Lane bought a crumbling villa and never left Tuscany. Because we'll be in Santiago in four days, and I'm having a hard time imagining how I'll ever say goodbye to all of this.

I stare down at Vi's texts. Raindrops coat my phone screen as I jab out my response to her.

It's a two-hundred-pound curio cabinet. I think you can find it.

Redondela is another adorable town with cobbled streets, medieval buildings, and undeniable charm. Even with the constant misty rain, there's a small market set up in the middle of town, with vendors under pop-up tents and patrons under umbrellas. Off to the side, there's a teenaged string quartet dressed like punk rockers playing eclectic covers of contemporary pop songs. It's just as we arrive in town that they end a stirring rendition of a Sabrina Carpenter bop and start playing something with a slow, gospel start.

Mal grabs my hand. "Oh shit, it's our song!" she shouts as she starts dragging me closer to the band. It still takes me a minute to place the tune, and then a teen dressed like Billy Idol starts singing the first verse. It's Madonna. "Like a Prayer." The song Mal and I danced to in Vila Praia de Âncora.

I laugh as I let myself be dragged across the square, but it soon becomes clear that Mal isn't joking at all. She fully intends to dance to this song in the middle of this Galician town, even though no one else is dancing. Even though it's raining and we're still wearing our packs.

"Mal . . ." I say her name like it's a warning that Mal won't heed. She's still holding my hand as she starts dramatically swaying to the music.

I'm frozen in place by embarrassment. There are people everywhere, and at least half of them are watching the tall woman with the blue mullet as she dances to Madonna. I'm sweating and blushing and cursing beside her, hoping she stops. Or that I somehow fall through the cobblestones and into another dimension where no one is looking at me.

But this is all going to be over in four days, and when I look back on my life, I don't regret the things I've done; I regret the experiences I've missed out on. So, I dance with Mal. She hoots, then pulls me into a bastardization of the tango. I let her lead. When she dips me, I dip as low as I can. And when she shakes her ass, I shake my ass too. And when she grinds against me, I grind right back, as robustly as I can, in tribute to every middle school dance I spent hiding in the bathroom.

I'm dancing in the street, and I'm not thinking about how silly we must look. I'm not spiraling about what others must think of us. I'm too busy watching the way Mal's hips rock side to side, and the way her bowed mouth looks curled into this goofy smile. The way she screams, "And now I'm dancing," along with the punk-rock teen. And I want Mal to take me there.

Someone in the audience catcalls us. I'm pretty sure it's Stefano.

Then Stefano is beside us, twirling Ari in ridiculous circles. Rebecca grabs Ro, and Vera grabs herself and does an impressive moonwalk into the middle of the dance floor that's forming around us. An older Spanish man offers Inez his hand, and she graciously accepts it, letting him waltz her around the square. More people join in. Couples and children and even a few reluctant teens, all of them dancing gleefully to an orchestral version of "Like a Prayer."

The grinding gives way to some kind of gentle sway, and we slow dance in front of tourists and locals and this teenage Billy Idol. I think about all the experiences I missed out on growing up: homecoming dances and prom and nights out in college. Pinning a boutonniere to the lapel of some beautifully handsome girl in a tux. Kissing strange women under strobe lights at an '80s night. Seeing a woman across the bar and having that fizzy, frothy feeling the first time our eyes meet.

But as Mal holds me close in the rain, it doesn't feel like I missed out on anything at all.

C'est La Vi with Me

HOME   ABOUT ME   DESTINATIONS   BLOG POSTS

When It Rains . . .

Sadie Wells
May 23, 2025 74 comments

It rained the entire 12 miles to Pontevedra. Not the light, misting rain we experienced yesterday, but a heavy, thick rain that soaked through even the best Pacific Northwest raincoat. It was the kind of rain that made it difficult to talk to each other, with our hoods up and our heads down, so we slogged along the path out of Redondela in silence, leaving plenty of time for contemplation.

The Camino took us into the woods and up the steep hills of the Alto de Lomba. The dirt path was slick with mud, and each step required my full attention as we climbed toward the top, where we were expecting a gorgeous view of the Vigo estuary. Instead, it was socked in by rain clouds and fog, everything painted in an undistinguishable gray that reminded me of Seattle. It was the first time in eleven days that the Camino's beauty disappointed me.

As the path briefly took us along the equally ugly N550, I started thinking about beauty. I've always cultivated a beautiful environment for myself: serene sounds, soothing aromas, and succulent flavors. An airy, open floor plan and a bucolic backyard paradise. My 500 thread-count sheets and my cashmere blankets. My William Morris wallpaper and my sound machine and my lavender diffuser.

But the Camino has taught me that the most beautiful things are the ones you can't control or plan for, like . . .

1. The sunrise over Viana do Castelo (absolutely worth the 4 a.m. wake up and the 700 stairs).

2. Jacaranda trees in bloom, the purple flowers drooping like amethyst.

3. A long, unbroken path in front of you.

4. An old Portuguese man on his morning walk, tipping his hat at every pilgrim that passes.

5. A cheap blue hat with an embroidered oyster shell to protect you from the sun.

6. A cone of pistachio gelato shared with a new friend.

7. The sounds of your tour group as you walk both together and at your own pace.

8. The Minho River from a rickety speed boat while a dozen nurses sing in harmony.

9. My bruised feet after a 19-mile day.

10. The place where the grass turns to rock, and the place where the rock turns to ocean, and the place where the ocean meets the sky.

11. A yellow scallop shell over a blue background on a mile-marker that notes your progress.

12. A yellow arrow that encourages you to keep going.

13. A basket of free bread and a full water bottle.

14. A tiny, twin bed with starched sheets when you're exhausted.

15. A hostel with an elevator.

16. And a bathtub.

17. The sound of waves crashing on Roman ruins outside of A Guarda.

18. My clean socks and underwear on laundry day.

19. Waking up while the rest of the world is still asleep.

20. A quiet day in the rain.

TWENTY-FIVE

REDONDELA, SPAIN
Friday, May 23, 2025

Mal

It makes the front page.

There's a side-by-side photo and everything. The first: a staged press image of handsome Valentim Costa, in a Valentino suit, cutting the ribbon at the newest vineyard in Rioja a few years ago. The second: a grainy, nighttime cell phone shot of his daughter in profile on the veranda at the Vigo vineyard, holding a wineglass while her body is draped all over a nameless redhead.

Only Sadie and I know that I was crying when this photo was taken, and that she was trying to comfort me; only we know that I was only holding that glass of wine because I absentmindedly took it with me when I fled the dinner table. But to the rest of the world, this photo makes me look like the drunk, hedonistic nepo baby of my father's nightmares. The splashy headline says it all: THE FUTURE OF THE COSTA FAMILY EMPIRE? With a fucking question mark.

The photos answer the question for anyone who might be unclear on *exactly* what that future is. The Costa family empire is now in the hands of a debauched lesbian who can't be trusted with your investments.

There was already a 6 a.m. phone call from the vice president of the board about whether I'm "fit for duty." (I'm not.) There was an email from stepmom-slash-interim CEO about strategic damage control that cc'd the entire publicity team; a dozen concerned text messages from Luzia; and a million WhatsApp missives from every person I've ever met from the Iberian Peninsula.

But I can't respond to any of them. I'm in the lobby of our Redondela hostel, clutching the first copy of *El País* I could find, immobilized as the world crumbles all around me. My eyes flicker over the Spanish article, my brain latching onto the most horrible highlights.

". . . Spain is still mourning the loss of a great man . . ."

". . . left his legacy to his absentee daughter . . ."

". . . wasted her twenties and thirties partying around the world . . ."

". . . the prodigal daughter returned, only to be seen cavorting with a buxom redhead . . ."

". . . sources say unpredictable Maëlys hasn't even visited the corporate offices in Lisbon since her father's passing . . ."

". . . Quinta Costa employs more than ten thousand people in Spain alone, and their livelihoods now depend on an aging party girl . . ."

They get uglier, and I punish myself by reading them over and over again. Because this is all my fault. I refused to face my inheritance directly, so now I'm facing the front page of a national newspaper.

My chest tightens, and there's a football in my throat, and all I can do is stare at that low-quality photo of Sadie and me. That's the worst part: the way this photo distorts an innocent moment, the way the article treats Sadie as a faceless object of temptation, the way I brought her into all of this, exposed her to public scrutiny, made her an accessory to my catastrophic mess.

I don't know who took this photo. No one on the tour would do something so cruel, something that could out Sadie before she's ready. But there were a dozen people from my father's staff wandering around the vineyard at any given moment. *My* staff. People who sold me out for a trite news story.

I hate that this photo ruins the perfect memories of those nights with Sadie at the vineyard, that it taints something I hold so sacred.

That *I* tainted it, ruined it, like I knew I would, and now I can barely breathe.

"Mal?"

My name sounds faint over the screaming thoughts inside my head. I turn, half-numb, and see Vera standing in the lobby in her matching silk pajama set. "I saw the news on my phone," she says to me in a quiet voice. "I'm so sorry they printed that garbage. That private picture of you and—"

"Don't tell Sadie." The entire newspaper crumples in my tightened fists. Vera watches me smash the photo and the article and the whole damn thing into a wad before tossing it in the nearest trash can.

"Of course," she says gently. "You should be the one to tell Sadie."

"No. I-I don't want her to know about it at all."

Vera stares at me through her giant, tortoise-shell glasses. "You . . . you're not going to tell her?"

"Please," is all I say in response. I feel like a crumpled newspaper in someone else's fist.

"*Please.*"

Vera doesn't say anything at all.

I'm avoiding Sadie again.

I avoid her at breakfast when she tries to ask me why I wasn't in bed this morning. I avoid her as we leave the hostel in the pouring rain, as we trudge through the wet countryside, as we push through the storm until we reach the N550. When we stop for morning tea, I finally tell her I have a headache. It's not a lie, exactly. It does feel like someone is drilling into my skull with a dull screw.

The lie is that I don't tell her everything else. I can't even look at her freckled face without drowning in guilt. It's not a particularly challenging day—only 19.5 kilometers to Ponteve-dra, with little elevation change after the initial hills— but I'm out of breath the entire time. I can't seem to fill my lungs all the way, and there's a stabbing pain every time I try. The more I gasp and choke for air, the more my headache intensifies, the more I worry I'll never be able to breathe again.

We arrive in Pontevedra a little after two, each of us soaked beyond reason. After checking into our private albergue, Inez sends us to our rooms to dry off and siesta before dinner. I can't get there fast enough.

I need to take off my too-heavy pack and my too-tight sneak-ers that I stole from my childhood bedroom in Vigo. I need to rip off these thick, wet wool socks and these waterlogged layers. I can't have any fabric touching my skin. Only then will I finally be able to catch my breath.

"Mal." Sadie's soft voice, usually such a comfort, grinds against the back of my teeth. I don't want her to see me like this. I don't want *anyone* to see me like this. I'm like one of those women who excuses herself from the dinner table when she starts to choke because she's too embarrassed to let anyone see her cough, one of those women who ends up dying alone in the kitchen.

"Mal, what's wrong?"

"Everything hurts and I can't breathe," I snarl as I forcefully kick off my shoes. One sneaker bangs against an Ikea wardrobe in the corner of the room and leaves behind a muddy print.

"You can't breathe?" Sadie repeats, stepping closer to me. A soothing hand finds my shoulder, but I yank myself away.

"I-I can't have anything touching me right now," I try to explain. I'm just lucid enough to realize how deranged this sounds.

But Sadie doesn't react like it's deranged at all. "Can I help?" She carefully untangles my arm from my wet raincoat, and my chest feels a little looser. Then she removes my damp fleece, my T-shirt, my soaked-through socks. My bare feet on the cold hardwood ground me. When I'm wearing nothing but my underwear and a tank top, Sadie leads me over to one of the twin beds. There's still a pain in my ribs, a sharpness in each shallow inhale.

"Why can't I breathe?" I ask her.

She perches on the bed next to me. "I think you're having a panic attack."

I cough out a strangled laugh. "I-I don't have panic attacks."

"Okay." She's as close to me as she can be without touching my skin, stripped down to her own underclothes as our outfits sit in a wet mound across from us. "Can you smell that?"

I inhale through my nose. "Smell what?"

"I don't know . . . something spicy, maybe? Or smoky?"

"The only thing I can smell is my own body odor," I tell her after sniffing the air. There's something especially potent about the mixture of sweat and wet clothes.

Sadie shakes her head. "No, not that. You don't smell it?"

She takes a long, deep breath through her nose, and I do the same. "I smell your wildflower shampoo," I tell her.

"Wildflower shampoo?" she touches her rain-soaked hair. "Oh, it's hibiscus. No, not that."

"And I can smell whatever cleaning products they used in this room."

"Not that either," she says, and she keeps taking long, deep inhales through her nose, like she's desperate to name the phantom smell, and I keep taking those long, deep breaths with her, until my ribs start to expand with each inhalation, until the pain in my lungs begins to subside, and *oh. Duh.*

There is no smell.

"Where did you learn that little trick?" I ask when I'm able to take several deep breaths in a row without asphyxiating.

Sadie offers me a small smile. "You pick up a few things growing up with a mom who has severe anxiety."

"I don't have anxiety."

"Okay," she says again. "How can I help with this non-anxiety, non–panic attack?"

I keep taking deep breaths, keep breathing in that hibiscus scent. "You've already helped."

She lifts her right hand and hesitates a second before she uses it to take mine. Our fingers stitch together. Her touch no longer feels suffocating. It feels like a slow, deep breath.

"Have . . . has this ever happened to you before?"

"No," I answer. But then I think about every paralyzing memory of my father's anger and disappointment. The way I freeze every time I remember the night I came out to him. The numbness and lightheadedness, the way it feels like there's a boulder on my chest sometimes. The racing thoughts and the fear of the quiet. The way I can't settle into anything, can't sit still, can't let myself stay in love.

"Sometimes," I quietly confess, "when I think about my dad, I get this . . . this tightness." I rub the heel of my palm over my sternum, over the place where the worst memories live, right behind my compass tattoo. "When I remember the night he rejected me, I get this sort of . . . I don't know."

I can't find the words to describe this kind of pain.

Sadie holds my hand in silence for a long time. "Do you think you might have some PTSD from all of that?"

"No," I say too quickly. "Or . . . maybe? I don't know."

Sadie doesn't press the issue. "What do you think triggered these feelings today?"

"There . . . there was this . . . *article*," and fuck. Now I'm crying for the millionth time. The tears are sticky and hot, but Sadie quickly brushes them away with the tips of her cool fingers.

I don't want her to see me like this, but Sadie always sees so much of me. *Too much.*

I brush away my own tears, brush away everything I want to keep hiding. "I'm not sure what part of your queer adolescence this is," I joke.

"Are you kidding?" Sadie squeezes my hand. "What could be more queer than comforting the woman you're having casual sex with through a mental health crisis?"

"Party girl?" Inez throws aside the newspaper in disgust. "I've only seen you truly drunk twice, and you wouldn't even do mushrooms with me when we trekked the West Highland Way."

She snorts, then takes a long drag of her cigarette.

"That's hardly the worst part," I tell her with my legs dangling off the balcony in her room. The rain stopped at some point in the night, and now Pontevedra smells damp and earthy. I keep breathing it in through my nose, keep finding calm in the early morning smells of an ancient city. "And I'd rather be a party girl than someone people depend on for their livelihood."

She studies me before leaning over to flick her cigarette against the edge of an ashtray. "Is that why you woke me up at four in the morning?"

I honestly don't know why I did it. After Sadie drew me a warm bath and went out to get us sandwiches from the super-mercado down the street so I wouldn't have to face everyone at dinner, we snuggled in the two twin beds we'd pushed together until I fell into a hard, deep sleep wrapped in her arms.

But at three in the morning, I startled awake in a cold sweat and couldn't quiet my brain.

In the silence of the night, the noise in my head had too much room, and my thoughts were running wild circles around dads and legacies and family empires; around the past I can't change and the future that's crowding in on me. First times and thousandth times, something both old and new, and falling and falling and never reaching the bottom, because what if there is no bottom? Thoughts of saying goodbye in Santiago.

Thoughts of rejection and shared Google Calendars. Thoughts of heartbreak and loneliness and living out of a single suitcase. Assembling IKEA furniture and Peanut the Elephant and somewhere that feels like home. Some*one*.

All of it—every single thought—sitting on my chest until I had to escape that sarcophagus of a hotel room. I tried going for a walk, tried calling Michelle, and when she didn't answer, I found myself knocking on Inez's door instead. Three cigarettes and thirty minutes of backstory later, and we're sitting on the cramped balcony, and I *still* don't know why I'm here, what I'm looking for.

"I woke you up because I'm having a panic attack!" I fidget under the blanket Inez threw over my bare legs.

"Are you having a panic attack about the article?" Inez asks with another leisurely inhale. "Or are you having a panic attack about Sadie?"

"It wasn't supposed to mean anything!" I explode. "I was just helping her experience her queer adolescence, just teaching her how to flirt and kiss and be comfortable with a woman, and it—" *Got out of hand? Snowballed into practice sex? Turned into something that feels too real?* Any attempt to describe it sounds ridiculous, so I lapse into silence, picking off bits of lint from my borrowed blanket.

Inez leans forward and flicks her cigarette over the ashtray again. "I told you not to fall for Sadie," she says. "But you did what you always do. *Such* a Gemini move."

"I think . . . I don't know . . . what if this thing with Sadie is . . . *more* than that?" A weird question mark asserts itself. It's the punctuation mark of emotional avoidance and cowardice.

"Do you want my honest take?" She stamps out her cigarette once and for all. "I think you're doing what you always do, Mal. You meet these women that you know it can never work out with long-term, you instantly fall in love with them, completely lose yourself in them. And like clockwork, as soon as the novelty wears off, you fall out of love and move onto the next thing."

Her honest take is a little *too* honest. It's the most direct she's ever been with me. No mysticism, no hiding behind a horoscope, no bullshit at all. "And you think that's what will happen with Sadie? That I'll . . . fall out of love with her?"

"Don't you always?"

I keep picking and picking at this blanket until I snag on a piece of fabric instead of lint. The string starts to unravel between my fingers.

"You've known Sadie for two weeks, which means you're in the height of your honeymoon phase. Everything is new and fun, distracting you from all the real shit you don't want to deal with."

Today didn't feel fun or distracting. When Sadie held me until I fell asleep, it felt like something else entirely.

"What happens when we get to Santiago?" she presses. "Sadie lives in Seattle, and you have to deal with things here, whether you want to or not. And let's say you *do* find a way to make it work with her."

Inez keeps pushing and pushing, and I keep unwinding the thread wrapped around my fingers. "What happens when things get too comfortable? When Sadie wants to settle into a life with you and realizes you never settle?"

What Inez is saying . . . It's everything Michelle has always said, everything I know, deep down, to be true about myself. I love beginnings—a new journal full of blank pages, the first few tracks of an album, the first few months with someone new.

But I'll only use the first five pages of that journal before I abandon it, and I've never listened to a thirteenth track in my life, and the middle was what ruined things with Ruth: the middle gave her time to see I wasn't worth the long haul.

I know all of this, yet here I am, still repeating the same cycle with Sadie, tricking myself into thinking that maybe, with her, the middle wouldn't be so intolerable.

"You don't think that maybe . . . maybe Sadie could be different?" I ask Inez with more hope than I care to admit.

"I'm sure she could be different," Inez says casually, "if *you* were different."

"Ouch."

"I'm not trying to hurt you, Mal. But I've designed this trek to be a journey deeper into yourself, and have you participated in any of that self-reflection? Did you do any soul-searching on this trip? Or did you dismiss it all with the same old flippancy? Because I think the woman sitting in front of me right now isn't any different from the woman I picked up from the Porto Airport. And *that* woman is going to hurt Sadie. She's going to hurt herself too."

I tug on the loose thread until the entire damn blanket comes apart on my lap. "Damn. You're unexpectedly brutal at four a.m."

Inez sighs. "And there's the flippancy, right on cue."

She slides out of her chair and disappears into her room for a moment. When she returns, she's holding a dark red crystal. She thrusts it into my hands.

"Seriously, where are these crystals coming from? Do you have an entire quarry in your pack?"

"It's jasper," she says bluntly. "To give you some courage."

The rock is silky smooth in my hands. "Courage for what?"

"To do the right thing," she says, like it's so easy.

But I have no idea what the right thing *is*.

TWENTY-SIX

Sadie

"Three more days and forty more miles," Inez says at morning tea, a few miles into our thirteen-mile day to Caldas de Reis. "You've all come so far, pushed yourselves *so far*. I am proud of each and every one of you."

She smiles at each of us in turn, and when she gets to me, I'm busy staring at Mal, trying to decipher the clench in her jaw. When I woke up in the middle of the night, she wasn't in bed with me, and it was hard to go back to sleep next to nothing but cool sheets. All morning, she's seemed distant, disconnected from the rest of us. Even now, she doesn't seem fully *here*. She's staring down at a red crystal clutched in her hands, rubbing her thumb in circles across the smooth surface.

"As we draw closer to the end, I want you to consider what you'll take away from your time on the Camino."

"Self-confidence," Rebecca blurts, like she has during every sharing circle for the past two weeks. "I did something I never thought I could do, and I will hold that close to my heart as I face the challenges I got waiting for me back home."

"The friendships," Vera says, and Ari drops her head onto Vera's shoulder with an *awww*.

"I want to take this newfound love for my body," Ro says, and Ari shouts, "Yes!" and snaps her fingers.

"Slowing down," Stefano shouts from his low squat.

"Gratitude," Rebecca adds.

"Time for self-reflection."

"Stillness."

"Pasteis de nata!"

Their voices all weave together with the banter of people who know each other too well, and when the chorus dies down, Inez fixes her gaze on me, like she's done at the end of every sharing circle for the past two weeks. "What about you, Sadie?"

All of it. Everything everyone else has already said and so much more. I want to gather up the entire Camino and put it in my backpack, keep the version of myself I was here forever.

But for right now, I want to give Inez the level of vulnerability she's always given us. "I want to keep the part of me that's learned to be okay with the unknown," I answer, and everyone turns to face me. "Thanks to this trip, to all of you," I gesture aimlessly around the circle, even though what I really mean is, thanks to *Mal.* "I finally let myself question my sexuality. I was so convinced that I had to have the right label, that if I didn't, my identity would be less valid somehow. But it was by living in the ambiguity that I was able to start uncovering who I really am and what I really want."

And I know I *don't* want to go back to the way things were. I don't want to keep holding everyone in my life at arm's length. I don't want a small life of never leaving that store. I want to go places, see things, have adventures. I want to keep doing things that surprise me. As much as I loved my Nan, I don't want to keep living someone else's dream.

I want to stop caring so much about what other people think of me. I want to be kinder to myself. I want to be *honest* with myself and with the people who matter to me.

I want all the things I've convinced myself I don't need. A partner. A family, someday. A thousand kisses with the same woman.

And there's a part of my vacation brain that wants that person to be Mal.

"Mal? It's your turn," Inez cajoles. "What do you want to take from the Camino?"

Her thumb keeps tracing the smooth stone. "I-I thought we didn't have to share?"

Nothing feels more uncertain than what happens with Mal when we get to Santiago.

"Trouble in the love bubble?"

I pull my eyes away from the Galician countryside to see Ari has fallen into step beside me. She gestures behind us, where Mal is drifting along the path behind even Vera. "There is no love bubble," I tell her.

"*Dude.*" Ari makes a show of dramatically rolling her eyes at me. "We all know that's not true."

I want to look over my shoulder again, but I already know what I'll see. I force my gaze to remain on the trail in front of me. "Whatever you think you know about me and Mal, it's not . . ."

It's not *what*? I don't even know what Mal and I are, or where we stand. Yesterday, she let me comfort her through a panic attack, let me see her in all her rawness, all her realness. But today, it feels like she's closing up again. "Mal and I . . . we're just . . . practice," I stammer.

"I'm sorry, you're *what*?"

"Mal has been helping me experience my second adolescence," I hear myself explain as we stomp along a dusty road. "And part of that was, um, practice kisses, and like . . . practice sex. It didn't mean anything. Our whole relationship has been about helping me gain confidence and explore my sexuality and—"

"I'm going to stop you right there," Ari snaps, thrusting her flat palm into my face. "*Practice sex*? Yeah, that's not a thing."

"They were more like . . . sex lessons, really. Friends-with-Educational-Benefits."

Ari gags. "I literally cannot."

"Are you repulsed by the idea of us having sex, or . . . ?"

"I am repulsed by the notion of *friends with educational benefits*." She sticks out her tongue. Ari has an uncanny ability to say rude things in a way that's strangely endearing. "That's not a thing people do. People don't have practice relationships."

"I know it sounds weird, but I am woefully inexperienced when it comes to . . . *everything*, and Mal—"

She cuts me off again. "Look, either you have feelings for someone, or you don't. You can't have *practice* feelings."

And she might actually have a point there.

"So, do you have feelings for Mal or not?"

I look over my shoulder once more. Mal has fallen even farther behind. "Of course I have feelings for her, but . . ."

"But what?" Ari demands.

But I have no idea how to tell her that.

But I don't know if she feels the same way.

But I'm still just an inexperienced baby gay, still the woman who came out to her on an airplane two weeks ago, still the woman who doesn't have the slightest idea how to love someone.

When I don't give Ari an answer, she scoffs. "You know, you remind me of my best friend back home."

"Thank you?"

"It's not a compliment."

Mal

"What crystal is that?"

I look up and see Sadie sitting on the floor of our Caldas de Reis albergue, her legs in a butterfly stretch. "Huh?"

"The crystal you've been clutching all day," she teases, but there's something sharp undercutting her tone.

"Jasper," I croak. My throat is dry from a long day of walking in silence.

Sadie moves her knees up and down, her legs flapping like butterfly wings. "What does it do?"

"Inez gave it to me for . . . for courage," I manage. "I-I looked it up, and it's supposed to nurture in times of stress. It . . . it helps you show up fully."

I'm aware of the irony: I haven't been present all day. My brain is twenty years in the past and two days in the future, and my body feels completely stuck.

Sadie unfurls her legs and stretches them out in front of her. "Why does Inez think you need courage?"

I shove the crystal into the pocket of my fleece. I'm still wearing all my Camino clothes, including my teenage sneakers, as I perch on the edge of my bed for the night. "I need the courage to . . ." *Break my old habits.* "To deal with my inheritance. With the company and my dad's funeral and . . . all of it. Finally."

I can feel Sadie's eyes on me even as she twists away in a deep, side body stretch. "I'm so sorry, Mal. When is the funeral?"

"In a week. Back in Porto. It's going to be . . . hard."

She comes out of her twist. "Would it help to have someone there with you?"

"What?"

"I could come to the funeral with you," she tentatively offers. "If that would be helpful."

I understand the words she's saying, but I can't wrap my brain around the enormity of what she's offering me, the way she's willing to show up for me. "You . . . *what?*"

Her eyes are on her bare feet. "When my Nan died, I think I would've liked to have somewhere there to hold my hand."

Would it be helpful to have this woman hold my hand at my father's funeral? It would be . . . *everything*.

"Or not," Sadie quickly amends. "You probably don't want a virtual stranger at your father's funeral."

I swallow and try to find the way to tell her exactly how much I do want that.

"Not sure how you'd explain the presence of your practice-girlfriend to your extended family." She laughs, but there's something beneath that laugh. Something that's not funny at all.

"Practice," I repeat. Hearing that word feels worse than looking at that photo on the front page. I touch my hand to my stomach and feel the jasper stone through the fabric of my fleece. *The courage to do what's right.* "I think having you come to the funeral might . . . confuse things. Between us."

Sadie contorts herself into another side body stretch, but this time, she's not looking at me. "Totally. Of course. That . . . that makes sense."

"It's just . . . we're going to be in Santiago in two days, and . . ." I take a long, deep breath through my nose. The room smells like dirty socks and hibiscus, like sweat and sunscreen, like Sadie's summertime sweetness. But summer never lasts, even if you chase it across hemispheres.

"I've been thinking about that, actually," Sadie blathers, "and since the trek is almost over, maybe it's for the best if we end our arrangement now. The . . . the sex arrangement, I mean." She cringes at herself, even as she keeps babbling. "I'll always be so grateful for you, Mal. Thank you for helping me experience my queer adolescence. Thank you for helping me question and explore. Thank you for the practice and the . . . the sex."

Sadie is thanking me *for sex*. A creeping numbness floats down my body, easing the growing pain in my chest. "And I'll always be grateful to you," I say, "for helping me open up about . . . everything. For listening."

"Of course." Her voice jumps an octave. "And I'm so sorry I invited myself to your dad's funeral. And I'm sorry if I got a bit . . . too attached. And I'm sorry that I—"

"Please stop apologizing." The words come from the pain, not the numbness, and I can hear the edge in my voice. Sadie stills on the floor.

"I'm sorry," she says again, apologizing for the apologizing. Then she pushes herself up off the floor. She sways on her feet, then catches herself against the edge of her own bed. "Friends, right?"

I meet her gaze.

"That was the deal," Sadie says. She's smiling, but there's something underneath that too. "We promised we'd stay friends."

I try to smile back. "Friends."

Sadie sweeps across the room and pulls out her toiletries bag like she's done every night for the past two weeks. "I'm going to get ready for bed," she tells me in that same false, high-pitched voice, and then she disappears behind the bathroom door.

And this is all for the best. Ending things now before either of us gets too hurt. I have to break my patterns. I have to find a way to focus on myself.

Ending things now is the right thing to do. So why does it feel like such utter shit when I fall asleep in a twin bed that isn't pushed together with hers?

C'est La Vi with Me

Things I Will Take with Me from the Camino de Santiago

Sadie Wells
May 24, 2025 81 comments

1. A love of walking. It's hard to believe that two weeks ago, I was terrified of the sheer volume of walking that awaited me, because now I can't imagine not starting every day this way.

2. An even more intense love of Bueno bars.

3. Approximately 12 blisters and self-confidence.

4. An appreciation for the simple pleasures in life: a cold Coke after a long day; a cheap glass of red wine; a free breadbasket; idle time with friends; taking the scenic route; long dinners where no one is in a hurry and food isn't the main course; soaking in a hot bath; a foot massage; drinking coffee with milk in the sunshine.

5. The box of pasteis de nata I plan to smuggle onto the plane.

6. Also, a bag of Sabor a Jamón chips.

7. Time for self-reflection. Back home, I'm always too busy, too tired, too stressed, but slowing down on this trip has taught me that I need to carve out time to sit with myself. Otherwise, what's the point in any of this?

8. A tattoo on my inner left wrist.

9. A small wooden arrow that a kind Spanish man passed out to pilgrims over his backyard fence.

10. At least two thousand photos.

11. A commitment to self-love and to actively trying to see the beauty in myself.

12. The travel bug. How am I supposed to stay in Seattle when there's so much beauty in the world I haven't seen yet?

13. Plans to do another Camino. I've heard that Caminos are like tattoos: once you do one, you won't be able to stop. I'm already scheming ways to get back here, to explore other routes to Santiago.

14. Plans to get another tattoo.

15. The contact info for some of the greatest people I've ever met. I'm not so naïve as to believe that I will stay close with everyone from my tour group. I know that realistically, I will never see most of these people again. We'll keep in touch in our WhatsApp group chat for a while, but eventually, our relationships will be reduced to liking each other's Instagram posts. But it won't matter, because I will carry my love for these people with me wherever I go from here. That's the thing about a Camino family. The very nature of your connection is fleeting, only meant to last until Santiago, but that doesn't diminish the impact they have on your life.

TWENTY-SEVEN

PADRÓN, SPAIN

Mal

"Yesterday, we talked about what we'll *take* from our experience on the Camino," Inez says to the seven other people crammed around a single table with her in Carracedo. "Today, on the penultimate day of our journey, I want you to think about what you're going to leave behind."

The table goes quiet as seven people all take a drink from their coffees at the same time to avoid answering the question.

"What we want to leave behind . . . ?" Rebecca echoes in confusion.

"I left behind two sweatshirts in Esposende," Ro says. "Is that what you mean?"

"Less literal." Inez smiles as sweetly as ever at them. "I want us to think about things that are no longer serving us. Habits or patterns or self-sabotaging cycles."

I feel Inez's eyes on me, but my eyes are on the crumbling monastery across the way.

Ro clears their throat beside me. "I can go first," they grumble, surprising everyone.

"Go ahead!" Inez encourages excitedly.

"I've realized that . . . that I've been self-isolating," they grumble. "Don't get me wrong—I love my corgis—"

"We *know*," Ari interrupts, and gentle laughter moves around the table. I couldn't tell you the names of any of Rebecca's human children, but we all know Copernicus, Newton, Daisy, and old, baby-food-eating Max.

Ro laughs at themself too. "But I think I've maybe, um . . . used my dogs as an excuse to, you know . . . not connect with people."

Their hands tremble around their café con leche, and Rebecca reaches over to place a comforting hand on their shoulder. "I've faced rejection all my life. For being brown, and queer, and Muslim, and fat, and trans . . . Most of my family doesn't talk to me anymore because of that last bit."

And then Ro starts crying. *Ro*, who started this journey hating all this touchy-feely shit. Rebecca scoots her chair closer so she can put her entire arm around them. Naturally, she's also crying. And Inez has been crying since Ro offered to share first.

Ro keeps talking through their tears. "I-I think I got so used to being rejected that I started rejecting the whole world first. I shut myself away with my dogs, and I acted like I didn't need anyone else. But . . . but I do. I need community. I . . . I needed all of you."

And *fuck*. Now I'm crying. I adjust my hat to try to hide my tears under the brim, and when that doesn't work, I simply tell myself to stop. I will the tears to reverse their path and suck themselves back into my tear ducts before anyone can see them. But when I glance around the table and see that Vera is crying too, my resolve weakens a little.

Then Ari reaches for a napkin to honk her nose. Cool, Portland-Hipster Ari.

And then Sadie starts crying, and she makes no attempt to pretend like she's not.

"I honestly came on this tour because I wanted to escape myself," Ro continues as the entire table weeps. "I-I never thought . . . I never thought it would change my life like this. Every one of you has had a huge impact on me."

Stefano is actively blowing his nose into his sweat band while still positioned in Warrior Two.

"Even if we didn't talk much, you helped me more than you could know," Ro says. "So, thank you, Inez, for this tour. And thank you, Rebecca, for never shutting the hell up."

Rebecca laughs through her tears. "Anytime, dear."

Inez dabs her eyes with a napkin. "Thank you so much for sharing, Ro."

"Fuck you for sharing," Ari sobs. "What is this? Degrassi High?"

Stefano babbles in Italian, reverses his Warrior, and never translates his comments. I catch the words *love*, *loss*, and *my beautiful friends*.

I fix my gaze on the crumbling monastery again. I'm still trying to keep it all in.

"Mal." I hear Inez say my name, but I don't turn toward her. "Do you have anything you want to share?"

She's once again opening a door for me, giving me the chance to finally be honest and vulnerable like everyone else.

"Do you have anything you want to leave behind?" she prods.

I wish I could leave behind my grief, all the complicated memories of my father, all the things we never said to each other. I want to leave behind that childhood trauma, move past it. I want to leave my father's rejection behind in a neat pile on my hotel bed in Padrón with a note that says "donate."

I would leave behind my fear of the silence, my fear of vulnerability, and my need to repress, my need to distract myself.

I would stop hopscotching across the world and between women. I would fall in love with Tuesdays and February and the middle of things. I would tell Sadie that none of it was practice, and I would learn to be comfortable in the stillness.

I wish I could leave behind my loneliness, but I don't know how.

"I want to leave behind these fucking blisters," I finally say, and I watch the disappointment paint itself across Inez's face.

In the midmorning sun, we walk along the Rio Vargas and through lush forests, but none of the beauty does anything to dull my misery.

A little before noon, we stop again, at Cafetería Bocateria, a café and market that's swarming with pilgrims. There's a tour of at least fifty Spanish people in matching red polka-dot necker-chiefs, another tour in yellow neon T-shirts, and while everyone else braves the crowds for drinks or snacks, I find myself a random cinder block out of the way and sit down.

Sadie makes it in and out of the market quickly, and when she comes to sit on a neighboring cinder block, she's holding a Bueno bar. She opens the package and passes me half. The simple gesture of this Bueno bar nearly rips me wide open. The bar tastes like lonely summers and kissing Sadie in my childhood bedroom. Ending things with her last night was definitely the wrong thing.

I want to tell Sadie that I started falling for her when we shared that pair of headphones on the flight here; I want to tell her that when I kissed her on that beach, it wasn't for science; I want to tell her that the sex was never for practice. That I spent two weeks trying so hard not to fall in love with her, and fell in love with her all the same.

"I talked to Inez," Sadie says, licking melted chocolate off her fingers. "And she said we can switch roommates for tonight. If it's okay with you, I'm going to room with Ari and Vera, and Stefano is going to stay with you."

"What? Why?"

"I thought it would make things easier," she says with her eyes on my Hokas.

And I want to tell her that I don't want *easier*. That I want *her*.

But that's what I always do, and I'm trying to do better.

"That sounds good," I say, even though it sounds completely intolerable.

When we get to Padrón, Sadie follows Ari and Vera up to the third floor, and Inez hands the final key to Stefano and me. As soon as the door to our room closes, Stefano pulls out two bottles of cheap Vinho Verde. "I got wines. We will drink wine, and you will tell me how you messed this all up, okay?"

C'est La Vi with Me

HOME	ABOUT ME	DESTINATIONS	BLOG POSTS

Things I'll Leave Behind on the Camino de Santiago

Sadie Wells
May 25, 2025 86 comments

1. My pinky toenail.

2. 18 inches of hair.

3. A pile of unnecessary items, neatly stacked on a bed in Vila do Conde—things I needed to stop lugging around.

4. Shame. All of it. Every last drop. I *really* need to stop lugging that around.

5. My fear of vulnerability.

6. My need to try to match someone else's pace or follow someone else's path.

7. My obsession with time, and with being *too late*.

8. My negative self-talk.

9. My need to have all the answers.

10. My heart. Is that a clichéd thing to say? Oh well. I'm a cliché.

TWENTY-EIGHT

Sadie

It's still dark outside when Inez has us wake up for our final day of walking. In fifteen miles, we will arrive in Santiago de Compostela.

I move tiredly around the hotel room, doing my morning stretches for the last time, putting on my wool socks for the last time, repacking my bag for the last time. It's the same routine I've done for fourteen days, but it feels wrong this morning, because I'm not doing the routine alongside Mal.

Vera's and Ari's noises are different. Vera's alarm is some loud techno bleating sound, and Ari turns on the overhead lighting as soon as she's awake. Vera wants to talk about the plan for the day, and Ari hogs the bathroom, and I keep bumping into both of them.

Fourteen days. Fourteen days of Mal sleeping in until the last minute, fourteen days of her water bottle clanging against the too-shallow sink as she tries to fill it for the day, fourteen days of her swift, purposeful movements. Fourteen days of smelling her deodorant and thinking about spring. Those few precious mornings where I woke up in her arms.

And now it's over.

It was always going to end in Santiago, in the same way our trek was always going to end there too.

I got what I wanted out of the arrangement. I got to experience the adolescence I missed out on. I cut off my hair and got a tattoo; I learned to flirt, learned what it feels like to have a crush. I had my first kiss with a woman. I had sex. I learned about what I want and how to ask for it. I feel at home in my body for the first time in thirty-five years, and when I look in the mirror, I see myself. A version of myself with short hair and a tattoo, but myself, nonetheless.

I've come out to seven more people than I was out to at the start of this trip, and when I return to Seattle, I will come out to my family, even if I don't have the perfect words.

So why do I still feel so unsatisfied?

Maybe because I went and did the most adolescent thing of all: I thought my first love might be my forever love. I went full Juliet, full Bella Swan, full teenage-girl-cliché and fell in love with someone I'd known for all of five minutes.

It would almost be funny if it weren't so tragic.

At five thirty, Vera, Ari, and I quietly leave our room and meet the rest of the group outside the hotel. Inez, Ro, and Mal have headlamps shining from their foreheads, and the rest of us have the flashlight app on our phones as we navigate our way out of sleepy Padrón.

It's the first time the tour group has walked before dawn, and there's something almost spooky about the empty cobblestone streets and old churches in the dark. Everything looks different in the shadows, and it reminds me of Viana do Castelo, that morning Mal forced me out of bed at four so we could see the sunrise.

We trek along country roads that take us past misty pastures, toward wooden paths cloaked in darkness aside from the ten pinpricks of light moving in a jagged line.

I can't make out much more than silhouettes, but I know Mal, even in the dark. Even only in shadow and outline.

We come over a small hill to a path through the trees lit up with solar-paneled lights, and we click off our own lights. The trail becomes thicker with other pilgrims, especially as the sun begins to rise over the valley. Blue-gray mist clings to everything as we make it to our first stop of the morning. The café is quiet, even as small groups come and go on their way to Santiago, all conversations hushed, almost reverent.

I order a cappuccino, and then I queue to use the restroom. By the time I join the rest of the group at the tables outside, there's only one chair left, the one right across from Mal.

In the pale morning sun, I see the purple bags under her eyes and the tired set of her bowed mouth.

"We're almost there. Only ten more miles," Inez says, and even her tone is hushed, as if the proximity to Santiago is too sacred for her normal excited tone. "As we walk this last bit of the Camino, I want you to think about what you hoped to find in Santiago de Compostela."

The truth is, I have no idea what I hoped to find.

I agreed to this trip to help my sister, to *run away* from my sister. I agreed because I needed more time. Time away from the store, away from the family pressure. Time to figure myself out. I thought if I managed to make it to Santiago, I would only find the things I wanted to escape waiting for me again.

We walk, and the path gets busier the closer we get to Santiago. Large Spanish tour groups guided by people holding colorful flags create blockades that we have to weave around. I get separated from the group more than once, lost in a sea of people in matching neon-yellow shirts for almost a mile, but I always end up alongside Ro and Rebecca, or Vera and Ari. We're all heading to the same place, after all.

What am I hoping to find in Santiago?

Closure, maybe? The ability to move on from my first love? The acceptance that this is part of what it means to be vulnerable with someone else. Sometimes, they shit all over your heart.

The path forks in front of us. The flocks of pilgrims all go one way, but Inez quietly beckons us with a hand to follow her in the other direction. "A more scenic route into the city," she promises.

We can see the buildings of Santiago over the copse of trees, closer than ever.

About a mile from town, we pass through a crosswalk that's been painted in the colors of the trans flag. Vera stops to take photos before realizing there's more.

There's a bench painted in the colors of the lesbian flag. Another one like the bi flag. They're at some kind of school or community center, and the courtyard is filled with gay benches and picnic tables, every surface painted like a different pride flag. Everyone takes photos with them, and it feels like some kind of sign, to come across the place so close to Santiago.

I just don't know what the sign *means*.

What am I hoping to find in Santiago?

Probably more than one city can give me.

It's a church.

That's what I find in Santiago.

We spill into the central square of Santiago de Compostela with dozens, if not hundreds, of other pilgrims after fourteen days and two hundred miles, and it's just a fucking church.

It's a cool church, I guess, but half of it is concealed behind construction scaffolding. The square is full of pilgrims triumphantly celebrating the end of the journey. Some take pictures, some reunite with old Camino friends, some sit in the middle of the square, backs propped against their packs, staring up at that stupid church like it has all the answers. I keep looking at it, trying to see what they see.

The tour group sticks together long enough to take a final group photo, then scatters. Most people go to line up to receive their pilgrim credentials. Ro and Rebecca go to find some brunch. Vera lingers behind with me for a while and takes a thousand photos, not of the church, but of the people watching the church.

I'm frozen in place. Fourteen days. Two hundred miles. And it's just a church?

"Do you want to go get our certificates?"

I turn, and there's Mal, appearing at my side like she did a dozen times in the last two weeks.

I shake my head. "It's just a church," I tell her.

Mal glances over her shoulder at the spires, then back at me. "Well, yeah."

Fourteen days, two hundred miles. Bruises and blisters. Shin splints and sunburns and side stitches. Horrible twin beds in horrible hostels. Laughter and tears. So much wine, and so little sleep.

"And it's under construction." I point to the ugly scaffolding. "What are people even looking at?"

"I don't really think the destination is the point," she says, her eyes on those half-covered spires. She's probably right. It shouldn't matter that this is how it ends: with the two of us standing an awkward distance apart, barely able to look at each other. All that should matter are those fourteen days, those two hundred miles we had together.

"Sadie," she says, and a silly bubble of hope rises in my chest at the sound of my name in her mouth. "I'm sorry . . . if you didn't find what you were looking for."

I let myself stare at her then. At her blue mullet and her sexy widow's peak. At her hazel eyes and her star tattoos and the perfect bow of her mouth. I stare at her mustard-orange fleece and her callused hands, and I try to memorize all of it now that it's over.

"I think I did find what I was looking for, actually," I tell her.

Mal opens her mouth, and for a moment, that stupid hope bubble makes me believe she's going to tell me that she loves me too. That she's going to admit that none of it was practice. That she'll kiss me and mean it, right here, in front of this church.

But what she actually says is, "I'm going to miss you, Freckles." And I realize this is goodbye.

I can't bring myself to say those words, so I'm quiet when she sweeps me into one last hug. I try to memorize the way it feels when she holds me. Her lean body and her springtime scent.

"Friends?" she asks me before she lets go.

"Friends," I say into her ear, and even though everything hurts, it's a promise I want to keep.

It isn't until I'm taking off my shoes at airport security that afternoon that I realize I'm still wearing Mal's Hokas.

My flight home includes a layover in Amsterdam, and I buy three packages of stroopwafels to eat on the plane. They're not nearly as good as nata, but nothing ever will be.

I have the window seat this time, and the man next to me watches *Wedding Crashers* on his iPad and never takes out his AirPods. There's light turbulence coming into Seattle, and I clutch my armrest until it settles.

When I pass through the final security doors at Arrivals, I'm ambushed by two redheads and a pair of crutches. I'm so jet-lagged, so supremely exhausted and utterly heartbroken, it takes me several seconds to realize the people hugging me are my mom and sister.

"You're home!" my mom cries.

"Thank fucking Christ!" Vi screams. "I can't handle one more day at the store!"

"You really did cut off all your hair," my mom says, clutching the ends of the short strands. "Your beautiful, beautiful hair."

"Let me see the tattoo!" Vi grabs my arm and pulls my wrist toward her. "Holy shit. Who the hell even are you?"

"I'm a lesbian," I answer.

My mom's hand stills in my hair. "Oh," she says.

It's not how I planned on telling them, not remotely the perfect way, but I can't take the words back now that they're lingering in the air at SeaTac. And I don't want to take them back. I will never have the perfect words or the perfect way to be myself, so this is as good as anything.

"What about the Portuguese guy you fell in love with on the Camino?" Vi asks, then catches herself. "Wait. Replaying that conversation. Not a dude. Got it."

"Not a dude," I say.

"Huh." My sister twirls her red hair around her finger. "But you've always dated *men*."

"Yeah. Heteronormativity is a bitch."

"Wait. Did that queer tour turn you gay?"

"Being gay turned me gay."

"Huh," Vi says again. "In retrospect, I probably should've seen this coming."

"Probably." I finally turn to my mom, bracing myself for her unpredictable emotions, preparing myself to have to care for her in this moment. "Are you . . . disappointed?"

"Disappointed? Honey, I am *thrilled*." My mom tackles me in another hug, squeezes me so tight I can barely breathe. "I'm so, so happy for you to start living your truth!" Her words aren't anxious, aren't sad. She's not asking me to take on any emotional labor. She's just . . . hugging me. I really need that.

I don't mind holding up my mom sometimes, but right now, it's nice to have someone else do the heavy lifting.

"I know so many women I can set you up with!" Vi squeals.

I slide my arms out of my backpack and let the heavy bag fall onto the airport carpet with a clunk, making the weight off my shoulders both physical and emotional. I didn't realize how fucking scared I still was to tell them until right now. I've always known that my family wouldn't care if I was gay, and coming out to them was *still* the hardest thing I've ever done, even harder than walking two hundred miles. Even harder than saying good-bye to Mal.

I can't imagine how hard it must have been for Ro or Rebecca, who didn't know what kind of reaction awaited them. How hard it must have been for eighteen-year-old Mal when she showed her dad her true heart and he scorned her for it.

"Oh, honey." My mom's hand is in my hair again. "You're crying."

I drop my head onto her shoulder.

"I think I'm ready to go home now."

Mal

Some people cut their hair after a bad breakup. I book international flights.

At least, that's what I've always done. Open the Kayak app on my phone. Choose some new, exciting destination. Hop on a plane, take off, run away. Meet a beautiful woman and follow her to Hong Kong or Laos or Wilmington, Indiana, to start the cycle all over again.

Right now, Alaska Airlines is running a special on flights to Costa Rica, and I have just enough Delta miles to get to Brisbane.

But I don't want to go to Brisbane. For the first time in my life, I don't want to get on an airplane at all.

Sadie is gone, and even scuba diving the Great Barrier Reef isn't going to make me feel better about it.

But I can't sit still, either, can't stop walking, stop moving. I can't sit in the silence for the next six days until my father's funeral back in Porto. So, when Stefano tells me his plan to extend his Camino a few more days and walk out to Finisterre on the far western coast of Spain, I decide to join him.

It's 120 kilometers to Finisterre via the seaside village of Muxía, and we do it in three days. We leave Santiago in the late afternoon, after a round of beers convinces me that this is a good idea, and we walk the twenty-two kilometers to Negreira in four and a half hours.

The next day, we push ourselves as far as we can—all the way to Muxía. Sixty kilometers over the course of fourteen hours, the most I've ever walked in a single day, and it's not just my feet that are killing me. It's every fucking part of my body and soul.

I'm punishing myself: for falling in love with Sadie, even when everyone told me not to; for falling into my same old patterns; for hurting myself, and Sadie, in the process.

But at least through all the screaming pain in my body, there's no room for silence.

So, we walk. And walk and walk and walk.

We walk until we reach Cape Finisterre, the rocky cliffsides overlooking the Atlantic, what medieval pilgrims believed was the end of the world. We walk until we can literally walk no farther.

I collapse onto a rock in a pitiful heap, half convinced they'll have to medevac me back to Santiago. Stefano, meanwhile, finds a smooth surface on which to begin his vinyasa.

"What. The. Fuck. Is wrong. With you?" It takes me nearly a minute to get out the question since I have to pause between every word to chug more water.

"What do you mean?" he asks from fucking Scorpion pose.

"This. Is not. Normal," I gasp. "What are you running from, dude?"

"I do not run from anything."

Stefano whips his body impossibly into a handstand.

"Then why are you incapable of sitting still? Why are you always moving?"

"I like to move," he says while upside down. "I've always liked to move, ever since I was little."

I am languishing on my rock in a pool of my own sweat, and this man continues to contort his body in unholy ways. "I'm sorry, but no one does *that* simply because they enjoy physical movement. You've got to be outrunning some demons, my dude."

Stefano flips himself like a pancake and ends up sitting cross-legged, facing me. "No demons," he says. "I do not run from anything. I run toward it."

I can barely lift my head, but I force myself to make eye contact with this ridiculous human when I ask him. "Run toward *what*?"

"Toward everything I want."

In the end, I don't need a medical helicopter to get me back to Santiago. The bus works just fine. Stefano and I say goodbye at the station before he gets on a train that will eventually take him all the way back to Naples, and I get on a bus that will take me all the way to my father's funeral.

Coming Out (and Coming of Age) on the Camino

Sadie Wells
May 30, 2025 213 comments

On the first day of my trek with Beatrix Tours, tour guide and owner Inez Oliveira asked us to share what brought us to the Camino. Because whether we realized it or not, no one does the Camino de Santiago just because they enjoy walking. We were all running from something, or running toward something, or trying to find the time we needed to figure ourselves out.

I didn't share that first day, but here is my truth: my sexual identity crisis is what called me to the Camino. It never occurred to me that I could be anything but straight until I was thirty-four, though in hindsight, there were clues. My childhood obsession with Amy Jo Johnson as the Pink Ranger. My later obsession with Mischa Barton's jean skirts on *The O.C.* I had my fair share of intense female friendships, and the only boys I ever had crushes on were the ones my friends liked, because I liked bonding with them over it.

When one of my friends in college came out as gay, I remember thinking that meant I couldn't be gay too, because if I was, I would've felt something when she told me. Instead, I felt weirdly numbed by the news. And when my sister told us she's bi, and my mom took it in stride, I told myself I couldn't be queer too. Because if I was, I would've told someone already. It was like I was waiting for the right sign, waiting for the universe to give me permission to question my sexuality. And in the meantime, I kept dating men, because that was the only path I could imagine for myself.

Even when I started feeling this desperate need to talk about questioning my queerness, I didn't have the language for it. And I thought I had to have the right words, the perfect label, for my identity to be valid.

So when my sister's injury meant she couldn't do the Camino tour, I jumped on the opportunity to escape my real-life responsibilities, to buy myself the time I needed to find the perfect words.

After two weeks and two hundred miles with Oliveira and a group of incredible queer people, I learned two things: there are no perfect words; and my sexuality is a small part of who I am and what I needed to figure out about myself.

I thought the Camino was about exploring my sexuality, but that wasn't the only thing I'd been ignoring about myself. It wasn't until I let myself question my queerness that I finally gave *myself* permission to question everything else. That's the truly special thing about Beatrix Tours, and Inez Oliveira as a person. She creates a culture of trust, vulnerability, and growth. She fosters a safe, loving community where pilgrims can choose to reflect as much or as little as they need to. And there's a beautiful power in getting to do that alongside queer family.

So, without further ado, one final list.

Things I Discovered About Myself on the Camino:

1. That I'm probably a lesbian.
2. But it's okay if I don't have all the answers.
3. And it's okay if the answers change over time.
4. That I need to stop drinking red wine.
5. That I don't like seafood (but I *especially* hate octopus).
6. That I cannot make rational decisions on limited sleep.
7. That I am the kind of person who gets a tattoo.
8. That I need to stop apologizing for taking up space.
9. That it's okay to make mistakes.
10. That sometimes, the best learning comes from those mistakes.
11. That I'm on a different timeline than other people.
12. And that's okay.

13. That I'm a giddy fool when I have a crush.

14. That I'm even worse when I fall in love.

15. That I want love, even if it doesn't always have a happy ending.

16. That I want a partner, and a family someday, and that it's okay to admit those things, even if they don't work out the way I want.

17. What it feels like when I have a broken heart.

18. What it feels like when I'm attracted to someone, when I *want* someone.

19. How to talk about what I want.

20. That there's something endlessly satisfying about the crunch of a dill pickle.

21. That I hate my job.

22. But that I love turning something forgotten into something beautiful.

23. That I do miss my family.

24. But that I don't miss twisting myself into something I'm not, to please my family.

25. That I'm not too late.

26. That I'm not too inexperienced.

27. That I am, in fact, exactly where I'm meant to be.

28. That life would be very boring if we already knew everything about ourselves.

Comments

The Rainbow Rocket
THANK YOU for letting us be part of this journey! I'm SOBBING. I didn't come out until I was 32, and this whole thing made me feel so seen!!!!

> **Cory O'Connor**
> SERIOUSLY SO SEEN!!! Mischa Barton made me gay too!!!!!

Rebecca.Hartley.1956

You are so brave, Peaches. I feel honored to have witnessed your journey

Jackie Jormp-Jomp

As a fellow late-bloomer, I'm so grateful for this!!

Clarissa Youn

I can't tell you how much this whole post means to me. Signing up for a Beatrix Camino tour right now!!!

Mal as in Bad

But what if I'm realizing I didn't learn anything about myself in two weeks and two hundred miles?

> ↳ **C'est La Vi**
> It's not too late

TWENTY-NINE

Mal

My father would have fucking loved this.

The Sé do Porto is standing-room-only as the pallbearers carry his fifty-thousand-dollar mahogany coffin away from the golden altar. The Portuguese prime minister is here, along with several lesser-known European royals that are crying in the front pews. I spot a daytime television starlet, a Eurovision runner-up, and at least three former reality television contestants. There's a cavalcade of ex-wives and mistresses who get incrementally younger and more grief-stricken, including my own mother.

"First wife and worst wife," he would tease. She's not crying at all; as far as I can tell, she's playing Wordle on her phone. His fifth wife, though, who I've only ever seen in pictures, is wearing something low-cut and skin-tight, and she's sobbing in a way that causes her impressive cleavage to heave up and down in a perfectly photographable way.

The bishop finishes delivering the service in Latin as the pallbearers make their final exit, and even though Valentim Costa was a half-assed Catholic, he would've loved the pomp and circumstance on his behalf.

I stare at the rose window ahead of me, and I try to make sense of how the man who would've delighted in this ostentatious funeral ever could've left his legacy to his utter disappointment of a daughter.

There is a tentative hand on my shoulder, then an entire arm wraps around me, and for a disorienting instant in this stuffy church, I think it's Sadie. That she came, even though I told her not to.

But when I turn, it's Inez's sympathetic expression that I see.

Of course Sadie isn't here.

It's Inez who holds my hand as a sixty-person church choir serenades my father with a hymn he would've hated.

"That was fucking ridiculous."

My mother takes an immodest sip of her drink—an aragonez port from 2018, according to the label on the bottle that a waiter held out on a silver tray. We're lingering in the gothic cloisters with at least a hundred other funeral goers. "Which deacon did Val have to blow to get wine served inside the cathedral?" my mother wonders *very* aloud.

Inez awkwardly clears her throat as several people turn to glare at my mother's indecency. "You didn't have to come, Mom," I tell her in a low voice.

She waves an irritated hand as she polishes off the rest of her wine. "Of course I came. I couldn't let you go through this by yourself."

I want to point out that she flew into Lisbon a week ago and didn't make any attempt to reach out to me, but alienating my one living parent at the funeral for the other seems unwise. "Do you want to go get dinner tonight?" I ask instead.

My mother isn't even looking at me. Her eyes dart around the courtyard, conspicuously aware of who is noticing her. "I can't, love. I'm on a flight to Paris tonight." Her head whips back around. "Come with me, Maëlys. We both deserve some retail therapy and French carbs."

"I can't." I don't provide further explanation, and Bianca Gonçalves doesn't ask for it. She doesn't really want me to come to Paris with her, anyway.

"There's that dumb bitch he left me for," Bianca hisses under her breath. Then, she raises her slender arm and twinkles her finger, making sure the giant engagement ring on her finger catches the light. "Isadora! Darling!" she calls out to my father's second wife. I watch them greet each other with air-kisses, as if they don't both actively loathe the other. Isadora ignores me, naturally, but she immediately fawns over my mom's engagement ring, peppers her with questions about the upcoming husband number three. Bianca shares every banal detail as the two of them disappear into the crowd together.

When I asked about the engagement ring before the service, the only thing my mom told me was, "It's going to be a private ceremony in the Maldives, and that's why I didn't invite you, sweetheart."

So when the waiter comes by again with his tray, I take a glass of red Vinho Verde and drown half in a single gulp. It's fucking delicious. My father made incredible wine, goddamn him.

"You are surprisingly well-adjusted," Inez concludes when my mom is out of earshot, "considering . . . all of this."

"*Surprisingly well-adjusted.* That's what I want it to say on my tombstone."

"I thought you wanted it to say *sapphic catnip*?"

"It can say more than one thing."

Inez takes me by the elbow, and we do a slow lap through the crowd, accepting condolences and collecting glares. It gives me a small surge of pleasure to know my father would've hated *this*: me in a tailored suit with a trans woman on my arm. It's clear

Inez knows this too, and she relishes in her role. She flaunts her sumptuously long legs and her gorgeously broad shoulders in a strapless dress that looks stunning on her.

"Thank you." I kiss her on the cheek. "For actually not letting me go through this alone."

Inez bends down and presses a kiss to my cheek in return. "Of course, irmãzinha." *Little sister.*

Someone pointedly clears their throat behind us. It's wife number five, hovering at my elbow, all cleavage and black-clad curves.

"Mal," she says, both softly and confidently. "We haven't met before but I'm—"

"Gloria," I cut in. "Wife number five."

The label doesn't even cause her to flinch. She's like most of my dad's wives: young and staggeringly beautiful, with an implacable and unruffled demeanor. I used to love trying to ruffle the wives as a kid. Which, come to think of it, is probably why Isadora refused to acknowledge me.

"I wanted to introduce myself," Gloria says with a corporate smile. I can see why the board nominated her as interim CEO.

"Are you hoping I'll call you mommy?" I ask. And wow. She's not ruffled by that at all. Gloria's eyes dart over to Inez.

"Do you think we could possibly speak in private for a moment?"

"Whatever you have to say to me, you can—" I start, but then Inez detaches herself from me. With another kiss on my cheek, she swans across the room, leaving me along with Wife Number 5.

"Thank you," Gloria begins, and I'm not sure what I've done to merit her gratitude. She continues, "I know you weren't on good terms with your father at the time of his passing, and I'm sure I feel like an extension of him. So, thank you for being willing to talk with me at all."

Well. Wife Number 5 is more perceptive than I gave her credit for.

"I also realize this is probably the last thing you want to hear today, but . . ." Gloria pauses, licks her lips, then forces out the words. "But he was so, so sorry."

"You're right," I bark. "That *is* the last thing I want to hear, Mommy Dearest."

Gloria *still* isn't ruffled. "I understand. I really do. But I know he would want me to tell you. He was sorry for what happened between you, and for never making it right."

"And he wanted his secretary to pass along that message?"

Her fake eyelashes flutter, but she doesn't break. "He knew he messed up beyond reproach. He was really trying to find a way to bridge the distance between you."

I think about all the inane texts he would send me about birds he saw from the back porch; the emails with links to articles I never read; the birthday cards with cash and a scribbled *Love, Papai*; the phone calls with voice messages that said, "Just had a minute as I was driving into town. No need to call me back."

That was really trying? Was I supposed to read between the lines on a *New Yorker* article about urban development and fucking decode his apology?

Bullshit.

"Why does the burden always fall on the queer kid to be the bigger person who forgives their ignorant parents who are *really trying*?" I yell at the woman in front of me, because it's too late to yell at him.

Because even when I had the chance, I never yelled at him.

"I know," Gloria says calmly.

"Do you know?"

"Yes. I'm bisexual." Her words are measured and unemotional. "My parents initially kicked me out when I was sixteen, and it took us years to repair that damage."

"Oh."

There's almost a hint of feeling in her voice as she says, "And I was so angry with Valentim when I learned he'd done the same thing to you. And worse, that he had it in his power to make it right and he hadn't."

"Why didn't he just make it right?" I ask, even though I know Wife Number 5 won't be able to give me the answers I really need.

"He had so much shame about how he reacted back then."

"Boo fucking hoo for him. He was embarrassed about how he reacted? Well, he taught me to be embarrassed of who I am, so it sounds like he got what he deserved."

A solemn nod. "He did."

"And if he was really trying to do better, he could've said *sorry*."

"He should have," she agrees. "But he didn't. He wasn't a perfect man. He was stubborn as hell. A trait, I think, you may have inherited from him."

"I've never been stubborn about anything a day in my life," I deadpan, and that almost gets Gloria to crack a genuine smile.

"I'm not trying to erase the pain and damage he caused you, Mal. I don't want to minimize it. He fucked up, and he was too proud to tell you that he fucked up." She sighs. "I just want you to know that he thought about you every day. He admired you."

I snort.

"No, really. He admired your free spirit, your independence, your passion for helping others. Whenever you started working for a new nonprofit, he always made sure to send an anonymous donation, because he wanted to support the causes you cared about."

I think about the money I gave to Inez to start Beatrix Tours as soon as I came into my trust, and her subsequent partnership with Quinta Costa's vineyards, a partnership *they* reached out about. My father wasn't trying to use Inez for the company's image; he was trying to support my investment.

"He would check your Instagram every morning like it was *Publico*, and he would always brag about whatever exciting place you were visiting. I think he wished he was more like you."

And that, somehow, is too much for me to handle. "Forgive me, but that's a weird thing to hear from your father's child bride."

Finally, my words crack her perfect veneer. I can see her take a deep breath to steady her response. "I'm thirty-four," she says calmly, "and not that I need to justify myself to you, but I was the COO of Quinta Costa—a job I *earned* before Val and I ever got together—before I had to step in to run the company because you were busy going for a *little walk*."

"Okay, so this whole loving stepmother act—" I angrily gesture toward her. "Is that just about getting his money? Are you angry that your Val didn't leave you a dime, and you figure your best bet to get your hands on a yacht or two is buttering up to his daughter with lies about what a good dad he secretly was?"

Her manicured hands fix themselves on her waist. "I'm Gloriana Silva," she says, *oh holy shit*. "Of the Silva Corporation. Have you ever heard of it?"

I feign ignorance. "I-I might have."

"Your father's wealth is *literal* dimes to me," she says with a dramatic swish of her hair. "I didn't need his money, or his houses, or his yachts. I work for Quinta Costa because I'm fucking good at it and I enjoy it, but I don't *need* it. The directives of your father's trust weren't a secret to me. We agreed *together* that he should leave everything to you. You were his only child. And nothing I said about him was a *lie* to butter you up."

Two things occur to me simultaneously: I had Gloria completely wrong, and I think she might actually be my favorite of the five wives. My own mother included.

"Sorry, I've been a dick to you."

Gloria takes a long, deep breath through her nose. "You have been," she agrees with a curt nod. "But this is your father's funeral, so I suppose I can grant you some grace."

"The thing is . . . I don't want the company," I tell her, and it's the closest I've gotten to a real decision. "I don't think I ever wanted the company. I-I wanted to have a choice."

Gloria's hands loosen their death grip on her trim waist. "I can appreciate that, one heiress to another."

I roll my eyes. "Okay, billionaire."

Gloria finally allows herself to crack a smile. "You *do* have a choice. You can choose to give up your majority shares, or sell the company, or whatever else you want. But I want to know that you're making that choice for the right reason. That you're rejecting your inheritance because it's not the right path for you, not because you want to spite a man who isn't even here anymore."

I nearly stagger backward in response to these words.

Everything I've done with my life for the last twenty years has been out of spite. I've defined my life by *not* being who he wanted me to be. I rejected every part of me that's tied to him, and I've drifted aimlessly from place to place, person to person, because it was the opposite of what he wanted for me. I've been so focused on refusing to become the daughter he wanted, that I don't even *know* what I really want.

An image surfaces in my mind: painted cabinets and plants beneath a window and tons of natural light. A place that feels like home.

I want *that*. I want a place that I miss when I'm away, somewhere to come home to that's mine. I want to visit the far-flung reaches of the world so I can appreciate the place I live even more. And I don't want that place to be Michelle's basement or the apartment of whoever I'm in love with at the moment. I'm tired of feeling like a guest in my own life.

I want roots. I want to be tied to something. And I haven't let myself have it because of him.

I let that smug motherfucker *win*.

Worse than that, I allowed his rejection that day to poison every single relationship I've had since. I was vulnerable with the person I loved most in the world, and he rejected me, and I let that moment convince me that if anyone ever knew the real me, they'd reject me too. I convinced myself that being vulnerable was never worth it, and I fell out of love with people before they could ever fall out of love with me.

I pushed Sadie away because I believed that if she saw this *mess* of a person, she'd leave.

Another image flashes in my mind: Sadie naked and eating pickles, the juice dripping down her curves.

Sadie's shy smile as we slow danced to Madonna the first time; Sadie dancing in front of all of Redondela the second time.

Sadie's soft hand in mine on the plane, on the Camino, in a hotel room when it was just the two of us.

Sadie's sweetness and her strength and her unending sense of awe; her freckles and her stubbornness; her blue-green eyes and her black Spandex and the way she learned to walk her own path at her own pace. The way she took care of me in Pontevedra. The way she made me feel special in A Guarda. The way she kissed me in Vila Praia de Âncora, and the way she loved the sunrise in Viana do Castelo. The way she let me rub her feet in Vila do Conde, and the way she let me cut her hair in Esposende.

Sadie, who made everything feel new. Sadie, who was so goddamn vulnerable with me from the beginning, even when I couldn't give her that vulnerability in return. The way she made me *want* to be vulnerable, if I could learn how.

What would it be like, to let myself stay in love? To plant myself next to another person so we could grow in our separate pots, twining our branches together?

That's when I start to cry. Choking, gasping sobs that cause other funeral goers to stare. Big, ugly tears that make my face hot and sticky as I stand here in front of my smoking-hot stepmom.

"Don't look at me," I grumble at Gloria as I attempt to dry my eyes on the sleeve of my suit.

"I wouldn't dare," she says, staring directly at my tearstained face.

"These tears aren't for him," I tell her.

"I didn't think they were," she says. "I assumed they were for you."

Gloria doesn't attempt to comfort me. She doesn't hand me a handkerchief or try to escort me away so no one else will witness my loud, snot-filled breakdown. No, all Gloria does is stand there with me through the snot and the stares, until Inez shows up at my side again and wraps me in her arms.

"Do you think . . . ?" Gloria says before I can walk away with Inez. "Could I maybe call you sometime, Mal?"

"Why?"

"Because I want to get to know you, Daughter Dearest."

I laugh through my hysterical tears, and Gloria smiles at me in return. "We're family, whether we want to be or not."

"I—I'm not sure I want to have a relationship with you," I tell her, because it's the truth. There's no malice in my voice now. No anger or resentment. Gloria isn't Valentim. And maybe even Valentim wasn't Valentim. Or, not the Valentim I thought he was.

"Nothing has to be decided today," Gloria says with a small shrug. Her manicured hand dips into her Prada clutch, and she pulls out a business card with a sharp flick of her wrist. "My personal cell is on the back. I'll be here whenever you're ready. And so will the company."

I stare down at the gold-foil-embossed business card in my hands as she walks away.

Gloriana Silva. Damn. My father did always have expensive taste.

THIRTY

Sadie

I must admit: I've truly outdone myself.

The seats from an old Windstar van have been converted into a mudroom bench. There's an antique chess set that makes a gorgeous statement end table. Six dressers with murals painted across the drawers, three refinished dining room tables, nine reupholstered accent chairs, a dilapidated chest saved by wallpaper and epoxy. Two cracked bathtubs that now work perfectly as raised garden beds. An armoire-turned–coffee bar, and a coffee bar–turned–wine hutch and a broken piano that's now a desk. Four bookshelves built out of vintage doors and one massive kitchen island rebuilt from two old rolltop desks.

I scroll through my new Etsy page. Three months of hard work, each piece beautifully photographed by Vera during her visit a few weeks ago.

Sadie Designs Wells has already sold seven items. Granted, three of them were purchased by my mother, who lives with me, but at least that saved money on shipping. The other sales were from Ari and Vera, and Rebecca, who bought a matching pair of Adirondack chairs I painted like pride flags, like the benches we saw on the way into Santiago.

Given that the Etsy page only went live an hour ago, I'm happy with those sales.

I close my laptop so I won't be tempted to stare at the screen until the first stranger makes a purchase from my page, and I survey the empty showroom on the other side of the counter. The badly scuffed floors, the dust outlines from pieces that sat unsellable for years. The walls are checkerboarded shades of green, darker in the places where mirrors or artwork hung, and lighter in places where the sun slowly faded the paint my Nan picked out almost thirty years ago.

This morning, the last van came to take the remainder of the furniture from Live Wells Antiques. It took three months to officially close the store. I sold off our expensive pieces to other stores and auction houses at a discount. I held weekend sales that Vi advertised on her Instagram. I kept the damaged items—the scuffed and stained, the wobbly and the well-worn, the things no one wanted—and I gave them new life using the skills my Nan taught me.

I scoured garage sales and Goodwills and the dump. I picked up the garbage people leave on the curb with FREE signs taped to them, and now I have a stockpile of broken furniture to repurpose.

I have no idea if I'll be able to support myself selling up-cycled furniture online; I don't even know if I'll enjoy it long-term. But for the first time in my life, I'm working toward finding my own dream, and I'm learning to live in the uncertainty. I have a sizable amount of money in savings, since before the Camino, I never had time to spend my earnings, and that should float me for a little while. It will at least give me time to figure out if this is the right path for me.

It's sad to see the empty, echoey space that once held my Nan's dream, but it's also *liberating*. This store has held me hostage my entire life, and I am finally free. No twelve-hour days, no working six days a week, no busyness to use as an excuse not to live. I'm no longer beholden to the store hours painted on the front door. I'm no longer trapped in this dark, dusty room with my ghosts.

Nan was the one who loved preserving history; I've always loved reimagining it.

I have plans to convert the store into an apartment that we can rent out for extra income, but the back room—the place where my Nan taught me to paint with the grain, and how to use a random orbital sander, and how to reupholster a chair without compromising the historical value—will serve as my workshop as I try to launch my own business selling upcycled, DIY furniture. I choose to believe Nan would have loved that for me.

I can hear two sets of footsteps on the backroom stairs, and I know what's coming for me even before Vi bursts in with my mom toddling after her. "How did it go?" Vi demands.

"It went well. The moving van left about an hour ago, and—"

"Stop." Vi holds up a hand. "I don't care about that. How was the *date*?"

"Tell us everything about her!" my mother squeals in excitement.

"Boundaries," I remind them.

My mom lowers the enthusiasm level. "I mean, if you feel like sharing with us, we would love to hear about your date last night."

I've been working on being more open with my mom and Vi, and they've been working on respecting my boundaries around my love life. It's a steep learning curve for all of us.

"The date was fine. She was . . . fine."

Vi smacks the counter. "You got to give us more than that! Now that you're finally dating women, we need *all the details*!"

There aren't really details, but I tell them what I can about Skye, the performance artist Ari set me up with. It was a beautiful, late-August evening, so we met at Green Lake Park, and eventually walked to Bluebird for ice cream. Skye told me about her upcoming one-woman show, *When the Pussy Calls*, and I showed her photos of my furniture. At the end of the night, I promised to buy tickets to her show, and she said she was going to buy one of my bathtub garden beds as soon as my Etsy page was up. Neither of us brought up the possibility of a second date.

Skye was my fourth first date since I got home from the Camino. None of them have been amazing, but it's shocking how different they've felt compared to dating men. I don't need a bet with my sister to cajole me into putting myself out there. I never check the time, never use excuses to end the date early if I'm not feeling it. I don't force myself to make it work, and I don't force myself to feel attraction.

On my first date with a woman, when I realized I wasn't attracted to her, I didn't feel suffocating shame about it. Just a flicker of disappointment.

Because I know when it's meant to work, it will work.

"Skye was cool and interesting," I try to explain, "but she wasn't—"

"Mal?" Vi interrupts with accusation in her eyebrows.

I roll my eyes. This is *always* where these conversations end up. "No, that's not—"

"Sadie. Darling." My mom gives me her most pitying mom-face. "I'm worried that you're wallowing, and that you won't be able to move on from this heartbreak."

"I think you might be projecting a little bit there . . ."

"You always have some weird excuse about why it can't work with these women," Vi points out in a well-executed mother-daughter double attack. "Just like you used to do with men."

"Always? It's been four women, and one of them was a former nun, so . . ."

"See? Excuses. You're not over Mal."

"I swear, I am."

"Oh yeah? Then explain *this*." Vi comes around the counter and yanks open a drawer hidden below where the register used to sit. She pulls something out, then slams it in front of me like it's damning evidence. Peanut the Elephant stares up at me.

"That," I say calmly, "is a Beanie Baby. You're probably too young to remember, but there was a time when people collected these because they believed they'd be worth money someday."

"I know what a Beanie Baby is," Vi huffs. "What I want to know is why you've been carrying around *this* Beanie Baby for the last three months?"

"Oh, well, you see, this one actually *is* worth money."

Mal's Hokas, her toe socks, her container of Vaseline—those are things I stole from her accidentally. But Peanut . . . Peanut, I stole with intention that night in Caldas de Reis. While she was in the bath, I snuck Peanut out of her pack and I hid him under my pillow.

I wanted one physical reminder of the *real* Mal—the version of herself she showed me at the vineyard. And now my sister is using Peanut as proof that I'm not over whatever it was between us.

"Peanut is a souvenir."

"Oh, Sadie." My mom also comes around the counter to wrap me in her soft, yet patronizing arms. "After your father left, I would sleep on top of a pile of the clothes he left behind. I understand."

I attempt to wriggle out of her suffocating embrace. "This is nothing like that."

I truly am over Mal. Sure, there were a few days in the beginning when I couldn't say her name without crying, a few nights when I slept with Peanut pressed against my cheek. There were times when all I could do was replay every conversation we had, wondering what I could've said differently to change the ending. There were times I would touch myself while thinking about her, the ache in me almost too much to bear.

When Vera uploaded over five thousand photos to the tour group's shared album, I spent hours clicking through every single one, searching for the candid shots of us: dancing in Âncora and Redondela, walking together along the Atlantic coast and through Galician countryside. Mal cutting my hair in Esposende and holding my hand while I got tattooed in A Guarda. The two of us sitting across from each other at every meal, sitting next to each other at every sharing circle. And I wept to see the expression on my face in those photos, so obviously and hopelessly in love with her.

Until one day, I could talk about what happened without crying at all. I could open the dating apps without feeling sick to my stomach, and I could watch *Property Brothers* without missing her, and I could hear the ding of a WhatsApp notification without deluding myself into thinking *that* message would be the one where she admits she misses me too.

Last night, I ate pistachio ice cream on my date with Skye, and I didn't feel heartbroken at all. One day I'll be able to listen to Madonna without feeling heartbroken too. I'll be able to look at the tattoo on my wrist or catch a glimpse of my short hair in a mirror and not feel Mal all over me.

"I am over Mal," I try to convince my mom and Vi. I try to convince *myself*.

Because I will be over her. Everyone gets over their first love eventually.

"In fact, we've been talking for the past several weeks, totally and completely as friends."

"Oh, of fucking course you have!" Vi throws her arms in the air. "Fucking *lesbians*!"

Sadie

As promised, here's the link to my Etsy page

Please don't feel obligated to buy something 12:14 p.m.

Mal

I won't buy something 12:16 p.m.

Mal

I'll buy *everything*! 12:16 p.m.

Sadie

Please don't. This is my entire inventory and it took me three months to get here. 12:17 p.m.

Mal

Okay, okay, I will try to show some restraint. 12:17 p.m.

Mal

I'm watching Buying and Selling right now, and here's what I want to know: where is this magical Property Brothers world where it's somehow always both a buyers' and sellers' market? 12:21 p.m.

Sadie

Calgary 12:22 p.m.

Mal

Ah. So is that where I should buy a house? 12:22 p.m.

Sadie

You're buying a house?? 12:23 p.m.

Mal

Well, technically, I already own like 12 houses. But I'm thinking about actually living in one. 12:24 p.m.

Sadie

Where??? 12:24 p.m.

Mal

Not Calgary, apparently

It's shockingly expensive

Isn't this place north of Montana????
12:25 p.m.

Sadie

You're a millionaire though . . .
12:26 p.m.

Mal

Which means I know a shoddy investment when I see one

But since I can do most of the work for the foundation remotely, I can basically choose to settle anywhere I want 12:28 p.m.

Sadie

OH MY GOD!!!!!

A stranger just bought something from my Etsy!!!!!!!! 12:29 p.m.

Mal

If they bought the rolltop desk kitchen island, I'm going to riot 12:30 p.m.

Sadie

No it was a bathtub garden bed
12:31 p.m.

Sadie

Never mind it doesn't count

I know the woman who bought it

12:35 p.m.

Sadie

We sort of went on a date yesterday

12:37 p.m.

Mal

Oh 12:37 p.m.

Sadie

I can't believe she actually bought it!
That's so kind! 12:38 p.m.

Mal

Definitely sounds like a keeper 12:39 p.m.

Sadie

Wait, so where are you going to buy a
house??? 1:15 p.m.

Mal

I have no idea 1:16 p.m.

THIRTY-ONE

Mal

"Are you watching porn at work?"

I slam my phone face down on my desk and look up to see Gloria standing in the open door of my office. "No, *Mother*, I am not watching porn. But you're welcome to change the parental controls on my phone if you don't trust me."

"If it's not porn, why are you grinning like that?" She sits down on the chair across from my desk. It's one of Sadie's chairs, with the wood painted deep sky blue, and the upholstery an old tapestry depicting wildflowers.

"I have so many questions. Do you grin while watching porn? And do you think porn is the only reason a person might be happy?"

Gloria primly crosses her legs at the ankle. "This is workplace sexual harassment."

"It's the weekend! And you're the one who came in here talking about porn!"

Gloria tilts her head to one side and studies me for three seconds before she deduces the truth. "You were talking to her again, weren't you?"

I shuffle around some papers on my desk. "We should really get down to business."

Without another word, Gloria flips open her iPad and slides a manicured finger across the screen. A series of charts and tables come into view, and I immediately lose interest. "I had accounting send over a summary of our first two quarters, along with projections of the tax breaks from starting the foundation, in preparation for our meeting with the board on Tuesday. Maëlys, put down your damn phone and pay attention. You're thirty-nine years old."

I reluctantly put my phone back on the desk, face up this time. "I mean this with all due respect, but I do not care about your charts. That's why you're the CEO, and I'm very much not."

She snaps the iPad closed and glares. "If the board approves the final plan for the foundation, then everything will be in place for you to leave Portugal."

So, it turns out I do care a little. I've been (for lack of a better term) trapped in Portugal for three months, bouncing between my office here, at the vineyard outside of Porto, and the corporate offices in Lisbon. At first, I was here to deal with the excruciatingly tedious process of naming Gloria as the official CEO of Quinta Costa, and then I stayed for the equally tedious process of establishing a corporate foundation *within* Quinta Costa.

As it turns out, Gloria was telling the truth at the funeral. My father followed my so-called career as I jumped around between nonprofits and NGOs, and the company gave millions to the causes I cared about over the course of twenty years. With generous tax benefits, of course. Which got me thinking . . .

I don't know shit-all about how to run a company, but I know some shit about how to run a nonprofit. Or how to work for one, at least.

The idea came together over a long weekend trip to La Rioja for the Batalla del Vino in June. Gloria and I had our own wine battle as we killed multiple bottles of red and hashed out a detailed business plan for starting a corporate-sponsored foundation that the company would fund and I would run. A foundation that would offer grants to existing nonprofit organizations locally and globally, especially those focused on uplifting women, children, queer people, and the trans community.

When we first presented our proposal, the board shot it down with excuses about overhead costs and bottom lines and fiduciary responsibilities to shareholders. We compromised: the board agreed that if I could provide the start-up capital to get the foundation off the ground and prove it was a sound investment, then the company would allocate ten percent of our overall earnings after the fourth quarter.

I suspect they thought I didn't have the follow-through or funds to make it happen.

But selling the Lake Como house more than covered it. As for the follow-through, well . . . I've been learning how to exist in this boring middle part.

The meeting in Lisbon is the final hoop to jump through before I'll be set up to run the foundation remotely from wherever I want in the world. I just have to figure out where that is.

The problem with figuring out what I want to do with my time and money is that it means listening to Gloria for thirty minutes while she goes over every chart, table, and graph her little heart desires. "Do you have any questions before the meeting?" she asks as she closes the iPad again.

"I think you covered it, Mommy Dearest."

Gloria sweeps her hair out of her face with the back of her hand. Every movement, every gesture, every word out of her mouth speaks of money—the kind of money that demands a childhood of etiquette training and an exacting emphasis on appearances. I see my own childhood mirrored back to me when I look at Gloria. She's who I would've been if I hadn't rejected the Costa part of me, and when Gloria looks at me, I think she sees a hypothetical version of herself too.

"I have reservations at O Paparico tonight at eight," Gloria says, still elegantly posed on Sadie's chair. "Would you like to join me?"

The funny thing is, I really would. "I can't tonight. Inez is in town before she leaves for a tour tomorrow morning, and I'm meeting up with her for tapas."

Gloria's smile is tight but polite, and I quickly add, "You're welcome to join us, though."

"You should enjoy your time with your friend." She rises from her chair as she smooths out the creases in her black dress. "I'm sure she has much to say about *that*."

My phone buzzes with another WhatsApp message, and I try to hide the notification. But Gloria has already seen it, and she's already giving me a knowing look before sashaying out of my office.

"I *do* have much to say about it."

I take another sip of my Verdelho, lean back in my patio chair, and resign myself to the inevitable. "Hit me with your best lecture."

"No one said anything about a lecture." Inez sweeps her Afro into a puff, like she's ready to get serious. "I simply want us to examine the facts of the situation."

"Uh-huh." I reach for the plate of pasteis de bacalhau.

"Do you still text Sadie every single day?"

"Not *every day*." Sometimes the time difference means we talk every *other* day. But ever since her final blog post, we've been talking consistently. Most of our messages are about boring, everyday things: updates about her fledgling furniture restoration business and my ever-evolving plans for the foundation; anecdotes about her mom's pitiful attempts at meddling less and Vi's even worse attempts at respecting Sadie's privacy; stories about my regular lunch dates with Luzia and my unexpected friendship with Gloria. I message her my reactions to episodes of various *Property Brothers* shows, and she messages me about her morning walks around Discovery Park. We only talk about our time on the Camino with oblique references; we never discuss the kisses we said were for practice.

"Every day?" Inez repeats, and I slowly, sheepishly nod.

"Yeah, every day. But!" I hold up a finger. "I also get daily voice memos from Stefano about his training, and daily photos of Ro's dogs, and I don't hear you attacking me over *that*."

"You didn't have sex with Stefano or Ro," Inez says plainly.

"Fair point. Carry on."

"Did you furnish your entire office with pieces from Sadie's Etsy page?"

I choke on cod fritter as I attempt to defend myself again. "Her furniture is *beautiful*. And I'm just trying to support a friend."

"And do you keep a framed photo of her on your desk?"

"It's a framed photo of the entire tour group."

Inez continues her interrogation. "And is it true you've been looking up houses in Seattle on Zillow?"

"Okay, yes, but only because that's where Michelle lives, and I want to be close to my godson."

"And have you refused to date at all since you and Sadie broke up?"

I sigh. "You know I have."

Inez has been a surprising constant in my life these last three months. I flew to Lisbon to meet her wife; she met me in the Algarve for my birthday. We've both driven hundreds of kilometers to see each other between her tours. I will miss that connection when I leave Portugal. But I also have faith that no matter where I end up, Inez and I will stay close, the way Michelle and I always have.

"And it's only been *three months* since I've sworn off dating, and *you* were the one who encouraged me to do that! So I can spend time working on myself, and focusing on my future, and becoming comfortable with the middle of things, and breaking old patterns, and blah blah blah."

"Blah blah blah?" She eyes me over her own glass of wine. "How profound. Speaking of, how's therapy going?"

"Horrible. Do you know therapists expect you to talk about *yourself* for an hour straight? The monsters."

My therapist isn't actually a monster. Sofia has been another staple in my post-Camino life. Twice a week, we meet over Zoom to unpack my childhood trauma, and I don't hate it as much as I thought I would. I've been surprised by how much time we've spent discussing my absentee mother and her impact on my self-esteem and my issues with commitment. But Valentim would be pleased to know he's still the star of the show when it comes to damaging my psyche.

There's been a lot of crying, a lot of unlearning and relearning, a lot of stand-up comedy routines in the place of genuine vulnerability, because I'm not perfect, and I'm still figuring out how to have a healthy relationship with my own thoughts.

Across the outdoor table, Inez strokes her chin like a philosophy professor contemplating the meaning of life. "I'm so proud of you. For slowing down. For going inward. For not jumping into the next relationship or the next distraction." Only Inez can say things like this without prompting a reflexively flippant response. Well, Inez and Michelle.

"Even your aura has changed." She lifts both hands and sweeps them into the shape of a rainbow around me. "An almost yellowish green now."

And *that* deserves a flippant comment. "I'm really glad we're sticking to the facts here."

Inez bites into a piece of cod fritter and glares at me. "The full moon lunar eclipse is in Pisces today."

"Which is relevant to this conversation because . . . ?"

"Heightened intuition today can guide us toward our best path. *If* we're willing to listen to it."

I have no idea what Inez or my intuition are trying to tell me right now. "Okay . . ."

"And if you can clearly communicate your needs, spiritual growth and transformation can occur."

"I *need* more wine." I point to my empty glass. "Do you think I should communicate that to the server?"

Inez rolls her eyes. "Such a fucking *Gemini*."

"Can you maybe give me the CliffsNotes version of what you're trying to tell me right now?"

The server divines my needs and appears with the bottle of wine, and Inez waits until they're gone again. "Why did you end things with Sadie in Caldas de Reis?"

"Because you told me to."

"Mal . . ."

I squirm in my chair, wishing I could squirm myself right out of this conversation. Our friendship was so much easier when it stuck to the shallows. But it was also less meaningful. "I ended things with Sadie because she represented an unhealthy pattern of jumping into relationships too quickly." I may or may not be quoting Sofia with that one. "And because you were right. We were in the honeymoon phase, and I was going to fall out of love with her eventually, like I always do."

Inez folds her hands into prayer position and presses her fingertips to her mouth. "And did you?"

"Did I *what*?"

"Fall out of love with her?"

I scramble for another defense, another justification, another joke. Did I fall out of love with Sadie? Is love constantly checking your phone because you always want to know what she has to say? Is love thinking about her every time I see a sunrise, every time I catch a whiff of the flowers in my garden, every time I eat a pasteis de nata? Is love saving her the second Bueno bar, even though she's five thousand miles away?

Is love wanting to tell her about what I ate for breakfast every morning, and what birds I see from my office window every afternoon? Is love wanting to hear about what she ate for dinner and what project she worked on that day? Is love wanting her opinion on every decision I make about the foundation? Is it hating the women she goes on dates with, even though I've never seen them? Is it buying a headboard she'd created out of a white picket fence and falling asleep in a bed that makes me think about having a home with her?

Of course it is. If anything, I am more in love with Sadie now than I was three months ago.

"I-I had to end things with Sadie before either of us got hurt," I say to an expectant Inez.

"But didn't you still get hurt?"

I sit in the silence of that question for a long time.

"That morning in Pontevedra." Inez exhales a deep breath. "You asked me if I thought Sadie might be different. And I thought you were doing what you always do—thinking each new woman is the exception to your toxic patterns."

I grimace. "Sheesh. Don't hold back, N. Give it to me straight."

She searches my face, and I'm not sure if she's reading my aura or my eyebrows, if there's something in my body language that tells her everything she needs to know. "But I think I should have realized that the fact that you *wanted* her to be different was the important part."

"What do you mean?"

"*This* is the boring middle part." She sweeps her hands wide, encompassing this table where we sit enjoying happy hour, this sidewalk in Porto. Sundays and 6 p.m. and September. "What I mean is, maybe you've found the person who makes the middles feel tolerable."

I shake my head. "No, no. It's . . . it's too late, with Sadie. I missed my chance. She's moved on, and she's happy, and it's . . . it's too late."

"Maëlys." She reaches across the table and puts her hand over mine. "That's the stupidest thing you've ever said to me."

I snort a laugh.

"We're all on different paths, all moving at our own paces," she says in her best wise mystic voice. And God, how I love it. "There's no such thing as *too late*. We all get to where we're going when we're ready. Not before."

She releases my hand and reaches into the beaded purse dangling off the back of her chair. She pulls out a crystal hanging from a gold chain and hands it to me.

"Rose quartz?" I ask, cupping the small, jagged stone in my palm.

Inez nods. "For love."

Mal

How are you feeling about your trip?
7:24 a.m.

Sadie

Excited! It's my first real vacation since launching Sadie Designs Wells
7:27 a.m.

Mal

Look at you go with your healthy work-life balance 7:28 a.m.

Sadie

What does someone pack to go to an Ironman??? 7:30 a.m.

Mal

Since you're watching, not participating, I think you'll be okay with normal human clothes 7:31 a.m.

Sadie

Is 4 pairs of shoes enough?!? 7:35 a.m.

Mal

For a 5-day trip? Yeah, that should cover it 7:35 a.m.

Sadie

Are you mocking me right now? 7:36 a.m.

Mal

A little bit 7:36 a.m.

Mal

But you're perfectly capable of packing your own bag 7:37 a.m.

Sadie

Am I though????? 7:37 a.m.

Mal

Yes. It's not like you have to carry all your belongings this time 7:38 a.m.

Sadie

GAHHHHH

I wish you were coming to Michigan with us

I need you to tell me how many coats to bring. 7:43 a.m.

Mal

One coat, Freckles. Always only one coat.
7:44 a.m.

Mal

And I wish I was coming too 7:49 a.m.

THIRTY-TWO

Sadie

"I can't believe I have to endure Seattle traffic home because of you," Vi grumbles from behind the wheel of my Subaru Forester.

I haul my bag over my shoulder and glare at her through the open passenger-side window. "Do you know how many times I've driven you to the airport during rush hour?" I ask from the Arrivals curb.

Vi rolls her eyes. "Once or twice, maybe."

"And I'm driving you to the airport in two weeks for your Camino," I remind her. Vi finally got the go-ahead from her doctor, and now she's going on her own tour with Inez. I have a difficult time imagining Vi participating in sharing circles with any level of sincerity, but I know Inez will crack her. And I'm curious to see what version of Vi comes home afterward.

"Fine. Whatever. You're an amazing big sister," Vi reluctantly admits. I give her a little wave before I turn toward the revolving door into the airport. "Wait!" Vi calls from the driver's seat, and I turn back.

"You *are* an amazing big sister," she says again, her tone serious this time. "Thank you for all the rides to the airport. And just for . . . *everything*."

I lean through the window to see her face up close. "What is this? What's going on? Are you dying?"

"Hardy har har," Vi monotones, but I swear I see a tear escape her right eye. "I just want you to know that I see how much you've done for me my entire life. I-I hope you can do something for yourself."

"Okay, weirdo." I clap the door. "Love you. See you in five days."

"Love you," she echoes in that same strangely serious voice before she chaotically merges back into the flow of Arrivals traffic, and there is a very good chance she might actually be dying. But I'll deal with that when I get home from Michigan.

The week I officially shuttered the doors on Live Wells Antiques, I went to Portland to stay with Ari for a few days. Given that we live only three hours apart, she's been adamant about us becoming best friends, especially since her *real* best friend got engaged while we were doing the Camino. Ari lives in a giant house she calls "Brideshead," with several other queer roommates, and we spent a long weekend sampling different food trucks and coffee. And when we FaceTimed Stefano together, he was shocked to learn we lived driving distance from each other.

"Are you driving distance from Michigan too?"

His first post-injury Ironman was going to be on Lake Michigan, and he begged us to come. "I really need my beautiful friends there," he said with a well-executed pout.

Neither of us could argue with that, even if his US geography is spotty.

Vi gave me some airline miles so I could go, because I promised myself I would travel more, and while it's not exactly on my bucket list, I've never seen the Great Lakes. When Rebecca heard Ari and I were going, she splurged on her own tickets and invited Ro to join us too. So the Ironman was going to be like a mini-Camino reunion, minus Vera and Inez. And minus Mal.

As I head to the security line, I think about the last time I was at SeaTac: crying into my mother's sweater after I got off the plane from Santiago. It was only four months ago, but it feels like a lifetime.

It also feels like no time has passed at all. Those feelings—of first love and first heartbreak—still feel so fresh sometimes.

But I *am* totally over Mal. I *will* be totally over her, someday.

Someday, I won't feel butterflies every time I hear the ding of a WhatsApp notification. But today, in this Hudson News, is not that day. My phone buzzes, and my stomach launches into my chest, and I immediately check her message.

ARE YOU AT THE AIRPORT YET?

I grab a Bueno bar from the display by the register and snap a pic to send. YEP. JUST STOCKING UP ON AIRPLANE SNACKS.

I can see from her read receipts that she saw the photo, but she doesn't respond, and I shove my phone back into the pocket of my jeans. I buy the candy. *Someday.*

Maybe it'll happen on Lake Michigan.

"Sadie Wells. If there is a passenger named Sadie Wells here, please come see us at the gate."

I hear the announcement when I'm still a few gates away, and I pick up the pace, almost breathless when I reach the Alaska Airlines counter. "I'm Sadie Wells. Is everything okay?"

"It's your lucky day!" The agent smiles at me. "You've been upgraded to first class! I just need to print you a new boarding pass."

"I've been upgraded?" I repeat. "Why? How?"

The woman behind the counter winks at me. "Someone must really love you."

Someone could only be my sister, who helped me buy the ticket with her elite mileage plan. *This* must be why she was acting so damn weird. I send Vi a thank you text as I board the plane early with all the other first-class passengers.

In first class, there is plenty of overhead bin space, and even more space in the seat for me to fully relax my body. But when the flight attendant swoops in to offer me champagne, I decline and decide to stick to water. No one needs a repeat of the last time I drank on an airplane.

I'm in the aisle seat, and the window seat next to me is empty. It remains empty as the rest of the plane starts to board, people staring at me as they pass like I'm some kind of fancy, potentially famous first-class person. I take out my phone, and even though Mal still hasn't replied to my previous message, I snap a pic of my ample legroom. UPGRADED TO FIRST CLASS! IS THIS WHAT IT FEELS LIKE TO BE RICH? IS THIS WHAT IT FEELS LIKE TO BE YOU????

She once again reads my message and once again does not respond. I close out of WhatsApp and close my eyes, holding my phone to my chest as I remind myself once again. *I have to get over her*.

Someone clears their throat and grumbles, "Sorry, but that's my seat."

I open my eyes to see someone pointing at the window seat next to me.

No. Not someone. *Mal*.

Mullet and widow's peak and Cupid's bow mouth. The poop-brown backpack and the Hydro Flask covered in gay stickers and the Cotopaxi fleece. Tattoos and visible nipples and *Mal*.

All the individual traits add up to her, but my brain can't fathom how she could be *here*. Not in Porto, but on an airplane in Seattle.

I don't move. I don't say anything. I don't know how to react to this impossibility.

The flight attendant starts coming through, closing overhead bins as she goes. Mal quickly shoves her pack into the bin above my seat, her shirt riding up to reveal an inch of the grapevine tattoo I once traced with my tongue. *Mal*.

She stands in the aisle for a few seconds, and when I remain immobile in my seat, she climbs over me in an awkward jangle of limbs.

"What . . ." I finally say. "What are you doing here?"

Mal fastens her seat belt as the airplane door is closed three rows ahead of us and a flight attendant starts pantomiming along with the overhead safety announcement. Mal turns her whole body toward mine and takes a long, deep breath. "I hate the Property Brothers," she says, and my brain has no idea what question she's answering with that little proclamation. "I can't explain it, but their faces make me irrationally angry. I'm sure they're very nice people, but I also want to punch them."

"What?"

She pushes her hair out of her eyes, and I realize her mullet isn't blue anymore. It's back to what I imagine is her natural dark-brown color. "On the Camino, I pretended to like the Property Brothers to have an excuse to spend time with you," she confesses. "And then I kept watching it on my own afterward so I'd have an excuse to message you."

"What?" I say again. I still have no idea why or how she's here. The plane is backing out of the gate, and Mal is in the seat next to me, and I can feel her presence in every bone of my body.

"And I bought like half the furniture from your Etsy page under several different fake accounts."

"What?" There's no other word for any of this.

"Not because I don't believe in you or anything!" she rushes to explain. "But because I genuinely love everything you make, and I wanted pieces of you at the vineyard in Porto."

At least one thing is starting to make sense. "Did you do this? Did you get me upgraded to first class?"

"Oh. Yes. I thought that was obvious."

"How did you get my flight info?"

"Your sister."

"You talked to *my sister*?"

"Yes, and she kept calling me Malcolm for some reason . . ."

The plane rattles as we begin takeoff, and Mal and I reach for the armrest between us at the same time. Her hand is warm, and I hold it on instinct as the plane leaves the ground. My stomach bungees into my rib cage.

"And the first CD I ever owned was Hootie and the Blow-fish, and the only person I invited to my eighth birthday was the woman who worked in the children's section at the library in Porto. She was seventy-two," she continues confessing, for no apparent reason. "And when I was twelve, I got really into this series of Nancy Drew mystery computer games, and I kept playing them until I was way too old." She pauses, then exhales again. "As in, I played the most recent one last year. I just never stopped playing them, and they are very much for children," she keeps blathering on, and this finally starts to make sense too.

Mal is telling me all of her secrets on an airplane, the way I did when we first met. People are turning to glare at her, but she doesn't stop. "I was afraid of the dark until I was in my mid-twenties, and I had to travel with a battery-powered night-light. And I'm still genuinely afraid no one will ever love me if they see all of me."

"You don't have to do this," I tell her, still clutching her hand.

"I do have to," Mal says with a nervous grimace. "Because it's what I should have done from the beginning. From the first day we met, you gave me so much of yourself."

"Yeah, and that's *weird*. Most people don't share all of their secrets with a stranger."

"But I love that you did." She stares at me with those hazel eyes, and my stomach is in my ribs again. "I have a habit of fall-ing in love with women I barely know, so when I immediately fell for you, I thought it was just the same thing I always do."

"You . . . you fell for me? Immediately?"

"Oh yeah. The second you shouted *I'm a virgin* on an airplane, I was a goner. And I should have known it was different with you. *You* are different. I-I can't explain it, but when you held my hand during that turbulence, I felt . . . at peace, somehow."

I hold tighter to her hand now. Whatever this thing is that she's doing, I am starting to suspect it might be about more than just sharing secrets with me.

"I almost kissed you on the plane to London," Mal says, giving me more and more of herself, "and if you'd given me even the slightest indication that you wanted me to, I would have."

I did want her to. From the moment I laid eyes on her and felt that jolt of familiarity for someone I'd never seen, all I wanted was to be closer to her. I think that's the real reason I came out to her when I thought the plane was going to crash. I didn't want to miss the chance to connect with her in whatever feeble, embarrassing way I could.

"When I found out we were on the same tour, I was pissed, because I knew I was never going to be able to resist you. But I tried. I really tried. Michelle and Inez both told me not to fall for you, but I-I couldn't help it. You made the silence tolerable."

I don't even know what this means, but I realize I'm holding my breath.

"None of it was for practice, Sadie," Mal says. "None of it was for the sake of science."

I exhale. "It . . . it wasn't?"

"I don't even care about science!" she shouts. "I just liked you. I flirted with you because I wanted to, and I kissed you because I wanted to, and I fucked you because I'd never wanted anyone like I wanted you."

"Ma'am, I'm going to need you to lower your voice." The flight attendant is back in the aisle beside us. "You're upsetting the other first-class passengers."

"I'm very sorry. I promise I'm almost done." Mal makes a

point of lowering her voice, of leaning closer to me. "I should have told you all of that from the beginning. And when you offered to come with me to my father's funeral, I should have told you that having you there would have meant the whole fucking world to me."

I close my eyes to stop the sting of tears.

"No woman I've ever been with has offered to do something like that for me, and I didn't know how to let you be there for me."

Fuck the tears. I open my eyes anyway. "You truly have the most deplorable taste in women."

She laughs. "I love that you always make me laugh when I need it most. I love seeing the world through your eyes, and I want to take you to every place I've ever been so I can experience it for the first time again, with you."

I almost don't notice the shift from past tense to present, but once I do, it's *all* I can notice. My heart is in my throat, and my stomach is in my chest, and my butterflies are in my stomach. A million foolishly hopeful butterflies, waiting for the first sign it's safe to take flight.

"And I just love you," Mal finally says with the most infuriatingly flippant shoulder shrug. "I don't care that we barely know each other, and I don't care that this is what I always do, because I've never done it with *you*. I-I think it could be different with you."

The butterflies take flight, and they take me with them, lifting me out of my seat and threatening to float away with me entirely.

"I want to kiss you a thousand times," Mal says, and gravity tugs me back down to my seat. "I want the boring middle parts with you. February and Tuesdays. Ikea furniture and an entire cupboard full of Tupperware and—"

"Oh my God," I gasp in horror. "You're not *proposing*, are you?"

"Oh, fuck no." She snorts. "No, no, I'm not proposing. Jesus. I just . . ." She takes our joint hands and brings them to her heart. "Sadie Wells, I would love to date you."

I'm kind of laughing, kind of crying, kind of floating. "But . . . but you live . . . wait, where do you live?"

"I have no idea," she says with a breathless laugh. "Seattle, maybe? To be close to Michelle and close to . . . you? If that's something you'd want. I thought maybe we could make that decision together."

Together.

The very idea makes me want to curl up against her warm skin and never leave.

"I love being your friend," Mal says, holding me as close as she can with the armrest between us. "But I would love to be more."

And I kiss her on this airplane to Michigan, the way she wanted to kiss me on the first one to London. But I wouldn't go back if I could; I wouldn't have her rewrite how it all played out. We took the long way round to get to this moment, but I wouldn't have it any other way.

At a cruising altitude of thirty-four-thousand feet somewhere over Oregon, we're exactly where we're supposed to be.

ACKNOWLEDGMENTS

Writing a book is kind of like walking two hundred miles through Portugal and Spain. Except writing is much, *much* harder.

I know this firsthand, because I decided to trek the Portuguese coastal route of the Camino de Santiago in the midst of a debilitating case of writer's block while working on my third book. I was, in essence, *running away* from my life when I hopped on that plane to Lisbon, and I've never been so grateful for my ADHD escapist behavior. Trekking the Camino was a transformative experience in the most clichéd way, and even as it was happening, I knew I would want to write about it someday. But it took me a while to find the right story—and the right character—for that journey.

At book events, I often jokingly refer to myself as a narcissist, because all my main characters are thinly veiled self-insert (and sometimes that veil is *so thin*, it leaves nothing to the imagination). They say to write what you know, but I'm not sure this is what they meant.

Each character and each book is almost like a time capsule, representing something I was working through (probably in therapy) when I wrote it. *Every Step She Takes* is slightly different.

The main character, Sadie Wells, is still a poorly disguised version of myself. (But she has red hair! And she's from *Seattle* instead of Portland! No one will ever figure it out!) But Sadie's story centers on two parallel journeys: the physical journey of trekking the Camino de Santiago and the internal journey of unlearning compulsive heterosexuality so she can live as her most authentic self. And these aren't journeys I was actively struggling with while writing this book.

I trekked the Camino in May 2022, and I came out to myself in February 2020 (though I am forever on the journey of unpacking heteronormativity). I didn't start writing *Every Step She Takes* until November 2023, when I was seven months pregnant, and my biggest struggles were round-ligament pain and holding in farts. Funnily enough, though, the arduous process of writing this book during some of the most challenging and transformative moments in my life (becoming a parent is wild, y'all) resembled Sadie's journey in unexpected ways.

For one thing, I was *always* concerned about my timeline and being "too late." Because I literally missed every single deadline (a serious difficulty for a recovering perfectionist). I spent a lot of time reconciling things in the past, in the way both Sadie and Mal do throughout the story. And like Sadie and Mal, I spent a lot of time figuring out how to accept that I was right where I was supposed to be.

And in the same way that Sadie needed an eclectic group of queers and a lot of Compeed to help her reach Santiago, this book required a lot of hands to get it to you, so let's get to the actual acknowledgment part!

This book, and all of my books, started with a conversation with my intrepid and *endlessly patient* agent, Bibi Lewis. I would always be lost without your guidance and support, but that was especially true with this book as I wrote through pregnancy and the newborn phase. Thank you for talking me through every deadline extension.

I am beyond fortunate to work with my remarkably sharp and insightful editor, Kaitlin Olson, who not only makes each of my books better, but also makes *me* a better writer throughout the process. (Thank you for also being patient with this one.)

To my beloved publicist, Megan Rudloff: it's been a true pleasure to work with you for FOUR (!!!) books now. You're a goddamn rock star! Nothing would ever get done on time without Ifeoma Anyoku, editorial assistant extraordinaire. Thank you for keeping everything organized and on track. Atria has the marketing and social media dream team of Jolena Podolsky, Morgan Pager, and Zakiya Jamal, and I am so lucky to have all of you in my corner.

This book would have a million *more* typos if it weren't for my copyeditor, Stacey Sakal. I don't know how I would've sorted out the timeline in this book without you. And the biggest thank-you to Sarah Horgan for each of my beautiful book covers.

To everyone else at Atria who does the indispensable work behind the scenes: Paige Lytle, Shelby Pumphrey, Lacee Burr, and Sofia Echeverry. To Liz Byer, for being an incredibly patient production editor. And to Libby McGuire, and all of Simon and Schuster, for supporting my gay little books. We need queer stories now more than ever.

Thank you to Rae Douglas at Bookink Services for your invaluable feedback, and thank you to everyone who talked to me during the research process!

I also could not have survived the writing process without help from early readers like Timothy Janovsky, Meredith Ryan, and Andie Sheridan. (Will I ever write a book without sending y'all anxious emails with the first fifty pages? I doubt it!)

And I couldn't have written this book at all without my personal support network. My therapist, Karen (one day I will no longer need to thank them in my acknowledgments but today is not that day). To my wife, Jordan, for doing the dishes while I was on deadline, for taking care of our son when I was catatonic, and for generally being the love of my life, my inspiration, etc. etc. Thank you to my parents, Erin and Bill, for all the free childcare. And as always, thank you to my sister, Heather, and my best friend, Michelle, for responding to every emotionally unstable text message.

Finally, thank you to my son, August, for giving me something to look forward to at the end of every workday. You are literally my favorite sunshine, and I hope you know how much I love you. (Sorry this book doesn't have Peek-a-Boo flaps for you to play with. I'll work on that for the next one.)

Oh, and one more! Thank you to *you*—to all my readers—for making this whole thing possible. Literally couldn't do it without all of you. Thanks for being on this trek with me.

ABOUT THE AUTHOR

Alison Cochrun is a Lambda Literary and Stonewall Honor Book award-winning author of queer romance novels, including *The Charm Offensive*, *Kiss Her Once for Me*, *Here We Go Again*, and *Every Step She Takes*. She lives outside of Portland, Oregon, with her wife, toddler, and three chaotic dogs. You can find her online at alisoncochrun.com or on Instagram at @alisoncochrun.